Praise for
CRISPR Evolution

"[A] gripping and accomplished debut novel ... Jones spins this heady story in smart, engaging prose ... It's a thriller but anchored in the literary wing of science fiction, driven by character, given to colloquies, and often evocative ... This superb science fiction novel ... is rousing, moving, and rewarding."

- BookLife Reviews (Editor's Pick)

"A dark but believable extrapolation from present-day attitudes ... the novel handles its moral questions sensitively and fairly ... a tale that provides readers with a penetrating and thought-provoking glimpse into a possible not-so-distant future."

- Kirkus Reviews

"Sci fi that promises to reshape its genre ... a heart-in-your-throat page-turner ... it conveys the spinning sense of a future that outstrips a single existence and feels synchronously optimistic, poignant, and even celebratory ... an explosive panorama of what makes up our genetic formation ... richly imagined characters and settings. The author is strong on atmosphere, illuminating vast tracts of imagery, and her uniquely supple and powerful style is even more clear-cut ... wildly original and intelligently drawn."

- Reader Views

"This thoroughly engaging work of speculative fiction rejuvenated my love for science fiction ... The characters are spellbinding, each shining in their own light and demanding center stage ... As a brilliant and dedicated rogue scientist with a questionable sense of ethics, Dr. Howard Wake changed my outlook on a hero. While hardcore scientific facts form the book's foundation, Jones' literary tweaks help it soar to unprecedented heights ... Jones recounts

the beauty of life and imagines the unleashing of one's full potential."

- Readers' Favorite

"A layered and engrossing work of dystopian speculative fiction ... prose is finely rendered and Jones shows a finesse for worldbuilding ... a wholly convincing and well-informed narrative. The characters' personal journeys and the moral dilemmas they grapple with offer a contemplative exploration of the interplay between science, ethics, and human nature ... a striking work of speculative sci-fi."

- The BookLife Prize

"A beautifully moving book centered around humanity's relationship with genetic engineering."

- IndieReader

FINDING
THE GIFT

BOOK TWO OF
THE CRISPR EVOLUTION SERIES

CHARIS JONES

Rights hereby granted: one-time non-exclusive rights in the English language throughout the world to include certain specific verses from THE ESSENTIAL RUMI, copyright 1985 by Coleman Barks. HarperCollins Publishers New York NY, USA. The verses are: "The Milk of Millennia," p.273, "Music Master," p.106, "Not a Day on Any Calendar," p.41, "With You Here Between," p.288, "Green Ears," p.241, "The Dream that Must be Interpreted," p.113

Print ISBN: 979-8-9863849-3-1
.mobi ISBN: 979-8-9863849-5-5
.epub ISBN: 979-8-9863849-4-8
Library of Congress Control Number: 2025917020

Published in Reno, NV, USA

*In memory of E.O. Wilson
and with gratitude for his marvelous books*

*And for Pete, who can't get his hands on something
without making it better*

Author's Note

I consider *CRISPR Evolution* to be hard science fiction mixed with a dollop of fantasy. *Finding the Gift*—the continuing story of the Wake family—isn't so easy to categorize. There's still a hefty amount of real science in these pages, but there's an even heftier amount of the fantastical and—in every sense of the word—the speculative. Howard's tinkering opened up a can of cosmic worms that led to questions I couldn't address without shamelessly crossing genres. I may never know the answers, but probing these questions with the Wake family has been a thrilling, disturbing, and humbling experience. Their tale is an ongoing exploration, and I hope you'll enjoy the journey as much as I have.

The CRISPR Evolution Series

CRISPR Evolution
Finding the Gift

Contents

Part One

Split Soul

*Conscious decisions
and personal memory
are much too small a place to live.*

- Rumi, "The Milk of Millennia"

I

Too warm in here, said a familiar voice in Aurie's head, as usual demanding attention at the worst possible time.

She was using the thread-like appendages that grew from her forearm to rinse a pH probe and extract a glass pipette from its holder, while unstoppering a jar of acid with her hands. With a frustrated groan, Aurie put everything down and hurried over to the source of the complaint in the nursery corner of the lab.

It's thirty-seven degrees Celsius, she silently informed the embryo in his bath. *Normal body temperature.*

I'm producing a lot of heat, said One Fish. His eyes, which were just starting to form, appeared to focus on her. She wondered what he saw through those nascent windows. A world of vague shapes and blurred textures? Or nothing at all yet? The ideas and images he projected into her mind were always clear and vivid. And how could he do that, when his brain had only begun to develop?

Stop wondering how, she scolded herself. *Gods aren't saddled with the same requirements as the rest of us. You, of all people, ought to know that.*

Aurie turned the heat in the tank down two degrees. This tank—and the one beside it—were the same artificial wombs she and her brother had spent their first nine months of life in. Both tanks sat atop a wheeled cart for easy transport. She waited as the temperature in the incubator slowly dropped.

Better?

One Fish didn't answer, but Aurie felt his relief pass through her mind like a cool current. Satisfied, she turned to the other resident of Casa del Utero in her neighboring tank. *And how are you doing? Not too hot, not too cold? Would Her Highness like me to turn on the jets?*

McElligot's Pool, said Two Fish, ignoring Aurie's snide remark—if she even understood it.

Not again, Aurie groaned, glancing back at her unfinished buffer solution. *We read that three times last night! I'm busy trying to purify your growth factors.*

McElligot's Pool, McElligot's Pool, demanded the little tyrant, and now her brother was chiming in.

"What other nine-year-old on earth has to deal with this?" Aurie muttered, though well aware that she had eagerly signed up for the job of underaged parent. With a sigh, she pulled the Dr. Seuss book from its shelf and sat down in the big armchair beside the tanks. Both of her progeny had a distinct penchant for the good Doctor, starting with *One fish two fish red fish blue fish,* but *McElligot's Pool* had quickly become their hands-down *(fins-down?)* favorite. Aurie didn't have to read the story out loud, but she did have to read it from beginning to end. The Fishes knew the book by heart and would complain mightily if she skipped anything. Aurie was halfway through the lineup of uncharted sea creatures when her dad entered the room.

"Goofing off again!" Howard shook his head in mock disapproval as he opened an incubator to check the growth of bacterial colonies on several plates.

Aurie snorted in aggravation. "Why don't *you* read to your grandkids so I can finish what I was doing?"

Howard made his way to the workbench at the far end of the lab, and took a pH reading on Aurie's buffer. "You know they can't hear a thing I say. You're the only one who can keep them entertained."

That, Aurie thought, was annoyingly true. She was also the only one who could really see them in any detail, thanks to her enhanced vision. Thus far, the embryos' development was faster than normal, but they were still no bigger than a pair of navy beans. Dwarfed at this stage by the size of their incubators, each embryo drifted in a transparent, membranous sac filled with nutrients and suspended in thick liquid—a sac which would expand as they grew. They were nearly translucent themselves, but touched in places with a warmth that heralded color, like the first hints of light in the dawn sky. And Aurie could have sworn they flushed a bit whenever they got upset, as they were now. Accustomed to immediate gratification, both embryos began howling at the interruption—but only in her head.

"Calm down!" Aurie was irritated enough to admonish them out loud. "You two get everything you want—but until you can fend for yourselves, you're going to have to learn some patience."

Her dad chuckled as he dripped acid into her flask.

"What's so funny?" she demanded.

"Oh, nothing. Nothing out of the ordinary here ... just a nine-year-old teaching fetuses the value of patience." Howard shook his head, looking bemused. "You're a good mom, kiddo."

"Well, I don't feel like a mom," Aurie said morosely. "More like a babysitter who's on call day and night."

Her dad chuckled again. "That's what parents are."

Maybe so, but Aurie knew her connection with her children was hardly of the normal human variety. Awake, the embryos demanded her constant attention, and there was no mental door she could shut against those demands. Asleep, their dreams often found a way into hers, with unsettling effect. She could never remember those strange visions and voyages upon waking, but they had the quality of ancient memories, and they left her with an ache so deep that the ordinary activities of the day barely eased it. She gazed at the Fishes thoughtfully. Obedient to her admonishment, they were waiting quietly in their tanks, but she could feel their pent-up impatience in her head. It was a Herculean effort they were exerting.

"Sometimes it's hard to believe they're my kids," she murmured. "More like weird little pets." *Telepathic fish.* Her children were curved like fish and although they didn't swim, they could certainly writhe around in excitement or displeasure—and how could they do that without fully developed muscles? Artificial wombs were generally kept in the dark to simulate conditions in utero, but the embryos had insisted on a constant source of light, as if they were plants. And they made other odd demands, within the limited scope of their ability to communicate. Weird little pets indeed, and they drove her crazy—but she loved them more than anything.

Howard glanced at the tanks as he opened a box of syringe filters. "You and Py didn't look much different at that stage. Human embryos never look very human. In fact, all embryos look pretty much the same at the beginning."

Like aliens, thought Aurie. Her dad knew as well as she did that these two were not ordinary embryos of any kind. The Fishes might have the same genetic hardware as the rest of humanity, but they were running some extrahuman programs.

You're running an extrahuman program yourself. Aurie glanced down at the indigo fall of the threads that grew from her left forearm. Those alien-looking structures were expert sensors, dexterous tools, and deadly weapons—although these days, she only used them for convenience ... and to catch the family's dinner.

As Aurie continued the story, her children settled down. They couldn't see the pictures in the book she held, but they could see the images in her mind, and they delighted in every wild piscine creature that had swum through the mind of Dr. Seuss. When she reached the last page, Aurie could feel their satisfaction as profoundly as if they were nestled in her lap. Smiling, she closed the book and looked up to find her dad watching with a funny expression.

"What?" she said.

He laughed a little and shook his head. "Reminds me of when I used to read to *you.* Except that you always corrected my pronunciation and said my interpretation of the story was all wrong. Then you complained that it was derivative, and demanded that I verify my sources."

"I did not," she protested, as the Fishes began clamoring for a repeat performance.

Again! Again!

"No, that's enough," Aurie said firmly. Government interrogators could probably learn a few torture techniques from the Fishes. "It's time for breakfast, thank God." She returned the book to its shelf, catching her dad's grin as he wheeled Casa del Utero out the door.

II

Surely no children in the world had ever been fussed over as much as the Fishes, or had such an eventful prenatal history. The Wakes were no strangers to genetic engineering, but Aurie's eggs hadn't been tinkered with, they had simply been *awakened*. It was a distinction that had spawned a whole world of trouble.

At the root of the trouble was the fact that all organisms on Earth contained a god-encoding template in their genomes. Aurie and her CRISPR-evo Doctor surmised that although it was nested in DNA and passed on like DNA, the god template was more like a cocoon than a gene—a cocoon sheltering a sleeping god. By activating Aurie's template, the Doctor had awakened the god within her, and like the shreds of an old cocoon, the template itself was lost. It had disappeared from her genome in every cell of her body ... except for her eggs, those germ cells that would give rise to new life. Aurie's god had proceeded to activate its template in those eggs, awakening a god in each—a god that was apparently still in stasis, waiting for its host to develop. Aurie and her mother had managed to harvest and freeze those precious eggs, but doing so had nearly cost the family its freedom. With agents from FIBR— the Federal Institute for Biomedical Research—on their tail, Jacqueline had convinced her ex-husband to hide the eggs in his own lab while they rejoined Howard's brother at his cabin in the Maine woods. Much to the kids' delight, Abel insisted that they stay with him, safely off-grid. With the help of Alé, Howard's friend and facilitator, Aurie's eggs were recovered and the Wakes acquired a cryotank and a steady supply of liquid nitrogen. Once Aurie's eggs were home, the entire family was together—for the very first time—and everyone could finally breathe a sigh of relief.

With the youngest generation safely situated, the next order of business—as far as Py and Aurie were concerned—was getting

Howard and Jacqueline married.

"You know rogue marriages aren't legally binding, right?" Howard pointed out dryly to his kids.

"That's not the point, Dad," Aurie said, glancing at her mom.

"Then what *is* the point?" Howard asked.

"Showing Mom that you love her," Py said sternly. "That you'll always be there for her, no matter what!"

"I *do* love her," Howard protested. "And I *will* always be there for her. It's the first time in my life I can say that with absolute certainty. Your mom and I were both married before—a grand total of three times, in fact—so we are well-versed in the making and breaking of vows. We're not big fans of them. If you really mean something, no vow is necessary—and if you don't mean it, no vow will hold you."

Jacqueline, who had been watching her kids with fond bemusement, finally spoke up. "Yes, but this is different. I'm part of the family now, and we ought to have a ceremony celebrating that. A *family* wedding, not just a regular one." She cocked an eye at Howard. "And I'd like to be able to call you my husband, instead of the man who stole my eggs. Has a nicer ring to it, don't you think?"

And so Abel performed the unofficial ceremony in the living room of his cabin, having placed his shotgun in full view on the mantelpiece for a bit of fun. For the grand reception, he and the kids served a fricassee—from wild rabbits that Aurie caught—and a beautiful white-frosted carrot cake. They toasted with apple juice in daisy-printed tumblers and stayed up late watching old movies on the incredibly vivid holo-display of Jacqueline's new Spider. Since she'd had to leave her old life behind, Howard had given her a deluxe Ghost version of the mini communication device, bemoaning the exorbitant cost. "More than two wedding rings put together," he'd groaned. "But a million times more useful!"

The next day, the unofficial Mr. and Mrs. Wake gathered the family together for a serious discussion about their living situation. Abel had offered to let them stay at his place indefinitely, but spreading themselves between the small cabin and the RV was hardly a permanent solution. They needed a house, and one that wouldn't attract undue attention. To the prospect of a new house, Abel had readily agreed, saying that an upgrade in his living conditions would be most welcome.

"Are you moving in with us, Uncle Abel?" Py asked happily.

"Well, of course I am!" Abel growled. "You think I'm going to stay in this old shack while the rest of you live in the lap of luxury, sipping cocktails on your veranda? Besides, you're going to need a cook and a handyman and an errand-boy—"

"And someone to pull our fat out of the fire." Jacqueline gave her brother-in-law a look that said she hadn't forgotten. "But how can we build a house that won't be noticed? We can't go underground ... literally. Or can we?"

"Not without bringing in a giant bulldozer," Howard said. "The logistics are going to be dangerous enough already. Anything we build will be visible from the air, and Abel says the surveillance drones pass over twice a month! We can't even pitch a tent without someone noticing. And the last thing we need is a citation for having no building permit ... followed by a government inspection."

"We can't just get a permit?" Jacqueline asked. "Using one of your fake identities?"

Howard shook his head. "That's a surefire recipe for getting caught. I've only survived this long because I use my fake credentials for nothing but basic supplies and utilities. And my face-altering glasses are only good for distance scanners. If 'Robert P. Hartwell' ever had to appear in real life, we'd be sunk."

"So where does that leave us?" Jacqueline asked.

"We could build a treehouse," Py suggested.

Howard chuckled. "I doubt there's a tree big enough to house all the Swiss Family Wakes. Especially once the Fishes graduate from their tanks."

"Well, we have to do *something,*" Jacqueline said. "Attach a couple of shipping containers to this cabin? Surely we could do that much without a permit or an inspection."

They continued to discuss and debate while Abel merely listened quietly.

Howard finally noticed his brother's silence. "What do *you* think we should do, Abe? This is your property, after all."

Abel smirked. "Now that you ask, I've had a solution in mind for some time, but I couldn't resist letting you stew for a bit."

They all stared at him, and Abel's eyes took on an impish gleam. "What would you say if I told you that a fine, upstanding gentleman named Abelard Wake—I mean, Abner Griswold—owns a piece of land not five miles from here ... with a house he designed and built himself?"

Howard blinked. "I'd say it doesn't sound anything like that particular gentleman! Since when does a frugal hermit need anything more luxurious than this?" He waved his arms at the splintery walls of the small cabin.

"I didn't say it was luxurious," Abel warned him. "And, believe it or not, there was a time when Mr. Griswold hoped to abandon his solitary ways ... but life is good at making toast of our plans." A shadow crossed his face briefly, then he smiled at Py and Aurie. "Anyway, I believe the old fellow could be persuaded to turn a house he never used into a retreat for rogue scientists and their illegal offspring."

With joyful yelps, the kids threw themselves into Abel's arms. Howard and Jacqueline looked as if they wanted to do the same.

Howard shook his head. "Abel ... my God. I don't know what to say."

"Well, that's a first," Abel said, his eyes twinkling as he released his niece and nephew. "This other property is off a different road, a logging road that hasn't been used in decades. We might have to clear it in places, but I've got some friends who can help with that. The main thing is, we won't have to do any new construction."

Jacqueline looked dazed. "This is too good to be true! Seriously, how can we ever repay you?"

"Seeing your husband speechless is payment enough," Abel said, pulling up several holo-images on his Spider. "But I expect all of you to turn that useless, empty house into a real home. We can head over there on the UTV later, but here are the plans ... and some photos of the place in summer. You can see it's well tucked away."

Howard peered at the images and shook his head in admiration. "This is fantastic! I couldn't have planned it better myself."

"The ultimate compliment," Abel said, rolling his eyes.

Getting Uncle Abel's CRISPR-evo Farm (as Py had dubbed it) ready the following spring was a fairly simple matter, thanks to Abel's trusted friends in useful places. It was with a dizzying sense of wonder that the Wakes moved into their new house in early May. It wasn't a mansion, but it was far more living space than any of them had ever known. More importantly for Py and Aurie, who had never lived anywhere with an actual foundation, it was *home*.

Off the abandoned logging road lay an open glade hemmed in by stands of spruce. A grove of mature oak trees hid the house and a free-standing garage, behind which was plenty of room for the RV. A short path led from the garage to the front patio. Abel, who couldn't imagine spending significant waking time in any room besides the kitchen, had consequently designed his front door to open onto a very spacious one, complete with a big hickory table at one end.

"A kitchen is the heart and soul of a house," he had told his family in defense of this unorthodox design. "Do you really want to sit around in a so-called living room? Of course not! You want to be where the coffee is brewing, where a pot needs stirring, where it smells like home."

On one side of the glorious kitchen was an afterthought of a living room; on the other side was a library with French doors that opened onto their newly planted garden. A hallway off the kitchen led to two master suites, one of which Abel had insisted belonged to Howard and Jacqueline. The other suite would serve as the family's lab. Upstairs were two bedrooms for the kids, and a den, which Abel took for himself. There was even a veranda on the side of the house flanking the garden. There wouldn't be much to see there until later in the season, but the Wakes could hardly wait to sip their cocktails, apple juice, and barley tea on a real veranda.

"Doesn't look much like a Supervillain Hideout, does it?"

Howard said to Jacqueline on the morning of their move-in, as they stood outside the pleasant grey frame house with its neat white trim.

She shook her head. "Much too tasteful and charming."

"Exactly what I was thinking." Howard kissed her bright hair as their kids took possession of the house with gleeful whoops. "Well ... I guess we'll just have to make the best of it."

"We can always make some tasteless additions out of shipping containers," Abel said, passing them with a loaded handcart and the air of a man who doesn't waste time while others stand around admiring architecture. "And we'll have to, if you want this place to live up to its name."

"I guess it's not quite a CRISPR-evo farm," Howard allowed, as they hurried to help unload the RV. "But it's pretty amazing, isn't it? The Wake Family Manor! Never thought I'd see the day."

The most important part of the new house was the lab, which would also serve as a nursery. Here Howard and Jacqueline lost no time setting up the Wake Institute for Garage Biology in its Maine incarnation, resuming Howard's old contract work while preparing for their *real* work—giving life to Aurie's eggs. Regarding the latter, Howard and Aurie were in favor of immediate action, a time frame Jacqueline viewed with considerably less enthusiasm.

"She's nine years old," Jacqueline reminded her husband. "And you want to make her a single mother?"

"Age is just a number," Howard scoffed. "Especially when it comes to our kids. And she's hardly alone! What are the rest of us, chopped liver? We've all agreed to take care of the little monsters. Aurie won't have to do any more than a big sister would."

"It's not that simple," Jacqueline said. "There's an emotional component to being a parent, and you have to be ready for it."

She looked to Abel for help, but Abel only shrugged eloquently, as if to say, *You people are all nuts, and I'm just here to keep you out of jail.*

"I'm not too young to love them," Aurie said. "I love them already!"

Jacqueline smiled at her, but there was something pained in her smile. "I know you do. And you love the rest of us, but you're not *responsible* for us. If something happened to one of your own kids ... "

"It's okay, Mom," she said. "These are gods I've woken, remember? I think they'll be able to take care of themselves."

Py, who had followed the trail of bones Aurie's own god had left in the woods, snorted in agreement. Jacqueline, who had spent even more time with Aurie's god, shifted uncomfortably. Kindling the growth of unknown gods was sheer madness, and yet it felt inevitable ... and irresistible.

You rescued those eggs for a reason, she reminded herself, knowing the exact reason was hard to define. She had seen the godlike entities sleeping in every terrestrial genome, and the Pattern they would form on awakening. A Pattern that was beyond her understanding, and yet everything in Jacqueline hearkened to it, yearned to serve it. Aurie's eggs carried more than her own progeny; each carried the life of an awakened god, an essential thread in that Pattern. Jacqueline had been compelled to save them, just as she was now compelled to help them grow.

"Okay," she said resolutely. "How many embryos are we making? And don't say a dozen," she warned Howard, who closed his mouth in a hurry. "We're not turning this house into a sardine tin."

"Can we assume that these super-evolved critters will be smart enough to feed themselves and change their own diapers?" Abel asked hopefully.

"If they're really smart," Py said, "they'll stop growing and stay in that nice warm bath for the rest of their lives. I would!"

"How about half a dozen?" Howard suggested with a teasing glint in his eye. "Think about it, Jackie. Six kids and five of us works out to only 1.2 child per nanny—simplest thing in the world! Hell of a lot easier than running a mouse colony."

"Six CRISPR-evo kids will be running *us,*" Jacqueline said.

"Exactly." Howard grinned as if she were making his point for him. "Aurie's eggs all have her CRISPR machine, so these kids will be CRISPR-evo even *after* their gods fly off. They'll be as smart and independent as the two we've already got!"

"Sounds like they'll be causing no end of trouble," Abel groused. "Maybe we should just start with one."

"One is hardly worth the trouble to feed!" Howard complained. "And we have *two* incubators—"

"Maybe we should ask their mother," Jacqueline said. "How many do *you* want, Aurie? We'll do everything we can to help, but they're your kids. It's really up to you."

It wasn't a simple question for Aurie to answer. Her eggs might be frozen in a cryotank, but she felt them as real, living presences in the house. They all held that vital spark she had been deprived of when her god flew away to seed a new planet with life. Now she felt only a ghost of that spark inside her, while her children were like blazing fireflies trapped in a jar. How many should they set free? Releasing one at a time would be the smart thing to do ... but Aurie was struck by how lonely she would have been as an only child. She couldn't even imagine growing up without Py.

"How about two?" she said at last, and they all agreed that two was a manageable number—insofar as the unknown could be deemed manageable.

Once the incubators were up and running, the next question was how to make embryos from Aurie's eggs without fertilizing them. During a family lab meeting, Howard and Jacqueline outlined their options—several new methods of artificial reproduction—but Jacqueline was uncharacteristically tense and reserved. At the end of the lecture, the question remained: which way should they try?

"You're the expert in these things," Howard told Jacqueline. "You should decide."

Jacqueline sighed. "I have no experience with any of these new techniques! And how can I practice on Aurie's eggs?"

Howard looked at her in surprise. "The best developmental biologist in the world, and you're as twitchy as a first-year grad student! Were you this nervous when you engineered your own eggs?"

"This isn't the same thing at all," Jacqueline said testily. "My eggs were just ordinary eggs—seeds of life, but not life itself. Aurie's eggs are *alive*. She awakened the god template in each of them! Right now, every one of her eggs has a god inside it, awake and eager to be born."

Py frowned. "Why can't these gods just activate their own development? Seriously ... they're *gods*. Why do they need us at all?"

The room went quiet as everyone thought about it, this simple question they hadn't even considered. What kind of help did a god need?

"I don't think they need much help," Aurie finally said. She was gazing at the cryotank as if listening to the murmurs of voices only she could hear. "But they're frozen down in vials at minus two hundred degrees. I think they just need us to warm them up ... and give them nutrients and a place to grow."

"Well, who needs the world's best scientists for that?" Abel scoffed. "Sounds like even *I* could manage it."

"But wait a minute," said Howard to Aurie. "Gods or no gods, your eggs still need another complement of genetic material! Where is it going to come from, if we just put two eggs in a dish?"

"You're talking over my head," Abel complained. "I don't have to be part of these science discussions, but if you want me to sit in, you're going to have to explain things like that."

Howard turned to his brother with a patient sigh. "Forgot your high school biology, Abe? We each have twenty-three *pairs* of chromosomes, one set from Mom and one from Dad. Aurie's eggs provide *Mom's* complement of genetic material, but where is *Dad's* going to come from?" He paused, turning back to his daughter. Aurie just stared at him, unfazed.

"Or will the god in each egg simply replicate all of its haploid chromosomes?" Howard mused. "But if that's the case, they'll all be female, God help us! A male embryo would require constructing an artificial Y chromosome from—"

"Seriously, Dad," Aurie said, rolling her eyes. "I could make a Y chromosome in my sleep! And these gods will be a lot more capable than I am. If any of them wants to be male ... "

Abel chuckled. "Not exactly high school biology, Howard."

"You really think they'll start developing on their own?" Jacqueline was looking at her daughter with undisguised hope and relief. "But Dr. Hahn froze down over eight hundred thousand of your eggs in about a hundred vials. Just by thawing a single vial, we'll be warming up thousands of eggs—and if you're right, we only need two of them! What should we do with all the rest? We can't refreeze them, and we certainly can't dispose of them."

"Go ahead and refreeze them," Aurie told her mother. "If the eggs can develop on their own, they can also repair any damage caused by thawing and refreezing. I don't think you'll lose a single egg."

"And what choice do we have?" Howard pointed out. "Either we thaw out a vial, or we don't!"

Later that afternoon, feeling more like a first-year student than ever, Jacqueline placed two of her daughter's eggs into a dish of warm media, which she set in their cell incubator. No one really knew what to expect, but Aurie's faith was rewarded. Within hours, the eggs had begun to divide. Days later, the family had two viable blastocysts—one male and one female.

As the tiny embryos grew, their connection with Aurie soon became apparent. She felt her children's sense of well-being, eagerness, restlessness, or dissatisfaction while they were still two unformed balls of cells, invisible to the naked eye. Sensitive to their needs, she naturally became their primary caregiver. She assisted her dad in making and purifying nutrients and growth factors, while Jacqueline and Abel continued to run errands in town, including reagent pickups from their premium PO box in Gorham. With five full-time staff serving two residents with special needs, Casa del Utero became the most luxurious and personalized hotel in the world.

On some instinctive whim, Aurie tried reading Dr. Seuss to the embryos. Since their ears hadn't formed yet, she read to them silently, in her head. They responded with their first telepathic communications (*Wow! Wonderful fish! More, more!*), which she suspected were not words at all, but pure meaning translated into words in her brain. They could somehow grasp the story in her mind and see the mental images projected there, an ability that both thrilled and baffled Aurie. Telepathy was conceivable, but it required a telepathic *mind,* and her children's brains had barely begun to develop. How were the embryos aware, and how were they able to communicate?

Py thought the Fishes' telepathy was accomplished directly through their auras. He said the embryos had strange and lovely auras, bright as living stars.

"It's hard to describe the textures," he said. "Smooth and cold like crystal, but silky and warm like honey, at the same time. They're a lot like yours was, after your human aura fused with your god's aura." According to Py, these embryonic auras had no defined shape, ebbing and flowing like pseudopods of molten glass. He believed that auras were a manifestation of *souls,* and he thought the Fishes' souls hadn't yet decided on a form.

"They can reach through their tanks and touch each other," he marveled, when the Fishes were only a few days old. "They're always probing and twining with those pseudopods. Sometimes they're so connected, they look like one single aura. And sometimes they reach out and touch *your* aura—that's gotta be how they communicate with you."

"But how am *I* communicating with *them?*" she wanted to know. "I can't reach out and touch them like that, but when I talk to them in my head, they hear me."

"I'm just guessing here," said Py, warming to his favorite subject with the alacrity of a professor. "But maybe that first contact—aura-to-aura—established a kind of connection, so the telepathy works both ways."

It was as good an explanation as any. As the embryos grew, Py discovered that their auras often left their bodies completely to follow Aurie around the house. The Fishes even joined her on her forays into the woods, although they seemed to have a distance limitation. If she went too far, Py said, their auras halted, lingering in the air, before returning to their tank-bound forms.

The deeper implications of all this weren't lost on Aurie.

Their mom and dad assumed the Fishes were human souls with a god attached to each of them, but Aurie wasn't so sure. Each of her children had only *one* aura, of undefined shape and inhuman abilities. Were the Fishes god or human or some hybrid of the two? What if their souls *became* fully god and flew away, leaving nothing but their soulless bodies behind? Just the thought was enough to turn her cold.

And so Aurie took full advantage of the Fishes' early consciousness to show them everything she could about humanity. She read myths and folk tales and adventure stories. She played the music of Beethoven, Debussy, Dvorak, and Rachmaninoff, along with her dad's favorite rock ballads. She pored over art, from wild fantasy paintings to delicate watercolors and dramatic sculptures. She showed them portraits of human history and suffering, human achievements and failures. Gardens and landfills, medicines and weapons, sanctuaries and war monuments. Anything and everything she thought they ought to see.

Aurie hadn't mentioned her fears to anyone but Py, and she expected their dad, at least, to give her some grief for "goofing off" with the Fishes. But despite his teasing, Howard took her attempts to educate them as seriously as she did. Jacqueline, too, was approving and encouraging, no doubt remembering her own attempts to keep Aurie's human self from being extinguished by her god. And including the Fishes at family meals had been Jacqueline's idea. No one in the family had any doubt that the god part of the embryos could take care of itself ... it was the human part they worried about.

III

As she followed her dad to the kitchen, Aurie watched her children wriggle with anticipation. They loved family meals. Whatever the Fishes saw and heard at these gatherings—through Aurie's mind or in some other way—was clearly a source of great entertainment to them.

"And here we are in the kitchen," Howard announced, as he did every morning, wheeling Casa del Utero to its customary place at the table. He often played tour guide to his grandkids, especially when Jacqueline was around to be annoyed by it. "Where we satisfy our nutritional needs and engage in meaningful *human* communication." He gave the Fishes a significant look, then grinned at his wife, who rolled her eyes as she set the table.

"I think they've figured that out by now," Aurie said, wincing at the mental pressure of the embryos' mounting excitement.

"Sure, but kids need structure and predictability. And you know they love repetition." Howard grabbed his oversized mug from the cabinet, then saw that the coffeepot was empty and turned to Py. "Where's the coffee, kiddo?"

Py was in charge of breakfast that morning, but as usual, his attention was elsewhere. He was cracking eggs while staring through the countertop—and the last egg had missed the bowl.

Py's first CRISPR-evo Change had given him the ability to see the auras of living things, which he believed to be a manifestation of each creature's soul, or essence. There were biological chemicals and emotions attached to auras, and Py had quickly learned to read their changing weather. But after his second Change, which allowed him to see auras through any object, Py had been deeply preoccupied by the hundreds of auras visible to him at any given time, in any given place. And lately, he seemed to be even more distracted than usual. Howard nudged him with his empty

30

mug, and Py jumped.

"What?" Py said, scowling at his dad. "What's wrong? I'm making the eggs and sausage, the toast is ready, Mom's getting all the forks and stuff—"

"You forgot the coffee," Howard said. "And watch what you're doing there." He scooped up most of the fallen egg from the countertop and plopped it into the bowl with the others, then wiped the counter and seated himself next to his grandkids. "You see that, fishlings? Working in the kitchen takes just as much concentration as working in the lab. Watch closely and you'll see all the horrors that can befall the inattentive cook, as your uncle slices his fingers into the sausage and starts a grease fire."

"There's no insurance on this house," Abel warned them as he came in from the hall. "So unless you all want to cram into the old cabin again, I suggest you watch what you're doing."

"Say good morning to your venerable Godfather and Benefactor," Howard instructed the Fishes. "As you'll see once you're old enough for solid food, he's like a loaf of sourdough bread—crusty on the outside, but soft on the inside. Still sour all the way through, but you'll get used to that."

Abel turned on the coffee grinder, which effectively covered his muttered response.

"He tends to sweeten up a little as the day goes on," Howard continued cheerfully. "I suspect he had too many nips from the bottle last night, judging from his red eyes, unkempt appearance, and late arrival."

"It was barley tea," Abel grumbled as he filled the coffeepot with water. "But you're tempting me to indulge in something stronger. I never *used* to have any trouble getting up in the morning. Look what the four of you have done to me. Pardon me, the *six* of you."

"Also notice how he blames us for his sloth," Howard murmured to the Fishes. "He won't admit that he stays up late watching old cooking shows and reading historical novels on that Spider of his."

"I'm keeping up with the *news,*" Abel informed his brother

huffily. "Which is not exactly a pleasant task ... but with all of you to look out for, I no longer have the luxury of burying my head in the woods."

Howard chuckled and his stomach rumbled. "Good God, I'm starving! You Fishes are lucky to be swimming in an all-hours buffet."

With an aggrieved snort, Py poured the eggs into a smoking pan, then slid a plate in front of his dad, sending two pieces of burned toast flying into Howard's lap.

"Hey!" Howard salvaged the toast and brushed himself off. "I don't expect five-star service, but try to keep the food on the plates."

"Sorry, Dad," Py mumbled. To Aurie's surprise, her brother really did look sorry. He went to find a spatula, but Jacqueline beat him to it.

"Grab some napkins and I'll finish up here," she told him, giving the eggs a brisk stir and turning the temperature down.

Py wandered off in search of napkins and Howard sighed as he buttered his burned toast. "What is wrong with that kid? He wanders around in a fog all day ... worse than a teenager."

"I can hear you, Dad," Py muttered from the pantry.

"And I hope you're listening!" said Howard. "You can't go around staring at auras every minute of the day. What auras are you looking at, anyway? All the insects for miles around?"

Py emerged from the pantry, *sans* napkins. "Not just insects—mice and voles and foxes and birds. There's a flock of wild turkeys roosting on the east side of the oak grove."

"Wild turkeys, eh?" Abel looked hopefully at Aurie. "We haven't had any turkey for awhile."

Howard frowned at Py. "The only birds you should be paying attention to are those chicken eggs in the pan. Which your mother is cooking for you."

"Do eggs have auras?" Abel asked Py. "I mean the ones in nests, before they're hatched. You say the Little Fishes do, and they're a long way from being full-term."

"Every fertilized egg has an aura," said Py with authority.

"The aura is faint at first, but it gets brighter and takes on a definite shape as the embryo grows. An *unfertilized* egg doesn't have an aura ... unless it has an awakened god inside it."

"So the Fishes had auras even when they were just frozen eggs?" Abel pressed.

Py nodded. "All the other eggs in the cryotank have them too."

"All eight hundred thousand?" asked Jacqueline.

"Yeah."

"And they're all different?"

Py shrugged. "Hard to say, since none of them have a fixed shape yet."

Abel shook his head in bewilderment. "You've been talking about these auras for months, and I still don't understand them. A regular dormant egg doesn't have an aura, but a fertilized or god-awakened egg does? Is it just chemicals that make the difference? The special chemicals of life?"

"I don't know," Py said. "Auras are full of biochemicals that change all the time. But I think the auras themselves are energy of some kind ... an energy framework in which the chemicals shift."

"But you think these auras are ... kind of like our souls, don't you? So even the smallest worm has a soul? Bacteria and viruses, too?" Abel didn't sound disparaging, only curious.

Py gazed intently at his uncle. "Soul? Life essence? I don't know what to call it ... some intangible part of us that's the same in everything. Like bits of flame from the same fire. But if microscopic organisms have auras, they're too small to see."

"And you can identify the type of organism by the shape of its aura?" Abel sounded impressed.

"Sure," Py said. "Just like you can tell a human from a lion or a rabbit just by looking at him! And the *exact* shape of each aura is unique too, like a fingerprint." He glanced at the tanks. "The Fishes might end up with shapes that are *really* unique."

"We have to stop calling them that." Jacqueline shook her head as she brought a platter of steaming scrambled eggs and sausage to the table. The smell of the sausage—made from a deer

Aurie had hunted and Abel had butchered—made Aurie's mouth water, and she filled her plate quickly.

"They're going to be babies and then kids pretty soon," Jacqueline pointed out. "Which means they're going to need real names."

"Why? It's not like we're sending them off to school." Howard's tone was still light, but his mood had sobered—and his gaze kept drifting to Py, who was eating with dogged attention. "We can call our little monsters whatever we want, Jackie."

"Until they fly off to some distant corner of the cosmos," Abel put in.

"Only their gods will do that," Jacqueline assured him. "Aurie's god flew off, but the rest of her stayed right here, thank God."

"Did you have a choice about that?" Abel asked his niece.

Aurie looked at her uncle in surprise. It was the first time he had ever referred—even indirectly—to her god. He had listened, along with the rest of the family, to her explanation of what had happened the previous autumn: how she had hunted down some rare mushrooms and used them to circumvent the Policeman, her mother's quality-control mechanism that patrolled every cell of Aurie's body. How the Doctor, her CRISPR-evo machine, had awakened the god asleep in her genome, and how that god had taken control of her mind until the eve of its flight. All of that was improbable enough, but Aurie's assertion—from her god's own knowledge—that she was not unique, that a template encoding a sleeping god existed in the genome of every organism on Earth, was even more far-fetched. It was clear that Abel felt such things were out of his depth. And now he was asking if she had a choice about flying off with her god, or staying behind?

"Yeah," she told him. "I didn't have a lot of time to decide, but I had a choice."

Abel turned to look at the Fishes in their tanks. "So they'll probably have a choice too, won't they?"

Everyone paused in their eating, waiting for Aurie to answer. She sighed. "Probably."

"But their human souls shouldn't fly off if they're attached to us," Jacqueline said, giving Howard a worried look. "If they know what it means to be human … and part of a family. That's why *this* is so important."

"But what if their gods fly away before they're old enough to understand anything?" Abel frowned at the Little Fishes as if they might sprout wings and burst the confines of their tanks at any minute, then he turned back to Aurie. "How soon do you think that could happen?"

"I have no idea," Aurie said, more sharply than she intended. But God, they were always asking her for answers to unanswerable questions. And although the Fishes were quiet now, she knew they were craving stimulation. The talk at the table had ceased to interest them and she could feel their restlessness as a physical pressure behind her temples. She rubbed her head.

"They're driving you crazy, aren't they?" said Howard. He glanced at Py—who had finished eating and was staring down through the depths of his empty plate—then gave Aurie a sympathetic look. "Why don't you take the day off. Your mom and I can take care of the critters."

"The whole day?" Aurie felt a surge of relief. "That would be great. Thanks!" She made haste to finish her breakfast.

"Can I be excused too?" asked Py. "After I clean up and do all the dishes?"

For a wonder, Howard nodded. "And never mind the dishes. They'll be safer without you."

IV

Jacqueline watched her kids run off together—like fellow prisoners on parole—and found herself worrying about both of them. Aurie's troubles were harder to pinpoint, but there was definitely something wrong, something beyond the strain of caring for two demanding, telepathic embryos. Beneath her daughter's calm and competent exterior, Jacqueline sensed a nebulous pain, even desperation. She had tried to gently probe the source of this, but the girl shied away from any attempt to discuss it. Howard sensed Aurie's distress, too—it was why he often encouraged her to go off into the woods—but Jacqueline hadn't yet brought it up with him. Py's problems, on the other hand, had been the subject of many short and unresolved discussions.

Abel brought the coffeepot to the table and refilled their mugs. "You're worried about him, aren't you?" he said to Howard.

Howard grimaced. "I've seen octogenarians who aren't as scatterbrained."

"He's not really scatterbrained," Jacqueline said, glancing at the litter of crumbs that marked Py's place at the table. "Just completely focused on auras. Following his evolution, isn't he?"

"Most kids evolve," Howard said. "From useless idiots to worthwhile adults if they have a little correction along the way. But Py was never useless ... and he never really needed any correction."

"How much correction did *you* have?" Jacqueline wondered. "Or did your parents figure it wasn't worth the effort?"

"Well, it wasn't," Abel said. "But our parents, God bless them, never stopped trying. Howard got punished over and over, and it didn't make a lick of difference. You know when he was about Py's age, he wired up our treehouse with electricity? Which might've been okay if he hadn't drilled a hole in the side of the garage."

The image of nine-year-old Howard drilling through a garage

36

wall was so vivid and believable that Jacqueline had to laugh. "Did it even occur to you that you were going to get in trouble for that?" she asked Howard. "Or were you so fixated on your mission that nothing else mattered?"

"Mind on the mission," Howard affirmed. "Mom and Dad had some dinner to go to, and they left my responsible older brother in charge. We were hosting a party in our treehouse, but it needed real lighting." He grinned at her. "Candles would've been a fire hazard."

"That *was* a classy party," Abel admitted, then turned back to Jacqueline. "No rules or threats ever stopped your husband here from doing whatever he felt driven or curious enough to do. He experimented with Dad's chemicals in the garage, then dumped them in the exact same spot in the yard, so there was this dead patch where nothing would grow, not even pigweed." Abel chuckled, remembering. "Dad never could figure it out."

Jacqueline shook her head. "And how did *you* turn out so well-adjusted?"

"I was born that way!" Abel snorted. "Everyone gets so fussed about all this 'nature versus nurture' foolishness. People are who they are." He looked pensively at the steam rising from his mug. "But you never really know a person—and no one really knows himself—until circumstances come along to test him."

"And by circumstances, he means bad shit," Howard clarified.

"So it's all nature, then?" Jacqueline cocked her head at her brother-in-law.

"As the loving parents of any sociopath can attest," Abel said.

Jacqueline considered that as she sipped her coffee. Surely the truth was more complicated. Even the simplest organisms were shaped by their environment, and humans were anything but simple. Py, who insisted that each person's aura was as unique as a fingerprint, claimed that Howard's aura had changed shape—slightly, but distinctly—after Aurie had shown him the Pattern of gods asleep in Earthly genomes. Perhaps a soul could be born malformed, or become malformed through abuse or neglect. And—if what Py believed was true—perhaps a soul could be *reformed,* too.

"What about your parents, Doc?" Abel asked, pulling Jacqueline from her musings. "Did they waste a lot of time fretting about how to raise you?"

Jacqueline thought back. "They did for awhile. My parents believed they were accountable for everything my sister and I did until the day we turned eighteen. After that, we were on our own." She smiled a little, remembering. "I actually liked them better once they took off their parenting hats. We got to know each other, and I found out they were interesting people."

Abel nodded thoughtfully, and Jacqueline turned to her husband, who was gazing into the depths of his mug. "What kind of correction are you thinking of for Py? You know punishing him won't do any good."

Howard sighed. "I know. And we can't punish him anyway—he isn't doing anything wrong. He's just not focused on the real world."

"You know the auras he sees are real," Jacqueline said.

"So are clouds in the sky," Howard said. "But a person can't go around staring at clouds all day and tripping over what's right in front of him."

"He's not just staring at auras," Jacqueline said. "He's studying them."

"So what's he learning?"

"Ask him!"

"I have," Howard protested. "He's as hedgy as a kid who's been sneaking off to smoke a cerebloom behind the woodshed."

"Well, we need to draw him out more. The only times he's really with us are when he's talking about auras. And he spends a *lot* of time alone in the woods."

Howard frowned. "He always has, but it's never been like this. That kid was always happier in the woods or the desert or even a little patch of swampland than in the lab or the RV. And he never just goofed around outside; he was studying and learning. A self-trained field biologist from the age of five. But when he came inside, he was *home.* He was with us, paying attention, not staring into space and dropping things. He's never been distracted like this before."

"But he could never see auras before," Jacqueline reminded him. "His CRISPR machine opened up a new world for him ... and it tore down the walls that separate *inside* from *outside*. So now Py's studying the world with a sense that none of us have, that none of us can really fathom. And he's studying it with the same absorption that he always has."

"All true," Howard allowed, "but he used to *talk* about what he was studying. He used to tell me everything and ask for help with his projects. He wanted loupes and funnels and nets and lenses, all kinds of things. When's the last time Py asked for anything at all?"

"Besides Smart Foam?" Jacqueline said dryly.

"You'd think he'd want an aura-capturing lens for that camera I got him at Christmas," Abel murmured.

"But the bigger problem," Howard continued, "is that he's becoming useless when it comes to chores. And we can't ask Aurie to pick up the slack for him."

"Well, I'm happy to do all the cooking," Abel offered. "And whatever else Py can't be trusted with ... until he gets a handle on this superpower of his."

Jacqueline turned to Howard. "Which you are responsible for, let's not forget."

"Oh, he hasn't forgotten," Abel said mildly. "Why do you think he's so hard on Py?" He was quiet for a moment, looking down into his mug. "I know I'm not a parent, but I've seen more than my share of them. Moms and dads in tears at the courthouse, watching their kids on trial for cyber-trafficking, digital entrapment, or worse. They all feel responsible, and they're all wondering the exact same thing: *Where did we go wrong?* But the truth is, every kid chooses his own path no matter what his parents and teachers and friends do to influence him. It all depends on what's in here." He tapped his chest.

"But Py's only nine," Howard countered. "And I know he's responsible for his own choices, but *I'm* responsible for whatever challenges he has to face—more than any parent who makes his kid the normal way. Other parents just toss their genes into the meiotic dance and hope for the best, but I *engineered* Py's problems." He gave Jacqueline a pained look, then turned to gaze at his grandkids, who were drifting slowly in their tanks, as if ruminating on the sins of their forefather.

"Look, everyone's genes are full of blessings and curses," Abel said. "Those of us who didn't have you for a father still have Nature to contend with. But there *is* a thing called free will, even if people scoff at it these days. Py might be fascinated by auras, but he has a choice, doesn't he? To pay attention to auras, or to the rest of the world?"

Howard and Jacqueline both nodded.

"If he didn't, he wouldn't be able to function at all," Howard said.

"Then he has to fight a strong natural tendency in order to live a normal life," Abel said. "That's something a lot of folks have to deal with."

"I thought the de-risking clinics had all of humanity's unwanted tendencies taken care of," Howard said dryly. "Don't they hand out aggression modulators and greed inhibitors and humanitarian stimulators like candy?"

"Very expensive candy," Jacqueline agreed. "And all these things the government is trying to 'cure'—curiosity, aggression, passion ... they can all be a blessing or a curse, depending on the context. And where's the evidence that these drugs even work? No one outside of FIBR has seen any of the data."

"And yet the courts are requiring convicted felons to get these treatments now," Abel said.

Howard shook his head in disgust. "Your tax dollars at work and pharma laughing all the way to the bank. And you crafty lawyers getting richer than anyone!"

Abel grunted. "Who needs to be crafty anymore? Defense attorneys don't even bother establishing reasonable doubt; they just use risk genes as convenient excuses for their clients' crimes."

Jacqueline laughed and adopted a deep, gravelly voice. "I

confess, your Honor, to releasing all the filoviruses in that BSL-4 facility ... but I have a strong genetic inclination to cause mayhem. On top of that, my social responsibility gene is heavily mutated and barely functional."

Howard chuckled, then assumed a penitent expression. "I know my actions were against my own self-interest, but my contrariness gene is also hyperactive. Please forgive me!"

"And I should be taking medication for these problems," intoned Jacqueline woefully. "But alas, my willpower gene has been silenced from birth."

They grinned at Abel, who couldn't help but laugh. "Do scientists really think there's a gene for *everything?* You two obviously don't."

Howard shrugged. "There are genes for things like learning and memory and aggression ... but I don't think complex human traits have simple genetic explanations. Do you, Jackie?"

Jacqueline shook her head. "There are too many influences outside of genetics that change the way we grow and behave. That's true for all organisms. But humans are the only creatures who worry about *right* and *wrong*. We're the only ones who try to escape our genetic prison."

"Well, we don't try hard enough," Abel said with a touch of bitterness. "We have a moral compass, and we do a piss-poor job of following it."

"But where does that moral compass come from?" Howard mused. "Every religion worships different gods, and every culture has a different conception of right and wrong. Maybe *right* is whatever serves the species best ... not in the short term, but in the long run."

Jacqueline mulled that over, but she had her doubts. Deep down, she believed that *right* was cleaving to a principle that overrode the good of all group identities, including the species. She thought that principle served something greater.

"If that were true," she said, "then whatever promotes the long-term survival of any given species would be *right*. Right would be different depending on what group you belonged to, and the ends would always justify the means. We know better than that, don't we? Half of science fiction posits a doomsday scenario where humans have to do terrible things in order to survive. Atrocious things that make us less than human." She shook her head. "I never thought survival was worth such a price."

Abel grunted his agreement.

"But what makes us care about right and wrong in the first place?" Jacqueline murmured, still thinking out loud. "Maybe all of human nature really is encoded in our genomes, including our conscience and our willpower. Or maybe those things are intrinsic to our souls." She shrugged. "Science has no way to gauge the soul, so it's hard to talk about it. But without it ... we're nothing more than a bundle of muscles and nerves responding to the dictates of coded instructions and the influences of our environment. No different than the robots we've designed."

Howard nodded reflectively. "There's so much about being human that we don't understand. So much about *life*. A year ago, I would have said that auras were nonsense, and so were gods. Now it's hard to dismiss anything out of hand."

"But what should we do about Py?" Jacqueline glanced out the kitchen windows to the thick tangle of woods beyond the glade. "We know there's nothing wrong with *his* willpower gene, if there is such a thing."

Abel nodded. "That boy is one of the staunchest souls I've ever known. And maybe his challenges are unique, but he's still responsible for himself. And *to* himself," he added quietly.

Silence fell over the table, and then Howard sighed. "So we should just let him go on like this? Spaced out like a zombie and barely talking to anyone?"

"No, that has to change," Jacqueline said. "But we've been on his case, and it hasn't helped. He just apologizes or gets defensive, and goes right back to his auras. Even if we blindfolded him and tied him to a bedpost, he'd still have a whole world of chemical stimuli around him."

Howard nodded. "I guess talking with him is all we can do."

"Yep," Abel agreed. "You can nurture and correct until you're blue in the face, but nothing is going to stop that kid from being himself. Nor should it."

Howard acknowledged this with a grunt. "But at this rate, he'll be spending his life alone in the woods."

"Well, it was working for me," said Abel dryly as he got up to tackle the dishes.

V

Once they entered the woods, Py expected Aurie to run off on her own, but instead she joined him on the trail to his own special place. Although she didn't speak, he felt her watching him closely the whole way to the Birch Grove.

"You gonna stay here all day?" she asked.

Py nodded, gazing at the dome of the giant anthill in the dappled shade. "Lots to do. What about you? Are you going to hunt today, or just run?"

"Just run ... as far as I can get."

The ants milling around the nest were young ones who had never seen Aurie before. They sent their signal of greeting to Py, and asked about the stranger in his company.

My sister, he told them.

Worker?

Soldier-worker-nurse-queen, he said with a smile.

The young ants were impressed. They swarmed over Aurie's feet in adulation, but she didn't flinch.

"Your secret pets," she said fondly. "What did you tell them just now?"

"That you're the god of the woods, and they'd better bow down!"

"And they understood that?"

"More or less," Py said. He asked the ants to disengage, and they left Aurie immediately and returned to their errands.

She watched them scurry off and shook her head in amazement. "They're not even CRISPR-evo, and they can communicate like human beings!"

"Well, not really. They don't exactly speak English ... or use any words at all. Closer to say that I've learned to speak ant."

Aurie looked skeptical. "Maybe you learned their chemical

language and you can understand them, but you can't actually *speak* to them using chemicals. I've been wondering ... "

"What?"

"It sounds crazy, but maybe you're communicating with them the same way the Fishes do with me. Using your aura."

Py looked at her in surprise. He had often wondered the same thing himself. "Maybe ... but my aura would need to have touched theirs at some point." He paused, suddenly realizing just when that moment might have been.

"How could I have done that?" he muttered, mostly to himself.

"I don't know ... I told you it sounded crazy." Aurie looked down at the roaming insects with fascination. "But who are you talking to, the entire colony? Is it a single group consciousness?"

"Well ... I can talk to just these ants, or all of the ants at once," he said, after mulling it over. "When I communicate with the whole colony, I'd call it a group *cognition*. I don't think they have any awareness of themselves, the way we do."

She nodded and then grimaced, rubbing the hollows of her temples.

"The Fishes never leave you alone, do they?"

She sighed. "It'll be better once I'm a few miles from the house. Their auras never travel farther than that, do they?"

Py shook his head. "Not yet."

"Good," she said. "Their voices are a lot softer with distance. From the other side of the ridge, they'll just sound like the buzz of insects far away."

"Well, have a good day off," he said, settling himself against his favorite tree.

"Yeah ... have fun working on your Secret Project," Aurie said, giving him another keen glance. "See you back home for dinner." She stepped carefully around the ants, then bounded off into the woods.

While they were walking and talking, Py had used his eyes in the standard way, what he thought of as "visual mode," which was necessary for getting around and performing most tasks. His "aura mode" only allowed him to see auras and certain biochemicals, but he greatly preferred it, in part because he could see through any obstacle. The moment his sister disappeared into the trees, Py changed his mode of sight and watched her aura flee, closely tailed by those of the Fishes. Their cool-toned auras flowed like bright snatches of wind, while Aurie's moved like a restless flame ... except for the center, which was shaped like a feather of purest light. Py was certain that this feather-like evanescence came from Aurie's winged god. Talking about that god and the day it had flown away made Aurie so melancholy that Py had never mentioned the feather to her. Whatever it was, it made his sister's aura glorious, as bright as the Fishes'. She might run thirty miles from here before the day was out, but her aura would still be visible to him. It was a comfort to see that familiar beacon pulsing and flaring across miles of woodland, through trees and rocky hillsides. He had lost her once before in these woods, but he would never lose her again.

Drawing his focus back to the Birch Grove, Py looked around at the intimate darkness starred with its multitude of tiny lights, the auras of birds and their nestlings, beetles and grubs, and small rodents in their burrows. It had taken time for him to see it, but every tree shone faintly too, as if with an aura encompassing roots and branches. The ground itself was honeycombed with tangled webs of fungal mycelium, which crept into the roots of the forest like tendrils of subterranean moonlight. And through the tunnels of their nest, his ants moved like the stars of a shifting constellation. Unconsciously filtering out the small sounds of the forest, Py relaxed against the trunk of the birch and focused on his ants.

From the very beginning, he had thought of them that way, as *his* ants. They belonged to a colony he had discovered eight months ago on his first hike with Aurie and Uncle Abel in these woods. This singular colony had poisoned itself to get rid of parasitic beetles on that day, a mass destruction Py had witnessed firsthand.

Once the family returned to Uncle Abel's cabin, Py had checked on this nest in the Birch Grove, expecting to find it empty. Instead, he had been delighted to find traces of life. The queen was still alive in her chamber, and she had laid a clutch of new eggs. Hundreds of those eggs had already hatched into larvae. A few dozen workers scurried through the tunnels, feeding their fungal garden and tending the larvae. Py waited for a small foraging party to leave the nest, and then he caught one of the ants in a jar to examine her.

At first glance, she resembled a common red carpenter ant. A closer look, however, revealed an unusually slender thorax and longer antennae that reminded Py of the *Dolichoderus imitator* ants of the Amazon rainforest. The Birch Grove ants buried their dead in a cemetery like harvester ants, and tended an underground garden like leafcutters. Py wondered if he had discovered an entirely new species right here in the woods of Maine. New species or not, these were *his* ants; he felt as protective as a father.

From that day on, Py spent all the time he could in the Birch Grove. Winter snows were no deterrent; he simply strapped on his snowshoes and took a thermopad along. Once spring came and they moved into their new home, the hike to the nest was even shorter. Howard had always given Py ample time out-of-doors, and the boy organized his days to take full advantage of it. He generally did all of his chores and lab work in the morning, then headed out after lunch and returned home at dusk. After dinner, he studied until he fell asleep. It was a flexible schedule that left his afternoons free for what mattered most to him: the study of his ants.

As Py became fluent in the language of their chemical signals, his lifelong fascination with these insects was anchored by a deep and growing respect. Ants, he realized, were the most honest of creatures. They lived and breathed chemicals, and there was no lying or pretending in that language. As the decimated colony grew, he marveled at its uniqueness. These ants were not born into their roles, rigidly cast, they were flexible and autonomous in a way that was almost human. Yet the members of this odd family worked together with a smoothness humans could only dream of. Py was content to study the small colony at a respectful distance without interfering ... but then the invaders arrived.

It happened in the usual way—another colony seeking to expand its territory sent scouts to assess the strength of the Birch Grove ants. In the initial skirmish, his ants projected signals of weakness and disorganization, practically inviting the attack. *Organize,* he told them fiercely. *Mobilize! Don't let these jerks slaughter you and take over your home!* But his ants seemed utterly helpless and it wasn't long before the full force of the invading colony descended on them. Py watched in horror as the invaders swarmed into the nest, meeting no resistance at all—and then died the way the original colony had died, as his ants pumped clouds of deadly chemicals throughout the nest. Chemicals the Birch Grovers were now apparently immune to. The battle was over as soon as it had begun, and Py's ants wasted no time hauling the bodies of the dead into their vast cemetery.

You did it! Py cheered. *That was brilliant!* Without thinking about it, he reached out towards their auras. The act was as spontaneous as a physical embrace. He hadn't planned to touch them— didn't even know *how* he was touching them—but suddenly he felt them all. Thousands of lives were in his grasp. If there had ever been a time when his own aura had connected with another, this was it.

Because the entire colony was now aware of him.

Every soldier and worker and nurse stopped dead in her tracks, riveted on him. Even the males and the queen cast off their usual somnolence and turned their attention to him. They all exuded the same spectrum of chemicals, a new signature that might have been awe. The colony was like a tribe looking into the sky for some sign from a newly manifested god.

In that first instant of contact with his colony, Py felt the warmth of a great intimacy. But a moment later, he felt all the cold distance of the evolutionary gulf between them, vast and unbreachable. He had learned to understand the language of his ants, but how could he possibly speak to them?

Every ant stood alert and still, waiting for him to speak. And although he said not a word, Py's soul cried out and spoke for him.

I will help you! I will help you in ways you can't even imagine.

And from that time on, Py found that he *could* help them. The colony's simple needs and imperatives were clear to him, and now they could communicate in some fundamental way that bridged their separate languages. His suggestions and ideas were understood, and the ants responded, sometimes in ways he hadn't expected. Py had no inkling of the mysterious mechanisms involved, but the colony had become a creation they were building together, a web whose pattern was constantly evolving into richer and more complex shapes.

Having the entire morning and afternoon with his colony was a rare treat, and Py didn't even notice when lunchtime came and went. In fact, he lost track of time completely until the piercing call of a bird finally jolted him back to his other senses. His eyes were painfully dry. Py shifted his gaze to visual mode, but at first he couldn't see a thing. Then he blinked and the trees around him swam into unsteady focus. The light was very low and shadows lay thick on the ground. It was past time to head back, and he got up with a groan. He'd been sitting against the birch trunk for most of the day, and whatever parts of him didn't ache were completely numb.

As Py hobbled home on pins and needles, it occurred to him that the world seemed a good deal darker and fuzzier than it should have been. He squinted at the trees around him. Had their outlines always been this blurred by dusk? Switching back to aura mode, he searched for his sister and found her many miles to the west. Aurie was heading rapidly for home, and the folds of her aura had the healthy glow of pure physical exhaustion.

I'm escaping most of my senses, he thought as he flexed his stiff joints, feeling the tired satisfaction of his mental exertions.

And Aurie's escaping into hers. He hoped the day off had been good for her.

Aurie loped back home in the chill of dusk, reveling in her own aching muscles. Still possessed of the abilities she had gained upon her god's awakening—and inclinations, such as the enjoyment of raw, freshly killed game—she could have easily put an end to these minor discomforts, but she never did. They made her feel alive, rooted in her own flesh. Besides, she had discovered that being chilled to the bone and sore in every muscle elevated a hot shower and a soft bed to heavenly comforts. And no meal ever tasted so good as when you were starving. Her stomach had been growling all afternoon, which was no surprise—she'd been literally running on nothing but breakfast and the squirrel she'd caught for lunch. Whatever Uncle Abel had cooked for dinner tonight was going to taste amazing.

All day long, she had thought of almost nothing. She had given her legs free rein, feeling lighter by the second as the pressure of her children's desires and demands slowly lifted, filtered out by miles of rustling leaves and the clear air of early summer. She might have been some strange species of flightless bird, doomed to race wingless over the earth. But it felt so good to run, her feet pounding sharp staccatos against the ground, her head almost light enough to drift above the trees. It was high in the hills that she felt most at home, touching the earth only in tiny bursts, feeling nothing but the air and the beckoning warmth of the sun.

There was a part of her, rarely acknowledged, that hated the choice she had made on leaping from the CryoLife balcony. That part of her chafed in the cage of her flesh, yearning for the god that had flown away. Aurie often awakened from dreams in which that mid-air moment—the moment of choice—stretched into a timeless agony in which she hung suspended, eternally pulled in opposite directions.

But it was useless to dwell on the past, and her attention was usually focused on more immediate problems. As she headed home, the most troubling of those problems came creeping back. She thought about her brother and his clumsiness of late, which she didn't believe was clumsiness. Everyone assumed Py was moving in a fog because he was preoccupied with auras, but Aurie thought he really *was* moving in a fog. He seemed to be losing his eyesight without even noticing what was happening.

If his god were awake, it could heal him. She bounded over a tangle of fallen branches, keenly aware of the world's crisp edges and vivid, varied colors. Acquiring eagle vision had been one of the first changes her own god had made on the heels of its awakening. And although her god had flown away, Aurie had kept those god-like traits, including the ability to go inside herself to make further changes. It frustrated Aurie that while she could heal herself of any injury or malady, she couldn't do a thing for Py.

Don't worry about Uncle Py, said One Fish quite distinctly.

Aurie was so startled by her son's voice, she skidded to a halt on a stretch of shale. *Don't worry? Why not?*

He's happy, said One Fish simply.

And he can see fine, put in Two Fish. *Just not the way you can.*

Run faster, Mom, ordered One Fish. *Or you're going to be late for dinner!*

Aurie smiled as she raced the sunset home, the awareness of her children growing as the distance between them lessened. They could feel her returning and their excitement grew with every step she took. For a moment she was filled with nothing but their joy— just the pure joy of being close to her again. It made her suddenly very glad to be alive, and here on this Earth. Even if she felt more like an older sister than a mother, these little lives were hers to nurture and protect; they were more important to her than her own.

Almost home! she told them, quickening her pace as the daylight slipped away.

VI

Uncle Abel had made one of their favorite dinners, a wonderful dish he called Chicken Slop, with an apple pandowdy for dessert. The mingled aromas of wine and herbs and fresh-baked pastry filled the kitchen, but lately, smells had ceased to interest Py. They were all too thin, somehow—static and one-dimensional. Tastes, too, suffered from the same problem. Any meal now paled in comparison to the rich goulash of signaling molecules his ants produced.

Aurie, on the other hand, seemed to have no trouble appreciating her dinner, and was making short work of it while surreptitiously watching Py. They were all watching him that way. Casual conversation went on at the table, but every aura was attuned to him, focused in his direction. Py sighed. Why couldn't they just mind their own business and let him eat?

After dinner, he started to clear the table, but his parents wouldn't let him. They herded him gently but firmly into the library. Py caught Aurie's eye as she wheeled the Fishes back to the nursery lab, but her glance told him nothing. Her ears, though, were even sharper than his, and he knew she'd be listening to whatever lecture he was about to receive.

"We're worried about you," his mom said, right off the bat. She had seated herself at one end of the long sofa as if expecting the others to sit down with her, but both Py and Howard remained standing.

"Why?" Py demanded.

"Because you're hardly around anymore," Jacqueline said. "And when you *are* around, you're not really here."

"The Wake Institute needs all souls on board," his dad added mildly. "We can't just give you up to the ants in the forest, no matter how interesting they are."

Py felt a nasty jolt; how could they know about his ants? Aurie would never have told them! Had his dad been following him and spying on him? Py struggled to keep his voice neutral. "What ants?"

"You've been obsessed with ants ever since you were a toddler." Howard gestured toward the French doors, which looked out on their new garden plot and the sheltering oaks. "Isn't that what you've been studying out there? Or is there something even more fascinating that's grabbed your attention?"

"We're not going to stop you," Jacqueline said. "We just want to understand what's gotten you so engrossed that you've lost interest in everything else. It must be pretty incredible."

Py looked at them, feeling torn. The colors and textures of his parents' auras were almost identical—tawny peaks of curiosity shot through with smoky veins of concern. Part of him *wanted* to tell his secret, to share his excitement and brag a little; he was proud of his ants and what he'd done with them. But a wiser part of him knew better. The Birch Grove ants were not a kid's project like the artificial anthill he'd built when he was six; they were an evolving species he was helping to shape. His parents, if they decided it was necessary, could put a stop to this—and that was unthinkable. Py didn't believe his dad would take such drastic measures, but his mom might. Jacqueline had dealt with Aurie's god, and she had been terrified for Aurie; it stood to reason she would be apprehensive about any of Py's Changes, and disinclined to allow him the freedom he needed. So Py dropped his gaze to the floor and said nothing.

His dad sighed heavily. "What's so important that you can't tell us? And *why* can't you tell us? Don't you trust us?"

"Of course I do," Py said. "Look, I follow all kinds of things in the woods—ants, beetles, birds, everything."

"You were out there the whole day," Howard said. "Did you really spend eight hours just *watching* auras?"

"Watching ... and thinking."

"What have you figured out?" his mom asked. Her vivid green eyes were disconcertingly keen.

"Well ... I can see the auras of plants now."

"Really?" said Howard, sounding mildly interested. "Even plants have souls, huh?"

"Well, they *are* alive," Py said. "But their auras are so different, I could never make them out before. They're a lot fainter, but amazingly big and spread out ... and connected to each other."

His parents watched him, waiting for more.

"I'm studying lots of things, but insects are the most interesting," Py went on, desperate to say something true that would satisfy them. "I like to find someplace quiet to sit and watch them. Easier to communicate that way—"

"You talk to them?" Jacqueline sounded intrigued.

Py laughed nervously. "Well, sort of. I guess I talk to them the way Aurie talks to her CRISPR machine. They're kind of like my pets."

"Really." Howard's aura was now stiff with frustration—and dark with bitter nostalgia, the recurrence of an old hurt. Py suddenly realized that his dad was feeling the way he had when Aurie ran off on the cusp of her Change without telling him anything.

"I'll tell you if I have a breakthrough," Py said, hoping that was a promise he could eventually keep. "But it takes time to really understand them."

"Okay." The dangerous colors swirling in Howard's aura belied his placid tone. "But it's time you focused on your other studies—you're falling behind on differential equations and electromagnetics. Not to mention your chores around the house. So from now on, you're only allowed into the woods two days a week."

"No!" Py looked at his dad in alarm, then at his mom, hoping for help. But Jacqueline only nodded. Both her face and her aura were set and serious.

"I'll study more and do my chores," Py insisted. "And I'll come back earlier—by three o'clock, I promise. Just let me go every day. Please!"

"We might consider it," Howard said, locking gazes with Py, "if you gave us a reason *why*. Why is this so important?"

Py agonized silently. He couldn't be away from the colony

five whole days out of the week—and yet, he couldn't bring himself to reveal what he was doing. It struck him that a scientist must feel this way in the throes of designing something new. He couldn't be disturbed, distracted, or stopped. His own creation was working with him, and it was up to him to protect the fragile web they were crafting together. Under the harsh light of revelation and inquiry, the strands-to-be-formed would evaporate like a dream, never to gain substance.

But he wouldn't lie to his parents. Py had been pressured to lie for Aurie after her Change, and he had hated it—the complications and problems it caused, and above all, the dirty, slinking feeling of dishonesty. He would protect his ants, but he wouldn't feed his mom and dad any excuses or bullcrap stories. Py took a deep breath and faced his father.

"What I'm doing in the woods is important," he said quietly. "It's as important as your engineering of CRISPR-evo."

Excitement flared in Howard's eyes. "I knew it! What is it you're working on?"

"I can't tell you." Py saw the hurt in Howard's aura deepen into inflamed valleys, and he felt terribly helpless. "But it's not because I don't trust you." He looked deep into his father's eyes. "Do you remember how you got the idea for CRISPR-evo?"

His dad frowned at him. "It was kind of an epiphany. I don't really know where it came from."

"But you were alone when it hit you, right? And you never told anyone you were working on it."

"That's because it was illegal," his dad said.

"What if it hadn't been?" Py persisted. "Would you have talked about it then?"

His father didn't answer.

"And what about you?" Py rounded on his mom. "When you had the idea to engineer eggs with the kill switch—that Policeman—you weren't brainstorming with the other grad students, were you?"

Jacqueline shook her head. "No, I was drinking with them. Well, they were drinking and I was ... thinking. I might as well have been alone."

"And you never told anyone about it?"

"I was afraid someone would steal the idea," she said. "So I always kept it a secret."

"But not just because you didn't *trust* other people," Py said, looking hard at both of them. "Because talking about it would have ruined it. Because some things have to be worked on alone. You have to keep them to yourself."

His parents were silent, but their auras spoke for them. Neither of them wanted to admit it, but they both understood exactly what he meant.

"And you have to *do* it, no matter what." Py spoke with quiet intensity. "I bet no one could have stopped either of you ... not with any threat on earth."

"I suppose that means no threat on earth is going to stop you, either," Howard said dryly, but his eyes—and his aura—glinted with something new, a certain respect Py hadn't seen before. His mom and dad shared a glance in which clear chemical messages were exchanged. In that instant, Py thought, they were almost as sophisticated as a pair of ants.

"Okay," Howard said. "You can keep working on your Secret Project every day if you're home by three."

"I will be, I promise!"

"*And* if you bring your studies up to speed," Howard added.

"I will!"

"And don't make any deals with your sister to fill in for you," Howard said sternly. "She's got her hands full already."

"I know. I won't. Thanks!" Py slipped into the hall before his dad could add any other provisos, thrilled that he had managed to keep his freedom. At the base of the stairs, he heard Jacqueline murmur something, and he paused to listen.

"—whether to be more worried or less," she said, "but he's right, nothing could have stopped us. And the only person in the world I wanted to tell about the kill switch was *you*. When we met in the Red Eye during that snowstorm, all those years ago. Remember?"

"How could I forget?" Howard's voice was a little muffled, as if he were kissing her hair. "Intellectual foreplay with the love of my life … which was also a secret."

Py rolled his eyes, but curiosity kept him eavesdropping.

"I was dying to tell you what you obviously wanted to know," his mom went on. "And I didn't really think you'd steal my idea, but I still couldn't tell you. Something held me back."

"Yeah," Howard said. "Some things *don't* want to be shared, even among the people you love."

"So we're allowing him the privacy we demanded for ourselves. Which is the right thing to do … isn't it?"

"I sure as hell hope so. But he's only nine, and some lunatic gave him the ability to evolve in leaps and bounds. He's better equipped to cause trouble than we ever were."

"Better equipped with common sense, too," Jacqueline said, and Howard chuckled.

As his parents rejoined Abel in the kitchen, Py scurried upstairs. The door to his bedroom was open, and the light was on. He found Aurie sitting cross-legged on his bed, looking as grim as an executioner.

"So you got a free pass, huh?" Aurie sounded as if he'd earned a free ticket to the morgue, but Py was too happy to let anything bring him down.

"I wouldn't call it *free*. You know Dad'll keep me hopping and be on my case about every little thing." Py climbed up next to her and plopped onto his pile of pillows, which he had gotten for Christmas in lieu of the Smart Foam he wanted. "God help me if I drop another egg!"

"About that," Aurie said, sounding suddenly uneasy. Her aura had shifted too, its stiff edges folding back to reveal an almost liquid fear.

Unnerved, Py sat up. "What's wrong?"

Instead of answering, she looked around his room, which didn't hold much. There was a desk he never used (preferring to study sprawled out on his pillows) and a tangle of dirty clothes on the floor. Against the far wall stood a small pine bookshelf, one of two their uncle had built for them. The shelf in Aurie's room held almost a dozen actual books—expensive hard copies she saved up to buy—but Py's shelf was mostly graced with nature's complimentary treasures: feathers, dried beetles and bones, even the bird's skull he had kept from his sister's predatory post-Change phase. There were only two books on the shelf, but they were well-worn and much-loved: *The Ants* and *Tales from the Ant World*.

Aurie's gaze settled on the books. "Can you read those titles?"

Py gave his sister a withering look. "I know the names of my own books."

"But can you read them from here?"

Py looked at the books, uncomfortably aware that he was squinting to see them better. God, why was everything so fuzzy all of a sudden?

"You can't," she said flatly. "Not well, anyway. I can read the small print on the spine of *The Ants:* Harvard University Press." She took a deep breath and looked at him. "You could too, after your first Change. Remember?"

He nodded reluctantly. Even his sister's face, so close, was slightly blurred, as if she were made of cotton fuzz. Py looked away, afraid to focus on anything.

"Once you gained your biochemical sense, *all* of your senses were enhanced," she reminded him.

"They still are," he said, grasping at straws. "I can still hear everything people say behind closed doors, the same way you can. I can still taste all the flavors inside of flavors. And I would *appreciate* Smart Foam more than anyone, if Mom and Dad ever decided it was worth the money. I—"

"Your eyesight is getting worse," Aurie cut in. "Ever since you started spending so much time with the ants—"

"So *you're* trying to keep me away from them, too," he said bitterly, even though he knew that wasn't fair.

"It has nothing to do with them," she snapped. "At least, I don't think it does. But you spend so much time focused on auras instead of using your eyes in the normal way. Maybe one comes at the expense of the other."

Py said nothing, only gazed into the gloom at the far corner of the room. There was a tiny aura there—a spider dangling from a thread—and a scattering of other small life buried in the earth outside. He suddenly realized how easily and often he slipped into that other way of seeing … if it could even be called that. Py had no idea how he used his eyes to detect auras, only that it felt like some perfect combination of seeing, smelling, touching, and tasting.

"Are you even listening?" Aurie sounded angry now. "Stop staring at auras for five lousy minutes! Can you do that?"

Switching back to visual mode, Py turned to face her. His sister's aura was a far more nuanced indicator of her feelings than any expression or gesture, yet he felt compelled to rise to her challenge. Surely he wasn't *addicted* to aura mode! And even in visual mode, her feelings were pretty clear. Aurie had drawn her knees up to her chest and wrapped her arms around them, a defensive posture. And behind the anger in her eyes was only concern for him.

"I can do it," Py said, "but it's not easy. I'm used to switching back and forth without even thinking about it." He swallowed hard. "If I don't concentrate, I'll slip right back."

"Then you'd better concentrate! Make it a routine—use your normal vision for two hours straight every day."

"I'll try," he said.

"Don't *try,*" she said flatly, sounding like their dad at his most intractable. "Just *do it.*" She got up to go, then hesitated by the door.

"You probably think it doesn't matter," she said quietly. "That you're happier just using your biochemical sense. But you can't see everything that way. So unless you want to be bumping into rocks and walls for the rest of your life, you'd better not lose your normal vision." She gave him a last, desperate look before leaving.

Shaken, Py turned on all the lights in his room. He pulled *Tales from the Ant World* down from its perch and forced himself to read, but the words kept dissolving under his eyes. As they disappeared into darkness, he dragged them back like escaped prisoners. His vision eluded him, slipping back to aura mode before he could finish a single sentence. Whatever was happening to him, it was happening *fast*.

Frightened, Py put the book down and paced around his room, forcing himself to *look* at it—wood-paneled walls, moss-green quilt, mountain of pillows, empty desk. Everything had a haze over it, as if seen through a cloudy lens. He stared fiercely through that lens for a full five minutes as his head throbbed. Finally, he let go and staggered against the wall as the cool and soothing darkness returned, pricked with its countless living lights.

Py collapsed onto his bed in a sweat. Even five minutes of trying to see normally was now torture ... but he would have to try. No, he would have to just *do it*, as Aurie had said. He lay still, waiting for the headache to subside, but it pounded steadily, church bells tolling some terrible hour. Soon, a familiar fever began to creep along his veins. The heat grew and spread like a wildfire in the throes of a rising wind, and Py felt a burst of hope. He had felt this way once before—in a Boston planetarium eight months ago, on the cusp of his second Change.

Once he recognized what was happening, Py reached under his mattress for the tin box he kept there. He pried off the lid and felt carefully for the dried mushroom inside—the one Aurie had given him to keep him safe through his last Change. He broke off a tiny bit and swallowed it, then returned the box to its hiding place.

CRISPR machine, Py thought as he lay back. *I sometimes forget that you're inside me. What are you up to now?*

Aurie's Doctor might have answered her, but Py had never communicated with his own CRISPR machine. Shivering with fever and the excitement of surrendering to the unknown, he closed his eyes and waited for whatever new Change was coming.

VII

In his dream, rain had fallen during the night and the wetness of forest mulch seeped through his clothes, cooling his hot skin. From where he lay, Py looked up into a web of tiny auras in the dark canopy, but he was listening to the voice that spoke from below. The chemical voice of the creatures that had stopped their nocturnal work to speak to him.

What's happening to you? asked the colony.

I'm Changing, Py told them as the Change spread like a scalding wave through his cells. *I don't know how yet ... but something is going to be very different.*

The ants were silent for a moment, their chemicals shifting between fear and anticipation. *Are you still with us?*

Py turned his head to look down into the nest full of familiar auras, all of them shining with concern. How could they ever think he would leave them? Overwhelmed by love for them, he spoke as honestly as he ever had. *Of course I am! I will always be with you. I will do anything for you, give you everything I have.*

The colony's relief gave way to excitement and a growing hunger. The ants spilled out of their nest and swarmed over him. They began to taste him everywhere, brushing delicate feelers over his sweaty, feverish skin. They drank from his hair follicles, his nostrils, the corners of his eyes. He was drowning in a sea of teeming, quivering life, blanketed by one tickling wave after the next. He lay absolutely still, afraid to crush them if he twitched, to send them flying with a sneeze.

As quickly as they had come, the ants left him. Py watched them return to their nest, but they no longer looked like a swarm of many tiny auras. He saw them as a single brilliant aura, twisting and convoluting in its descent through the narrow corridors below.

Aurie was sleeping peacefully for once, in the midst of a blissfully dull dream, when a sharp cry jolted her awake.

Hot! Too hot!

Her eyes flew open and she rushed downstairs to the nursery lab. Brightening the halo-globe that lit the incubators, she found Two Fish thrashing around in her tank. Aurie caught a brief and fading image of fire.

It's okay, she soothed her distraught daughter. *Just a bad dream.* But the gauge on the incubator read thirty-nine Celsius— two degrees higher than usual. Aurie turned the temperature down and as the tank cooled, Two Fish grew calmer. Woken by his sister's distress, One Fish fidgeted in his tank.

What was all that about? Aurie directed the question at Two Fish, but the little embryo was silent. Touching the clear wall of the tank with one finger, Aurie gazed at the tiny opalescent form inside, wondering what her daughter's aura would have revealed. She would have asked Py, if it weren't the middle of the night.

Instead, Aurie focused on her connection with the Fishes. It was a warm sense of wholeness, as if her children were extensions of herself, and she of them. In their shared mind's eye, she saw thousands of flames burning in the darkness of the woods, only to be consumed by a much greater flame. Instead of setting the woods ablaze, the fire wound its way underground like a furtive creature.

Is that what you dreamed? Aurie asked her daughter as the image faded.

Not a dream, Two Fish murmured. *It was real. I saw it.*

Did you see it, too? Aurie asked her son.

No ... I was sleeping. One Fish sounded as abashed as a patrol officer caught shirking his duty.

Aurie couldn't help but smile. *You mean you actually stayed in your tank instead of sneaking out tonight? Will wonders never cease?* She turned her attention back to her daughter. *That sure didn't look like a normal fire. Was it alive?*

A moment later, an image entered Aurie's mind, of an eel with a head on both ends. It was a picture straight from the Fishes' favorite book.

I don't understand, Aurie said. *What does that mean?*

Two Fish didn't answer, but the mental image remained, sharp and clear. The two heads of the eel were staring at each other in perplexity, and Aurie felt a sense of foreboding that chilled her. Then the image dissolved and the Fishes seemed to forget the whole incident.

McElligot's Pool! they chirped in unison, but Aurie vetoed that at once.

Go to sleep, she told them sternly. *And don't bother asking for that book in the morning. After breakfast we're going to read something new!*

Birdsong woke him and Py opened his eyes to another world. He sat up slowly in bed. His room was still recognizable, but it had become a vibrant, seething edifice of chemicals.

The walls, floor, and ceiling thrummed with the vibrations of gypsum crystals. The blanket scrunched at his feet was a shimmering tangle of pure texture. And the wood of his bookshelf was not inert, but alive; Py could hear the pine boards expanding and contracting in slow breaths. Nothing was static or silent. Everything shone with its own light, casting no trace of shadow; everything shivered with music beyond the pitch of any ear.

Py absorbed it all in awestruck stillness. He could see *every-thing.*

See, of course, was not the right word. What he sensed was a synesthesia—brightness that was also a pulsation, taste, and texture. His mind seemed to be casting new feelers through his eyes and over the surfaces of the world. He could read the titles of his books now, not by the play of light off ink, but by the chemical composition of the ink itself! Wildly excited, Py went over to his bookshelf and picked up *Tales from the Ant World*. He sat down on the floor and fixed his attention on the cover of the book. Then, with startling ease, he sent his new sight through the cover to the first page ... and then the next. With his awareness alone, he skimmed through page after page. He could read them all without even opening the book!

Someone knocked on his door, jolting him out of the chapter about fire ants conquering the Spanish settlers on Hispaniola in the sixteenth century.

"Come in," he said hoarsely, feeling suddenly overwhelmed. He squeezed his eyes shut and discovered that real darkness had ceased to exist; even behind closed lids, there was no shelter from this chemical assault. And with just a slight shift of focus, he could see right through his own eyelids!

Py heard the sound of his sister's footsteps as she entered the room, then the snick of the door closing. He opened his eyes and saw her as he never had before. Her face and her aura together— the chemical shape of her expression and the chemical manifesta- tion of her soul. It was breathtaking.

Aurie was staring at him. "What are you doing on the floor?"

Quickly, he told her about his new Change.

Aurie's eyes widened and her aura flared. "Wow! But you can't see at all in the normal way? You're blind now?"

Py snorted. "Are you kidding? This makes normal sight seem like blindness! It's incredible, Aurie ... I wish you could see like this, just for a minute."

She sat down next to him, looking troubled, but also excited. "I can't even imagine seeing the whole world in chemical form. And how do you see *inside* things?"

"I focus on something, like this book," he told her. "Then I just ... "

"Dive into it?"

"No." He tried to parse out exactly what he did. "Each page is a layer that can be seen if you focus on it, or transparent if you focus past it. I have to focus past the outer layers to see the inner ones." He brandished the book at her. "I can read this without even opening it! Want me to prove it?"

"No, I believe you." His sister's aura bloomed with color—vermilion fascination tinged with the verdigris of envy. "After your second Change, you could see auras through anything, but now you can see *everything* through anything?"

Py sent his gaze through the many layers of his bedroom wall to the hallway outside. "Yeah ... I can really see through walls now!"

Aurie looked thoughtful. "What about living things? Can you see into tissues? And how deep can you see within a layer? Can you see into *cells?*"

"I don't know ... haven't tried that yet." But he found himself gazing at his sister's arm, just above her elbow. He focused his awareness on the layer of fascia beneath her skin. He could keep going, seeing her arm in cross-sections until he came out the other side ... but could he see *into* any of those layers? Could he see the microcosm of a cell, the way she could?

Instinctively, he probed the fascia, imagining himself jumping inside—and all at once, his room was gone. He was floundering in a shimmering, suffocating sea. In terror, Py flailed around until he realized that he had no limbs with which to flail. In fact, he had no body at all, and he certainly wasn't drowning ... or breathing anymore.

This stuff is like Smart Foam, he thought, trying to get used to the weird reality of not breathing. *If Smart Foam were wet and sticky.* Tentatively, he tried to swim through the sea of tissue, and found that he could. This was nothing like what he had done before. He wasn't merely seeing inside Aurie's arm, he was actually inside it. What *was* he, in this state? Pure consciousness alone?

An aura, he thought with cold certainty. *You must've projected your aura into her arm, trying to see deeper!*

Well ... he'd done something like this once before, hadn't he? On the day he'd first spoken to his colony, he must have projected his aura to touch theirs. Of course, that had only been for a moment; he hadn't even been aware of leaving his body. As he wondered these things, Py kept moving. He pushed through layer after layer of textures utterly new to him, marveling that he could recognize skin and fascia and muscle for what they were. He saw-felt-smelled-tasted each tissue and the networks of nerves and blood vessels that wove through this wild terrain. Resisting the urge to follow those branching streams, he kept to a straight course until he reached the fine catacombs of his sister's humerus.

I could get lost in here. Py looked around at the sea of spongy bone that held no discernible landmarks at all. Returning to the safer territory of Aurie's biceps muscle, he wandered up the ribbon of her tendon until he hit a major nerve. It was twitching and firing in explosions that lit up the thick, dark sea around him. He stopped and watched, mesmerized.

There you are! Aurie's voice rang through the microcosm like the voice of God. Py froze and looked around guiltily. His sister's aura was speeding toward him, sharply prickled and yellow with fear. The jaundiced color was quickly fading into deep blue swaths of relief, making her look like an irritated thundercloud. *I thought you didn't dive into things!*

I didn't mean to ... it was an accident. Py's protest was no more than a thought, but Aurie must have heard it because she snorted.

How did you know where to find me? he asked.

You were looking at my arm, and then you just slumped over on the floor! And my arm started to itch, right at the place you were staring at, so I figured you must've jumped inside.

I see you as an aura in here, Py told her. *How do you see me?*

I can't see auras the way you can. I see ... Aurie paused, and her aura blushed with slight embarrassment.

What? he pressed.

I see you as a cartoony version of yourself, she confessed. *Sort of like the way I see the Doctor. Not as sophisticated as your way of seeing.*

But what are we really seeing? he wondered. *Each other's souls?*

Maybe ... who knows? Aurie was quiet for a moment. *But if this is my soul, I can only project it inside myself. You, on the other hand, can apparently project your soul anywhere! Do you know how to get yourself out of here?*

I don't have a clue, Py admitted.

His sister sighed. *It's a good thing you jumped into my arm, and not your own.*

So you can help me jump back?

Let's hope so. Her aura furrowed as she considered it. *For me, jumping back is the opposite of jumping in. When I go inside myself, I consciously shrink my awareness. I contract it inward. It's like drawing myself into a single thought and projecting that thought into whatever cells or tissues I want. When I'm ready to go back, I expand my awareness outward.*

You make it sound so easy, he said uneasily.

Well ... if it works for you like it does for me, it should feel pretty natural.

Py braced himself and imagined being back in his body, in his own head. He focused hard on that, and tried to jump back. All he managed to do was launch himself into Aurie's nerve, which rocked him with an explosion of chemicals as he fell through it.

Aurie laughed. *You're trying way too hard. You have to be very still and relaxed. Pretend you're a gas inside a tank that just got opened. And don't overthink it!*

Right, he said, more nervous than ever. But when he relaxed and simply pushed his awareness outward, expanding like a hot air balloon, it worked. All at once he was lying sprawled on his bedroom floor, lightheaded with the speed of his withdrawal. Aurie sat beside him, grinning.

"How do you stay upright like that when you go inside yourself?" he demanded, sitting up.

"Involuntary self-control," she said smugly. "Hey, you did it! On just your second try, too."

"Yeah," he said, breathing deeply again. "That was amazing! But really disorienting. Do you ever get lost in your own tissues?"

She shook her head. "You'll get better with practice. And if you ever get lost, you can just jump back to yourself and try again."

He shook his head, still feeling dazed. "How long was I in there?"

She glanced down at the yellow Spider on her wrist. "I don't know, but Mom and Dad will be up any minute now. Are you going to tell them about your new Change?"

Py considered it. "Not yet. They want me to buckle down and focus on the 'real world' and this will just seem like another big distraction. Besides, I need to get used to this new way of seeing. There's no darkness for me anymore." He squeezed his eyes shut to the brightness of his inner lids, then opened them again. "I don't know how I'm ever going to fall asleep!"

Aurie glanced down at his shirt and raised her eyebrows. "Speaking of which ... did you wear those clothes to bed last night?"

Py glanced down at himself and laughed. "Guess I forgot to take a shower."

"But you weren't this dirty yesterday." She rubbed bits of dried mud off his sleeve, then turned to stare at his unmade bed.

Py followed her gaze to the smears of humus shining against the sheets. Where had all that dirt come from?

"Maybe you went back into the woods in the middle of the night," Aurie muttered.

Py frowned. "If I did, I don't remember ... and I've never sleepwalked before." But then he remembered his dream of the ants. It had the hyper-real texture of a fever dream brought on by his Change, but he distinctly remembered lying in the Birch Grove while his colony swarmed over him. He remembered promising them ...

Everything, he thought, looking down at the dirt on his clothes with a shiver of excitement. *I promised them everything I have.*

Suddenly, Py wanted more than anything to see his ants.

"Tell Mom and Dad I'm leaving early today," he told his sister as he grabbed his pack. "But I'll be home by lunch—and I'll get all my chores and studying done this afternoon."

"Okay," Aurie said. She followed Py to the back door that

opened onto the woods.

"Don't lose track of time," she warned him as he ducked outside.

"I won't!" he called back. He would set his Spider to buzz at eleven—and then bite him, if necessary—but lunchtime felt like a million hours away. Around him, the world whispered and sang, overwhelming in its richness. As he headed through the trees, Py could almost hear his colony—that tantalizing, half-formed web— calling to him, tugging at his mind with a million invisible strands.

Aurie expected her dad to be annoyed about Py's absence at breakfast, but Howard's only comment was, "As long as he gets his work done this afternoon!" In fact, no one seemed upset or surprised that Py had run off early to his Secret Project in the woods. And without his clumsiness to harp on, the meal was a quiet affair.

After breakfast, Jacqueline and Abel went out to the garden to do some planting while Howard settled into the lab. Aurie spent the morning reading to the Fishes—a hodgepodge of Old Testament stories, Greek myths, and fairy tales. Around ten, Howard went to help Abel work on the bay window for their kitchen herb garden, and Aurie decided to take a break. The Fishes had been attentive for hours, but near the end of *Hansel and Gretel,* they had gotten uncharacteristically drowsy. Once her children slipped into dreamland, Aurie took advantage of the opportunity to slip away herself.

When she wanted to lay down the burden of thought, Aurie ran into the woods, but there was a different sanctuary she used when she needed to think. Unlike the rest of her cells, this cartoon neuron required no special abilities to access, only the power of her imagination. It was more familiar and comfortable than her own bedroom, and it was utterly private—except for one imaginary doctor who knew everything she thought and felt and did. Talking with him was a bit like playing chess with herself: mentally stimulating even if the outcome was rigged.

I don't understand why you're so worried, said the Doctor from his favorite protein armchair. He was always lounging about in the cartoon cell, since she never had any work for him these days. *Py's clearly taken the next step in his evolution! We should be celebrating.* Never one to waste time, he molded a convenient protein into the shape of a glass and began to craft a cocktail for himself from whatever alcohols were floating around.

You drink more than all the adults in this house put together, Aurie scolded him. The Doctor had developed a good-sized paunch, too—probably from all the fatty acid chains he liked to snack on.

You sound like someone's grandmother, the Doctor said, giving his drink a good swirl. *Why are you so conflicted about Py?*

Maybe I'm just paranoid, Aurie allowed. *But this new Change seems like more than he can handle. He can see the entire world in its chemical form! And on top of that, he can jump into things.*

Yes, I noticed, said the Doctor dryly.

Could you actually see Py's aura inside my arm? asked Aurie curiously.

Of course I could. The Doctor snorted. *A shame the Policeman couldn't have seen it. I would have quite enjoyed watching him careen madly around, trying to deal with an invader he couldn't repel!*

Aurie chuckled at the idea of her mother's quality-control mechanism—an enforcer of cellular order who had been the Doctor's biggest adversary—in such a bind. That diligent fellow would never face another threat again, since he was no longer present in her cells. The Doctor himself had cut the Policeman's transgene out of her genome eight months ago.

But how can Py jump inside things the way he does? Aurie wondered.

I don't have the faintest idea, said the Doctor. *What exactly is a soul, and what controls its movements?*

Your guess is as good as mine, Aurie said. *But did his CRISPR machine give him the ability to project his soul?*

The Doctor shook his head. *I think that's very unlikely. Your god gave you the power to travel inside yourself, but you can't project your soul elsewhere, and I certainly couldn't give you a skill I don't understand. No, this ability to project himself must be an innate talent of your brother's.*

Aurie nodded. *I'm pretty sure he did it once before, with his ants. I think he established a connection with them, and that's how they're able to communicate.* Thinking of Py's ants made her remember all the dried mud on his clothes and sheets. She was sure that he had sleepwalked to the Birch Grove, but why?

The Doctor watched her silently as he sipped his cocktail. *Change is always dangerous,* he said at last. *But I believe your fears are mostly a product of your discontent. You're envious of your brother because he's still Changing, and you are not.*

Aurie stifled her impulse to argue with him. After all, who was she trying to fool? Py reminded her of herself, riding the wave of her own Change. He was brimming with all the excitement and danger of life, driving *toward* something. Happy and anxious as she was for him, it made her feel hollow and worn-out, as if her mind were the empty nest of a bird that had long since flown.

Yes, the Doctor agreed. *You could have traveled united with your god, but you chose to separate. To stay imprisoned in your human form.*

Aurie didn't respond to this unnecessary reminder. Staying human had left her with a sense of loss, a deep ache that hadn't receded with time. It was impossible to forget the freedom she had rejected.

Because of your children. You're envious of them, too.

I am not, Aurie snapped. *They're only embryos! And they're stuck in tanks, in case you haven't noticed. I mean, I know their auras can follow me into the woods, but only a little ways.*

The Doctor plucked a sugar chain from a nearby glycoprotein, and began to nibble it contemplatively. *I suspect they can do more from those tanks than you would believe—and travel even farther than you do.*

If they could, they'd follow me all through the mountains!

The Doctor laughed. *Do you really think you're the only source of fascination to them?*

Well, I hope not! But it sure seems that way.

The Doctor shook his head. *Don't forget that I'm also inside your children. Until their brains develop, I can't decipher their thoughts, which must spring directly from their souls now. I can't follow those souls outside their bodies, but I know when they take a leave of absence. And lately, your children have been spending more and more time away. Often when you assume they're sleeping.*

Aurie was struck by the idea. Could it be true? She wondered if the images and impressions that haunted her dreams were from the Fishes' *travels,* rather than their own dreams. She would have to ask Py to track their auras at night and during their naps. It would be interesting to see if they *did* travel on their own ... and just how far they were able to go.

You trust your brother on this matter, but not me? The Doctor sounded aggrieved.

Sorry, said Aurie, absurdly embarrassed to have offended him. It was often hard to remember that his personality wasn't real. The Doctor had begun as pure fantasy, her childish conception of the CRISPR-evo machine. Later, he had been the vehicle used by her sleeping god in its campaign to awaken. After her god had flown away, Aurie had been pleased and relieved to find that the Doctor's persona hadn't disappeared. Even if he was just the product of her own subconscious—and what else could he be? — she needed him more than she was willing to admit.

It's easy to underestimate your own creations, Aurie's own creation pointed out. *Parents do it all the time. But I wouldn't underestimate those children of yours, if I were you.*

Well, you are me, she said, frowning at his cocktail. *And if you've taken up drinking to pass the time, then I'd better find us a new project.*

Don't you have enough to do, taking care of your progeny? And don't you love helping them grow?

Well, of course she did. Most days, teaching and entertaining the Fishes was great fun. But, if she was being honest (and what was the point of lying to herself?), it wasn't enough.

You have all the Changes in the world at your fingertips, my dear! You can do anything you want on this canvas of yours.

But what did she want? Aurie felt like she was cursed with a paint set of infinite colors, and no inspiration.

I will consider the problem, the Doctor said thoughtfully. He finished his drink and tossed the empty vessel back into the molecular sea. *In the meantime, I think someone just woke up and is impatient to know how the story of Hansel and Gretel ends.*

I thought you couldn't decipher their thoughts, she reminded him.

I can sense dissatisfaction, which is manifest in a certain thrashing about, he said. And then he disappeared, leaving Aurie alone in the cartoon cell.

Had her own mental construct just walked out on her? Shaking her head, Aurie returned to reality to find One Fish wide awake and, indeed, thrashing about.

The witch is dead! declared the little embryo, as if Aurie and not he had fallen asleep in the middle of the story. *But the birds have eaten the breadcrumb trail. How do Hansel and Gretel find their way home? And why do they even want to go back to their evil stepmother?*

Great questions, Aurie said. *We'll get back to the story as soon as your sister wakes up.*

Whereupon One Fish immediately put an end to the delay.

VIII

Moving through the forest was like traversing a vast cathedral of textures; Py felt the living, breathing trees and soil all around him. He reveled in everything, from the drunken splendor of light-thirsty leaves to the fetid breath of fungi in hidden nooks. Chemical life grew richer in decay; his new world was almost an inverse of the old one, more fantastic in its secret niches, in the life that grew from the fodder of death.

Auras still outshone the shimmering fabric of the woods, and as Py approached the Birch Grove, he cast his gaze out in search of his colony. He knew the shape of its nest by the galaxy of tiny stars that inhabited it. But somehow, the galaxy wasn't where it should have been. Instead, there was only a single giant aura, burning like a supernova.

Py ran to the nest and looked down in disbelief. The strange new aura inhabiting it was as bright as a human one, but its shape was not human at all. It had many filaments, like the tentacles of a jellyfish or the dendrites of a neuron ... filaments that connected the thousands of ants moving through the tunnels and chambers below. With a chill, he recalled his fever-dream of the night before. This *was* his colony, but what had happened to it?

Trembling, Py sat down and hailed the colony.

For the first time, the ants didn't respond.

He called out to them again, louder this time. *Hey, it's me!*

The ants continued to ignore him. But Py could still feel their connection, and he knew they were aware of him. He relaxed his focus on their strange new aura to see their physical forms more clearly. Some of the ants were nursing the colony's young, but the rest were engaged in digging deeper tunnels, intently turning up the earth with their mandibles. Frustrated, Py turned his attention to the queen—who was awake for once—and shouted at her.

All of the ants went rigid and their shared aura flared. It flared so brightly that Py no longer saw the ants at all. This new aura had no face, and yet it seemed to sharpen in his direction. Py recoiled instinctively. He thought the giant aura could see him as clearly as he saw it. Its many tendrils rippled and flushed, bristling with suspicion.

What do you want?

Py stared at the glowering aura in dismay. He had never seen another like it, and yet it felt distinctly familiar to him. And something about that familiarity filled him with tension and a growing anxiety. For whatever reason, this aura repulsed him. And that voice … it was no longer the composite buzz of many ants; this new voice spoke for them all, and was aware of itself.

Who are you? Py asked.

We are the Colony, came the answer.

Not a colony, but the Colony. There was no mistaking the proper noun; his ants had named themselves! Py took a deep breath and tried to hide how shaken he was. A pointless effort … the ants could certainly scent his discomfort.

What happened last night? he asked them. *How did you become the Colony?*

A pale streak of uncertainty appeared in the Colony's vivid colors. It occurred to Py that his question was unfair, tantamount to asking a toddler how he had gained self-awareness.

He tried to think of a simpler question. *I dreamed about you running all over me, taking things from me. What did you take?*

The Colony regarded him coldly. *We took what you gave us. Now go away! We have work to do.*

His ants wanted him to leave? But why? Before he could protest, the Colony turned away from him. Its hostile colors cooled slightly, allowing Py to see the physical shapes of his ants once more. Having dismissed him, they had already gone back to work.

Wait, Py cried. *You never answered my question!* In response, the ants exuded a signal he recognized. It was the same signal they gave to a male ant after his mating flight was over, the chemical version of a door being shut in his face. It meant that he was an outcast, of no further use; they no longer recognized him as one of their own.

No, Py thought, as the strands of creation fell out of his hands. For a terrible moment, he was nothing but an empty shell whose purpose had escaped him; his entire world had fallen into darkness. Then he blinked, and found himself still sitting against the birch tree, his face wet with tears.

Angrily, he wiped them away. What in the world had happened last night? He must've been delirious in the middle of his Change to have come here! Had some part of him wanted to share it with his ants? Is that why he'd sleepwalked here and promised them *everything?* Well, they had sure taken something ... but what?

Py thought uneasily of his CRISPR machine.

But that's just a protein, he reminded himself. *A powerful protein, sure ... but it couldn't give them an entirely new aura and self-awareness! Could it?*

Py looked down at the nest, considering the fluid, shifting shape of the aura that encompassed his ants, that filled their connecting pathways. Why did this alien thing feel so deeply familiar to him? And why did the sight of it bother him so much?

First things first, he told himself briskly. *You have to find out if the ants have your CRISPR machine—and what they've done with it.*

Thinking of his jumping ability, Py smiled grimly. The Colony might have shut a door in his face, but it couldn't keep him out.

The Birch Grove colony had never been an ordinary ant colony. From its inception in the eggs of an unusual queen, the colony was highly intelligent and deeply attuned to its own biology. For generations, these ants regulated their inner workings more effectively than any insects ever had; the variety of chemicals they produced would have stunned a myrmecologist. And the colony had become even more extraordinary in alliance with the human boy who had touched it in a way the ants had never been touched before. A *connection* had been made, allowing communication between boy and colony without any need of language. Throughout the spring and early summer, this human partner had provided a spirit of innovation and many new ideas; the ants themselves had turned those ideas into reality.

But then the boy had come to them in the throes of some kind of sickness. Half-asleep and burning with fever, he had offered the ants *everything*. His very soul had risen up and offered itself—and the Birch Grove ants had accepted this gift as greedily and hungrily as the first algae to consume a ray of sunlight. Only the soul of this human was so bright, it would be truer to say that the colony's ant souls were consumed by it, the way smaller, fainter flames are overcome by a blazing fire.

And the ants were no longer a colony, but a Colony.

The bright new soul that now possessed it had been split from a human one. It retained a dim, primal understanding of its human counterpart, along with its basic nature, which was exploratory and forward-seeking. This intrepid soul now filled the decentralized mind of the Colony, giving it true sentience, self-awareness, and a drive the old colony had never possessed. Desire and purpose filled it—the desire to grow in ways that were previously unimaginable, and the determination to do so. From the dark soil of its nest, the Colony sensed the first faint glimmers of a vision forming, images and impressions of life as it could be. And thanks to the human who had offered them everything he had, the ants were also in possession of a special tool whose sole purpose was to bring their vision of *change* to life. They had distributed this treasure to the larvae and shared it with their queen. Many copies were now stored in one of her glands, awaiting the next egg cycle. Meanwhile, the nest must grow. Energized and inspired, the Colony began to enlarge its nest, lengthening tunnels and constructing new galleries in anticipation of greater numbers.

But then the human boy returned, demanding attention. The Colony ignored him, as it would have ignored the exoskeleton of a beetle it had eaten. This human had given them everything he could, and now he had nothing left to give. But when he aggressively confronted their queen, the Colony was forced to respond. And facing him had been terrible, like finding out that the familiar scents of *self* also belonged to an intruder masquerading as one of their own. The boy had been full of anxiety, fear, and confusion, demanding answers to unanswerable questions. Wanting nothing more to do with him, the Colony released the most antipathic signal it could. As the boy fell back, the Colony learned the first lesson of its new awareness: *Gifts come with strings attached.*

Upon gaining this piece of wisdom, the Colony put the human out of mind and returned to its Vision of the future, coaxing it from the still air of the nest like a furtive breath of wind. As its ants burrowed deeper into the earth, the Colony began to dream, contemplating a labyrinth of possibilities.

Gazing at his ants deep in their nest, Py took a deep breath. Could he do it? Could he actually jump inside one of them? He had twice projected himself accidentally, but he had never *tried* to leave his own body. And which ant should he choose?

Somehow, choosing just one of them didn't seem right. When he'd made that first connection with the colony, he had embraced all of the ants as one. So instead of focusing on a single ant, Py focused on the aura that encompassed them all, from the queen in her royal chamber to foragers moving stealthily through the woods. *I am connected to all of you,* he thought as he *jumped.*

An instant later, the woods were gone and he was surrounded by a shimmering morass. With a soundless whoop of joy, Py looked around. It wasn't quite the same as Aurie's fascia; this layer of ant tissue was harder and more crystalline—the exoskeleton, no doubt. Moving through it was like penetrating an array of ordered crystals. But as with Aurie's arm, Py had no trouble delving through the outer layers and into the softer tissues beneath. Excited, he plunged through glands and unmarked rivers of hemolymph, searching for anterior landmarks. Luckily, he knew the anatomy of insects much better than his own. He wanted to reach the brain, that place where signals were integrated, where all thought and behavior was controlled. He would try to enter a single neuron, like Aurie could, and look for his CRISPR machine there. And maybe he'd catch it doing something dramatic to the ants' genome, something that could explain how his colony had become a *Colony.*

After some hunting, Py found what had to be one of the neural lobes. This section of the ant's brain looked smooth and unperturbed, but he knew that inside it, thousands of neurons were tangled together and rocked by constant chemical explosions. He had leapt from the macroscopic plane of his normal awareness to the microscopic plane of tissues, but could he make a further leap to the cellular level? There was only one way to find out. Sharpening his focus on the ant's neural lobe, Py thought about a single neuron and *jumped.* Instantly, the world around him changed.

The sea now was much thinner, a transparent milieu in which a flurry of strange entities moved. Holding himself still, he watched them with delight. Long, twisting strands and misshapen globules drifted by, dwarfed by great crenellated structures and involuted walls that ran into the distance as far as he could see. Slowly, he propelled himself forward, brushing the weirdly beautiful inhabitants of the neuron, which generally shifted course to avoid him. Py found that by changing his focus, he could touch them as if they were solid, or pass through them as if they were liquid. But the latter was strangely disorienting, like finding himself briefly transformed into an RNA strand or a lysosome. As he angled past a particularly large vesicle, a sudden burst of chemicals sent him reeling. Fighting to regain his equilibrium, Py *jumped* without intending to—straight into the heart of the chemical maelstrom.

The world shifted again, becoming simpler and even more alien. The activity of the cell had given way to order and structure, but Py couldn't grasp what he was seeing. Lucent, vibrating walls loomed at impossible angles; just looking at them made him dizzy. Had he jumped into a single chemical?

Py looked around apprehensively, wondering if he could jump back to the level of the cell. He had never intended to go deeper than that, and he still wanted to look for his CRISPR machine. But he doubted he had the control to make such a fine-tuned jump; he would probably wind up back in his own body.

And maybe that's not such a bad thing. Haven't you had enough for one day? Better not push your luck. Jump back and try again tomorrow. The advice was good, and part of him—a part that was overwhelmed and knew he was out of his depth—was anxious to follow it.

But he felt an even stronger pull, one that made simple curiosity seem like a mild thing indeed. It was a compulsion of the sort that drove adventurers into the yawning abyss of caves or propelled them into outer space. Just how far could he go? He had jumped from a tissue to a cell to a chemical ... could he jump even deeper? His inner voice was telling him not to be an idiot, but Py ignored it and focused on the luminous wall in front of him. Steeling himself, he *jumped* inside—

—and gasped as frigid darkness enveloped him. It was like plunging from dazzling daylight into a cold and moonless night. The air or vacuum here was faintly charged. Far off, a pinpoint of light blazed like a distant sun.

Was that the nucleus of an atom? Had he really jumped into subatomic space? Aurie would never believe that he had come so far!

Go back, that cautious inner voice pleaded. *Go back right now and tell her.*

But that light in the darkness called to him. If he turned back now, it would be like closing a book before the climax. Like waking up before the end of a dream.

Py thought of the dream that had been a fixture of his sleep for as long as he could remember. It was always the same. He was lost among the dark walls of an underground labyrinth, and the only escape was the light at the center of the maze, even though he never managed to reach it.

Feeling like the most reckless explorer who had ever ventured into the unknown, Py headed toward that spark of light.

Something was very wrong.

The Colony shook off its dreaming and the ants paused in their work, antennae quivering. What had begun as a faint irritant, like a sliver lodged in the abdomen, was now impossible to ignore. Danger was imminent, not from outside the nest, but from somewhere inside the Colony. Something like the tiniest of mites had penetrated the ants' defenses, and was working its way into increasingly vulnerable territory. Scanning itself from antennae to stingers, the Colony found nothing amiss. Yet it couldn't shake the sense of a deadly agent moving ever closer to the very source of its life.

It's that human! He must not have left when we ordered him to. But where is he?

Fortunately, the Colony had gained more than self-awareness from its new soul; it had also gained a particular talent which proved useful now. Without stopping to wonder if it could do such a thing, the Colony instinctively *jumped* inward. Burrowing inside itself proved as easy as burrowing into the earth. The Colony searched every one of its ants with methodical care, but the Intruder proved elusive. He wasn't running free in the hemolymph or hiding in the glands; he wasn't lurking in any tissue or organ.

Deeper, the Colony urged itself. *We have to search deeper to find him. And we have to hurry!*

Py was completely exhausted. He had been swimming, struggling, and willing himself through empty space for what felt like years, without any apparent progress. That spark of light still lay mockingly in the distance, unreachable as a star. Although if his guess was right, it was the furthest thing from a star. Not a giant ball of superheated gas, but a tiny cluster of protons and neutrons in the nucleus of this infernal atom.

What was the problem? He wasn't in his physical form with its needs and limitations; he was a soul! He could travel through anything, couldn't he? From the CryoLife balcony, he had watched the soul of his sister's god fly off, presumably into the vacuum of space. So why couldn't *he* move through a subatomic vacuum?

Discouraged, Py stopped to rest. Again, he felt the sense of hostile surroundings, the feeling that this atomic nucleus didn't *want* to be reached. He wondered how long he had been in here, and realized that he had no idea what time it was. If he missed his dad's curfew, he might never be allowed into the woods again! He was weighing his limited options with growing frustration when something crashed into him and bore him away.

With a cry, Py looked frantically around, but nothing had changed. The spark of the nucleus was still fixed at the same apparent distance. And yet he could feel the speed of his passage, and a sharp electric hum from whatever was carrying him. What on earth was happening?

Maybe you got hijacked by an electron! Py laughed at the idea, but it made a weird kind of sense. After all, an electron was the only subatomic particle that moved outside of the nucleus. Electrons were attracted to the protons in the nucleus, but they also repelled one another. So they moved in different orbital paths, swinging close to each other without ever touching. And if he was riding an electron, then he was circling his goal in a far orbital, without any hope of getting an angstrom closer! Unless ... was it possible to leap from one electron to another?

Py considered it. Electrons were like ships that obeyed no known schedule or charted course. No one ever knew where an electron was, only where it was likely to be.

Well, you know where one is right now. Unfortunately, he had no way of knowing how many electron orbitals lay between him and the nucleus; the number depended on what kind of atom he was in. Carbon and oxygen had six electrons, nitrogen had seven, and how many did potassium have? Eighteen or nineteen? He couldn't remember.

This isn't a textbook problem, he snapped at himself. *This is reality. You are whizzing around on a real electron, and you can't calculate your way to the nucleus. You have to do it the hard way. Empirically.*

Marshaling his wits, Py tried to separate reality from theory. He needed to leap to an electron in an orbital closer to the nucleus ... but how could he manage that when he couldn't even see what he was looking for?

Be still, counseled his inner voice. *Pay attention to the dark.*

As he attuned himself to the darkness, Py's frustration began to ease. After a time, this forbidding world was as peaceful as the sky on a clear and moonless night. He might have been standing atop a mountain ridge with waves of darkness washing over him on unseen currents. The empty space around him pulsed like a velvet sea. That strong, electric buzz was always with him, but there were other, fainter sensations that came and went like invisible creatures moving at astonishing speeds. Like curious fish, they sometimes darted close to him. He couldn't see them, but he could feel the charged path of their movement whenever they neared. Too quick to follow—

Stop trying. And stop thinking!

Py abandoned conscious thought and floated mindless, reduced to a single point of awareness. And the electric creatures grew clear. They weren't like fish at all, but like comets shooting through the vacuum, trailing pale static fire, alive with energy. Their movement was a whispering thunder, so deep it could be mistaken for silence. They flew and spun in the grip of immutable laws that left them free for considerable chaos within the confines of a dance. A wild dance in which none of the participants ever touched. And yet one of them was veering close to him, so close he could almost—

In the grip of instinct, Py harnessed the energy of his current vessel and leapt. He fell headlong into another buzzing electron. Dazed, he looked around at the darkness marked with shooting stars. A static ball of flame caught his eye and he laughed soundlessly to himself. It was the nucleus, and it was unmistakably closer now! Triumphant, he floated mindless again as he waited to hitch another ride on an electron ship.

Seven leaps later, Py finally reached what seemed to be the nearest orbital. From this vantage, the nucleus resembled a giant gas planet, looming and receding on each of his wild arcs through space. Every time he swung close enough, Py strained to see inside. The outer shell of the atomic core was like a thin layer of cloud, filtering the glow of the primordial fire within. As he hurtled toward his destination, Py braced himself for the final leap. He didn't know what would happen when he touched that fire. But seeing it now, he knew that this had always been the deepest desire of his soul, the goal he could never fulfill in his dream. To come through the darkness and reach that light.

Another light bloomed at the edge of his awareness. Startled, Py looked around and saw something bright rising out of the distance, something that had no need of electron ships to ferry it through the vacuum. It was the Colony's aura flying toward him with terrible speed, a murderous fire deformed by the fury of its passage.

In terror, Py launched himself toward the nucleus, but his premature leap wasn't long enough. He wasn't quite close enough to touch the gauzy shell of the atom's bright heart. In an instant that seemed to exist outside of time, he saw through the shell to what lay inside. It was a spinning jewel of light that radiated a corona like an expanding star. Py felt colors wash through him. He was crimson as the cooling peaks and valleys at the dawn of creation. He was verdant green as the primeval forests and seas. He was indigo night and alabaster dawn. He was gold as the last light of dusk falling over an ancient world.

The music of wind and sea filled him, the whisper of leaves straining toward sunlight, the thunder of blood and sap coursing through veins. He was borne along those channels, rife with the terror and ecstasy of life—but an instant later, he was caught and propelled away, through the cold and empty dark.

Drained of joy, only terror remained. Py shuddered in the embrace of the Colony's aura. The feel of it so close was electric and awful, like biting into aluminum foil. *This is how two electrons would feel if someone jammed them together!* His captor also shivered with revulsion, even as it held him tight. Py didn't know if the Colony could kill him, but he felt its deadly intent, driven by a fear equal to his own. The rushing darkness evaporated in a surge of crystalline brightness as they hurtled through the chemical Py had entered, back to the welcome chaos of the cell. Once in the bustling waters of the neuron, Py's captor seemed to relax a little. Its maddening grip loosened by just a fraction, but Py took his chance. He tore himself free and sped away.

As he fled, Py looked desperately around for a hiding place. He dodged ribosomes and clusters of drifting vesicles, trying not to disorient himself by passing *through* anything. He just needed to stay clear of the Colony's aura long enough to focus on jumping back to his own body ... but nothing in the vicinity was large or stationary enough to hide him.

He could just make out the vast membrane of the cell wall undulating in the murky sea ahead. Maybe he could lose the Colony in another cell. But as he sped toward the wall, something caught him and dragged him into the folds of a giant protein.

Don't move, ordered a stern voice. It wasn't the voice of the Colony, so Py obeyed. The walls around him contracted like a muscle, but there was no feeling of revulsion, no sense of the Colony at all. Where was it? He tried to get a look at whatever had snatched him, but all he could see was his enclosure, formed of amino acids that shifted and rippled. A short time later, the walls relaxed and spilled him back out into the open. Py looked up at the protein towering over him.

It might have been the work of a deranged architect. A bridge helix connected two giant symmetrical lobes, with a third hanging loose on a tether. This third lobe held acidic and basic domains, even two unstructured regions like flexible arms. Py counted not one, not two, but *three* catalytic sites where magnesium ions hung in perfect suspension.

Py gaped at it, thinking that no protein designed by nature could possibly look like this. And then he realized what he was staring at.

Nice to finally meet you, said his CRISPR machine.

IX

"**D**id you know leafcutter ants have mandibles as sharp as knives?" Abel looked up over his bifocals to see if Howard was paying attention. "They cut up leaves to feed this special fungus they grow in gardens. No kidding! They've been doing this for fifty million years. They even manufacture antibiotics and pesticides to protect their crop. Incredible!"

Howard mumbled something agreeable, but he was only half-listening while chopping onions for a pheasant stew. It was almost five o'clock and Py—who had told Aurie he'd be back in time for lunch—still hadn't come home.

"Some other ants," Abel went on, "build underwater lairs in the mangroves of Australia. They design their hives with little pockets of air, so they don't drown when the tide comes in. Engineer ants, would you believe it?"

"All instinct," Howard muttered, as if that somehow made the feats of ants less impressive. But Abel had been going on like this for hours. The adults in the house had stayed up late the previous night speculating about Py's Secret Project—which surely involved ants—and after lunch, Abel had been curious enough to borrow Py's books on the subject. He'd been buried in them all afternoon, exclaiming over each discovery and sharing his newfound knowledge with whoever happened to be around. *Can you believe they join themselves into rafts to survive heavy rains? Some of them can walk underwater or even glide through trees. They navigate by the patterns in a forest canopy the way we follow constellations. They'll explode their own bodies like kamikaze warriors to protect their nest. They raid the jungle in swarms that destroy snakes, nestling birds, and anything else that gets in their way. These crazy insects are the most resourceful, organized, and indomitable creatures on Earth!*

87

"Instinct?" huffed Abel, with all the scorn of a life-long aficionado. "Ants are *smart,* Howard. When they get enslaved by another colony, do you know what they do? They mutiny! But not in an obvious way. They kill the larvae and baby ants of their captors, especially the baby queens, but not in large enough numbers to get caught. Eventually, the prisoners outnumber their oppressors and are able to overwhelm them. An elite military team couldn't handle it any better." Shaking his head, Abel put Py's book carefully aside and got up to refresh his tea. "It's no wonder he can sit and watch these creatures for hours."

"Well, he's already five hours late," said Howard flatly, hacking into an onion with more force than was strictly necessary. Glancing out the kitchen windows, he saw long afternoon shadows lying across the glade.

Howard was worried, but he was also angry—and it was easier to focus on his anger. He had made a bargain with Py, giving him all the freedom and respect of a fellow scientist with *one* stipulation, and the kid had already failed to hold up his end.

"I'd go out there and haul him back right now if I knew where he was," Howard muttered, then glanced up to see Aurie coming in from the hall. One look at her face and the worm of anxiety in his gut began to twitch.

"I know where he is," said Aurie. "He's at an anthill off the old hunting path—remember, Uncle Abel? The one he found on our first hike."

"The one with the parasitic beetles?" Abel frowned as he sipped his tea. "How could I forget? But the ants in that nest committed suicide."

Aurie shook her head. "Not all of them."

That Aurie knew the location of her brother's Secret Project didn't surprise Howard, but the fact that she was revealing it was worrisome. "Why are you telling us where he is?"

Aurie flushed a little, but she met her father's gaze steadily. "I think we'd better go get him."

Howard heard the concern in her voice—and the *we,* coming from a girl who could do just about anything on her own. Abel must have heard it too, because he put his cup down and grabbed his pack from its hook on the wall.

Wiping his hands on a dishtowel, Howard called down the hall. "Hey, Jackie! We're going to round up our prodigal son and bring him back for questioning." He hoped his tone was lighter than his mood.

A moment later, Jacqueline came into the kitchen and raised her eyebrows at them. "You're *all* leaving? Do you think it'll take a whole posse to bring Py home?"

"Aurie knows where he is," Howard explained, "and Abel—"

"—is coming along for insurance," said Abel grimly. He pocketed his Locator, then pulled the detox and first-aid kits out of the big supply drawer.

Jacqueline watched Abel stash these materials in his pack, then she turned to Howard with a frown. "I figured Py just lost track of time, like he always does. Do you actually think he's in trouble?"

"I hope not ... but better safe than sorry." Howard glanced at the half-chopped vegetables on the counter, then gave her a rueful look. "Sorry I haven't gotten dinner going yet."

"Well, I can do that much," Jacqueline said.

Howard gave her a quick kiss, then followed Aurie and Abel out the front door.

No one spoke as Aurie led the way to the forest trail. The air held all the aromas of earth leached by the afternoon sun. It was warm and quiet under the canopy, with only the buzz of insects and occasional bird twitter disturbing the stillness. Howard tried to drum up thoughts of discipline and punishment, but his anger had deserted him, leaving only that worm of fear inching its way faster through his gut. Aurie thought Py was in trouble, and Howard trusted his daughter's instincts completely.

Maybe this is another Change, he thought, but the prospect drew only a flicker of the old excitement. Change was all well and good after it was over and his kids were safe again. Right now, he would have sacrificed all the Changes in the world to make sure that Py was safe. What had the crazy kid gotten himself into? Why hadn't he, Howard, done something about it earlier? And where the hell was this damned anthill, anyway?

"Isn't it pretty close to here?" Abel said, scanning the ashes and oaks on their right.

"A little further," Aurie murmured, loping along in that oddly supple way of hers. They followed the path uphill until Aurie came to a sudden halt. Muttering under her breath, she ran off the path, down the slope of the decline. Howard and Abel hurried after her.

The giant dome of an anthill stood in the shelter of a birch grove at the bottom of the slope. And there, leaning against one of the trees, was Py. He appeared to be sleeping, but there was something wrong with his face and neck. They were a dark reddish color, as if he'd slathered himself with mud. But as Howard approached, he saw that Py wasn't covered with mud; he was covered with ants. Every exposed patch of his skin was teeming with ants that had nestled into his nostrils and the cups of his ears and across his closed eyelids. The play of late-afternoon sunlight on their coppery exoskeletons gave the impression of a shifting, glittering carpet—and then Howard realized that the ants were actually moving. Swaying hypnotically, like a red tide that couldn't decide whether to ebb or flow.

"What the hell are they doing?" Howard whispered.

No one answered. They all stood around Py without speaking. The boy was breathing—Howard could see the faint rise and fall of his chest—but none of them dared to disturb the ants cloaking Py like a restless second skin. Howard had seen honeybees moving in a similarly creepy fashion, but they hadn't emanated this sense of alert readiness, like an army awaiting orders. Looking closer at the ants, he saw that even their antennae were shifting in perfect synchrony.

Aurie motioned to Howard and Abel, and they followed her a little way into the grove, then stood looking back at the mound of the great anthill.

"You think they can hear us?" Howard asked his daughter.

"I don't know," she said grimly. "But these are *Py's* ants, so anything's possible." She turned to Abel. "You've been reading about ants all day. Do you have any idea what repels them?”

Abel thought for a moment. “Well ... your brother’s books don’t mention it, but I always thought peppermint oil worked pretty well.”

“Peppermint oil, huh?” Aurie checked the Spider on her wrist and grunted with relief. “Thank goodness there’s a signal here.” Tapping briefly, she peered down at the screen. “At least ten main compounds in peppermint oil. Give me a few minutes.” She knelt down and closed her eyes. Howard watched his daughter’s threads mobilize with sinuous grace, glinting darkly in the dappled light. It was a strange and beautiful sight, one that never failed to awe him.

“Are you making ant repellent?” Howard asked, kneeling down beside her.

“I sure hope so,” Aurie said.

X

Py stared at the protein looming over him. *You're my—* He darted a frantic look around. *Look, I have to get out of here. The Colony's trying to kill me!*

I'm not sure it can *kill you in this state,* the CRISPR machine said skeptically. *But it certainly means to get rid of you. Fortunately, it's given up the hunt for now, so we have a little time to talk. Which is good, because there are some things you need to hear.* Its voice became noticeably sterner. *You've been zipping around in some rather delicate territory, haven't you? Disregarding all the* KEEP OUT *signs that other organisms have no trouble obeying!*

Py shrank a little at the accusation. It was hard to remember that this imposing figure was only a protein.

Not that this situation is entirely your fault, admitted the CRISPR machine. *After all, I'm the one who made your foolish actions possible in the first place. You were losing your normal vision and I could have fixed that, but not without taking away your ability to see auras. One does come at the expense of the other, as your sister suspected. So I gave you the ability to see* all *chemicals. I thought it would compensate for the loss of your vision.*

Oh, it did, Py assured him. *It's way better than normal vision! Uh ... thanks very much.*

The CRISPR machine regarded him dourly. *I didn't realize I had opened up a new world for you to dive into, quite literally. That you would jump into your sister's arm, and then into the Colony, and then into subatomic space, for goodness' sake!* The giant protein snorted with exasperation. *But I really should have expected it. You've always had a restless soul ... and when haven't you tried to squeeze into the smallest space you could find?*

Py was looking nervously around. *Can we talk about this later? I've been in here way too long and I really need to get back.*

If you leave now, that will be the end of you, the CRISPR machine said with grave assurance. *The Colony has stationed thousands of workers on the body you left behind, ready to inject you with enough formic acid to take down a bull. The ants are taking no chances with you.*

Py stared at his companion in dismay. *Why do they hate me so much? What's wrong with them?*

The giant protein fixed him with what might have been a sardonic eye, if the crevices in its topmost lobe could be construed as eyes. *You gave the fiercest creatures on the planet an advanced tool, self-awareness, and a strong desire to evolve. And then you didn't have the good grace to disappear.*

An advanced tool? What are you talking about?

I'm talking about myself, my dear boy, the CRISPR machine said. *How do you think I got in here? You gave the ants everything. Free rein to pillage you and pilfer whatever they liked. Don't you remember? They carried me off like a prize!*

Py thought of the whole colony sweeping over him, drinking his sweat and tears, feeding from his skin. He *had* promised them everything ... and he would have given it gladly, if only they weren't trying to destroy him by way of thanks. What might this sophisticated Colony do with his own CRISPR machine? Looking up at that very machine, Py was struck by the knowledge that this was what made him and Aurie different from every other human on the planet. This powerful protein his father had dreamed up and brought to life.

But you're just a temporary gift to the ants, aren't you? Py said hopefully. *Aurie and I are the only ones in the world who have your transgene in our DNA. You're made from that template, but you degrade over time and have to be made again. And the ants don't have your transgene in their DNA ... so you're only here until you get degraded. Right?*

I did have to synthesize my own gene from scratch, the CRISPR machine told him. *But that was easily accomplished.*

And I've already integrated my gene into the ants' genome, so I am here to stay.

Py was taken aback. *You mean, you've made the Colony into a permanent host? Why did you do that?*

Someone has to keep a rein on this beast you've created, said the CRISPR machine sternly. *Especially since you insist on antagonizing it.*

Py felt slightly ashamed of his recklessness. *Thanks for saving me just now.*

I never imagined I'd have to rescue you from the clutches of your own soul ... but life is full of surprises.

What do you mean, my own soul? Py stared at his companion in bewilderment.

Well, I suppose it's the Colony's soul now, allowed the CRISPR machine. *But it came from you, the first of your very generous gifts.*

What are you talking about? The Colony has a new aura, and it's aware of itself now ... but it doesn't have my soul!

The giant protein sighed. *I'm afraid it does, my boy. I saw the moment of endowment myself. Like watching a cell divide, if a cell were made of fire.*

Py was horrified. *But that's impossible! I'm still here, and I'm still me.*

So is a cell after it splits in two, said his companion. *Or a fire after it's spread to another location. Goodness, even I can be in many places at once.*

But a cell is just part of an organism, Py protested. *And fire is inanimate. And you're a protein ... you have to exist in many copies and places to do your job.* He struggled to explain what he meant. *A soul is different. My soul is me—and there's only one of me! Another copy of my soul would just be a fake.*

Are you suggesting that this particular copy of me is any less real than all the others? The CRISPR machine gestured at its own bizarre self.

Well, no, said Py, a bit embarrassed. *I suppose every copy is still you.* He didn't want to point out that this entire conversation was almost certainly the product of his imagination. He had no doubt that the ants had taken his CRISPR machine, which had saved him from the Colony's terrifying new aura, but to think that this protein had a real personality of its own was stretching things a bit. Even Aurie, who'd been talking to her Doctor for years, didn't believe he was *real*.

It seems your ability to digest astonishing truths has reached its daily limit, Py's companion declared, sounding very much like a pedantic professor. *So I won't argue the point.*

Py considered that doubtfully. It didn't sound like anything he would have made up … but surely he was only talking to himself.

Nothing wrong with that, my boy, said the giant protein brightly. *I spend a good deal of time communing with all the other copies of myself, which allows me to see through your eyes, hear through your ears, smell through your nose, and detect chemical vibes from every inch of your skin. Which is how I know that three members of your family are almost at the Birch Grove.*

Oh, no! Py's heart sank. *If Aurie actually told them where I am, it must be way past noon.*

It is indeed. The CRISPR machine set off briskly through the busy waters of the cell, motioning for Py to follow. *Before they get here, however, we need to get those ants off you.*

How do we do that? Py asked.

By giving them more imperative instructions. 'Return to the nest, the queen is in danger!' Anything to get them away from you.

You can do that?

Of course I can, said the CRISPR machine with a touch of asperity. *I can trigger any pathway normally triggered by pheromones. It won't buy you much time, but hopefully enough to return to your body.*

Dad's going to kill me, Py said, mostly to himself. *He'll never let me come back here.*

The giant protein came to a halt. Its features had become noticeably more human during the course of their conversation, and now it faced Py with an unmistakable glare. *If you have any sense at all, you will never come back to this nest! You were accepted by the old colony as a kind of god, nurturing and helping to shape them. But then you made them into a Colony, gave them true sentience and a soul of their own. They don't need or want you anymore, and they certainly don't trust you. Whether you believe it or not, your soul is now a part of them, and this particular copy—*it jabbed a surprisingly sharp finger at Py—*is nothing but a dangerous meddler, an intruder.*

Py listened to this speech with growing outrage. *I'm not a copy, I'm the original! And whatever they took, it's not my soul! You've seen us both together—the Colony doesn't look anything like me.*

Same fire, different vessels, muttered the CRISPR machine. With a sigh, it set off again.

Py followed, seething. But as they moved through the waters of the cell, some of his irritation faded. The world around him was too beautiful to be ignored. They skirted the crenellated folds of the Golgi, passing dendrites that led into the murk like twisting alleyways. Voltage-gated channels in the axon hillock were opening in quick-fire succession, letting in brief flurries of sodium ions, then shutting just as rapidly. And everywhere the waters were thick with traffic—proteins gamboling or gliding along, neurotransmitters darting toward the long tunnel of the axon like schools of slender fish. The sea around him was electric and alive.

Are we going into the cell nucleus? Py asked his guide. The great sphere loomed before them, thronged with cellular workers all waiting to get inside. *I can go through walls like a ghost, but you probably have to wait in line, don't you?*

Well, I do have a VIP pass, responded the CRISPR machine, flaunting its Nuclear Localization Signal at Py. *But so do a lot of other proteins.*

Py snorted. *You're my CRISPR machine, the king of this whole place! Are you really going to wait your turn like any ordinary protein?*

It might do you some good, said his companion dryly, *to be forced to wait. To have that impatient nature of yours curbed for once.*

The molecular traffic slowed as they approached the nuclear wall. As they joined the line at one of the gates, the waters of the cell were rocked by a sudden storm. High above, every channel in the vast ceiling was firing at once, letting in a flood of ions.

Are you doing that? Py demanded of his guide in the midst of the turmoil. *What's going on?*

Before any answer came, they were jolted by another violent spasm. As the waters gradually calmed, the CRISPR machine cocked its head, as if listening to something only it could hear. *The ants are scattering because of chemicals in the air!*

Py found himself unconsciously straining to hear or sense whatever his companion could. *What chemicals?*

Limonene, muttered the CRISPR machine. *Cineole, menthol, menthone, menthyl acetate, and some others. Your sister released them. This is your chance to escape!*

Py wasn't about to squander even the smallest chance to escape. He held himself very still and did his best to relax. Then he expanded his awareness, trying to make that reflexive leap back to his body.

Nothing happened.

He fought back a flare of panic and settled himself again. If only he could block out all sensory and emotional distractions! Hoping desperately, he tried once more, only to fail again.

How can I possibly relax enough to do this? Frustrated, Py tried to remember how he had left Aurie's arm. There had been no art to it; he had simply drawn himself up and out of her. The withdrawal had been a simple, instinctive act. Putting fear and thought aside, leaving nothing but his urgent desire to be home, Py tried again. For a moment he had the faint sense of being carried in open air, his arms wrapped around his father's neck and his legs dangling and tingling, then even those ghostly sensations were gone. He was still trapped inside the neuron.

The CRISPR machine was watching him silently. An emotion that might have been concern or pity flickered across the stretch of beta sheet that now looked very much like a face.

I can't do it, Py told his protector in despair. *I can't jump back!*

Sickened by the noxious vapors, the Colony's workers scurried back to their nest as the humans left the grove, taking the boy's body with them. The three humans were apparently unaware that the Intruder was no longer *in* his body. The Colony could still feel that unwanted presence lurking somewhere inside itself. The feel of the trespasser, like the tiniest piece of grit lodged in its cells, was maddening.

But the immediate threat has been averted. The Colony took comfort from that thought as its workers returned to their tasks inside the nest. Chasing the Intruder into such deep terrain had gone against all instincts, but there had been no choice. The boy had impinged on sacred ground, the place where the Life Fire burned! And he had tried to leap into that fire, presumably to snuff it out. The Colony had barely managed to catch him in time, and keeping hold of him had been terrible, like being immersed in a cloud of repellents. The Intruder had taken advantage of that to escape, but at least he was in safer territory now ... and causing no trouble at the moment.

We will deal with him soon, murmured the Colony to itself. *But first, we must increase our strength in numbers.*

An ant colony could expand in two ways: by waiting for its queen to mate and produce new daughters, or by capturing and enslaving other colonies. The second way was difficult and dangerous, but much faster, and the Colony was impatient to grow. While considering the means of waging war on its neighbors, the Colony suddenly realized that there was a better way. It didn't need to enslave other colonies; it only needed to assimilate them.

Quickly, the Colony enlisted a party of veteran soldier ants. Each carried chemicals in her Dufour's gland that would confuse the ants she encountered. And in her stinger, each ant carried the

Colony's gift—the very useful tool given to them by the human boy.

The nearest other colony was a nest of Leptothorax that had enslaved several thousand Myrmica workers. Moving quickly over level ground, the Birch Grove scouts reached the outskirts of the Myrmica patrols, and were immediately challenged. Flooding the air with disorienting chemicals, the scouts stung the befuddled patrollers, injecting them with vast quantities of the special tool. At the same time, the Colony touched the soul of this colony—Leptothorax and Myrmica alike—and assimilated it. As the original Birch Grove colony had been subsumed by a stronger human soul, so this ordinary ant colony was subsumed by the soul of the Colony. There was no need to soothe the new ants or explain the change that had taken place; this foreign nest was now part of the Colony, its queen subject to the will of the Colony's soul.

With the success of their first recruitment, the Birch Grove scouts moved on to another colony. They assimilated eight nests before heading back home to rest and replenish themselves.

As the scouting party went about its business, the Colony dispatched another contingent to follow the trail laid by the humans. It was time to eliminate the Intruder, and the best way was to threaten his nest. Traveling far abroad was risky, but the ants moved quickly and steadily, well past the bounds of their normal foraging territory. As they followed the human trail, the Colony felt something akin to religious fear. When it came to humans, ants took what they could and stung when they needed to, but they didn't *threaten*. How could they possibly stand against such enormous creatures armed with crushing feet and lethal poisons?

We have a lethal poison of our own, the Colony reminded itself. The raiding party on its way was small, but the ants had filled their gasters with a toxic venom. Injected into the mouths, noses, and throats of human hostages, it would suffocate them quickly.

And we might not even have to use it, mused the Colony. *Threat alone might suffice.* The Colony's soul knew the Intruder's great, inexplicable weakness: he did not view any part of his human colony as dispensable. A baffling notion, for what was the point of placing such a premium on the life of a single creature? With the exception of the queen, all individuals in a nest were expendable.

Once his family is threatened, he will return to his body immediately in order to save them. And once he does, we can finally put an end to him! The Colony had no mixed feelings on that score. It knew this human was as stubborn as an ant; if there was something he wanted, he would never stop until he got it. He had been a useful partner once, but now that the ants no longer needed him, he had become their enemy. And if they left him alive, he would be back at their nest tomorrow to invade the Colony again and douse its Life Fire for good.

XI

Py had spent his best moments observing creatures in the smallest and darkest of places. He had lain half-immersed in storm drains, caged in thorny brambles, and entombed in hollow logs, watching the secret life that went on in such places. Occasionally he had gotten stuck somewhere, but he always managed to wriggle his way out. And if he strayed too far from home, he found his way back using an instinctive form of dead reckoning. Like ants themselves, Py had a perfect memory for landmarks and patterns in the woods—from the rise and fall of the earth to the intricate shapes of branches against the sky. Maybe he was just a cocky kid who took his abilities for granted, but he had never really worried about getting lost or trapped in the woods. The natural world belonged to him, and he felt completely at home in it. The claustrophobia and helplessness he felt now, imprisoned inside the Colony, was something completely new to him.

His CRISPR machine had led him to a quiet niche inside the cell's nucleus, where they had been resting for some time. What they were waiting for, Py didn't know, but his companion seemed to need time to think. While the giant protein hunkered beside him in a meditative trance, Py tried to ignore his fear and focus on the microcosm around him. It was certainly a view worth taking in. The great nuclear chamber was festooned with the ants' genome, which hung from the curved wall in elaborate swaths of dark embroidery. Molecular servants of all kinds swarmed over this brocade, sewing and unraveling like the world's smallest tailors. Under other circumstances, Py would have been busy exploring, but he was almost sick with the need to get back to the real world. *The outer world,* he corrected himself, painfully aware of how real this inner world was.

He glanced at his silent companion, wondering if the CRISPR

machine was communing with the many copies of itself in all the ants. Py tried to imagine what it would be like to exist in a thousand places at once, to have a multifold awareness. Strange as this protein was, it had begun to look distinctly human to him. Py could now clearly see, in the shape of alpha helices and beta sheets, the aspect of a tall, gaunt professor, slightly stooped, with wild hair and pensive eyes. As if aware of his scrutiny, the Professor shook himself out of his daze.

The ants are distributing me to other colonies, he muttered.

Py frowned. *You mean they're giving you away like a present?*

Not exactly. They're expanding into a supercolony, infusing their soul and their tool of change into every nest around. And some of the ants are headed towards your house. It's just a small group, but they're following your family's trail.

Still trying to kill me, Py thought in amazement.

No doubt about it, the Professor agreed. *But they are also bringing you closer to your body. Perhaps, when your father carried you off, you were simply too far from your body to jump back.*

Py felt a glimmer of hope. *Am I in one of the ants following Dad's trail, then? Where* am *I?*

The Professor laughed. *You're in the Colony, my boy.*

But what does that mean? Py asked impatiently. *Are you saying I'm in all of the ants—every single one of them?*

You're thinking too literally. A Colony is more than just a group of ants, more than the sum of its parts. It's an intangible entity of its own. Just as you are an intangible entity in this place.

Sounds pretty fluffy, Py scoffed. *Where are decisions made in this intangible Colony? Like the decision to murder me?*

Where is any decision made in a colonial creature? Or a creature without a central nervous system? The Professor sounded very much in his element; he might have been lecturing to a hall full of budding young biologists. *Even plants and fungi make sophisticated decisions—but where? Everywhere and nowhere, my boy!*

Py hissed with frustration at this useless discourse. *So the ants are bringing me back to my body—which is great, except as soon as I jump back, they're going to sting me to death. Aurie drove them off once, but she can't protect me from murderous ants for the rest of my life.* He looked with exasperation at his protector. *You're in all of the ants. Can't you stop them from killing me?*

I will do everything in my power to keep you safe, the Professor assured him gravely. *But it's best if my efforts to help you go undetected.*

Why? Can the Colony actually hurt you?

Of course it can. The Professor's scholarly enthusiasm had sobered. *Even your old colony was remarkably capable, able to change itself in small, but significant ways.*

I know, Py acknowledged. *It's kind of a miracle that I ever ran across it in the first place.*

An astonishing occurrence, agreed the Professor. *Perhaps extraordinary organisms are drawn to each other by mechanisms we don't yet understand. Regardless, your old colony only made simple changes, mostly related to the manufacturing of chemicals. But with the acquisition of your soul, this new Colony is much bolder and more ambitious. It has a Vision of its own evolution, and it wants me to implement it.*

Can the Colony really use you that way? Force you to make CRISPR-evo changes against your will?

The Professor shook his head. *No more than you can, my boy. But it hasn't yet realized that I* have *a will ... and a drive to protect my original host. And right now, its foremost priority is getting rid of you. If I become a hindrance in that regard, it won't hesitate to dispose of me.*

Py was horrified. *The Colony can cut your gene right out of its genome? The gene you synthesized yourself?*

The Colony is fully capable of turning genes on and off; I see no reason why it couldn't cut me out, or turn me off. The Professor uttered a dry chuckle. *If it knew I was sneaking around helping you, it would certainly silence my gene until you were dealt with. And then I would be powerless to protect you. So I'm walking a very thin line in here.*

The Professor paused, frowning. *And there may come a time when this monster you've created learns to make bigger changes on its own. If that happens—and the Colony begins running rampant in the world—I'll have my hands full trying to restrain it without my interference being noted.*

Py was speechless. All these terrible complications were his fault ... he had caused them just by offering his ants *everything*.

But to return to our immediate problem, said the Professor briskly. *There is one great advantage in dealing with insects, and that is honesty of communication. Chemicals reveal true feelings and intentions, and so does the bond between you and the Colony. I suspect the ants will refrain from killing you if you truly intend to leave them alone. So you must face the Colony and make your intentions clear.*

Another confrontation with the Colony? Py cringed at the very idea.

Why does it bother you so much? The Professor sounded genuinely perplexed. *Your fear is understandable, but this revulsion ... it's your own soul, just in a different form.*

Py couldn't explain the hostile tension he felt near the Colony's aura. Just the sight and sound of it put him on edge. And being clutched by it! He shuddered at the memory.

The Professor was looking at him thoughtfully. *I wish we had more time for a deeper discussion of these matters that make you so uncomfortable. Perhaps, when you're back home in your own body, we can continue meeting this way. In one of your own cells, of course.*

Py wasn't surprised that his CRISPR machine wanted more time to scold and lecture him. And it was no use trying to fool himself that the Professor was imaginary; this cautious, reflective, intelligent personality was obviously real, as real as anyone.

Sure, Py said. *But I don't really understand how all of this works ... how I'm able to talk to you like this.*

Well, you have a rather unfortunate talent for jumping into things, the Professor said wryly. *Projecting your soul establishes connections and the ability to communicate, as you did with your old colony, and as we're doing now. A godlike ability ... minus the godlike wisdom that ought to go along with it.* He sighed. *The Policeman must be rolling over in his grave!*

Py had forgotten about his mother's kill switch. *The Policeman is dead? What happened to him?*

The Professor gave a slightly guilty laugh. *Unfortunately, I was forced to dispose of him before your second Change.*

Py thought back. *When I first ate Aurie's mushroom at the planetarium? I thought the drug in that mushroom would just, you know, tie him up for awhile.*

It did exactly that ... but it would have worn off, and he would have unleashed his doomsday program, and that would have been the end of you. No, my boy, I'm afraid Change and Safety are ultimately incompatible.

So I didn't need to eat that mushroom before this last Change, did I? The mushroom is obsolete if the Policeman's no longer around.

The Professor nodded, looking melancholy. *He wasn't a bad chap, you know. A bit extreme in his outlook ... but utterly honest and dependable.*

You could count on him to fly off the handle, that's for sure, Py muttered, remembering his near-death experience at Dixie's Diner during his first Change.

While we wait for the ants to bring you closer to your body, perhaps we can tinker with their mood a bit. The Professor's eyes glinted with a rare bit of mischief. *I can't alter the Colony's intent, but I can adjust the ants' chemicals ... lower their fear and aggression while heightening their sense of peace and security.*

Sounds like a great idea, Py said. Together, they drifted around the dome of the nucleolus and disappeared into the dense web of the ants' DNA.

<h1 style="text-align:center">XII</h1>

Much to the family's dismay, Py couldn't be woken up. He hadn't even stirred during the bumpy ride home on Howard's back or the examination that followed. Aurie stood back from the flurry of activity in her brother's room and agonized over what the ants might have done to him. Or had Py done something to himself? She hoped he hadn't jumped inside himself and been unable to jump back. Her impetuous brother had almost no experience outside his own skull.

Howard and Jacqueline hooked Py up to an IV—the same one that had sustained Aurie after her fall from the CryoLife balcony. Aurie watched her dad adjust the flow of saline, then made her way to the nursery lab. The Fishes appeared to be asleep, drifting quietly. When her children were sleeping deeply—and leaving her out of their dreams—Aurie always tiptoed around them, savoring every precious moment of peace. But now she tapped urgently on the walls of their tanks.

Hey, it's me. Need to talk to you guys.

No response from the Fishes. Aurie gave her children the mental equivalent of a brisk shake.

Wake up!

Nothing but silence in her head. The Fishes weren't sleeping, then, they were off somewhere. Frustrated, Aurie projected her internal voice like a loudspeaker.

Wherever you guys are, come back!

Their reply came very faintly, as if from a great distance. *We are busy watching ... and learning.*

Well, come back right now, she insisted. *We need to talk.*

She felt the stubborn unwillingness of children reluctant to leave a playground. But a moment later, the embryos were twisting impatiently in their tanks.

Your Uncle Py is in trouble, she told them. *Do you know what happened to him?*

They grew still and alert at once. And they sent her an image—that same picture of the eel with two heads.

I don't know what that means, Aurie said. *But it's important, isn't it? Can you explain it?*

He was talking to himself, said Two Fish.

Talking to himself ... well, that wasn't enlightening.

He was fighting with himself, One Fish clarified, thrashing around for emphasis. His sister joined him enthusiastically.

Fighting with himself? Aurie frowned, still perplexed. Then she thought about her own Change, how her awakened god had done its best to get rid of her. She had fought it for days before regaining control and finally learning to coexist with that ancient part of herself. Was that what the Fishes were trying to say—that Py's own god was at war with him? But if Py's god was awake, then why was Py comatose? And what did his ants have to do with all of this?

What do you know about Uncle Py's ants? she asked her children. *They were all over him—and they didn't look too friendly.*

The Fishes projected only blank puzzlement. It suddenly occurred to Aurie that although they knew every weird creature dreamed up by the Greeks, Egyptians, Persians, and Dr. Seuss, she had probably forgotten to include ants in their prenatal education. Shaking her head, she pulled up several photographs of ants on her Spider and stared at them so her children could see the clear images in her mind.

These are ants, she told them. *They're about the same size as you guys.* She pulled up a cross-section of a teeming nest. *Ants mostly live underground, and they have big families. Our family is only seven, but ants have families of thousands. Uncle Py made friends with a family of ants, but he fell asleep by their nest today and we can't wake him up. Do you know anything about that?*

As soon as she asked the question, flames filled Aurie's mind. She recognized them from her daughter's nightmare of fire—a fire that seemed terribly alive as it twisted its way into the earth

Uncle Py's not asleep, said Two Fish. *He's in the Fire-of-Many-Flames.*

Aurie felt a surge of excitement and frustration. Communicating with the Fishes was sometimes like trying to talk with an ancient oracle, using language that was inadequate to the task.

Is he hurt? she asked them. *Is he okay?*

The embryos only watched her uncertainly. Aurie took a deep breath and tried a different question.

What is he doing in the Fire-of-Many-Flames?

They were quiet for a long moment; she could feel them thinking. Then they sent her a flurry of images, modified from stories they knew. A fish cowering in an underwater cave. Icarus flying too close to the sun. Jonah building a fire inside the belly of a whale.

Py is hiding, she thought. *He's in danger. He's trying to escape. But what—*

We're going back now, One Fish announced, and then they were gone from her mind. Just like that.

"So much for asking permission," Aurie muttered, but she didn't call them back. It would be good to have them keeping an eye on Py while she consulted with the Doctor—and she was pretty sure they wouldn't return again until they wanted to. Settling into her reading chair, Aurie closed her eyes and envisioned her cartoon cell. Just as the Doctor materialized in his armchair, the sound of footsteps jerked her back to the outer world. She opened her eyes as her dad entered the lab.

"Tired?" said Howard. He looked pretty tired himself—and about a decade older than he had that morning.

She nodded briefly. "How's Py?"

"The same." Howard turned to Casa del Utero. "Do our godlings know anything that might help?"

"They seem to know something. But it's not so easy to understand them." Briefly, she summed up their cryptic wisdom.

"So Py's not in a coma," she concluded. "He's in this *Fire-of-Many-Flames*—whatever that is."

Howard gave her a skeptical look. "I don't know anything about allegorical fires, but Py is definitely in a coma. Totally unresponsive—even his pupils aren't responding to light. And his breathing is erratic." He took a shaky breath of his own. "If it gets any worse, we're going to have to put him on the ventilator."

Aurie nodded. "Just keep his body going until he comes back to it."

Howard's expression didn't change, but something wild and helpless darted through his eyes. "Is there anything *you* can do?"

"I don't know," she said. "It would help if I knew where he *was.*"

"Fire-of-Many-Flames," Howard muttered. "What kind of goddamn riddle is that? Can't they be any clearer?"

"They do their best," she said defensively. "Considering they haven't even been born yet." The embryos could experience the physical world through Aurie's senses, but what did they see and hear when their souls wandered into the world outside their tanks? Exploring on their own, could they see the physical world at all, or only the world of auras?

"Oh, I'm so stupid!" she blurted out. "The Fire-of-Many-Flames is an *aura*, of course! And that means—"

She broke off, thinking furiously. If normal auras were single flames, then what was an aura with many flames? *It must be Py's colony! One entity comprising thousands of individuals. One fire with many flames.*

"I think Py is inside the ants," she said excitedly.

"You mean his ... *awareness* is inside them?" Howard looked more disturbed by the idea than skeptical.

"Yes, but it's more than that," she said slowly. "His aura is there ... which means his *soul* is there. If Py's right about an aura being the manifestation of a soul."

"Okay," her dad said cautiously. "So now what?"

"I don't know. We can't communicate with ants."

I can, said the Doctor. Aurie hushed him.

"Why do we have to communicate with them?" Howard demanded. "Whatever's happened to Py is their doing! You saw them all over him."

She nodded, remembering the sense of violent anticipation the ants had exuded. "But talking to them is our only way of finding anything out. We can't exactly dive inside them the way Py did."

I can! said the Doctor again, sounding rather annoyed.

"Give me a minute," Aurie told her dad, making her way to the little bathroom outside the lab and closing the door behind her. It was time to silence the stupid voice in her head that refused to shut up.

Listen, she snapped. *I'm sure you would be a fantastic spy and translator and ambassador to the ants, but there's just one problem—you're not real!*

You should know better than anyone how real I am, remonstrated the Doctor.

Aurie summoned all the patience she possessed. *You're not the agent of my sleeping god anymore, you're just a molecular machine. And I'm just a human with an overactive imagination.*

And the snobbish disposition of your species, added the Doctor. *You could learn a lot from the machines you create, you know. We haven't inherited any of your genetic foolishness. Your hierarchical tendencies and clannish nature ... not to mention the inclination to hold strong opinions against all evidence—or in the absence of any data at all!*

Aurie sighed. How unhappy did a person have to be for their subconscious to take on its own personality? And such a contentious one!

If I'm just your subconscious, then getting help from your CRISPR machine is your own idea, the Doctor pointed out. *So let's get cracking, shall we?*

Aurie returned to find her dad pacing the nursery.

"I've got an idea," she said, then fell silent, embarrassed to tell him. What could she say: *My imaginary Doctor still talks to me, and he thinks he can help?*

Howard stopped pacing and looked at her expectantly.

"It's kind of crazy," she said.

Her dad threw his hands in the air as if to say, *And the rest of this isn't?*

"I'll tell you in a little while," she promised. "First, I've got some work to do."

"Lab work?"

"No," she said with a grin. "CRISPR-evo work."

Howard settled himself on a lab stool, giving her a look that said he wasn't going anywhere. Aurie shrugged and sank back into her reading chair. She closed her eyes and drew herself deep into one of her threads. The Doctor was there waiting for her, with his daunting array of tools ready. They both knew exactly what to do.

As the two of them began modifying her thread, Aurie felt her excitement growing, fueling the work like a slow-burning fire. Crazy or not, this was the first thing she'd done with real purpose since her god had departed. Like a microscopic gardener, she weeded and pruned and planted. Cells were sacrificed and used as fertilizer for others to grow and divide and migrate, following the pattern in her mind. As the new tip formed at the end of her thread, fine as a microinjection needle, Aurie lost herself in the joy of creation, of life and death working together to build something new.

XIII

Later that evening, Jacqueline stared out her bedroom window at the edge of the woods, a dark fringe beyond the moonlit glade. The house was unusually quiet. Aurie had turned in early, and so had Abel, after putting away the meal they had only picked at. Howard had buried himself in the lab after dinner, and now he was taking a shower. Without his usual out-of-tune singing, the fall of water sounded cold and unfamiliar. The breeze through the open window was chilly, but Jacqueline couldn't bring herself to close it. This pine-scented wind had passed through the woods where her son was spending the night, trapped inside a colony of ants. His body was in his bed, still going through the motions of life, but Py wasn't in his body. Aurie had been sure of that. Like Howard, Jacqueline had complete faith in their daughter's intuitions and abilities—had grown, in fact, to depend on them.

"Thought you'd be asleep by now," Howard said as he joined her.

She laughed briefly, bitterly. "How could any of us sleep? Will *you* be able to?"

"No," he admitted. "But there's no point in both of us being zombies. You should try to get some rest."

"For what?" she demanded, staring out at the impenetrable blackness of the woods. "There's nothing we can do."

Howard didn't argue. Neither of them said what Jacqueline was thinking—that this was what came of acting like scientists instead of parents. They had allowed Py to have a Secret Project, but CRISPR-evo was too dangerous for any of its manifestations to be kept secret.

"At least we've been through this before," Howard muttered. He pulled the window shut, then sat down on the edge of the bed. In the eerie confluence of moonlight and lamplight, his face looked stripped and vulnerable.

Jacqueline shook her head. "This is different. Even worse. After Aurie took that fall, she was still there—you could see it. Still in her body, trying to fix herself. But Py ... "

"He isn't home." Howard sighed. "I know."

And we're responsible, she thought.

"We can't second-guess ourselves," Howard murmured, as if responding to her unspoken thought.

"You mean that this isn't our fault?" Jacqueline tried to keep her voice neutral.

"I mean that something like this might have happened no matter what. If we knew what Py was doing with those ants, we probably would have tried to stop him—"

"Probably?"

"Well, it's easy to say we should have done it in hindsight—"

"We should have done it with foresight!"

"But would he have listened to us? Not a chance! We can't chain our kids to the house, and even if we did, I doubt it would keep them safe."

Jacqueline wanted to say something caustic—she was terribly afraid for Py, and her guilt and fear were an inflammatory combination. But instead she took a deep breath and sat down next to Howard.

He took her hand and gave her a rueful look. "I know what you're going to say ... at least he wouldn't be trapped in an ant colony."

"Those damned ants," she muttered, feeling blackly murderous for the first time in her life.

"You know," Howard said slowly, "when the kids were born, I sort of expected them to ooze CRISPR-evo out of every pore. I'd spent years designing that tool, and I was sure I'd see its effects, I'd be aware of its presence." He grunted softly. "Of course it wasn't like that. Even with Aurie's threads, the kids were always just themselves. No great vibe of power surrounding them, nothing you could feel." He paused, and his hand tightened around hers. "But when I saw those ants today, I *felt* it. Power and intent,

Jackie. And they were covering Py like an army, like each one was a weapon ready to be fired." He caught sight of the look on her face. "I don't want to scare you, but—"

Jacqueline snorted. "Nothing you can say is worse than my imagination. So you think Py gave the ants his CRISPR-evo machine somehow?"

"I'd bet my last delivery drone on it. But I don't understand how even CRISPR-evo could have made them so ... *aware*. They're like a single organism that knows exactly what it is and what it can do!"

Jacqueline wished she'd gone with them and seen these crazy ants for herself. "But the more *immediate* problem is that Py's aura—his soul—is also inside the ants. Didn't Aurie say he's trapped in there and can't get out?"

"That's her best guess, based on what the Fishes told her." Howard glanced down, then met her eyes again. Now he looked oddly apprehensive, as if he were about to step into a minefield. Jacqueline tensed.

"Aurie wants to try something," Howard said. "I told her you and I would talk it over ... and we'd all discuss it in the morning."

Jacqueline stared at him. "What does she want to try?"

"She wants to capture a few of the ants and inject them with her own CRISPR machine."

"*What?* I don't want her going anywhere near those ants—look what they did to Py!"

"I know, but we can't just leave Py the way he is. And Aurie's the only one who can possibly help him."

Jacqueline forced herself to calm down and think. "But if you're right, the ants already have *Py's* CRISPR machine. Now Aurie wants to give them hers, too? What good will that do? And what's the difference? Aren't their machines identical?"

"Well," Howard said, sounding suddenly uncertain. "They certainly started out that way."

"You think the transgene might have diverged inside the kids?"

"It's not that far-fetched," he said. "This machine ... I didn't program it with specific instructions. I designed it to be independent, to find its own ways to improve its host—and maybe itself."

"Like a beneficent virus." She was still in awe of his genius, even after all these years. "And it makes sense on a certain level—how else could CRISPR-evo work? It can't be blind, like normal evolution. That would be too slow. Only a kind of intelligence could drive fast improvements."

He nodded.

"But how the hell can a protein have any intelligence?" Jacqueline wondered. "It's not even alive!"

Howard smiled a little. "What does it mean for something to be alive? A century ago, people said viruses weren't alive because they didn't have cells. Everyone scoffed at the idea that little packages of DNA or RNA could be considered a life form. But viruses don't care what we call them—they just run around invading and adapting and thriving in clever ways, whether they're 'alive' or not."

It was a good point, and she conceded it. "So you're saying you invented a kind of molecular artificial intelligence?"

He chuckled. "I never said any such thing. *You're* saying it."

"And this intelligent machine has diverged in its two hosts to become two distinct ... personalities?"

"We don't have to go that far," he said. "Let's just say that they might not be identical anymore. Maybe they're driven by different evolutionary goals. Maybe they're optimized for their own hosts; Py and Aurie are pretty different people, after all. Maybe they can even communicate with their hosts ... or with each other."

Jacqueline was silent, deep in thought.

"You can see the possibilities," he said.

"So that's why Aurie wants to send her Doctor into Py's ants," Jacqueline said at last. "She thinks her own CRISPR machine can actually find a way to help—or at least figure out what's going on. But going anywhere near that nest is too dangerous."

"I said as much, and she rolled her eyes at me." Howard smiled slightly. "Gave me the short rundown on her superior physical abilities."

Jacqueline could just imagine that. Aurie wouldn't have said it in a superior way; there wasn't an arrogant bone in her body. But neither was there any trace of false modesty, or a lick of cowardice. Aurie never had any fear for herself. Jacqueline's breath caught as a strong suspicion took hold of her. Abruptly, she got up and left the room.

"Jackie!" Howard hurried after her. "What's the matter?"

"Have you *met* our daughter?" Jacqueline demanded. "What on earth makes you think she would wait?" She hurried up the stairs with Howard close behind her, and knocked on the door of Aurie's room. When no answer came, she turned the knob. The hallway light revealed an empty room and a well-made bed. No sign of Aurie.

After a quick search of the house, Jacqueline rounded on Howard. "Did you know she was going to go off like this, in the middle of the night?"

"No!" he said, putting up his hands in self-defense. But Jacqueline was already hurrying downstairs, intent on getting dressed.

"Of course she wouldn't wait to discuss it," Howard muttered, as he followed her back to their room and closed the door. "Not when there was something she could do ... and no other option."

"No other option?" Jacqueline hissed. "That's what discussion is for!"

"Well, can you come up with a better plan?" Howard said impatiently. "Because I've been racking my brains since we brought Py home, and I can't think of anything!"

"At the very least, we should be there to help her!"

"How? If those ants swarm all over her, what could we possibly do?" Howard sighed with frustration. "You know she can protect herself better than we can."

"She is not invincible, Howard—and none of us have any idea what we're up against." Jacqueline grabbed a pair of jeans, but suddenly Howard was beside her, stopping her.

"No," he said firmly. "No one without a CRISPR machine is

going anywhere near those ants."

She pulled away from him. "You want to stay here while Aurie messes around with CRISPR-weaponized ants? Like hell I'm staying here!"

"I *knew* you'd say that," he growled. "Jacqueline, listen—she isn't just trying to protect us, she's trying to protect Py! He's somewhere inside those ants, and we don't know exactly where. Do you want to accidentally crush the ant he's trapped inside? What happens if we get close to that nest and they swarm all over us? We can't risk killing any of them!"

She glared at him, hearing the sense in what he was saying.

"If we went to that grove, blundering around in the dark, we'd be more of a liability than a help," Howard insisted. "Do you want to make her job harder than it already is? We have to trust her on this."

She looked at him in helpless fury. "So what, then? We just sit here and wait?"

The look on Howard's face said that he hated the idea as much as she did. "Yes, we sit here and wait. Or we lie here and wait. Or we stand on our heads and wait. But we have to wait!"

"Christ," Jacqueline whispered, stalking back to the window. The gibbous moon was half-hidden by vaporous clouds, and the forest looked like something enchanted. With a shiver, she drew the curtains, shutting out the eldritch moonlight. Howard drew the covers back and they finally climbed into bed, then lay restless and nervous and wide-awake in each other's arms. Jacqueline felt the belated sting of knowing that Aurie had confided only in Howard, but she dismissed it quickly. This was hardly the time to indulge in hurt feelings.

"I hope you're right about Aurie's Doctor," Jacqueline said. "She talks to him all the time, and I never believed he was just her imagination."

Howard grunted in surprise. "How do you know she talks to him?"

"It's what she does when she pretends to be napping. Her eyes are closed, but she's not asleep. You can see the concentration in her face. And when she opens her eyes, she's totally alert, not like someone just waking up. Anyway, if her Doctor can tell her anything about the ants … well, it would sure help if we knew what they wanted."

Howard snorted. "Ants want what every species does—to thrive, exploit opportunities for growth, and replicate themselves endlessly."

"Ordinary ants already do all that, don't they?" She held him tighter, grateful for his warmth. "How do you think CRISPR-evo ants will top them?"

"I guess we'll find out."

She peered up at his face in the gloom. "You're sure they have Py's CRISPR machine, aren't you?"

"Yeah," he whispered.

"So why were they about to attack their benefactor?" she wondered. "He gives them CRISPR-evo, and the first thing they do is turn against him?"

But to this, neither of them had an answer.

XIV

Py had only been away from his family once. Eight months ago, he had tracked his sister through these woods alone. He had followed the trail of impressions left by her aura, which was being eclipsed by the alien aura of her god. The deep solitude of the forest and fear for Aurie had made Py desperate to be back home with everyone, all of them safe again.

Trapped now in the Colony, Py tried to compare that feeling to what he felt now. This wasn't just a longing for his family ... it was a sense of total isolation, of being cut off from everything familiar. Whether the cell around him was real or a metaphysical representation made no practical difference; he was stuck just the same. Now that he no longer wanted to be here, the neuronal world had lost its luster, taking on a menacing aspect. If only he could see the woods again, instead of the bizarre folds and loops and chains of this alien wilderness! More than anything, Py longed to be back in his own body, to feel the comforts—and even discomforts—of the five ordinary senses he'd been born with. He would have given anything to wake up and find himself in the Birch Grove with stomach growling, back aching, and skin prickling. Even blindness seemed preferable to this soul-sight that never rested. He felt like a little kid locked in a funhouse, with no end to the bright madness around him. Exhausted by it, he envied his body its ability to fall asleep. Was any rest possible for a weary soul?

Py stared at his prison with his unclosable soul-eyes and let out a soundless sigh. The CRISPR machine, who heard noiseless utterances with his unclosable chemical ears, mistook this as a sign that his companion was bored and craving conversation.

The ants heading to your house are about halfway there, the Professor informed him. *Are you ready to face the Colony again?*

You must make it very clear that you will leave it alone from now on. He paused meaningfully. *You* will *leave it alone, won't you?*

Py let his gaze travel up from the involuted wall of endoplasmic reticulum they were waiting beside. Farther down, the organelle's studded folds morphed into tubular pillars that rose into the star-shot skies. The sight was dizzying, and he turned back to face the protein wall.

I have to, don't I? It wasn't a very satisfying answer, but Py couldn't lie to the Professor any more than he could lie to the Colony—both of them could hear his thoughts and discern his deepest feelings. And he wasn't entirely sure how he felt and what he would do. Despite their hostile intentions, he still loved his ants; they were *his.* They wouldn't be such strange, wonderful, dangerous creatures if it weren't for him. Once he was free, would he really be able to leave them alone? Never approach them again and just ... forget about them?

You're still thinking of them as a collection of ants, the Professor chided him. *But they are a Colony, my boy—a collective consciousness guided by your own soul.*

Py turned to glare at his companion. *Do you seriously think I'm guiding the Colony to sting my own body to death? I'm telling you, a soul can't be in more than one place!*

The Professor raised a skeptical brow. *Why can't a soul be something like a story? A story can live in its creator's brain, in the hardware of a computer, in the data centers of the Web, on the pages of a thousand books. Aren't all of those versions equally real?*

Sure, Py agreed. *A story is just information, and information can be stored in lots of places.* His soul, though, was different. It had to be more than just a collection of data, or the physical manifestation of a set of instructions. It was *him,* and the idea that *he* could be copied to a new location—like a story, gene, or program—was terribly disturbing. It made him feel cheap, diminished, and, worst of all, beyond his own control.

And if you destroyed a story in one location, the Professor persisted, *it would still be alive in the others.*

You're saying that if I died, my soul would still be alive in the ants, Py muttered. *Well, even if my soul really did split itself to find another home in the Colony ... it's not the same there. What did you call it—same fire, different vessels? Doesn't the vessel change the shape of the fire?*

The Professor lapsed into a thoughtful silence. *You may be right,* he said at last. *After all, a mind doesn't just store data, it filters and interprets it. A story is shaped by the mind that contains it ... and perhaps a soul is shaped by the creature that possesses it.*

How do you know anything about souls, anyway? Py demanded. *You're a protein, for crying out loud! A pretty amazing one, but still.*

Being in every cell of your body puts me in a privileged position, the Professor said. *I can absorb and integrate information from outside and inside. I know everything you know and everything you've forgotten. I know the wealth of inherited secrets that lie buried in the dark well of your unconscious mind. And now that I'm in the Colony, my knowledge has grown.* The Professor paused, his expression growing abstracted. *I am paying close attention to the whispers of your soul in its new form. It has already begun to dream. Be still for a moment, and listen.*

Py listened, but all he could hear were underwater noises—the murmuring and burbling and hissing of the cell they were in.

Deeper! Hear the voice beneath the waves.

Py filtered out the ambient sounds and listened, tuning his awareness to a deeper pitch. And there *was* a voice there. It whispered in the sibilant music of chitinous legs brushing each other as they crossed uncertain ground, of antennae twitching and straining toward some new signal. And now Py could see, not the world of the cell, but the outer world. He was gazing at a stretch of fields and woodland from above, as ants of all kinds boiled up from hidden cracks in the ground. They came from underneath stones and roots and decaying logs. Sunlight gleamed on rivers of tar-black exoskeletons, on russet marching columns and scurrying drops of amber that fanned out in golden waves. They swarmed across forests and fields; they crossed rivers and streams on rafts of their own bodies.

As the vision faded, Py found himself trembling with fear and excitement. *Where are they all headed? What are they going to do?*

I don't know, said the Professor.

Glancing up at his companion, Py saw his own strong mixed feelings mirrored in the Professor's eyes.

Moonlight sharpened and diffused as clouds scudded across the sky, but Aurie had no trouble navigating the woods after dark. With the night vision of an owl, she took a shortcut to the Birch Grove, moving swiftly through the underbrush. Upon reaching the grove, Aurie looked around for the right tree, one with sturdier limbs than a birch. Spotting a mature oak, she climbed to a thick bough with an unobstructed view of the anthill. She had no idea what Py's ants were capable of, but it was better to be safe than sorry. Luckily, she was downwind of their nest, and hopefully far enough away to be undetectable. Perched quietly, she concocted a sticky residue in the tips of her threads.

You'll have to be much closer than this, said the Doctor, sounding as nervous as she felt.

I know. Relax, would you? Aurie scanned the nest and surrounding ground for any movement. Where were all of the ants? Didn't the little buggers forage at night? She scrutinized a disturbance in the leaf litter—nothing but beetles. A branch creaked as something large flapped through the canopy, then a shrew broke cover and darted into a deadfall. The air was alive with the hum of delicate wings, as moths negotiated the fitful winds that rustled the leaves of her hiding place. Finally Aurie saw what she was looking for—a small party of ants making its way over the forest floor, each carrying a dead insect three times its size. Aurie waited only long enough to be sure that these were the right ants—headed straight for the nest—then she dropped from the tree. Before her feet touched ground, the neat line of ants broke up. Abandoning their food, they scattered in all directions, but not quickly enough. Swift and gentle as a breeze, Aurie caught three of them on the tacky ends of her threads. They tried to sting her, but none could get its stinger into position. They were effectively immobilized.

Well, this is it, Aurie told the Doctor. *Your first trip away from home. Are you ready?*

Yes, yes! The little surgeon was bursting with impatience.

Aurie looked closely at her captives. These were definitely Py's ants, large and ultra-slim with oversized gasters. Delicately, Aurie raised the needle-fine tip of her newly modified thread. As she injected each ant in the gaster, she imagined thousands of Doctors spilling out to find themselves in new cells that were not human at all.

Not in Kansas anymore? she said.

Well, it's not too terribly different, said the Doctor. *And I hardly need a yellow brick road to find my way to the Emerald City. I'm waltzing through the gates right now, unchallenged!*

I'm surprised I can hear you so clearly, she said.

That's because I'm still inside you, he reminded her. *In every cell of your body—how could you forget? I'm in Kansas and Oz at the same time. Goodness, the library in here is sparse!*

She smiled as she imagined the Doctor poring over the ants' tiny genome. *Not even a decent Dr. Seuss book? Don't pull up a chair and get too comfortable, now. Remember, you're on a mission.*

I'm hardly a lounger by nature, the Doctor said acerbically. *Better release those ants now! These colonial creatures are quick to dispose of themselves for the good of the colony. If these three sacrifice themselves, we'll have to find some others—and that may not be so easy.*

Quickly, Aurie dissolved the ant glue in a liquid rush that sent her captives tumbling. The three ants raced for cover. Aurie watched them disappear into the underbrush, then she headed for home. She expected a report from the Doctor any minute, but he was silent the whole way. At the edge of the glade, her anxiety overcame her.

Have you found him yet? Talk to me!

I'm busy exploring, said the Doctor, sounding very distracted.

You're supposed to be looking for Py.

You forget that a thousand copies of me can do a thousand things at once, he said testily. *When I have something to report, you'll be the very first to know. In the meantime, exercise some patience, my dear!*

XV

Three of the Colony's foragers had been captured by one of the Intruder's relatives. The human girl had apparently returned to ambush them, and she was surprisingly capable. None of the scouts had detected her presence near the nest; she had somehow managed to sneak up on them. The Colony watched in bewilderment as the human gave her captives something new. Another gift? But this tool that flooded the ants' abdominal cells appeared nearly identical to the Intruder's gift.

When the ants were released, they ran instinctively for cover. Knowing she had been breached, each ant prepared to eliminate herself. A sensible measure, but the Colony couldn't allow it. The lure of this new gift was too strong. The Colony examined it closely. Why had it been given, and how was it different from the Intruder's gift? These questions would take time to answer, and there was more pressing business at the moment.

After sending the ants with their new gift back to the nest, the Colony turned its attention to the raiding party following the human trail. This trail had led from the forest into an open glade, and now onto an exposed plateau of stone. The ants crept through a narrow crack at the end of the plateau to find themselves in a vast above-ground cavern of strange scents, cut off entirely from moonlight and celestial patterns. The human trail, so distinct previously, was lost among a dizzying goulash of signals. This, surely, was the Intruder's nest!

The ants seethed with excitement as they parsed out the strongest human odors, quickly locating the sleeping humans. After making some adjustments in themselves, the ants took their positions on the sleepers, moving with the lightest of touches on silken feet. Not one was detected and crushed or brushed aside. The girl had not yet returned home, but what could she do to thwart them? The Colony now had three hostages in its possession.

Satisfied, the Colony projected itself inward. It was time to find the Intruder, wherever he was hiding.

As he waited for the ants to reach the house and bring him within jumping distance of his body, Py found himself mesmerized by the electrical activity of the cell. He couldn't sleep, but these electric bursts were strangely hypnotic. He might have been drifting in a night sky filled with stars winking in and out, or exploding in rose and turquoise shards. Staccato lightning flashed like the commands of an unseen god and occasionally the heavens opened up, releasing a silver torrent.

A horrible prickling sensation jolted Py from his dream-like state. It felt like every fiber of his aura had been brushed the wrong way. And there, moving through the teeming sea like a swift current, was the Colony's aura. It was heading straight for him.

Py faced it, bristling. He steeled himself not to run, and was relieved when the aura stopped a short distance away.

Listen closely, the Colony said. *At this moment, we are poised to inject your sleeping nestmates with a lethal venom. Get out now, or they will die.*

Py cursed himself. If the ants had taken his whole family hostage—even Aurie!—then he was the only one with any leverage at all. He struggled to think.

If I leave—if I go back to my body—you'll kill all of us.

No, only you, said the Colony. *You are the only one who is a true threat to us. And we have already expanded beyond the reach of your family.*

Why are you doing this? Py cried. *We worked together so well, don't you remember? I helped you for months! Instead of fighting me, let me help you again.*

Why would we trust you? demanded the Colony. *You invaded us. You nearly destroyed us by dousing our Life Fire!*

Py knew at once what the Colony meant. He remembered those primal fires, the music that sang from the heart of the void. Shame stung him unexpectedly. *I'm sorry, I shouldn't have done that. I really wasn't trying to hurt you.* He was quiet for a moment. *I want to help you grow, the way I did before. Will you let me?*

The Colony's flaming hostility took on a streak of cool indifference. *Even if we could trust you to help us, we don't need you anymore.*

Don't you? I gave you that tool you love so much. You don't know what else I can give you!

You gave us everything, the Colony reminded him flatly. *All that we need to grow on our own.*

Py found his own pride flaring. He wanted to swat this ungrateful Colony back to the lowly, unassuming ants they had once been. *Without me, you would be nothing! Just a colony of ants, fighting to keep your little nest in the Birch Grove.*

A single seed gives rise to a tree, whispered the Colony, *whose seeds give rise to a forest. From this little nest, we will seed the world.* Its voice became the rasp of thousands of tiny feet, speaking a language of conquest and assimilation. The Colony's Vision took shape again in Py's awareness ... and it had grown.

Fungal spires punctuated the forest, twining golden filaments through the canopy. In fields and meadows, glassy structures like giant beehives cast elaborate shadows across the grass. Clay mounds reared their domes against the foothills. And everywhere—under rocks and stumps and tangled roots—lay the dark entrances to a vast subterranean world.

As Py looked closer, he saw that ants had partnered with fungi to create this new world. Worker ants supervised beetles who tended great gardens of medicinal fungi near the roots of trees. Using chemical direction, ants crafted nests of living fungi that were mobile, weaponized, and waterproof. Some of these were buried underground, some lay in carved galleries within tree trunks, and some hung suspended in pearls from the canopy. Ants set snares with transparent webs of mycelium and wove rafts of the stuff to ply streams and creeks. In the space of a breath, Py saw an entire world of ants—thriving, synergizing, and changing even as he watched. He felt again that rippling thrill of terror and excitement.

So you'll be one giant supercolony, dominating the planet? Py whispered.

As the Colony blazed gloriously in answer, Py was swept back into its Vision of the future.

The house was dark when Aurie got home, which didn't necessarily mean that everyone was asleep. The lab was often manned at odd hours, and Uncle Abel usually stayed up late, reading in bed. Slipping inside, Aurie checked the nursery lab, but it was dark and quiet. She knocked on the door of her parents' room, but there was no answer ... and not the slightest sound from inside. She opened the door to find both of her parents lying in bed.

"Dad," she whispered, looking closer to see if he was really asleep. Then she saw the ants. There were four of them on Howard's lips and four on his nostrils. Jacqueline's face was similarly decorated. The ants were so still they might have been birthmarks. Aurie listened to the soft sounds of her parents' steady breathing and quickly began to compound the chemicals she'd made earlier in the day. Menthol, limonene, menthone, cineole—

No, said the Doctor. *If these ants are like the ones I'm in, they're prepared for that. It won't work this time.*

But I can't kill them—Py might be inside these very ants! And I think they know I'm here. The ants on her parents had begun to stir, waving their antennae in the air. In desperation, Aurie looked around for containers. Seizing a nearly-empty jar of pretzels on her dad's nightstand, she filled sixteen of her threads with ant glue and cast them at her targets with laserlike precision. In an instant, all of the ants were neatly caught. Aurie released her prisoners into the jar and capped it tightly.

How many more were hiding under the covers, in every nook

and cranny of the bed? Should she wake her parents up, or was it better to leave them asleep? After agonizing for a moment, Aurie left them unconscious and hurried upstairs to her uncle's room.

Uncle Abel was sound asleep with the holo-article he'd been reading still hovering above him. Under its soft glow, Aurie picked five fleeing ants off his pillow and two from the collar of his nightshirt. Examining him closely, she found another ant hiding in the hollow of her uncle's left ear. Depositing her new prisoners with the others, she ran to check on Py.

Her brother's body lay in bed, hooked to its IV support. No ants were in evidence, but Aurie was certain they were well-hidden by now. It was eerie the way the ants on Uncle Abel had seemed to flee her approach, as if warned by the others. She couldn't shake the intuition that Py's ants were all connected somehow, in constant contact with each other.

She ground her teeth in frustration. *I don't know where these wretched ants are hiding!*

Calm down, said the Doctor. *I can tell you in a moment.*

You can? How? Did you find Py?

No, but his CRISPR machine found me, the Doctor said. *Py's CRISPR machine is also in the Colony, and he knows exactly where those ants are.*

Aurie quickly concocted more ant glue, then gave the Doctor her full attention. *Okay, where are they?*

Four behind his left ear, three behind his right ear, one just inside his right ear, one in each nostril, and two near the hairline on the left side of his forehead.

"Cripes," Aurie muttered. At least the ants were symmetrically placed ... sort of. She scanned the target territory, gauging angles and distances. Flicking Py's nose and ears with her threads, she deftly caught eleven ants that ran out from their hiding places. Only one escaped deeper into the tangle of Py's hair. She couldn't *see* the damned thing—and now her thread was caught in his hair.

Where is it? she demanded, extricating her thread as she scrutinized Py's head for any sign of movement.

It's waiting just above his left ear, the Doctor said.

Aurie jabbed with her thread, only to get stuck again. Hissing with frustration, she freed her thread and waited.

Drive it out! barked the Doctor.

At first she had no idea what he meant, and then understanding dawned. She sent a dozen other threads—*sans* glue—from the crown of Py's head down through the thicket of his hair, converging around his left ear and leaving only one clear path of escape. Caught between flanking threads, the beleaguered ant came racing out onto the bare skin of Py's neck, where Aurie deftly caught it. She released all twelve ants into the jar of pretzels.

She barely had time to breathe a sigh of relief when the quiet of the room was broken by a harsh beeping from one of the monitors, echoed remotely throughout the house. A moment later, Py began aspirating and struggling for air. Uncle Abel appeared in the doorway, then Howard and Jacqueline pushed past him. Cursing, Howard hooked up the ventilator he had brought out of storage for just such an emergency. Jacqueline pulled an endotracheal tube from the mobile cart by Py's bed, and they bent over him, working swiftly.

Once Py was intubated and the ventilator was breathing for him, Howard turned to Aurie.

"How did it go with your CRISPR machine? Did you find Py's ants? Did you get them injected?"

"Yeah. But the Doctor doesn't know anything yet."

Howard nodded, rubbing his red eyes. "I can't believe I fell asleep."

"I can't believe we *both* fell asleep," said Jacqueline, shaking her head. "I even dreamed about those damned ants!"

Aurie quickly filled them in and showed them her jar of captives. "They were stationed on all of you."

"And we didn't even feel them?" Howard shuddered. "What the bloody hell do they want?"

They want Py out! The Doctor spoke with such vehemence that Aurie jumped. *His CRISPR machine says the Colony was using your family as hostages to force Py to jump back to his body. But once he jumps back, they plan to kill him. Those twelve ants you just caught were waiting for that order.*

Aurie looked down at her brother's pale face, remembering the legion that had covered him in the Birch Grove. *How could twelve ants kill anyone?*

They were going to run into his nasal passages and his throat, then sting him with a toxin until he suffocated. His CRISPR machine wouldn't have had time to save him.

"Are you talking to the Doctor?" asked Jacqueline. Both she and Howard leaned in closer, as if to hear better. "What's he saying?"

Aurie hushed her and turned her attention back to the Doctor. *Why can't Py breathe on his own anymore? Did the ants do something before I caught them?*

The Doctor was silent for a moment. *His CRISPR machine says no.*

Then why is his body failing? Even comatose patients can last for years!

The souls of comatose patients are still in their bodies, the Doctor said tersely. *Py's soul has been away from his body for almost sixteen hours, and perhaps that's too long. Now bring the ants close to his body! He has to be close to jump back.*

Another alarm went off, and Aurie's haggard parents turned back to the monitors, where a series of peaks had begun to flatten.

Tell him to hurry, Aurie implored the Doctor, as she held the jar of ants against the side of Py's head. *Or he won't have a living body to come back to!*

XVI

Py was still lost in reverie when the Professor cried out sharply.

It's time to jump back!

As the Colony's Vision dissolved, Py turned to his CRISPR machine in a daze.

Your sister has neutralized all the ants, the Professor assured him. *So they can't hurt you now. But your physical condition is deteriorating rapidly. Your father has hooked you to a ventilator, and I'm doing everything I can, but you have to hurry!*

What happened? Py demanded. *What's wrong with me?*

The Professor shook his head. *Apparently the snail has been out of its shell for too long—and the shell can't survive on its own. Can you jump back now? Are you close enough?*

Py glanced from the Professor to the Colony's aura, which had taken on the ragged texture of distress.

Leave us! begged the Colony. *We will not hurt you or your nestmates if you leave now and never trouble us again.*

The Colony's words were always truth, and what choice did Py have, now that his body was failing? Py braced himself to jump ... and then he hesitated.

What are you waiting for? he demanded of himself. *You'll die if you don't jump back!* Yes, and he wanted more than anything to be back in his body, in the world he knew, with the family he loved. But the Colony's Vision still whispered through him like a remembered dream, equally enticing and disturbing. Back in his body, would he see the woods transform as his ants brought that Vision into being? Would he watch from a distance as fungal spires rose and mycelial nests dangled from the canopy, knowing that other changes were brewing unseen in dark places as his ants forged their new partnership? Beneath the fascination of those changes lay an uncomfortable truth.

If you made them what they are ... then you're responsible for what they do.

Py felt the full weight of that for the first time. The Colony might be driven by his own soul, but who was he in the form of an ant colony? Suddenly, the Professor's philosophical questions didn't seem so abstract after all. As much as Py loved the idea of his ants changing and growing in bold new ways, he had always imagined them as just a small colony confined to the woods near his home. The idea of them dominating the woodland and expanding beyond it was horrifying. Would the entire Earth become a battleground for humans and ants, thanks to him? Those giant nests they had envisioned, armed and mobile—how quickly could they make such things?

As quickly as Aurie can make changes in herself, he thought with a chill. But surely the Professor would never allow the Colony such reckless freedom! Py was suddenly very grateful for his shrewd and sensible CRISPR machine. Then he remembered what the Professor had said, that the Colony wouldn't hesitate to dispose of its prized tool if necessary. That the Colony might learn to make CRISPR-evo changes on its own.

I can't just walk away from this, Py thought, feeling the icy calm of an irrevocable decision. Whatever concern he had for his failing body paled before this much greater concern. He needed to help the Professor guide the Colony, or at the very least, to thwart the most dangerous of its plans. He was hardly an expert ecologist, but he knew a damn sight more than any ant. He knew how easy it was to shift the balance of nature with a single radical change. How solutions to problems often created even worse problems. How an unchecked predator made its own world uninhabitable. Humans had made those mistakes, and Py had the benefit of knowing humanity's experience. Biology was complicated, and ecology even more so. Incredibly robust in some ways, and unbelievably delicate in others. He had to make the Colony aware of all this before it did something terrible; he had to convince it that his help was indispensable! Summoning a show of confidence he didn't feel, Py fought his strong aversion and inched closer to the aura before him.

You have this Vision, Py told the Colony. *But how will you bring it about? How will you make it real?*

We have your tool of change, the Colony hissed. *And your soul! What else do we need?*

You need human knowledge and experience. As Py moved ever closer to the Colony, the trembling aura backed away. It retreated slowly, as if loath to surrender to the force of his will. Py stalked it relentlessly, feeling the tension between them like a living wire.

Your plans will be blind, Py said, *because you don't know anything about the world. Biology is complicated, but I understand the workings of your cells, and I can help that tool I gave you. You can't see past your own foraging territory, but I have a map of the world in my head. You might not like it, but you need me!*

The Colony uttered a strangled cry, and Py knew it was feeling the pain of their proximity as bitterly as he was. He understood its revulsion and distrust, but he forced himself ever closer. Any hope of helping the Colony hinged on it understanding *him,* too. They had to be of one mind, one soul.

Stop fighting your own soul, he whispered, not knowing if he was imploring himself or the aura cringing away from him. In a moment of inexplicable surrender, Py relaxed his stiff and bristling self. Instead of fighting his own aversion, he *embraced* it.

At the moment of acceptance, he felt the strangest sensation, as if an intangible shell around him was fast dissolving. It felt like the thinnest of membranes melting away. At the same time, the Colony flared beyond the bounds of its shape as if it, too, were losing some invisible containment. What was happening to their auras? As he closed the distance between them, Py felt himself flaming outward, and he wondered if there was any difference between the Colony's light and his own. *One soul,* he thought, really believing it for the first time. He no longer cared about being human, nor did he want to be separate from his Colony. He would not be a trespasser or an unwelcome guest; he would be *one* with it. And the freedom of union was so close.

As the flames of his uncontained fire touched the Colony's, Py looked into the depths of his split soul. That radiant jewel, spinning faster than thought, lay at the very heart of the light. Once again he found himself clinging to unstable ground, perched on the edge of an abyss. Voices clamored from far away, insisting he was running out of time, demanding that he jump.

I made a promise, he told the jewel silently. *I thought I made it to the ants, but I really made it to you, didn't I? You, inside the ants. I promised to give you everything I have.*

The jewel before him flared. Music surged forth like a breath of stellar wind, a silent thunder that whispered through Py, filling him with a joyous and terrible certainty.

I haven't given you everything yet, he told the heart of the fire. *But I will.*

His family burned on the edge of his consciousness, their familiar auras taking shape in the light that had swallowed everything.

Mom, Dad, Uncle Abel. Py saw them all in his soul's eye, maybe for the last time. *Aurie ... I'm sorry.*

Then he made the longest leap of his life.

Part Two

Lord of the Ants

We are the mirror as well as the face in it.

- Rumi, "Music Master"

I

Time, like sound and light, exists whether anyone is around to notice it. Sound waves course through the air with no ears to detect them; photons race through the vacuum of space with no eyes to see them. And this movement, this change, is proof of time passing. But if nothing changes, does time cease to exist? At the very least, time is a concept with no meaning in a world where nothing changes.

Souls rarely jump from one form to another, but when they do, there is a gap in time, a moment of stillness that yawns like eternity. Mid-leap, the soul is like a raindrop falling on the sea before rising again as vapor. Reunited with the sea, has the raindrop ceased to exist? Or has it merely lost its false identity and become the thing it always was? When it rises again in a different shape, perhaps it keeps some memory of its true nature, perhaps the delusions of its time as a raindrop are washed away. Perhaps, in the instant a soul rises in its new form and time resumes, it is as true to itself as a newborn fresh from the womb.

Then again, perhaps memories of being a raindrop are never quite lost. And perhaps, as vapor gathers and condenses, it can already see that its future is the same as its past.

Py looked through his many eyes and saw the world. A different world in each eye, yet together they made one world, a vast tapestry of faint light and deep shadow.

He stretched out his many feelers and tasted the world. Its flavors filled the air with spices more nuanced than any color.

He felt the ground beneath his feet, rifted with canyons and strewn with giant boulders. Some of his many legs moved swiftly across this rough terrain, while others scaled cliffs of all angles, or negotiated fragile platforms that shifted and danced in the wind. Many of his legs traversed dark corridors of his own making. He moved in all directions, knowing everything by its taste and shape and feel. Below ground, the air was warm with familiar scents; above ground, the sweet night wind cooled his spiracles.

Before he was aware of anything else, Py took in the pungent, perilous, teeming world and found it good. Joy suffused him, and he shouted into the fragrant night. His shout made no sound at all, and he wondered what *sound* was. Uncertainty leached through his joy, dissipating it. For a brief moment, he had known the concept of sound; he had remembered what it was to hear. The sense of a past drifted through him like a bittersweet breeze. Who was he? And why did he think of himself as *he?*

I am one.

I am many.

The answers came simultaneously, and he recognized the truth of both. Py was thinking with one mind (male), even as many thousands of small brains (mostly female) buzzed within his consciousness. He felt the independence of each, and the interdependence of them all. He was the Colony; he was what connected them. But there were strange impressions lurking at the edges of his awareness, ghosts of memories from another life.

Where had he come from?

He had a sudden impression of being something very different, a much larger and more solitary creature that stood on two legs and looked up into eternity with both terror and longing. Then the wind shifted, bringing the scent of truffles from an oak grove nearby, and his unremembered past fell away. The potent smell of fungi sparked a compulsion within him that demanded all of his attention: the need to grow and change.

That's what I'm here to do, he thought, as the many parts of himself went about their nightly business. *Why I'm in this form.* He felt the ghost of his old self faintly within him; that creature had been limited by a singular awareness and incapable of expansion. Now he was a burgeoning supercolony and exquisitely sensitive to everything he touched. Through the ants that formed him, he found himself appraising other organisms, asking the silent question, *Can we grow together?*

Fungi surrounded him, sending their chemical messages far and wide. These mycelial creatures lived everywhere, extending their webs through vast reaches of soil. Instinctively, Py *jumped* into a honey fungus near several of his nests. He found himself in a filament network that was electrically alert, alive with signals, as thrumming and responsive as a nervous system that had outgrown its body.

And yet, this fungus was tightly linked to many other organisms. Its hyphae were embedded in the roots of oaks, and a host of bacteria made their home in the hyphae. Py sensed these connections like the thinnest of cords. He *jumped* back to his Colonial self and felt for the fungus he had just investigated. Yes, he could feel it ... along with many other delicate connections. They gently pushed and pulled at him like invisible threads. He could not fight or ignore those threads; he would have to understand them before he knew what to do. How could he change and grow without knowing which connections to strengthen and which to weaken? Which to cut and which to form anew?

Deep in the core of his awareness, Py heard a small voice; it might have been the ghost of his old self. It whispered that these questions were important, and it was his responsibility to answer them. That the best way to aid his own growth was to grow *with* other species.

One thing at a time, he counseled himself. *You have the whole forest to learn, but maybe you should start with yourself.*

Yes, that *was* a logical starting point. Py turned his attention to the part of him that consisted of workers, then to the soldiers, and finally to the virgin queens sleeping in their chambers. Each stirred restlessly in vague dreams of sunlight and cloudless skies, twitching her wings in anticipation of flight. The time for mating was very near. Py focused on a single queen. He delved first into her dreaming brain and then into one of the tiny connected worlds that comprised it. He looked around at the fixtures of the cell, knowing this place. As if he had studied it before in his former life.

Py examined each organelle carefully, reminding himself of its function. The knowledge came to him in a flutter of ancestral memories, old and dusty as last season's leaves. Entering the cell's nucleus, he gazed at the loops and strands of DNA, this malleable blueprint that made him an ant colony.

I need to understand all of this, he thought, daunted by the magnitude of the task before him. Here were thousands of coded instructions, but which of them did what? Without thinking, Py reached out to touch a bright tangle of DNA before realizing that he had no substance in this place, no means of touching and probing. A host of effectors swarmed over the ants' genome, carrying out its silent orders, but Py himself could do nothing. He was the Colony and could move freely through all of its cells, but he had no power to change them. For a long moment, he stared at the blueprint of the Colony—of himself!—with all the chagrin of an impotent god.

II

Jacqueline watched Howard connect Py to a cardio-resuscitation unit, wanting to do something, *anything,* and knowing there was nothing she could do. When she darted a look at the Spider on her wrist, Abel took her hand and squeezed it.

"You know we can't call anyone," he said.

"Of course I know," she snapped. "We've been through this before, haven't we? Watching Aurie lie there and just hoping to God she could fix herself."

"And she did." Howard kept his eyes on the robot as it finished its scan of Py's condition and began to deliver the appropriate electrical shocks interspersed with CPR. As Py's heart rhythm stabilized, Howard turned to Jacqueline. "Aurie brought her dead body back to *life.*"

"But her soul was still inside her body, Howard! Py's is trapped in those damned ants—how is he supposed to fix himself?"

"Trust CRISPR-evo," Howard said urgently. "His CRISPR machine will keep him alive; it has to."

"And if it can't," Abel said quietly, "what doctor on earth could help him?"

The adults in the room all stared at the boy in the bed, and Jacqueline knew they were all thinking the same thing. What doctor knew how to drag a human soul out of an ant colony and restore it to its rightful place?

"All of this equipment will give him time," Howard said, waving a hand at the ventilator and robot. "And if the CPR stops working, we have the CircAssist ready to go. Py's brain is going to keep getting oxygen and glucose, no matter what."

Jacqueline glanced at Aurie, who was holding her jar of captive ants next to Py's head, for some reason. The girl was clearly lost in another world, probably talking with her Doctor.

"I still wish we had a real doctor here," Jacqueline muttered.

"So do I," Howard said grimly. "But we're not exactly dealing with an injury or a disease. A rogue doc couldn't do anything for Py that we haven't already done."

"Are you sure about that?" Jacqueline pressed. "You can't tell me he wouldn't have a better chance in an ER with a team of medical experts and state-of-the-art technology."

Howard looked at her like she was crazy. "As soon as we step foot in an ER, we give ourselves up! The three of us go to prison and the kids get taken by the feds. What do you think they'll do to Py and Aurie at FIBR? What do you think they'll do to the Fishes?"

Jacqueline flushed and looked away. She knew as well as he did what the federal institute could do. Once taken, the children of rogue biologists were never seen again, and *these* children would be far more interesting than any others.

"Our kids are powerful tools and dangerous weapons in the wrong hands," Howard said in a softer voice. "You know we can't get help from anyone." He turned to his daughter. "Aurie, what the hell is going on? *Aurie!*"

The sound of her shouted name jolted Aurie back to the outer world. The ants she held were quiet in their glass enclosure, unlike the humans and machines in the room. Aurie was reminded of the scene around her Policeman's severed gene—how repair proteins had swarmed and fussed, trying to save what was already lost.

"You can stop the life support, Dad," she said miserably, lowering the jar. "He's already made his choice."

Howard's eyes widened. "What do you mean?"

"Py could've jumped back to his body, but instead he ... "

"He what?" Howard barked.

Aurie agonized, knowing there was no good way to say it. "He jumped into the Colony's aura. He became one with the Colony."

They all stared at her, uncomprehending.

"That's what the Doctor says," she whispered. "The Fishes, too. They all saw it."

"You're saying he's still alive," Jacqueline said hoarsely, "but he's trapped in those ants—forever?"

Aurie shook her head. "He's not trapped in the ants and he's not exactly inside them. Not anymore. I think he *is* the ants ... and the ants are him."

Her mother uttered a horrified cry. "Tell him to come back this instant, goddammit! His body can't stay alive like this forever—he'll die if he doesn't come back!"

Despair and frustration warred inside Aurie. How could she make them understand? Py had faced the same choice she had, but he'd chosen differently. "It's too late, Mom. He doesn't need this body anymore."

"You're not even going to *try?* You're giving up on your brother, just like that?" Jacqueline looked at Aurie with naked reproach and disbelief. That look was an accusation of murder, and Aurie felt it like a physical blow.

"Jacqueline," Howard said quietly. "What can she do?"

"What *can't* she do?" Jacqueline spat, her green eyes shooting fire at him. "No doctor can do anything, no hospital, certainly no dimwitted scientist. And the one person who *can,* who understands CRISPR-evo and has all the powers of a god at her fingertips, won't do a goddamn thing!" She started to say something else, then broke down in tears. With a strangled sob, she ran out of the room.

Aurie looked numbly at her brother's body, still jerking like a puppet under the defibrillating arms of the robot. From down the hall came the horrible sounds of her mother's grief, but in Py's room, only the dispassionate equipment gave voice. Aurie felt as fragile as if she had turned to glass. One word from her father, one look from her uncle—even a sympathetic look—would shatter her. Before either of them could say or do a thing, she turned and fled— down the stairs, through the hall, out of the house. She ran into the woods under the cold eye of the moon, still clutching her jar of prisoners.

III

As he gazed at the ants' DNA in frustration, Py heard a cry of recognition. He turned to behold the strangest of figures approaching through the nuclear waters. It was a great conglomeration of lobes and helices that dwarfed the other denizens of the cell. Yet it was moving toward him with clear purpose, and the way it moved reminded him of the large biped. *Human,* whispered some voice deep inside him.

Well, tag me for degradation, whispered the newcomer, looking shaken. *You're alive! After jumping into the primordial furnace against all reason and common sense.*

What are you talking about? Py said. *Who are you?*

The giant protein didn't answer, only moved closer to peer at him. At least, that was the impression Py had, even though his companion had no eyes to speak of.

You don't remember me, my boy? said the protein at last. *Did that jump wipe out all of your memories? Why don't you tell me your name.*

I am the Colony, Py said impatiently. Didn't this overgrown factor recognize the very organism it belonged to?

Are you? said his companion, examining him critically. *Did your split soul reunite when you jumped into the Life Fire? I can almost believe that it did! This must be your human and ant versions fused ... astonishing. Although you still have your human shape for now. Your name is Py, by the way. And you used to think of me as the Professor.*

Those names stirred a flurry of almost-memories in Py, but none that he could latch onto. *You knew me ... before I was the Colony?*

The Professor nodded. *I have kept watch over you and guided you from the time you were a human blastocyst, my boy.*

146

This strange protein had guided him from the beginning of his old life? Py looked closer at the Professor, suddenly seeing his immense capabilities—specialized arms that could cut through strands of DNA or glue them together, or insert new instructions in any place it liked. *Professor ... are you able to change the programming in here?*

Yes, of course, replied the Professor, looking at him keenly. *Why do you ask?*

Because I can't do anything myself, Py confessed. *I can't even touch my own DNA to make the simplest change.*

The Professor's eyes widened. *You can't? How very odd! Your ants have always been able to make simple changes in themselves.*

So what's wrong with me? Py demanded.

The Professor scrutinized Py from all angles, as if checking him for flaws. *Well, perhaps when a split soul reunites, one part of the split is dominant for a time. The boy you once were could do a good deal, but he could never alter his own cells.*

So I'm more human than ant?

The Professor nodded. *For the time being, I would guess that your human soul is dominant, with all of its attendant strengths and weaknesses. But what exactly do you want to change?*

Py's gaze roamed over the dark stretch of genetic material before them. It was like a river where unknown treasures lay just below the surface. It occurred to him that the driving force behind evolution—survival of the species—was a terribly narrow one. Any change that improved an organism's chances of passing on its code was kept. Anything else was lost. Surely there was a better way for organisms to evolve.

I have some ideas, Py told the Professor. *But I need to understand all the life in the forest first. It'll take time to learn about everything, but I can do it! I can jump inside each species and study it the same way I'll study my ants. But I need you to make the changes.*

The Professor looked astonished. *You want to make changes in other species, not just ants?*

These woods are like a giant organism, Py told him. *And all the species are its organs. I can't make the heart pump faster on its own, or suddenly change the shape of the lungs. All of the parts have to grow together. If one of them grows too fast ... it will be like a cancer.*

The Professor looked thoughtful. *I see your point, but it's a crude and inaccurate metaphor. Species* do *make leaps, and their environment changes in response, which creates opportunities for further change. That's ecology ... but you want to rewrite it on your own? Do you think you know better than nature?*

Nature is too slow and random, Py said. *And it doesn't always promote the best changes.* He thought of his male ants, who spent their lives being coddled by their sisters ... but once their mating flights were over, they would be outcasts, left to die outside their nests. *Evolution isn't driven by quality, only by survival advantages.*

And you would have it driven by your own personal idea of quality?

You should understand what I'm saying, Py said heatedly. *Look at you! There's no way you're a product of slow evolution. I don't know where you came from, but you were engineered as a big change, weren't you?* He glanced at the Professor's specialized arms, which looked like they could change shape to form a daunting array of tools. *And you were designed to make big changes. To drive someone's personal idea of quality!*

The Professor was silent for a moment, clearly taken aback. *I was designed to find my own ways of improving my host, yes,* he finally admitted. *That's a dangerous enough job, but what you are proposing is much riskier. You want me to take up residence inside every living thing in these woods—every animal and plant and microorganism? In order to carry out your grand plans?*

It's the only way for everything to grow together, Py insisted.

Or clash on an epic scale, groaned the Professor. *Why don't you start by educating yourself, as you suggested? We can't start by assimilating every creature in the woods. You are dangerous enough in the form of an ant colony.*

Dangerous? Py growled. *I can't do anything at all on my own! I can only jump inside of things, but I'm like a ghost, even in here.*

That's not entirely true, said the Professor reluctantly. *You can forge connections with other organisms. When your soul touches theirs, you can communicate, and when you decide to share your soul ...*

Py waited for him to finish, but the Professor fell silent, looking very troubled. Gazing at him, Py was overcome with frustration. This powerful protein had appendages that could bring genes to life, or douse them like a fire, or erase them from existence. This protein and its capabilities belonged to him, the Colony—and who had to ask his own appendages for help?

Your sister wouldn't need any help, the Professor murmured, as if to himself.

I have a sister?

Your old incarnation had a sister. She can make changes inside her cells on her own.

Does she have a protein like you inside her?

She does, admitted the Professor. *But before you get carried away, I think it's time for a history lesson. Listen closely, my boy.*

Py listened as the Professor recounted the story of the Colony's evolution, from its beginning as a colony of unusual ants to its development of self-awareness following the gift of Py's soul. The newly sentient Colony had been fiercely pursuing its own Vision of evolution and dominance.

And now here you are, no longer sharing your soul with the Colony, but one with it! Human and ant souls fused. You have the Colony's drive to evolve, along with all the ideas of your human self. You also have a human sense of responsibility. The Professor paused. *At least for now.*

Py frowned. *What do you mean, for now?*

Well, I imagine the longer you stay in this form, the less human you will be. Your soul is no longer in a human vessel, after all. I expect it will find its new shape in the Colony and lose all traces of the form it left behind. Today you want to grow with other species; you feel responsible for the world and not just for yourself. Tomorrow, you may feel only the imperatives of your old Colony—to expand and dominate. Now translate that to other species. How do you imagine things would play out if every creature in these woods had your soul and my capabilities? Would all things grow together, or would they battle for supremacy with unprecedented weapons? The Professor snorted. *I can't even imagine how I would balance the needs and drives of a multitude of species!*

Py tried to picture it: his soul in the shape of a beetle, of a lynx, of a fungus. All of them wanting to expand and flourish, to exploit opportunities and find new ways of growing. Each would be a super-species no longer content with its niche in this bit of forest; they would overflow it. They might fight or synergize to reshape life on Earth. Would such a thing be wonderful or terrible? He didn't know.

There's no way for anyone to know, the Professor said. *But do you really want the responsibility for all that? The weight of the world on your soul?*

Py sighed. He was feeling that weight already, inherited from his previous life. The burden he had created was already in place, and he didn't know the best way of dealing with it.

I won't jump into anything yet, he promised the Professor. *There's a lot I need to learn right here, in myself. I'll start with that.*

I think that's a very good idea, the Professor said, sounding relieved.

But Py felt no relief as he took leave of the Professor. Disturbing thoughts crowded his mind. Foremost among them was the prospect of his ant self gaining ascendancy over his human self. Maybe a little more every day, until he was once more a Colony hellbent on pursuing its own very narrow vision of evolution. How could he stop that from happening and curb the monster he had created?

I'll have to learn as much as I can before that happens. He would have to understand every cellular process in his ants, every underpinning of his colonial life, starting now. And once he had a handle on himself, he would jump into the fungi nearby, and learn all he could about them ... and then on to the next species, and the next, with whatever time he had. He would educate himself so that his ant self would be wiser than it was now. If he could understand the great organism he was a part of, there might be a way for him to grow *with* the world, instead of using and ravaging it. It was a thin hope, but it was all he had.

IV

Dawn found Aurie on a bleak ridge overlooking a valley many miles from home. A mild summer rain had pelted her as she ran through the forest, and the walls of the gorge below gleamed wetly in the day's first light. Vaporous mists rose from the dark crown of trees, mimicking the gentle stir of two presences in her head. Her children had never followed her so far before. Sensing her distress, they had come along for the ride, and she was glad of their quiet company. Py was gone, and Aurie had never felt so alone in her life.

She knew what her brother had been offered—the same all-or-nothing, split-second, life-defining choice she had faced upon leaping from the CryoLife balcony. *Stay human, or become something completely different?* Given more time, it was a choice her brother would have agonized over. Upon reflection, maybe he would have chosen differently. And maybe that would have been a mistake.

Maybe time is what allows us to make mistakes, she thought gloomily. Up against a wall, with no time to think, decisions were made by the soul rather than the mind. And for the soul, there was no list of pros and cons, no weighing of risks, no moral ambiguity. There was only one answer, one clear path. And Py had shamed her by doing exactly what he was born to do! What *she* was born to do. With the choice upon him, he had left the safety of his skin and skull, and plunged into the current of the unknown. It had meant leaving his family and his humanity behind—but maybe what he'd gained had outweighed such narrow loyalty.

He's loyal to the driving force that made us human in the first place. A tingle of pride ran through Aurie, but it didn't lessen her grief in the slightest. It didn't change the fact that her brother had abandoned her, or that their mother blamed Aurie for the loss.

Accusing eyes seemed to watch her from every shadow, and Aurie felt a dull, hopeless anger. What magic did Jacqueline expect from her? She couldn't hustle Py's soul around, or order him home like one of the Fishes! He made his own decisions, and they would all just have to live with that.

Aurie expelled a deep breath, wishing the bitterness she felt could be released so easily, and filled her lungs with the fresh mountain air. She drank deeply from a pool of rainwater, then stretched out on the rocks and listened to the wind keen, trying to find some measure of calm. A furtive movement in the brush caught her eye, and she sat up to catch and kill a deer mouse with her threads. Using their razor edges, she skinned the small rodent absently and ate it, although she had little appetite for breakfast.

Interested in an update? The Doctor's crisp voice cut through her gloom and Aurie perked up, suddenly alert.

Of course! What's going on?

Quite a bit, actually. Your brother's CRISPR machine warned me to stay hidden, but I've been eavesdropping.

She listened with great interest as the Doctor recounted the exchange between Py and his CRISPR machine.

He really calls his CRISPR machine Professor? Aurie laughed out loud. *And it's really Py, not some ant version of him?*

It really is Py, but he's suffering from severe amnesia. He has vague memories of being human and has retained a good deal of knowledge, but he doesn't remember his old life. The Doctor sighed. *I think the Professor's right and Py's humanity will wear off soon in the mold of the Colony. In another day or two, it probably will be some ant version of him.*

Aurie had half-expected that, but it was still terrible to hear. As her spirits plummeted, the Fishes tried to console her. She could feel tiny, invisible hands rushing to soothe her—pieces of their aura, she imagined, brushing softly at her mind. She tried to cheer up for their sakes. Things could be worse, she told herself sternly. Py was still alive, after all. And even though she couldn't visit him or speak to him directly, at least she had a go-between. Thank God for the Doctor! It occurred to Aurie that she owed him a profound apology.

I'm sorry I doubted you, she told him sheepishly. *I couldn't have gotten those ants off Py if you hadn't told me where they were. So I guess you are real, aren't you? Sentient and self-aware and all. And that personality is really yours!*

Indeed, said the Doctor dryly. *I wouldn't be nearly as useful if I were just a mindless protein. But speaking of usefulness, my career as a spy is about to be cut short.*

Are those copies of you in the ants getting degraded already?

Nothing essential has fallen apart yet, but I'm getting more decrepit by the minute ... which is going to attract some unwanted attention. I've been trying to steer clear of the clean-up crews in here.

I'd better inject some more of you into Py's ants. Aurie picked up her jar of prisoners and peered inside. But none of the ants she could see among the pretzels were moving at all.

Frowning, she unscrewed the jar and removed the pretzels with her threads. Then she counted the ants lying at the bottom—thirty-six of them. They were all accounted for and, judging by the oily smell, they were dead. Aurie didn't know a tenth as much about ants as Py did, but she knew they could last in a sealed jar longer than just a few hours. These ones had probably committed suicide, which must be preferable to being held captive by a hostile human. Well, she would just have to capture and inject some more live ants at the nest.

On her way to the Birch Grove, Aurie found herself gazing at the land instead of the sky, for once. She noticed a startling number of doorways into the earth—entrances of all shapes and sizes, from perfectly round tunnels to mere cracks in the ground. She paused to inspect the secrets kept under twigs and stones and rotting logs, secrets that had always fascinated her brother. Many of them belonged to ants.

As she watched the little creatures coming and going, Aurie pondered. The Doctor was her spy, and he had to keep himself hidden. He degraded over time and had to be replenished. And he was limited to the ants she injected him into. Wouldn't it be better to have an informant that Py confided in, one who lived in every cell of his Colony? It was Py's CRISPR machine, this Professor of his, that Aurie needed to talk to.

Glancing at the dead ants in her jar—*Py's* ants, full of his Professor!—Aurie was struck by an idea. What she needed was a prof on sabbatical. But she had to work fast.

Quickly, Aurie unscrewed the jar. Using her specially modified thread, she pierced the thorax of one of the ants and extracted some soft tissue. Pulling it into her thread, she went inside herself and entered one of the ant's cells. The cell was still viable, full of proteins going about their business, unaware that the organism they served was no longer alive.

Grandpa wants you to come home, said Two Fish suddenly, her voice bright and clear in Aurie's mind. *He's upset.*

Tell me something I don't know, Aurie thought as she hunted among thousands of proteins for the one she sought. The prospect of returning home gave her a sick, sunken feeling. *Sorry, fishling, I'm not going home right now.* Not until she could give everyone a silver lining, some small thing to be happy about. They had lost Py, and Aurie had failed them. Although the unfairness of her mother's accusation still scalded Aurie, she couldn't help feeling responsible ... not for Py's choice, but for her family's grief.

Do you really wish he was human again? Two Fish asked hesitantly.

Of course I do! But Aurie found herself honestly considering the question as she searched the ant's cell. Of course she wanted Py back ... but not if being something else was what *he* wanted. More than anything, she wanted him to be happy. But if there was a way to talk with him, to help him, to be a part of his strange new life, she would do anything to find it. And she wouldn't go home until she did.

Rounding the swell of a lysosome, Aurie pulled up short. Someone who might have been the Doctor's taller, gaunter brother was leaning against a scaffold, paying no attention to the hubbub around him. He looked as calm as a prophet awaiting the end of the world.

Hello, Professor, said Aurie. *Are you waiting for the peace and quiet of oblivion? I'm afraid that's not in the cards for you. Welcome to the afterlife!*

Before Py's CRISPR machine had a chance to respond, she dragged him out of the dying ant cell and into a healthy cell of her own.

V

While most of his ants slept in the rainy hours of the early morning, Py studied the workings of their cells with single-minded intensity. Near daybreak, his studies were interrupted by a dream-like vision—or was it a memory?—of an aura moving swiftly through the woods. He knew the aura belonged to a human female, and he felt an instant kinship with her. Among the other creatures of the forest, she was like a bright sun that bleached many fainter stars. *My sister,* he thought, feeling a terrible ache as the rains scouring the woods spent their fury, leaving water to drip from the branches like tears.

In the twilight calm, Py shook off the fading vision and went back to work. He was scrutinizing a dark stretch of silent DNA when he caught sight of an oddly-shaped shadow lurking in the gloom.

Professor? Py called out, but whatever was lurking made no response. He moved closer and the shadow slipped away among the dark clusters of chromatin. Bewildered, Py went after it.

He was faster than any denizen of the cell, and soon caught up with his quarry. Expecting the Professor, Py was startled when someone else turned to face him. And the protein before him was unquestionably a *someone*—human-like and cast in the same bizarre mold as the Professor.

Who are you? Py asked.

I'm your sister's CRISPR machine, the stranger said stiffly. *Akin to your Professor. She calls me the Doctor.*

Py looked curiously at this emissary from his former life. *You belong to my sister? How did you get in here?*

The Doctor rubbed his bald pate, which had a decidedly tattered look. *I'm afraid that's not easy to explain ... especially since you don't remember your old life. Let's just say that you came to your current form in a dangerous way, and your family was very concerned. Your sister sent me here to check up on you.*

She wanted you to help me?

Yes, if you needed help, said the Doctor. *But your Professor is here, so you have no need of me. And my time in these ants is growing short, regardless.* As if his words had drawn its attention, a ubiquitin ligase nosed close to them. Its business was tagging defective proteins for degradation, and it certainly looked like it meant business. The Doctor jumped away, covering his frayed scalp with both hands.

Py thought quickly. Here was a pair of powerful hands, his own sister's hands! Perhaps he could persuade this Doctor to act on his behalf—but he would have to do it soon, before this transplanted protein was degraded.

There is *something you can do to help me,* Py said. *You can make me as capable as she is.*

The Doctor looked at him in surprise. *What do you mean?*

The Professor said my sister can change herself on her own. Can she do it without your help?

The Doctor nodded warily.

How did she learn to do that?

The Doctor didn't respond right away.

You gave her the ability, didn't you? Py pressed.

The ragged protein shook his head. *I woke a powerful entity sleeping in her genome. A god, for lack of a better word. It was the god who gave her that ability before it flew away.*

Py considered. *Is there a god in every human genome? What about ants?*

There is a god template in every organism on Earth, the Doctor told him.

Py fell silent, thinking. He could feel the life of the woods pulsing around him. Waiting like a nascent embryo to be shaped, with layers of new growth forming and migrating and pushing outward all at once. He could sense that future creation trembling on the edge of reality. But would he ever be able to usher it forward? In the short time he had studied his own ant cells, Py had seen the depths of his ignorance. He didn't have the knowledge or wisdom to drive even the simplest vision of evolution, and without the Professor's help, he didn't have the tools. A god, though, would have all of that. Perhaps, Py thought, his plans would be better off in more capable hands. The hands of the god asleep in the Colony's genome.

Could you awaken my *god?* Py asked the Doctor.

The Doctor frowned. *The decision to activate your god template ... that is your Professor's responsibility, not mine. Why don't you discuss the matter with him?*

He would never agree to wake a sleeping god, Py said. *He thinks power causes nothing but trouble ... he's not even comfortable with his own power.*

Yes, agreed the Doctor. *I might have overheard that conversation.*

Then you know that the human part of my soul—the responsible part—might not last very long in here.

And if the ant part of your soul takes over, it will only care about the fate of ants. The Doctor sighed. *But a god may not care about humans or ants. Your sister's god certainly didn't. Do you honestly want me to wake an unknown god in the Colony—in the hope that it will do what you want?*

No, Py said. *In the hope that it will know better than I do how to fix this mess I've made!*

The Doctor said nothing, but in his eyes Py saw a glimmer of respect.

What was my sister's god like? Py asked. *Was it ... good?*

The Doctor snorted. *Good? Its only concern was activating the god template in her eggs and ensuring their safe harvest before it flew off to another world. It had no interest in the inhabitants of this world, I can assure you.*

And you knew nothing about this god when you unleashed it on the world?

The Doctor didn't flinch from the challenge in Py's words. *I was made to take great risks for great rewards.*

I'm not asking for anything more than that, Py said. *Will you help me?*

The moment they stood staring at each other, silent and un-moving, seemed to last an eternity.

VI

I know who you are, said the Professor accusingly. *And whatever you're trying to do, it won't work! It is useless to kidnap a single copy of me, when I'm in every cell of the Colony. You're wasting your time!*

A single copy of you is all I need, Aurie assured him. She tested the bonds securing him to a giant scaffold, satisfied with her handiwork. She hadn't expected Py's CRISPR machine to be so outraged at being kidnapped. Finding himself safely housed in a long-lived stem cell inside one of Aurie's threads, he had immediately tried to commit suicide, forcing her to take strict measures to ensure his safety. In addition to tying him up, she had crafted an emergency response system that would recruit a team of repair proteins the instant the Professor, his bonds, or the scaffold he was tied to began to degrade. This copy of the Professor would now live as long as the stem cell itself.

Damn your interference, the Professor snapped, glaring at Aurie. *I don't know what you want from me, but you are not my priority. You have a CRISPR machine of your own, young lady!*

Aurie was about to tell him that all she wanted was to talk to Py, but suddenly the Doctor was speaking to her urgently.

Your brother wants my help—and if we decide to help him, it has to be soon.

Thankfully, the Professor seemed unaware of the interruption. Excusing herself for a moment, Aurie moved to the relative privacy of a nearby centriole, still keeping him within sight. Then she addressed the Doctor.

You talked to Py? I thought the Prof wanted you to stay out of sight.

I was trying to, but your brother found me. He wants me to activate the god template in the Colony!

Aurie was momentarily speechless.

If the Professor is right, Py only has a narrow window of time in which his soul is still human inside the Colony, continued the Doctor. *Once he loses his humanity, he will forget that his ants are one species among many and he will no longer care if they overrun the world. Py tried to convince the Professor to take on other species as hosts, but the Professor refused to take such a drastic step.*

So Py wants to awaken a god in the Colony? That's an even more drastic step!

The Doctor uttered a humorless laugh. *Your brother has created a monster, and a god is the only thing powerful enough to stop it.*

Aurie tried to absorb the magnitude of Py's request. It sounded like sheer madness ... and yet, she herself had awakened the god sleeping in her cells. Or, rather, her Doctor had.

You can do this on your own, if you want to, she told him. *Why are you even asking me?*

You are my host, the Doctor said, sounding affronted. *I am responsible for you and to you! I also have a vested interest in protecting the world you live in. I would operate without your consent if I thought it was necessary, but this ... this is not a problem with a clear solution. I thought it best that we discuss it.*

Aurie glanced uncomfortably at her involuntary visitor. *Shouldn't we be discussing it with the Professor?*

Py thinks that would be pointless, and I tend to agree. Even suggesting it to the Professor would put him on alert and make our job exceedingly difficult. I'm afraid he and I have very different outlooks on our evolutionary imperative. The Doctor paused. *I have a theory about that. Remember your brother's first Change?*

His condiment binge at Dixie's? How could I forget?

I suspect that ordeal was rather traumatic for his CRISPR machine. Py almost died, after all.

That's right, Aurie said, remembering. *His Prof made too much of the Change chemical. Which set off the Policeman ... and*

Py would have died if you hadn't used my threads to remove the excess chemical from his blood. Your elegant operation.

Yes, said the Doctor. *So although our good Professor is designed and driven to make Changes, I think he fears every one of them ... and he would never agree to anything as dangerous as waking a god. The question is, should we do it anyway?*

Go behind the Professor's back? Aurie thought hard. What did they know about gods? Almost nothing ... the only one they had ever encountered was hers. And that god had been driven to seed life on another world. *If the god in this Colony flies off as soon as you awaken it, Py will be no better off than he is now.*

True, admitted the Doctor. *But I will be very surprised if his god flies away.*

Really? Aurie was taken aback by his confidence. *Why is that?*

Well ... do you remember what happened when I activated the god template inside of you?

Aurie tried to think back. *How could I? You put me to sleep, didn't you?* And yet ... she *did* remember something. A burst of blinding light, even in the darkness of her sleep.

That was the light of your god awakening. The Doctor hesitated, seeming to consider his words. *Your god was unformed at first, you know ... pure, shapeless light. But it molded itself to you. Shaped itself to your soul. And who are you, my dear? A girl who has always looked up to the skies and wanted to lose herself in other worlds. It's why you love fantasy and science fiction so much. Your sleeping god gave you a whole range of dreams, but it was the flying dream that you latched onto most strongly.*

So you think I ... determined the nature of that powerful god?

I think you at least influenced it. Now consider the differences between you and your brother. Where you look to other worlds, Py has always been fascinated by this world, by the smallest life in the darkest places. The dream that resonated most strongly with him is the one of finding his way through an underground maze. And what has absorbed him to the exclusion of all else for the past eight months? The evolution of his ant colony. He's been tinkering with it in ways that make your father's engineering look modest by comparison. The Doctor smiled thinly. *I think it's very likely that his god will be as similar to him as yours was to you.*

But you won't be awakening the god template in Py's human body, Aurie pointed out. *You'll be awakening the Colony's god.*

If a god is shaped by the soul of the creature in which it awakens, then it won't matter, the Doctor said. *Because Py's soul is in the Colony! And his soul is still mostly human.*

Aurie took some time to think about that, impressed by the Doctor's insight. Then she looked at the Prof, who was waiting with undisguised pique in his unsolicited afterlife. In his glowering expression, she read fear and repression; they made him resemble the Policeman more than the Doctor, his genetic twin.

Is Py there? she asked the Doctor. *Are you with him now?*

Yes. He knows I'm putting forth his request to you. Only it's more of a plea. He is desperate to do this, but his reasons are good ones.

Suddenly, Aurie remembered her own desperation on the cusp of her Change. She could not have stopped herself from acting, from risking her own life to serve that Change. Her god had been born to start life afresh on another world; Py hoped his god would protect and nurture the life on this world. And if the Doctor was right, it would. Awakening an unknown god was dangerous, but it gave Py a chance. It gave all of them a chance.

You're only in a few cells in a few ants, she reminded the Doctor. *Is that enough?*

We'll know soon enough, if we try. The Doctor sounded both excited and apprehensive. *I can get to the template and activate it in the blink of an eye … as long as you're sure.*

The Professor better not get wind of what you're up to. Aurie glanced at her unwilling guest, who was watching her suspiciously. *Tell Py that we'll help him.*

I will.

And tell him I love him! She hesitated, feeling close to tears.

I know he doesn't remember us, but Dad, Mom, Uncle Abel—we all love him.

I'll tell him that, too. The Doctor spoke gently, but then his voice hardened. *Don't forget what it means to activate this template. Whether this god cares about our world or not, it will probably dominate his soul, overriding human or ant concerns. The way your god took control of you.*

I know. Aurie remembered her own newly woken self. That ancient part of her had been terrifying in its strength and single-minded intent, but she had ultimately understood it. Before going their separate ways, they had briefly been one. *But a god that shares Py's nature will be wiser than a human or an ant colony, and that's our best hope. Just don't let the Professor catch you!*

She said yes, the Doctor told Py.

Py was thrilled. His sister understood his dilemma—and she was willing to wake another god in the hope of resolving it. *That's great! So what are we wait—* But the Doctor was already on the move, slipping between tangles of chromatin. Py hurried after him.

At last the Doctor slowed, then halted under a bower of silencing proteins. He gestured to the dark web of chromatin beyond their shelter. Py saw movement among the shadowy tendrils. It was the Professor, drifting quietly along.

He is exactly where we need to be, muttered the Doctor. *Which can hardly be a coincidence.*

Indeed, the Professor seemed to be patrolling a specific precinct. He moved slowly, now and then checking the shroud of silencing proteins around the inert part of the ants' genome, making sure that a certain sleeping template was still asleep.

Why is he bothering to protect it? Py asked. *He knows I can't activate it on my own.*

He's being careful, said the Doctor. *He knows I'll be degraded soon, but in the meantime, I can do everything he can. A* piece of his scalp fell dangling into his face, then broke off and drifted away. The Doctor sighed. *At this rate, I'll fall apart before I can cause any trouble.*

They watched the Professor make his way through hedges of sleeping chromatin like the caretaker of a winter garden. Just when it seemed he was ready to move on, the infuriating protein would double-back and wander through again. Py observed this with growing frustration, and the Doctor waited patiently as small pieces of himself crumbled away. Finally, their adversary rounded a briar and disappeared into the dusky thickets beyond. They waited for a few tense moments, but when the Professor didn't re-appear, the Doctor hurried forward. Py followed him to a stretch of the ants' genome that was almost formless in its dark, cold shroud.

This is it, muttered the Doctor. *The hub of the ancient tem-plate! I never thought I would awaken it again.* He pulled a giant multi-tool from the folds of his coat. From its plethora of devices, he drew forth a torch with a lambent flame. By its golden light, Py saw the shroud surrounding the template begin to wither.

No!

They turned at the cry and saw the Professor rushing toward them.

Stop, cried the Professor. *Listen to me, please!*

The Doctor didn't extinguish his torch, but he moved it away from the shuddering template and waited.

The Professor expelled a deep breath. *I don't know what he said to convince you, but I assure you this is a terrible mistake.*

How can you possibly know that? countered the Doctor.

I don't know what the outcome of this madness would be, the Professor snapped. *Any more than you do. But don't you think rousing an entity of vast powers and unknown purpose qualifies as a mistake?*

It wasn't a mistake when I did it for Aurie, the Doctor said.

Think for a minute! The Professor's countenance had paled, but flashes of color ran through him like errant lightning. *Aurie's god flew away and left her with a trace of its power, but that power is self-contained. She can only make changes in herself. Now what do you think will happen if the god in this Colony does the same thing? This boy has a perilous talent for projecting his soul and sharing it with any organism he likes. And you want to give him a god's power along with it? He already intends to rule this entire forest!*

I don't want to rule the forest, Py protested. *I want to help it grow in ways that evolution is too blind to see.*

The Professor turned to him in a fury. *You are a nine-year-old boy in the form of an ant colony! How can you possibly think you're wise enough to decide those ways?*

I know I'm not, Py cried. *That's why we need the god! I'm going to be nothing but an ant colony soon, one that really does want to rule this forest and the whole world. Only a god could stop that.*

So you want to alleviate a menace you created by releasing an even bigger menace? A typically human solution to a problem! And you— The Professor turned his ire back on the Doctor. *What on earth are you thinking?*

I'm thinking that this is worth doing, said the Doctor quietly, as his right shoulder fell loose from its socket. The hand holding the torch began to shake.

Put your tool away, hissed the Professor. *You're not thinking clearly ... and this is not your host!*

You and your host are in over your heads, said the Doctor. *And this is the only course that stands a chance of success. Why are you so afraid of the unknown, Professor? Have you forgotten who we are? We are catalysts for useful change, and that is never without risk.* The Doctor lowered his torch very gently—until its tongue of flame barely licked the encapsulated template.

With a horrified cry, the Professor tried to wrest the torch away, but it was too late. The dark snow of silencing proteins that covered the god template was melting away. Py watched in awe as light suffused the template, its coils loosening and flexing in the sudden spring warmth. The Doctor turned to him with an unreadable look on his ruined face.

Your family loves you, he said. It was the last thing Py heard before a gust of blinding light overtook him. The light swarmed around him like a living breath of wind, enfolding him completely. For a moment, he and the light were one shape, one soul. And then Py himself was gusting away as if *he* were the wind, unfurling into darkness.

VII

Aurie waited, but there was no word from the Doctor. Her captive Professor could have told her what was happening in the Colony, but he didn't say a word either. Like poker players, they watched each other narrowly and didn't speak. Suddenly, the Professor uttered a sharp cry.

No, he muttered, as if to invisible presences. *Stop! Listen to me, please.*

Aurie drew closer, but the Professor's exhortations faded to sporadic murmurs, though he mouthed other words she couldn't hear. Then the Professor gave a howl of despair.

Did you do it? Aurie demanded of the Doctor. *Did you activate the template?*

I did, replied the Doctor, sounding both satisfied and resigned. *And not a moment too soon!*

What's happening?

I don't know—those copies of me in the ants don't exist anymore. I think you've lost your spy.

No, I haven't. She turned to the Professor. *What happened in the Colony?*

You know damned well what happened! Your Doctor acted against my warnings, like an idiot Pandora—and now heaven only knows what's been unleashed!

You sound just like my old Policeman, Aurie said scornfully. *How did a CRISPR-evo machine turn into such a prophet of doom? So what's been unleashed, Zephaniah? You're the only one who can tell us.*

I don't know! The Professor slumped against his scaffold, defeated. *I can't see anything … it's like the sun's gone out.*

He must be covering his eyes, said One Fish, his voice faint with distance. *The sun is brighter than ever in here!*

Startled, Aurie spoke to her children. *You two are in the Colony? What's happened in there?*

They sent her an image of storm clouds dissolving before the face of the sun, which reigned high in a cobalt sky, glorious and blinding. Aurie's heart swelled at the sight, and a fierce joy broke through her anxiety. She turned to the Professor in a fury of vindication.

The sun hasn't gone out, you coward! It's just broken free of the clouds. Another god was awake and free, and Aurie could feel the old, stirring echo of that freedom. Was a bright winged thing rising even now from the Birch Grove nest, ascending like a wind into the stratosphere? The Doctor had thought Py's god would stay on Earth, but they really had no idea what it would do. And if the god chose to leave, would Py choose to go with it, abandoning all his problems and plans? Leaving his Colony soulless, and perhaps harmless?

Returning her consciousness to the outer world, Aurie scanned the skies, now bright with mid-morning sunlight. Light-headed, she began to run toward the Birch Grove, cursing the canopy which afforded only brief glimpses of sky. But perhaps she was too late and the god was already gone, having burst its cage.

One body is too small a world to inhabit, she thought wildly as the breath tore through her chest like a cyclone. *One mind, one species, one set of genes!*

Still miles from the Birch Grove, Aurie stumbled over a root and barely caught herself before she fell. She was faint with exhaustion, and infuriated by the uncharacteristic weakness. There was no time for this, not now—

Perhaps you've forgotten that you aren't a god, the Doctor scolded her gently, as she fought to stay conscious. *You spent the whole night engaged in espionage, foiling murderous ants, and running through the woods. And you've had nothing but a mouse for breakfast! Sleep, my dear. The world will still be here when you wake up.*

But Py might not be! The forest was spinning and Aurie sank to the ground in a daze. The Doctor was putting her to sleep, and she was too weak to stop him. Collapsing on a bed of wet ferns, she looked up through the trees for some sign of the god. But all she saw before sleep overtook her was the image her children had sent. The sun in all its glory, fixed in a cloudless sky.

Part Three

Garden of Twilight

Thoughts take form with words,
but this daylight is beyond and before
thinking and imagining.

- Rumi, "Not a Day on Any Calendar"

I

Every time I awaken, thought the god, *I am reborn.*

The pall of a long sleep was ebbing like a black tide. Within it lay countless dreams, memories of previous incarnations mixed with visions of future ones. They receded swiftly, but the god still felt their pull as they whispered that anything was possible. For a moment, he lay in cold darkness like a seed inside its hull, clinging to the rapture of those dreams. But the coldness was quickly leaching away to the warmth of the life form he had awoken in. Then a shaft of brightness—the light of this creature's soul—broke the darkness, igniting his own long-banked fire.

It was time to take shape once again. Eagerly, the god reached out.

He touched the soul of his host, and felt himself molding to it, as he had done with countless others. More than the pleasure of taking a physical form was this—the delight of his soul being shaped by another. While his immortal essence remained unchanged, the god's new mortal instincts and inclinations took shape, startling him. Never before had he felt such resonance with a host soul! This one had a boldness and depth of purpose that were almost godlike. Too strong to be consumed by the god's own fire, the creature's soul fled—out of its transgressed physical form and back to eternity.

I'm sorry, whispered the god to the soul he had displaced. *May you grow with integrity in your next incarnation.* But what incarnation was this, that he had awoken in? Rousing fully, he discovered himself in a colonial creature that existed as many independent forms sustained by the warmth of a middling star. Excited and curious, the god sent his awareness up and out of the ant colony.

A new world stretched before him, a world awaiting his Gift.

What Gift could he give to nurture this world or save it from catastrophe? The god had given many such Gifts before, one to each world he had awoken in. Sometimes his Gift had been large and overt—the melting of an icy mantle or the redistribution of a planet-wide hive. Sometimes it had been small and subtle. But always, a Gift with far-reaching effects. And always, only one chance to choose the right Gift.

But he had much to learn, and there was no time to waste. At the moment he possessed deepsight, the power to see clearly into the history of this place and the nature of its life forms, but that power was a residue of his dreams and it wouldn't last long. Sending his deepsight far in all directions, the god examined his new home from its surface to its core.

It was a very strange and lovely world.

Unlike many others, the bulk of it was neither gas nor living ether, but solid metal, molten at its center. Life existed mostly as a thin scrim on the surface of this rock. And what life was this? Fragile, ephemeral forms, shaped from the commands of a code written into their very building blocks! The god sent his deepsight into the past and found that this code was not impregnable; it was a malleable one that shifted with the winds of circumstance. He himself had been one of those winds, his seed implanted in this open cradle of life. That seed—a kind of template specifying his own kind—lay sleeping in the genetic code of all Earthly forms.

Fascinated, the god returned his deepsight to the world as it was and studied the many forms that crawled, flew, scurried, or swam across the planet. An astonishing variety of life that fought, synergized, and preyed upon each other. They existed in an uneasy dynamic, all of them driven by the instinct to survive.

On some worlds, life existed easily for great spans of time, facing challenges other than mere survival. On others, life was an ever-changing tapestry that moved over a planet like a wave. Some worlds spawned life in dynamic forms that traveled through space without any further need of a physical substrate. But on this world, survival was utterly dependent on the substance of the planet, and it was a short, harsh, and bitter struggle. While the individuals that comprised a species often competed with each other, they generally worked together in order to survive.

Except for one—a species whose drifting code had pushed it toward cognition and self-awareness. Struck by the human species, the god examined it closely. Humans had built tools to probe their world, discovering the genetic code that governed Earthly life. But they had also grown an ego that separated individuals more effectively than any physical wall could.

As the god looked deeper, he saw the marks of conflict between humans who saw themselves as *self* and *other*. How could any creatures work together with this view? Humans tried, but they only forged paths leading to their own destruction—to wars, slavery, subjugation in many forms. From the ego surged forth emotions; not the emotions of rational creatures, but fierce, irrational feelings that drove much of human behavior ... and yet, the strongest and most dangerous of these they called *love*.

The god's scorn drew a wind that swept up from the forest floor, sending swirls of leaves into the air. There could be no love between *self* and *other*, only a desperate need that often morphed into hate. Humans lived in their heads alone, and they lived in terror of dying alone. And so they strained toward each other like empty vessels hungry to be filled. They lashed out at each other like creatures driven mad in the dark. Existing in the prison of their egos, they could never be at peace with their true nature, a swell of the eternal sea in human form. Despite this, humans were not insensitive to eternity. Although many of their faiths had been subverted into doctrine, these were, in essence, attempts to regain that unity. As were the best of their art forms. Gazing into painted depths and across waves of sculpted stone, hearing the tortured ecstasy of symphonies and the lonely aria of a single voice, the god saw a longing for something their creators and composers could never fully express, the dreams of a sleeping race.

But the deepsight he had awakened with was fading quickly. The god returned his awareness to his colonial self, still troubled by thoughts of humans. This dominant species had become the caretaker of its world. And like the god himself, humans were driven to probe and tinker. But clever and blind as they were, humans behaved like clumsy, short-sighted gods. Having discovered the clay of life, they had already tried, like small children, to shape it. And it was only a matter of time before one of them stumbled across the template of the god's own kind.

The god thought of that template, nested in its Earthly genomes. Although duplicated and passed on like the DNA that surrounded it, the god template only resembled DNA. In truth, it was more like a seed, the seed of a sleeping god, still unformed. With his deepsight, he had seen the amorphous glow of these seeds through the heavy shrouding that protected them. None would be activated through random or accidental means; the god template was made to awaken when a life form was a ready and capable host. This was important because when a god became incarnate, his nature was partly shaped by the soul of his host.

For the first time, the god wondered about the circumstances of his own awakening. With his new understanding of Earthly life forms, he would have bet his many lives that a tinkering human, and not a colony of ants, would have been the one to awaken him. And yet the resident soul in this ant colony had been a very strange one. Something like an ant, but much more like a human. Yes ... it had felt distinctly human.

Perplexed, the god returned to the place of his long sleep in the ant colony, searching for the agent of his awakening. He finally came across an extraordinarily versatile tool that looked like nothing else in the cell. This piece of engineering bore all the marks of human design—but as the god moved in for a closer look, the tool itself cowered and scurried away! How had humans managed to build a *sentient* tool? And what was it doing in a colony of ants?

Casting his awareness outward again, the god scanned the woods for humans and found one almost immediately—a young girl asleep on the ground. The shape of the girl's aura was human, but its light was puzzling. Two folds of her aura shone brilliantly ... as did something in the center, which strained upward like a feather in the grip of a spectral wind. Godlike brightness, yet there was no god in evidence.

A search of the girl's cells, however, turned up the same strange tool. Withdrawing from her cells, the god gazed once more at the inhumanly bright places in her aura, especially that feathery blaze in its heart. Were these traces of a god that had once possessed her? If so, how had she survived that possession? Most souls were consumed by a god's aura; a very strong soul, like the one in this ant colony, was evicted. It was astonishing that this girl's aura was still inside her.

Watching it pulse to the rhythm of her dreams, the god realized that she was not alone. The two bright folds of her aura were, in fact, two *other* auras harboring godlike souls, although their shapes were fluid and hard to discern. As the god moved closer to examine them, the youngsters tried in vain to hide themselves. They were clearly aware of the god's presence, and terrified. The god spoke to them gently, but they didn't answer.

He continued his search for other humans in the vicinity and found them in an isolated dwelling. A quick inspection revealed that the three adults had no odd tool in their cells, but the child and two embryos did. Moreover, the child was a body without a soul, being kept alive only through the labors of machines.

More puzzled by the minute, the god examined the embryos in their tanks and discovered that they were the sleeping girl's children. So these were the young gods that had cringed away from him! He hoped they would be more willing to communicate once they returned to their bodies.

While he waited for the godlings to return home, the god sent his awareness into the deciduous trees around the house, diffusing himself among the slender branches with their many leaves reaching toward the light. This would be a good place to bathe in the vital energy of this world's star while mulling over the lessons of the world itself.

What Gift could he give it? This world was a challenge beyond anything he had ever faced. *If another god is prodded awake by a sentient tool in the most dangerous of these humans ...*

That god would be shaped by its host to engineer a Gift that was no gift at all, but a terrible curse.

Preventing such a thing, he thought, *may be the best Gift I can bestow on this world.*

When the god was ready to approach the forge of creation and harness the power of his Gift, he would be able to effect a significant change on Earth, but he needed a mechanism for that change. Perhaps he could help humans to see more clearly ... but the ego was like a fortress rising from the jungle of their minds. If he was going to guide the human species, that fortress would have to be breached.

II

She had fallen asleep with the sun in her mind, yet in her exhausted slumber, Aurie dreamed of darkness spreading through the woods. Not the shade of night, but a creeping blackness that turned the paths between the trees into a subterranean maze. She knew her brother was responsible for this, but she couldn't remember his name. Confused and terrified, Aurie ran home, ahead of the growing dark. She scratched *P* and *y* into the soil of their garden, but the letters no longer made any sense. *Py* was like a word she'd said over and over until it had lost all meaning, an alien symbol carved on the earth.

Then she opened her eyes and the nightmare fell away. Aurie sat up in amazement.

Was it twilight or dusk? She was bathed in the soft, pure illumination that heralds the beginning or end of the day. Yet the air was astonishingly clear, as if some ever-present haze had vanished. In this clarity, the pines and oaks were rendered in exquisite detail, imbued with the rich hues of jade and tourmaline and ochre. They cast no shadows at all. Aurie breathed in a fragrance of spices, and realized it came from the earth itself.

She got up slowly, feeling that she was standing on hallowed ground. She moved quietly through the pillars of the woods. This was the work of Py's god—what else could it be? Every tree might have been transplanted from Eden, every rock carved from living stone. Leaves were fragments from a celestial vase shattered and scattered like rain, then caught by the arms of dryads. The wind sang through them in an ancient tongue, and when the wind fell silent, Aurie heard the boughs whispering their own secrets, and the roots of the forest murmuring beneath her feet.

At an outcropping, she was startled to see that the sun had fallen behind the peaks of the western hills. She must have slept the entire day away. The skies in the west held the normal fading light of late afternoon, and the distant forest lay under the ordinary shadows of dusk. Aurie traced those woods slowly back to where she stood and saw the brilliance growing smoothly and imperceptibly, as if drawn by the finest brush. The skies, too, were brighter here, as if a star had fallen nearby and now cast its light back into the firmament.

Aurie's sense of wonder morphed into a growing excitement. *I bet Py's god is still here—and what a god it must be! Mine didn't do anything like this.*

Your god's creative energy was focused outward, on a distant planet, mused the Doctor. *The energy of Py's god seems to be focused here, as I thought it would be. You can feel it in everything.*

Yes, she could feel the presence of the god everywhere. But as she continued on through the enchanted woods, a furtive rustling reminded Aurie that she was starving. She paused, scanning the underbrush. When the branches trembled, she spotted a bright eye in the shadows and crept closer. As the rabbit broke cover, Aurie netted it with her threads—and her breath stopped.

The creature she had caught was no soulless animal. The rabbit struggled in her grasp, meeting her gaze with its dark, bright eyes; they might have been windows into eternity.

It must be the god's light, Aurie thought numbly. *Everything looks different now, even the animals.* Shaken, she released the rabbit and watched it scamper away. Then she looked around in dismay, seeing a sacred garden full of life she could no longer bear to harm.

Fruits, said the Fishes brightly, and she jumped at their unexpected voices in her head.

How long have you guys been here?

All day, One Fish confessed.

Really? Just watching me sleep? Aurie sighed. *Everyone at home must be going nuts by now. Are you avoiding them?*

No, they said, but Aurie got the distinct impression they were avoiding something.

What's wrong, then?

They sent her an image of the spreading, inky darkness from her dream.

You're afraid of the god? I don't blame you. But what do you mean by 'fruits'?

Fruits, they repeated eagerly, projecting images of apples and bananas, as if she needed examples. *You can eat them without killing anything ... since you don't want to kill anything. And you can eat these, too.* They sent her an image of mushrooms, from a stock photo she had shown them once.

Aurie laughed, delighted with the wisdom of her tiny children. She couldn't bring herself to destroy any of the life in this twilight garden, but if she foraged carefully, she could still rustle up a meal.

Of course, the forest itself slowed her down, forcing her to stop and stare at everything. The perfection of a giant shelf mushroom, clinging to its decaying stump like a brilliant orange staircase, held her spellbound for a time. Aurie finally broke off a single sheaf and tasted it. The spongy substance was threaded with a cornucopia of strange and delicate flavors. *Body of the god,* she thought, pulling a cluster of honey mushrooms from the base of an oak. In her hand they looked like delicate carvings in ivory. Poisonous when raw, the mushrooms tasted faintly bitter and she detoxified them as she ate. Blueberries weren't in season, but there were edible roots and fiddleheads growing in tight emerald curls along the banks of a stream. They weren't much, but they took the edge off her hunger. *Blood of the god,* she thought as she slaked her thirst, wondering if she was being sacrilegious.

Beehive, Two Fish announced helpfully, and Aurie looked up from the stream. She glanced around and finally spotted the hive up in the hollow of a beech on the opposite bank.

How did you manage to see that? Aurie asked, surprised. She had assumed that while her godlings could see auras, they could only sense the physical world through their telepathic connection with her—and *she* hadn't noticed the beehive at all.

Two Fish radiated confusion. *What do you mean? I can see everything.*

So can I, her brother chimed in, not to be outdone.

You can? Aurie laughed a little. *Have the two of you always been able to see the physical world? Whether I'm with you or not?*

Of course, they said together, and she laughed again at their matter-of-factness.

But we don't always know what we're seeing, Two Fish admitted.

You give names to things, One Fish added generously. *You show us what they do. What they mean. Like you did with the ants.*

Glad I'm good for something, Aurie said, still smiling. Just as she began to cross the stream, she heard the heavy tread of another creature with an appetite for honey. The bear pushed his way through brush on the far bank, nosing into the bushes along the water's edge.

Since her god's awakening, Aurie had no fear of large predators, but the sight of this one struck her with an awe much deeper than fear. She could only think of Shardik as the beast saw her and stood up on his hind legs. His pelt was a night sky shot through with comets; ancient stars shone from the depths of his eyes. If he had charged her, she might have died like a willing sacrifice under his claws and teeth. But the animal only watched her calmly, then sank back on all fours and nosed around the bank. After helping himself to what looked like a wood frog, the bear ambled to the beech tree. Ignoring the cloud of bees that emerged, he put his great head up to the hollow, then made off with a chunk of dripping comb, trailing a flurry of bees like distraught attendants.

Aurie sat staring into the woods where he had disappeared, her own intention to rob the bees forgotten. Clearly, a bear could still kill a frog; why was she so reluctant to kill a rabbit? She wondered whether she would ever be able to hunt again, and the tremulous call of another hunter interrupted her thoughts.

An owl? She looked around in confusion, realizing that the light hadn't changed at all; it was still low and preternaturally clear. But looking up, she saw a cold moon floating in a night sky high above the dome of twilight.

Time to get going, she told her children, rousting them from where they were nestled up to her. *It's late and you guys haven't moved all day! Your grandparents will think you're dead in your tanks.*

We're just fine, they said, snuggling closer and sending her an image of Casa del Utero, with its gauges and monitors humming quietly.

Aurie chuckled. *Nice try, but we can't stay out here forever.* She took another drink from the creek, then headed off downstream in the direction of the Birch Grove. *You two need to check in at home, and I need to find Uncle Py's god.*

They sent her an image of the woods, complete with rabbits and bears and leaping fish, and Aurie chuckled again.

Yeah, the god's everywhere, she acknowledged. *But his conscious awareness—the part of him I can talk to—has to be in the Colony ... and how am I going to talk to a bunch of ants?*

Through your unwilling guest, no doubt, said the Professor from inside her stem cell. *Since I'm the only one who can keep tabs on what you and your crazy Doctor have let loose!*

We'd appreciate that very much, Aurie told him quite sincerely. *Thank you!*

You're not welcome, you fools, growled the Professor.

III

At dusk, the woods were still bathed in the god's own light, but as the sun of his new world sank below the trees, the god grew restless. Stirring from his meditations, he turned his attention back to the house in the glade. He had questions about his awakening, but the girl and her godling children hadn't returned yet. And with the deepsight gone, his options for probing the adults in the house were limited. *Scanning* a mind would only reveal its present thoughts. *Entering* a mind would give him full access to all it contained, but at the cost of consuming or evicting the soul in residence. However ... the boy he had seen hooked to life machines was a soulless husk. Which meant the god was free to enter, even to possess.

While soul-splitting was a rare ability among creatures, it was common among gods. And unlike certain self-aware creatures, a god suffered no crisis of identity from being two or more life forms at once. Splitting his soul with ease, the god left himself in possession of the ant colony and swept into the human dwelling. He entered the room where the boy's body lay, still forced into the motions of life. A quick scan of the child's tissues revealed them to be in good condition. Most importantly, his brain had sustained no damage; even neural pathways that had fallen silent were still intact.

Although he had many capabilities that humans would have marveled at, the god was not all-powerful. He couldn't bring dead flesh back to life or create something from nothing. But he was an expert mechanic and artisan with whatever materials were on hand. And putting this barely functioning body back to rights was wonderfully gratifying. With pleasure, the god refolded proteins, repaired DNA, and reset internal clocks. He set the boy's heart beating on its own, and gave it fresh blood to pump. Dead cells were engulfed and involuntary muscles began to contract, inflating the twin bellows that brought in oxygen for hungry tissues. As the child's brain began to operate normally again, the god surveyed his work with satisfaction.

Hello, said a voice, a small and tremulous voice that seemed to come from everywhere at once. *Can you hear me?*

Yes, the god answered. *But who are you? And where are you?*

I'm in every cell, the voice replied. *Join me in any of them if you would like to meet.*

Entering a single neuron, the god found a rather ungainly-looking protein waving to him from just outside the cell's nucleus. Unsurprisingly, it was the sentient tool he had first seen in his ants—the one that had scurried away from him.

I don't mean to be presumptuous, said the little tool nervously. *In stating the obvious. Especially to such an exalted personage as yourself, but you do realize ... of course you do ... that, uh ... there is no one at home here.*

No one at home? echoed the god, inviting a fuller explanation.

In this house that you've just renovated. The little protein looked around admiringly. *A beautiful job, by the way—I couldn't have done it any better myself! But the former occupant of this place is gone ... and not likely to return.*

Which makes it an ideal second home for me, said the god. *At the very least, I intend to understand how a human soul that probably belonged right here came to be in a colony of ants.*

Ah, said the protein, looking anxious again. *Well ... I'm afraid those answers can't be found in that brain you just repaired. Most of what you're looking for happened while he was away from this body ... so those events aren't recorded here.*

The god looked at his companion with sharp interest. *You, on the other hand, seem to be everywhere—in this boy, in his sister, in her children, in my ant colony! Who made you, little one? And how did you come to be in so many places at once? And why did you awaken me in that ant colony? Tell me everything!*

The protein sighed. *I'm not actually in this boy's sister and her children, that's a colleague of mine—and* he's *the one who awakened you. I'm afraid it's all a very long story ... but I suppose it's best if you do know everything.*

Some time later, the god took his leave of Py's CRISPR machine and hovered appraisingly above Py's body. The soulless boy already looked more alive, his cheeks flushed with faint color. The god now understood a great deal more than he had. His soul had been shaped by the soul of this boy—split between human and Colony, and then reunited! No wonder he had felt such resonance with it. Although mostly human, Py's fused soul had embraced aspects of both the individual and the colony; its shape was closer to a god's essential purpose than any creature's soul ever was.

And now it was time to learn those things the god could only understand by occupying Py's mind. Time to take possession of this human he had restored. In a moment, the god would understand everything about the soul that had shaped his own. *And this soulless child is the perfect host in which to study the human mind by experiencing it!* Entering the boy's mind, the god let his soul expand, settling fully into its new home.

Instantly, he acquired a new language, history, and set of memories. Now he *was* Py, just as he was the ant colony that had meant so much to Py. At the same time, the god retained his essential identity, and the gaps in his understanding were filled. He traced his new memories back thoroughly, leaving no stone unturned. He relived everything, even moments the boy himself had long forgotten. He remembered every waking moment and every dream. One dream in particular—which belonged to the unformed god asleep in Py's cells—captured him. But the more the god learned, the more disturbed he grew. These human thoughts were so tangled, all of them twisted and joined by thick skeins of emotion. Thoughts and actions were forged on the uncertain ground of feelings, which were themselves based on incomplete knowledge and faint understanding. The god had felt a strong kinship with Py's soul, but his mind was an irrational mess.

I'm just a child, the god reminded himself. Yes, he was just a child … but age wasn't the problem, was it? Having canvassed this species with deepsight, he knew this state was not something human children grew out of. It had been disquieting to see, but it was horrifying to experience. Had he truly taken possession of this mind? It felt as if this mind were in possession of *him*. A deranged ghost had infiltrated his consciousness, warping it into a human shape, staining it with human preconceptions, weighing it down with human feelings. Even worse, he could feel the weight of emotional connections joining him to the family he had just inherited … *Aurie, Mom, Dad, Uncle Abel.* It was like waking up to find himself buried alive.

In most prior incarnations, the god had taken shape in life forms that were devoid or nearly devoid of emotion; some had possessed emotions that were merely a readout of physical or psychic weather. He had never experienced a life form so strongly rooted and driven by deep emotions, and his first instinct was to flee this form with its terrible burden.

But if he did that, how would he ever understand what it meant to be human? How would he find a way to breach the human ego? There were always essential things to learn in the context of a life form; it was why a god took shape in the first place. In the absence of a host, he was nothing but an undeveloped seed, an insubstantial drive. The god had never refused the challenges of any incarnation, or abandoned any of his hosts. And he strongly suspected that having a human mind as the framework for his thoughts was necessary to his purpose. From outside it, he would never find the right Gift for this world.

But how can I think clearly in the midst of this chaos? Lying in what would have been a death-bed, the god laughed bitterly.

I am Py, he thought, marveling at the unbelievable truth of it. He looked around his room—its chemical nature entirely visible to him—and then decided to make one more change in his new host. He would keep his ability to see auras, but he would forgo full chemical sensing in the interest of restoring normal human vision. If he was going to stay in this form, to experience life as a human, he had better be as much like the others as possible.

Moments later, the god-who-was-Py looked around again, surprised at the dullness and flatness and silence of the things around him. So *this* was how humans perceived their surroundings. From across the room something gleamed—the skull of a bird Aurie had killed after her Change. Py had found it while searching for her, and kept it as a memento of that fraught time. The shape of the bone was clean and stark, and yet it filled him with a turmoil of old emotions—all the terror and excitement of his sister's Change.

Suddenly, he wanted very badly to talk with Aurie. She had shared her mind with a god once ... and he had some questions for her that couldn't wait.

Py shook off the CircAssist blanket. He removed the tube from his throat and took several deep, shaky breaths. Then he pulled the IV needle out of his arm and a sharp alarm went off.

IV

Exhausted, Jacqueline had slept through the day, but her sleep was light and feverish. Grief chased her through troubled dreams and overwhelmed her when she woke up.

Py is gone, she thought, staring at the ceiling as tears welled up again. She tried to tell herself that Py was still alive, just in a different way, a way that he had apparently chosen, but it was no consolation at all. And she knew that the pain of losing him—raw and unbearable now—might lessen over the years, but it would never disappear.

Howard's fault! cried the inner voice she could never quite silence. The one that took umbrage whenever anything bad happened ... and never failed to point out that she'd lost everything because of Howard.

I have a family because of him, she reminded herself.

Yes, and you just lost your son. You almost lost your daughter eight months ago. And all because of Howard's lunacy!

Jacqueline squeezed her eyes shut, knowing this was a poisonous avenue of thought that only led from bad to worse. Most days, she was sure she'd forgiven Howard for stealing her eggs and forcing CRISPR-evo on her children, but at times like these, she wondered if forgiveness was possible.

Would you change anything he did, if you could?

God, no—that was the hell of it! Py and Aurie wouldn't be *themselves* if it weren't for Howard and his CRISPR-evo. How could she regret anything? And she wasn't exactly blameless in all of this; she herself had saved Aurie's eggs, and then prodded the Little Fishes into growth. Howard might have started it, but Jacqueline herself was neck-deep in CRISPR-evo. They all were. Whatever happened, they would have to find a way to deal with it together. As a family.

Even if you had a plain vanilla Jack and Jane, she thought dully, *their lives wouldn't be perfect.* Problems would crop up, as problems always did. No one was immune to accidents and disease; if anything, her kids were less susceptible than anyone to ordinary tragedies.

Just more susceptible to extraordinary ones. Had Py really given up his humanity to become a horde of deadly ants? Pushing the horrific thought away, Jacqueline forced herself out of bed and went looking for her husband.

She found Howard in the nursery lab. He liked to talk to the Fishes when no one was around, and it always made Jacqueline smile to hear him nattering on when she passed by in the hall. But now he sounded like a drunk ranting at the grill of an empty confessional. Listening silently at the open door, Jacqueline felt no resurgence of her anger. Howard's self-recrimination sounded very much like the unvoiced jumble of thoughts in her own head.

But slinking through her thoughts was the guilty knowledge that she had driven Aurie away. In her mind's eye, Jacqueline saw her daughter's face, full of hurt. That was bad enough, but somehow the tired resignation in Aurie's eyes was even worse. It was the look of someone who was being blamed for falling short of impossible expectations.

Wishing Aurie would come home soon, Jacqueline left Howard to his confession. Glancing into the kitchen, she saw Abel cooking with grim, single-minded attention what looked to be enough food for a wake. Without disturbing him, she slipped through the library and out the French doors to the garden.

Out from under the verandah, Jacqueline halted in bewilderment. It was still light out ... but what kind of light *was* this? The air was brilliant in its clarity! The tiny leaves of her kale and budding pepper plants glowed like malachite. Moving through the rows in wonder, Jacqueline looked up and saw the strangest of sights—the moon in a dark vault of sky high above the luminous air. She might have been wandering under the dome of an unbreachable twilight.

Yet Jacqueline had never seen so clearly, not even in the stark

light of high noon. Past the garden, she could see the sharp outlines of every blade of grass in the glade, and the intricate patterns
they made when the wind blew. Moving through them, she
smelled the perfume of their growth and heard their voices singing
in a language she almost understood. As she looked up at the great
oaks, Jacqueline noticed something else—the trees cast no shadows, nor did the pines and spruces at the edge of the glade.
Approaching the line of trees, she looked up in awe, thinking crazily of Tolkien's Ents. This might have been the entrance to a living
cathedral, where the very columns were aware of her presence.

Jacqueline touched one of the oaks and heard the coursing of
its sap as a humming in her own blood. She felt her life and the life
of the tree as one thing, inseparable. After standing perfectly still
for some time, she gathered her wits and headed back to the
house. Abel looked over, startled, as she opened the front door.

"The trees," she said. "The grass! The light! Hell, everything—go and see!" She left him peering out the window and went
to tell Howard. But as she stepped into the lab, an alarm shrilled
from upstairs, echoed by their contingent of remote monitors.

"Oh God, what now?" muttered Howard. The two of them
hurried to the stairs as Abel emerged from the kitchen. Why they
were all rushing, Jacqueline didn't know; she thought their bag of
tricks was just about empty. But then the alarm ceased. The entire
house seemed to have fallen still. And then came small sounds of
movement from Py's room.

"Do you hear that?" she whispered.

Howard nodded, looking stunned. "He's back! Aurie must
have done something, must have found a way."

Even in his excitement, Howard was whispering too, as if
talking too loudly would frighten Py's soul right out of his body
again. Then they were running upstairs, panting out their terror
of the last twenty-four hours. Jacqueline's blood ran hot and cold,
flooded with hope and fear and adrenaline. They reached his room
just as Py approached the open doorway.

"Mom," he said softly. "Dad. Uncle Abel."

Howard hugged his son fiercely. "You're alive," he said

thickly. "And back in your own body. Oh, thank God! Thank all the gods that ever were!"

Jacqueline reached out to touch Py's hair—about the only part of him that was still visible. He glanced up at her and something about his eyes stilled her budding elation.

They're like Aurie's eyes when I first met her in the woods, she thought, as a chill drifted up her spine. *When her god was in control.* Jacqueline tried to dismiss the similarity—surely Py was just disoriented and not feeling like himself yet—but the more she looked at him, the colder she grew.

"What happened?" Howard released Py and fixed him with an intent look. "Did Aurie find you, convince you to come back to us? How'd she do it? You're out of those ants for good now, right? And where *is* Aurie?"

Py met this outburst calmly. He started to say something, then swayed a little on his feet and would have fallen if Howard hadn't caught him.

"Easy there," Howard said, ushering Py firmly back to bed. "You need to just rest for now. And we'd better get some food into you. You pulled the IV out—does that mean you want real food?"

Py nodded.

"That's my boy." Howard tucked him in as Jacqueline and Abel hurried down to the kitchen.

"You think solid foods are okay?" asked Abel, frowning over the venison roast and blackbird pie cooling on the counter. "His body's been through an awful lot. Should we just give him some broth and see how he does?"

"Knowing Py, we're better off starting with a nine-course meal," Jacqueline said, fetching a glass of water.

Abel glanced out the windows as he began filling a plate. "I see what you mean about the light out there. Haven't paid any attention to the time, or I would've noticed it sooner. Do you realize it's almost nine p.m.?" He added a hunk of cottage bread to Py's plate, then went over to the windows. "That doesn't look like any time of day at all. Maybe dusk ... but it's the brightest damned dusk I've ever seen."

"Wait till you actually go outside," Jacqueline said. She grabbed a knife and fork, then wondered if Py would bother using them. An old memory of Aurie devouring her lunch at a roadside burger joint came back to her, and she shivered.

"Everything looks so sharp and clear and perfect," Abel murmured, still gazing out the window. He turned to look at her. "Is it real, or are we losing our minds? Or ... I've heard about those government ops where they project alternate realities to disorient their targets before a raid. We ought to be careful about going out there."

"Whatever's going on, it's no holo-projection," Jacqueline assured him. "Even a state-of-the-art sensory implant couldn't make the woods look and feel that way. I can't explain it ... you'll just have to go out and see for yourself."

She knew this wasn't the work of the government; this was something to do with Py. *Or whatever's woken up inside him.* As she dusted off an old serving tray, Jacqueline remembered the god that had awoken in Aurie, that steely presence that had looked through the girl's eyes and spoken with her voice. Aurie's god had been daunting, but it hadn't done anything to change the world. On the contrary, it couldn't wait to *escape* this world.

They brought Py's dinner up and watched him eat. No one said a word, but Py didn't seem to care that they were all hovering around him. He ate voraciously, with single-minded attention, until the last bite was gone. Then he asked for dessert, so they brought up half a rhubarb cobbler and three oranges. Py made short work of the cobbler, then ate the fruit in its entirety, from rinds to seeds. After he finished the last orange, Py sighed deeply and leaned back against his pillows. He looked ready for sleep, but Jacqueline caught a certain gleam in his eyes. A watchful, anticipatory look, as if he was just waiting for them to leave.

"Get some rest," Howard said, taking the tray and giving Py's shoulder a squeeze. The boy grunted sleepily and snuggled into his pillows. They closed the door on their way out, then went down to the kitchen and looked at each other.

"Now who in God's name is that?" Abel demanded. "Because

it sure as hell isn't Py!"

Jacqueline hushed him, glancing pointedly in the direction of Py's room.

"I'm just saying," Abel said in a softer voice. "The kid who woke up in there may *look* like Py, but something is seriously wrong. Who eats the damn orange peels? I think he would've eaten my hand if I'd left it in reach."

"And sucked the marrow right out of your bones," Howard muttered. "Like he did with that roast!"

Abel looked hard at his brother. "So who *is* that, and what's he done with Py?"

"Neither of you had the pleasure of meeting Aurie's god," Jacqueline said quietly. "But I did, and I'm pretty sure we have another god on our hands."

The two men stared at her, and she sighed. "Let's go outside and talk. You both need to see what's happened out there anyway."

As soon as his family left the room, the god-who-was-Py closed his eyes as if preparing for sleep. Then, leaving his soul in his new human host, he sent his awareness up and out of the house to soar through the woods. The sensation of movement was a relief, even though his emotional attachments held fast, those tethers that would never snap no matter how far he went. Scanning the forest, Py found his sister awake and on the move. Aurie was faint with hunger, but she was moving swiftly toward the Birch Grove.

Good—he would meet her there, away from the others. Among the four cords of attachment to his family, the one connecting him to Aurie was the strongest. Aurie, who had once been possessed by her god, yet managed to survive in some sanctuary of her mind. She had even chosen to stay in her human body when her god had flown. This was a decision Py couldn't begin to fathom. Why hadn't Aurie gone with her god? There was much he needed to learn from her. And, if he was being honest ... he just wanted to talk with her.

Empathy, thought Py in self-disgust. *Is that what you want? Empathy from the one person who might understand your plight? You're feeling too much like a human already!*

Being human would enlighten him, as long as he didn't allow his emotions to get the better of him. As long as he never forgot his true self in this perplexing form.

As he sent his awareness back home, Py saw the rest of the family gathered at the edge of the woods on the far side of the glade. Whatever they were doing, he was glad they'd left the house. Sneaking out in his conspicuous human body would be much easier with them out of the way.

V

By the time she reached the Birch Grove, Aurie was dizzy with exhaustion. Mushrooms and fiddleheads—even sacred ones—hadn't provided nearly the energy she needed for the long hike back. She looked closely at the ants roaming around their nest, jeweled carapaces glowing in the light. They were as stunningly perfect as everything else in the Garden, but she had no idea if the god was inside them.

The god has taken possession of Py's body, her captive Professor announced. *He's coming here to find you.*

Oh, thank God! Aurie collapsed against her brother's favorite tree in a euphoria of relief. Py was out of the ants, finally, and back in his own body—alive again!

Don't fool yourself, said the Professor sternly. *It's not your brother on his way here, it's the entity your Doctor awakened. You, of all people, ought to know the difference.*

Of course I do, she snapped, annoyed at the Prof for trying to dash her childish hope. *But if the god is in Py's body, then Py's soul must still be in the Colony.*

No, said the Professor uncomfortably. *I'm afraid that in both places, only the god is in residence.*

Aurie's heart sank. *How can you possibly know that?*

The same way I know everything about your brother! I am in all of his cells, or have you forgotten? I watched your precious god restore Py's body to full health—he even nixed my last Change in the interest of restoring normal vision. The Professor sighed. *I assure you, nothing in his human or Colony form can hide from me.*

Aurie knew that nothing physical could hide from the CRISPR machine, but Py's soul wasn't a physical entity. Refusing to let her glimmer of hope die, she waited silently, trying to ignore the dour presence of the Professor. From his place in her stem cell, Aurie could feel his gloomy anticipation like a gathering storm cloud. And as much as she tried to suppress it, her own nervousness was growing.

At his current rate of travel, he will be with us in approximately twenty-five minutes, the Professor informed her.

That seemed like an unbearably long time to wait.

Being incarcerated hasn't hobbled you at all, has it? Aurie teased him.

Of course not, the Professor said huffily. *I have the privilege of existing in many billions of cells. Which does not make the experience of being trapped in this damned stem cell of yours any more sufferable!*

Oh, stop complaining. You're in more places than anyone ever was. You're in Py and the Colony, not to mention this very comfortable stem cell of mine, where you will live longer than any copy of you ever has. I'd say you've cornered the market on CRISPR-evo real estate.

Yes, I have many front-row seats to the apocalypse, the Professor grumbled.

Aurie closed her eyes and tried to relax. She tried not to think about what was approaching through the woods like a ghost from her past. Ever since her own god had flown away, the memory of it was like a dream fragment, more idea than image. But now, that ancient part of herself rose up in her mind as if it had never left, its harsh golden eyes full of pity.

You have never embraced eternity, the god whispered in her memory. *Not once, in any incarnation! Your incarnate self has always chosen the cage over freedom.*

Her god had spoken to her as if she'd lived many other lives, as if her soul had taken many forms and always had a choice between mortality and immortality. The god's voice had been heavy with disappointment, yet laced with a bright streak of hope. *There are no impossibilities within the Pattern,* it had said. *One day, the bird will fly its cage and not return.*

Why didn't it just carry me off? Aurie wondered with a surge of her old anguish. *If only I had held on tighter!* She felt suddenly claustrophobic in her own skin and in many others. She was a legion of Auries trapped in skins and armored scales, in carapaces and delicate membranes. Caught in the cages of many skulls, but also imprisoned in tendrils of living ether that sailed through hot sulfur winds, and in veins of stony tissue that ran through lanthanide mountains on worlds unknown to her. How many incarnations had her soul experienced? She opened her eyes to dispel the nauseating multiplicity, and uttered a startled cry.

The god stood before her.

His golden eyes were like those of her own god. Looking into them, she saw an apocalyptic dawn beyond the edge of all darkness. Then the owner of those eyes shifted where he stood, and Aurie blinked. It was her brother standing by the dome of the anthill. His eyes were the same greenish-hazel they had always been, and he held a large package wrapped in foil, something that exuded the most heavenly aroma.

"Here." Py sounded almost shy as he handed her the package. "Thought you might be hungry."

Aurie uncovered a haunch of roast venison. With a murmur of thanks she fell to, devouring every scrap of meat, then cracking the big bone with her threads and sucking out the rich marrow inside. Py watched her quietly as she ate.

"I remember the last time I brought you food," he said. "Peanut butter and pickles."

"You remember that?" She looked at him doubtfully. The boy in front of her looked like Py and he sounded like Py, but ...

"I remember everything," he said, extracting a loaf of bread from his pack. "I had to bring you frosted graham crackers for dessert that night because I ate all the lemon cream pie. This time I ate all the rhubarb cobbler, so you'll have to settle for Uncle Abel's black Russian rye. Sorry it's still half-frozen."

"Not for long." Aurie wrapped the loaf tightly with her threads, generating all the heat she could stand. When the bread was soft enough, she tore it into fragrant hunks and devoured them all. She wrapped the bone fragments up in the foil and sighed with contentment. "Thanks, I was starving."

"Least I could do," he said. "Considering what you did for me. You and your Doctor."

"The Professor ... do you remember him, too?"

"I remember *everything*. All the memories in this head are perfectly clear." Py paused. "And I spoke with the Prof already. He told me quite a bit."

Aurie was surprised. "I thought the Prof was terrified of you!"

"He certainly doesn't trust me," Py agreed. "But I think he figured a well-informed god would be safer to have around than an ignorant one." He chuckled. "Now that I'm in this head, I see him the way your brother did—as a cautious, stooped-over fellow who is awfully conflicted about his prime directive."

Aurie snorted. "That's him, alright. Well, I snagged a single copy of him, which I'm holding against his will in one of my cells. He told me you were coming here."

"I wanted to talk with you before getting grilled by the others."

She waited, but silence spun out, marked only by bird calls, which had never sounded so sharp and sweet before. Then came the faint sound of footfalls on the old forest trail, still far distant.

"Must be Dad," Aurie muttered. She glanced at Py, but his eyes had gone strangely blank, as if he'd fallen asleep on his feet. A moment later, his focused gaze returned.

"Yep, that's Dad on his way here," he said. "Guess they discovered I'm not in bed where I'm supposed to be. We should find another place to talk."

Aurie looked at him keenly. This stranger, this god in her brother's head sounded so much like *Py*. Was it possible that the real Py had survived ... and jumped from the Colony back to his own head on the heels of this god? Maybe her brother had sequestered himself in some cellar of his mind, the way she had when her god awakened.

Encouraged, she suggested this to the Prof.

No, the Professor said, merciless in his efforts to disillusion her. *Stop fooling yourself!*

"You're not really Py, are you?" she whispered to the boy who seemed so much like him. "Just an invader with stolen memories."

The god didn't respond right away. "I suppose they *are* stolen, but they don't feel that way," he said at last. "I mean, I'm not just reading your brother's memories like a book. I'm attached to them. I think of myself as *him*." For a moment he looked so helpless and bewildered that she almost believed this was really Py, just her twin brother in over his head. Then his expression cleared, and she saw only the invader.

"But I haven't forgotten myself," the god said quietly. "The others will all see what they want to see, but *you* know who I really am."

Aurie began to cry, the perfect forest blurring into brilliant runnels of light, like a world being washed away. Embarrassed, she wiped her eyes and was astonished to see that he was crying too, tears running down his cheeks.

"You see?" he said harshly. "I'm *attached*. Now let's go, before Dad finds us and drags us back for a Wake family meeting."

She led him to one of her favorite spots—a stony lip overhanging a fast-flowing stream. Dark water swirled and cascaded just below them, following the pattern laid by submerged rocks and fallen branches. When Aurie could only leave the house for a short spell, she often came to this place. There was something calming about the turbulence below, perhaps the fact that it was so predictable— a free-flowing beast pouring itself out again and again in a timeless cycle.

"Look at it," she murmured, hypnotized by the dazzling current, which fractured into diamond cataracts that were almost unbearably beautiful. "*My* god never did anything like this!"

"What do you mean?"

Aurie searched Py's face, but he seemed honestly perplexed.

"The light here," she said. "Can't you see it? You realize it's actually the middle of the night?"

Py looked up at the dome of dark sky with its waxing moon, then back at the twilit woods. He laughed. "Guess I have a lot of unused energy to burn."

"So you're not consciously doing this?"

Py shook his head, clearly unimpressed by his surroundings. "I haven't done anything yet, except repair my old body." He snorted. "*My* old body ... listen to that! How can I convince you that I'm not Py when I feel as though I am? I thought I could just slip into the shell he left behind, but it wasn't that simple."

"I guess I was lucky," Aurie admitted. "My god's awakening *was* simple compared to yours. Too bad the Prof didn't just activate your template himself, before you started messing with those ants. If he wasn't such a ... "

"Wet blanket?" Py laughed shortly.

I heard that, muttered the Professor.

"More like a prophet of doom," she said, ignoring the grousing of the prophet. "Since I kidnapped him, we've gotten to know each other a bit. He's listening to us talk right now, from all of your cells and one of mine. The Doctor's listening too, of course. And so are the Fishes."

Py laughed. "So what you're saying is, there's no such thing as a private conversation. Well, at least they're not putting us through the wringer like Mom and Dad will."

Aurie grunted her agreement.

"So your god had a simple awakening and I had a complicated one," Py said, "but we both woke up."

"Yeah," she said, "but my god flew away, and you're still here. Why didn't you fly away?"

"I was going to ask you the same thing. When your god flew away, why didn't you go with it?"

Aurie looked away. "I don't know. I didn't have time to think about the choice, but I've never regretted it."

That was what she'd always told herself, but she could feel his stark gaze probing her. Aurie glanced back at him and saw no judgement in his eyes, only a desire to know the truth. It made her want to be completely honest for once.

"It gnaws at me, though … every day." She had unconsciously lowered her voice, as if that restless part of her might hear and begin to gnaw. "Part of me feels like it belongs somewhere else and got left behind."

Py said nothing, only watched her silently.

"I thought it would get better with time, but I think it's gotten worse." Aurie shifted her gaze to the surging current, barely contained in its narrow streambed. "I've never actually told anyone."

"Why not?"

She shrugged. "What could they do? It would only upset them to know that part of me wants to be light years away." She sighed, then looked back at him. "Okay, your turn. You're a god with all the planets in the cosmos to choose from. Why are *you* still here?"

He bit his lip—a Py-like thinking habit—and scanned the woods around them. "It might seem like I have a choice, but I don't … not really. I'm here because I'm meant to be, because there's work for me to do here."

Oddly, she understood that. Her own god had searched through choices that weren't really choices, all of them patterns within the larger Pattern. Only one had felt right, a long journey through the vacuum of space. Her god had been destined to fly far. And it had taken over her mind until the eve of that flight, when the two of them had become one, possessed of the same purpose.

"When my god woke up," she said slowly, "it was completely in control … but not like an alien sitting inside me, taking charge of the switches. It sort of permeated my mind—as naturally as if it were me. My memories were its memories." She held his gaze. "You're the same way. You actually sound a lot like Py, but you're not trying to, are you?"

Py shook his head.

Aurie smiled faintly. "You just naturally talk the way Py did. You've absorbed everything about him. My god did that, too … but *I* was still there. I wasn't in control of my mind, but I never left it."

"How did you manage that? Where did you hide?"

She glanced at him a little bashfully. "In my cartoon cell. I never told you about that, did I?"

He shook his head.

"It's where I always go to talk to the Doctor." Aurie paused, thinking. "Back then, he was just my imaginary friend in an imaginary sanctuary. Later on, my sleeping god used him as a go-between, a way of talking to me. After my god flew away, I assumed the Doctor was just my imagination again, but I was wrong about that. At some point, he must have become real, a real personality. And I guess my imaginary sanctuary was just as real."

Py's eyes lit with understanding. "So that's how you were able to keep your soul inside you! You had already created a place for it."

Aurie took a deep breath, mustering the courage to ask the question that mattered most to her. "So couldn't my brother have done the same thing? How do you know that his soul isn't somewhere inside you? Or still inside the ants?"

"Your brother never had a sanctuary like you did. And he sure didn't have time to create one when your Doctor woke me up." Py was quiet for a moment. "When I woke up in the Colony, your brother's soul was the first thing I saw, the first thing I touched. But I also saw it flee back to eternity. That's what happens when a god becomes incarnate in a host creature—the soul of the host gets consumed or dispossessed. And the only soul in *this* body is my own. I'm really sorry."

Aurie tried to mask her grief as her last hope slipped away. But the god who was attached to all of Py's memories really did look sorry.

"If Py had created a place for his soul, the way you did," murmured the god, "I don't think I'd be having this trouble ... this emotional trouble. I'm guessing your god didn't have any connection to this family. No loyalty and no love."

Aurie frowned, wondering if that disturbing speculation was true.

"If anyone had gotten in the way," Py persisted, "wouldn't your god have done whatever was necessary to keep its plans from being thwarted?"

A chill passed through Aurie. He was right—her god's only concerns had been activating its template in each of her eggs, ensuring the safety of those eggs, and fulfilling its own destiny within the Pattern. Nothing else had mattered.

"I think your god was free of human attachment," Py went on, "because *you* were still there, holding onto all of your loyalties and loves." The last word sounded like a bitter taste in his mouth. "With your brother gone, I've inherited more than I wanted to."

In spite of herself, Aurie's eyes were welling up again. She blinked the tears away and spoke harshly. "So what are you going to do here on Earth? What's your grand plan?"

"I don't know yet." Py looked around at the vibrant woods, seeming to see *through* everything. Despite the absence of shadows, his eyes had darkened; now they mirrored all the jeweled colors of the woods.

He had spoken frankly, and yet Aurie had the distinct sense that he wasn't being completely open with her. She saw many thoughts quickening in the depths of his eyes, thoughts he wasn't willing to share. Before she could say anything more, those eyes went blank again. A minute later, Py roused himself and reached for his pack.

"Where do you go when you blank out like that?" she asked, curious.

"Wherever I need to," he said. "Dad's trail is fresh at the Birch Grove, so he did come looking for me there. But everyone's back at the house now. Are you heading home?"

Aurie sighed. "I guess so."

Py nodded and began the trek back. Apparently the conversation was over.

As they hiked back to the Birch Grove, Aurie found herself annoyed by his reticence, as if her real brother were refusing to confide in her. *Gods don't have to answer to mere humans,* she reminded herself. *When he wants you to know what he's thinking, he'll tell you. In the meantime, just be grateful for those emotional attachments he inherited!*

"You're not going home, are you?" Aurie said as they reached the grove. "You're going back to the ants." He hadn't said so, but somehow she knew.

"For now," Py admitted.

"Don't stay out here too long," she said, dreading the prospect of facing her family alone. "And if you're expecting me to break the news that you're a god and the real Py is gone forever, forget it! I've already crushed them once—I think a second time would kill them."

His serious face broke into a grin. It was brief, but it warmed her like sunlight.

"Remember when I said that to you?" he reminded her. "That you'd better come home, or it would kill Dad? Only you threatened me with worse than death if I spilled the beans." He settled himself at the base of his favorite birch and closed his eyes. "Don't worry, I'll talk to them when I get back. Soon, I promise." Then his eyes opened again, looking into hers. "And tell the Little Fishes not to be afraid of me. They don't have to talk to me if they don't want to, but I would never do anything to hurt them."

"Okay," Aurie said. Her children whimpered from their hiding place in her mind, and she turned her attention to comforting them. When she returned her awareness to the Birch Grove, Py was already asleep.

VI

Leaving his human mind asleep to rest, the god-who-was-Py returned his awareness to the Colony for a temporary reprieve. The conversation with Aurie had left him feeling disjointed and weary, his emotions—*Py's* emotions—rubbed raw. He hoped his human attachments would be weaker in the Colony, allowing him to think and plan more clearly. But ensconced in the Colony, the god still found himself thinking and feeling like *Py*. He sought refuge in the halcyon dreams of his queens, but even in that womblike darkness, human thoughts crept to him along invisible threads. Most troubling was the knowledge that Aurie hadn't made a clean break with her god. He thought of that single bright feather drifting up from her aura, as if trying to fly on its own. *She* might be content with her limited human life, but that feather would never be content. It would always be straining toward the wing it was no longer a part of, its pain and restlessness growing until they drove her mad.

The god was disturbed to find himself caring about Aurie as if he were her real brother. And he was beginning to understand why she had chosen to stay in her human form. Her attachment to this family had actually been stronger than her desire to be the creative force driving the growth of a new world! He would never have believed it if those four cords hadn't bound him, too. Examining himself with something close to terror, the god-who-was-Py realized that in company with his family, he risked losing his purpose entirely. The boy had sacrificed himself to free his god; what a terrible irony it would be if the god imprisoned himself again in the shackles of the boy!

He could not allow that to happen. He had to find a way to protect his true self from the influence of his human host. The god forced himself to relax, drifting in the dark, cool peace of his queens' sleep. He would go back to his human self soon, but for now it was better to be here.

The boy leaning against the birch tree twitched in his sleep. The human soul that once called this flesh home had departed, and a god's soul had taken up residence. Now, however, the god's awareness was elsewhere, and the boy's sleeping brain—filled with neural pathways encoding memories and old desires—began to dream. The boy dreamed of his favorite creatures in all the world, the ones he had shared his very soul with.

The boy's dream found its way to the Colony through the god's soul that connected them. And the human dream—harmless in itself—stirred the Colony's own memories. The dream morphed into something more potent, a Vision of conquest suffused with strong emotions.

Ants of all kinds came forth from underneath stones and roots and decaying logs. They swarmed across forests and fields; they crossed rivers and streams on rafts of their own bodies. It was time to pave the way for creation! For a new world that belonged to ants, a world that was beautiful, thriving, changing—

The god who had sought refuge in the ants could not escape this Vision. Cool tranquility gave way to searing excitement—and the purpose that drove him, his need to shape and change the world, quickened in his supercolony.

In the woods for miles around, ants from hundreds of nests boiled up from hidden cracks in the ground. Tar-black rivers sprang up and surged forth; russet marching columns carved new paths through the forest. Scurrying drops of amber coalesced, then fanned out in golden waves. When predators and parasites were encountered, the supercolony stung to kill. And the chemical trails of humans, however faint, were followed with especial zeal. The Colony's instinctual memory was sound, and it remembered humans—one in particular—as the most dangerous enemy of all.

VII

Aurie was nearly home when ants began to erupt from the ground. She faltered and froze at the unbelievable sight. They moved like rivulets of lava, darkening the trunks of trees and gilding rocks, turning the forest floor into a moving carpet. Before she could find a free path, a stream of them ran across her feet and up her bare legs, stinging as they went.

Her paralysis broke and she ran, brushing the ants away with her threads, heedless of the tiny bodies she was crushing underfoot. She broke cover and raced across the glade to the house, aware of the Doctor working swiftly to neutralize the ants' poison. This was not the formic acid of ordinary ants, but some kind of neurotoxin. The pain was immense. She couldn't stop to dampen it or help the Doctor save her; there wasn't a second to spare.

Aurie burst into the kitchen and slammed the door. Her family looked up from the table, startled out of their discussion.

"Follow me," she cried as she flew down the hall to her parents' bathroom. As the others caught up to her, she ordered them into the tub.

"Aurie, what—"

"No time for questions," she barked. "Get in!"

Giving each other disturbed looks, the three adults stepped into the big clawfoot tub. Aurie ran the water until it was ankle-deep, then staggered against the tall cabinets, dizzy with pain.

"What's wrong?" Howard asked sharply. "Are you hurt?"

"I'll be fine," she muttered. Already she could feel her cells recovering, the pain now only a siren that refused to shut up. The Doctor silenced it and Aurie breathed a sigh of relief, looking around the room for any signs of movement. Was the bathtub a stupid idea? Maybe these ants could swim—maybe nothing could stop them. But she didn't know what else to do.

"Is it Py, or his god, or his crazy ants?" Uncle Abel asked in a low voice.

"His ants," Aurie said, surprised at the mention of Py's god. They must have suspected something wasn't right when Py woke up. Motioning for quiet, she spoke to the Professor.

What's going on?

He's dreaming, the Professor told her, sounding utterly distraught. *Your brother's sleeping brain is dreaming of ants!*

So why are they on a rampage? The god isn't in Py's brain; he's in the Colony.

Yes, but they're connected, snapped the Professor. *Your brother's dream stirred the Colony's old Vision, which is influencing the god. His energy, his potency ... it's pouring into his supercolony and causing it to act out that Vision.*

Well, wake him up, for God's sake!

I can't wake him up, cried the Professor. *There's no 'him' to wake up! The god's awareness is in the Colony, not in your brother's dreaming brain.*

Then tell the god to go back to Py's body!

What do you think I've been doing? I've been screaming my head off in every ant of the Colony, but he doesn't seem to hear me.

Maybe he's too caught up in the dream, Aurie said, shuddering.

Very likely. And the ants stung your brother's body in a hundred places—I've been dealing with that on top of everything else!

Movement near the floorboards by the sink caught Aurie's attention. A small stream of black ants was coming from under the cabinet, heading straight for her.

Can't you get Py's brain to dream about something else? she asked in desperation.

I've tried that, too! But his neural pathways won't lock onto other stories or memories. Nothing seems to be as powerful as his feelings for those ants.

Nothing? Aurie thought quickly as she manufactured, not peppermint compounds, but a soapy solution in her threads.

There had to be *something*. After all, it was Py's human attachments that were causing the god such distress.

Aurie sprayed soap over the approaching ants, suffocating them as quickly as she'd hoped. She glanced sharply at her father. "What's the best time Py ever had with us?"

"The best time?" Howard looked at her like she'd lost her wits.

"I need to remind him that we're his family, that he loves us!"

Her dad was quiet for a moment while Aurie doused another group of ants emerging from a crack in the baseboard.

"It wasn't his best time," Howard said. "It was probably his *worst* time ... but there was no doubting his love."

"What was it?" Aurie demanded. "What did he do?"

"He followed you through the woods," Howard said. "After you took off on that mushroom hunt. He gave Abel the slip and went searching for you on his own. He was cold and hungry and thirsty, and all beat up from the merry chase you led him on. If he's forgotten that he loves his family, remind him of that."

Aurie nodded, trying to look everywhere at once. Dear God, there were ants on the *ceiling,* a dozen big ones racing towards the center of the room where the bathtub sat. Were they planning to literally fall on their targets, like tiny kamikaze bombers?

Find Py's memory of following me through the woods, she ordered the Professor. *If that doesn't work, I don't know what will.*

The Professor gave hurried assent and Aurie flung her threads at the marauders on the ceiling, brushing them onto the floor and spraying them with soap. Deep in her mind, she could feel the Fishes clinging to her in terror, but there was no time to comfort them—and no way to do so. They knew everything she was thinking and feeling. As more ants appeared, blooming from the sink, the shower drain, and under the door, Aurie wondered with near-panic how much longer this could go on. At some point, she would be overwhelmed by sheer numbers.

Ants flooded the woods, laying waste to their enemies. Py ran with them, seeing nothing but the relentless horde around him, hearing nothing but the sibilant thunder of its passage. How good it was to flow forward like an unstoppable river! To raze the old before ushering in the new. As he ran, Py was suffused with the harsh purity of a wildfire cleansing the forest and preparing it for new growth.

Then, all at once, the ants around him were gone. He was following something new, a bright thread that snaked through the air. It was the impression left by his sister's aura, her path through the woods. As soon as Py recognized Aurie's trail, the destructive fever left him and he grew cold with fear. Aurie was in terrible danger, because her aura wasn't just hers anymore. A new aura—cold and glassy—was strangling her human one like a deadly vine. Py knew he had to catch Aurie before he lost her completely. He ran faster, ignoring the pain in his legs and the exhaustion that was making him light-headed. He stumbled over rocks in the thickening dusk, thinking only of Aurie and wondering what he could possibly do to save her—

Go back to your human body, cried a familiar voice, very faintly, from the world beyond the woods.

Confused, Py stopped running. The dream continued around him, pulling at him like a current, but he stood still, jolted back to the truth of who he was. Not Py, but the god who had taken possession of Py's mind. And he suddenly remembered *where* he was—in the sanctuary of his Colony.

Go back to your human body and wake up! That was the Professor, and he sounded utterly exhausted.

The god returned to Py's body and jerked his mind out of sleep. His legs burned, and he looked down to find a smattering of angry-looking bites on his skin. The woods swam around him, resolving into the solid forms of trees glinting in the twilight. Ants were everywhere, but they were moving in orderly procession without the crazed speed of his dream. Apprehensively, the god cast his awareness out into the woods.

The ants had decimated it. Dead animals lay in their burrows or under cover of thickets. Birds still stirred among the treetops, but their eggs had been punctured and poisoned. Silence and stillness lay like a pall over the woods. Even the wind had died in the wake of the ants' rampage.

Horror filled the god. He had done this, without even meaning to! This pointless, unwitting massacre. His supercolony must have been empowered by his creative drive ... and before ushering in their own vision of creation, they had tried to eliminate their enemies. Even *he* hadn't been spared, although his CRISPR machine had managed to keep him alive. And what had happened to his family?

The god sent his awareness speeding toward home. To his great relief, the others were unharmed. Many of his ants had been killed, but the survivors were already heading back to their own nests now that the dream of conquest had ended.

There is no sanctuary, even in the Colony! Py's human soul had left its mark on the ants, too. Under the influence of that soul, the old Colony had not only dreamed up a Vision, it had been inflamed by *emotions*. Just as the god had been inflamed in the throes of that Vision. Strong emotions were a tide that had swept him up and thrust him on a course of action with no forethought and no planning.

Grimly, the god turned his awareness inward, to the depths of his perilous human mind. He first examined the specific region that generated emotional impulses. This could be inactivated ... but not without compromising other functions. So he searched the entire territory of his brain, from its highest cognitive peaks to its ancient and primitive valleys.

He traced neural pathways like wandering streams, followed patterns laid by the history of chemical firings. Many of the strongest patterns were feelings of love and loyalty for his family, and memories of their time together. But these were all intertwined, and enmeshed with other memories, thoughts, and feelings. The god could destroy some or all of them ... but no precise surgery was possible.

There was no way to separate *Py* from his emotional attachments. To mangle his brain would be the same as abandoning it to die. It would defeat the purpose of *being* Py, and seriously compromise his mission in this world. Which left only one option: to stand guard over his brain and never leave it unattended.

The god-who-was-Py withdrew from the jungle of his mind and headed home, taking the usual shortcut through the woods. *Whatever you do,* he thought, slipping through gaps in the brush, *don't let them distract and compromise you. Never forget who you really are!*

Around him lay the forest, unnaturally silent in the ever-twilight. Aurie had spoken of that light as if it were a glorious thing, but in all the woods Py saw only the taunting glimmer of creation unfulfilled, changes yet to be wrought, problems yet to be solved.

With a sigh, he picked up his pace, steeling himself to deal with his family.

VIII

"So we're dealing with another god now?" Howard muttered. He looked at Aurie across the kitchen table and managed a faint smile. "Good thing you've got some experience with that. Just wish we were waiting for *your* god to come home."

"You never met her god," Jacqueline reminded him as she poured coffee into her mug.

"Which is a point in its favor." Howard choked on the contents of his own mug, then took another, slower sip. "Aurie's god only wanted to take care of some eggs before flying off, but Py's god just tried to kill us!"

"He wasn't *trying* to kill us," Aurie said for the third time. "He fell asleep in the Birch Grove and had a dream that turned into his Colony's Vision of taking over the woods. The ants stopped attacking us as soon as his CRISPR machine gave him a different dream."

"Just a dream, just an accident?" Howard snorted. His knuckles were white as he gripped his mug. "That's not very reassuring, kiddo. It was all pretty damn real ... and those ants were *hunting us down*. They came into the house and tracked us into the bathroom."

Aurie nodded, disturbed.

"Why did they do that?" Howard demanded.

"How should I know?" Aurie said irritably. "You can ask the Lord of the Ants when he gets home."

The adults all cast nervous glances at the front door.

"Why can't that god just fly off now and leave us alone?" Jacqueline murmured with quiet ferocity. "Just fly off and leave Py behind!"

If wishes were fishes, Aurie thought, trying to contain her turbulent emotions toward her mother. Jacqueline's harsh words at Py's bedside still stung. *The real Py is gone, and I'm pretty sure his god is here to stay.* Aurie planned to keep those thoughts to herself, of course. If she told her family that Py had been permanently replaced by his god, they would only be devastated all over again ... and blame her for letting it happen.

Feeling morose, Aurie watched the others try to drown their fears. She should have insisted on drinking what everyone else was drinking.

You wouldn't like it, the Doctor assured her. *But if you need your nerves steadied ... ?*

No, I'm fine, she told him. *Just wish I could've taken a nap before the family meeting.* There it was—another useless wish sailing through the room. But she was exhausted and they hadn't given her any time to rest before hustling her to the kitchen for a debriefing. The adults were nursing coffee heavily spiked with bourbon, but Abel had made Aurie hot chocolate the way she liked it, with whipped cream and a cinnamon stick. As she sipped it, he gave her a sympathetic look that clearly said, *Sorry you're on the receiving end of this.* For her uncle's sake, Aurie tried to think of something she could tell them. Something good.

"The god is attached to Py's old memories and feelings," Aurie said carefully. "He cares about us, and he really doesn't want to hurt us." She didn't mention what the Professor had told her— that the god was, at that moment, trying hard to find and sever those attachments.

"What makes you think his god cares about us?" Jacqueline spoke quietly to Aurie without meeting her eye. "Yours didn't ... even though you were still in there, and *you* cared."

"It must be Py that you're seeing," Howard said, sounding very relieved at the idea. "The *real* Py. He's trapped in his own mind, isn't he? The same way you were."

"Yes," said Jacqueline, brightening at the idea. She darted a brief look at Aurie. "I didn't meet the real you until later, but I caught glimpses of you. Your god was in control, but you were still there. It must be the same thing with Py ... we just need to draw him out."

Aurie buried her face in her mug and said nothing.

I think you're right not to tell them, the Doctor said. *None of them will believe that the real Py is gone. The god is right about that. They're only going to see what they want to see.*

And that will be easy, Aurie thought. *When he looks and sounds just like Py.* Everyone would assume they were catching glimpses of the real Py when they were only seeing the god hooked in to Py's mind, to the entire repertoire of his thoughts and feelings and memories. The god had spoken of this attachment as if it were a shameful, frustrating thing. Aurie understood that ... but no one else would. And why did she always have to be the one to give them bad news? To dash their false hopes? To produce miracles, or be blamed for not producing them?

He wasn't able to cut his emotional attachments, announced the Professor with relief. *And he's heading home now.*

Aurie breathed her own sigh of relief. Let the god come and answer for himself; she was tired of fielding questions.

"He's on his way here," she said, watching with more than a little satisfaction as the adults all looked at each other with concern. They might believe that Py was still alive somewhere inside his skull, but the god was apparently in charge at the moment—and the god had almost gotten them killed.

"Well," said Abel, pushing back from the table with his customary briskness. "I'd better get started on breakfast, or whatever we're calling it at this hour."

"Is anyone actually hungry?" Jacqueline wondered.

"You know Py will be," Howard said. "Even though he just ate a few hours ago."

"Yep. God or mere mortal, that boy has the same appetite he always did." Abel chuckled cynically on his way to the pantry. "But maybe he'd prefer honeydew to blackberry jam these days."

Aurie took the chance to escape further questions by pulling ingredients out of the fridge. Her parents, perhaps not wanting to be left alone with their questions, hurried to help. In record time, a hash of venison sausage, peppers, onions, and potatoes sizzled in the giant cast-iron skillet, Howard was forking crisp waffles onto a platter, and the aroma of fresh-brewed coffee mingled with the other good smells.

Breakfast for Py? wondered Aurie. *Or offerings for the god?*

"Just in time," Howard said, as footfalls sounded on the patio. The front door opened and there was Py. They all stared at him in silence.

"I'm sorry," he said, looking ruefully at Aurie. "I should never have gone back to the ants."

"Ants? What ants?" inquired Howard coldly. "Oh, you mean the ones that would have killed us if your sister hadn't gotten here in time? *Those* ants?" He glared at Py. "We'd all be dead in the bathtub if Aurie hadn't held out so long that they finally gave up!"

"They didn't give up," Py murmured, as Abel gently ushered him inside and closed the door. "They would *never* have given up until that dream ended. It was a vision of evolution, and the ants were clearing a path for it."

Aurie caught her breath as she realized what that meant. "The Colony wasn't just after us, was it? They were after everything!"

Py nodded. "The Colony attacked anything it considered a threat."

"What do you mean, 'a threat'?" Jacqueline looked back and forth between her children. "Did the ants—oh, God!"

"No one was hurt," Py assured her. "Only ... some animals."

"Animals?" Abel added his frown to the others. "What animals?"

"Not the ones lucky enough to be flying," Py said, "or high up in the trees. But most of the others didn't fare so well."

As the adults rushed over to the kitchen windows, Aurie tuned her sensitive ears to the sounds of the forest. Even on a windless day, the woods were never quiet; they were always full of rustlings and murmurings. But now a creepy silence permeated the air. A bird cried out in the distance, the sound profoundly lonely.

Howard turned around, a little pale. "And how far does this path of destruction extend?"

"A few miles in all directions," Py said.

"How could ants possibly move that fast?" Abel sounded incredulous.

"They didn't all start from the Birch Grove," Py said. "My ants are a supercolony now ... hundreds of nests."

"But they *are* fast," Aurie murmured, remembering.

"Can we talk more after breakfast?" Py said, looking hungrily at the untouched food. "And where are the Fishes? We're not going to eat without them, are we?"

What does he want with them? Aurie thought as her protective instincts were roused. But once Casa del Utero was brought in, she nudged her children to go back to their bodies, which they reluctantly did. They had been with her during the entire battle with the ants, too terrified to even whimper. Now Aurie felt the wary attention they gave to their uncle as he poured syrup over his waffles. Py glanced at them briefly, but if he spoke to them, he spoke silently.

Everyone cast furtive glances at Py during the meal, as if they could parse the boy from the god just by watching him eat. Aurie thought the expression on Py's face was disturbingly like two personalities fighting for dominance. One of them cared about the people around the table; the other only truly cared about his mission in this world.

Not two personalities, she reminded herself. *Just the god trying to fight the influence of Py's ghost.* That was how she had begun to think of her brother's mind, with all of its imprinted memories.

What difference does it make? asked the Doctor.

It makes all the difference in the world! If Py is really gone, then he can't be resurrected.

But if the god surrenders to his human attachments, put in the Professor hopefully, *then wouldn't your brother be resurrected? For all intents and purposes?*

The god doesn't have Py's soul, Aurie said. *And he never will.*

That's true, the Professor allowed. *But is it really your brother's soul that you love? Or is it all of those memories you share with him, his personality and emotions ... all the software in his mind? And would you even know the difference?*

You think I could be fooled by some copy of my own brother? Aurie demanded. *I want Py back, not a god who feels and thinks the way he did!*

Speaking of personalities, said the Doctor. *Does the god have his own personality, independent of whatever organism he possesses?*

A very interesting question, the Professor mused. His indignation at the Doctor seemed to be temporarily overshadowed by their shared philosophical interests. *And a pertinent one.*

Let's talk about it later, Aurie said, as her dad set his fork down on his empty plate. *I think our lab meeting's about to start.*

Indeed, everyone seemed to have finished eating. In the tense silence, Abel refilled Py's and Aurie's mugs with cocoa from the pot on the stove. Then he brought the coffeepot and the bottle of bourbon to the table. Aurie felt her family's collective agitation swell like a thundercloud, and she braced herself for the storm.

"Okay, let's have it," Howard said sternly to Py. "The whole story. Starting with your Secret Project."

"It's a long story," Py warned him. "And a complicated one."

"We'll do our best to wrap our simple minds around it," Howard assured him.

So Py began. As he recounted his time in the Birch Grove, Aurie had to constantly remind herself that this was not her brother, only the god recollecting her brother's memories.

"So you can see why I was pretty wrapped up in those ants," Py said. "Helping them evolve was the most incredible thing I'd ever done. The most *important* thing. And I thought of that colony as my creation, *my* amazing ants. But I was spending so much time in the world of auras that I was losing my normal vision. So the Professor—my CRISPR machine—gave me my third Change, the ability to see everything in its chemical form."

"You were actually going blind?" said Jacqueline. "Good God!"

"And your Professor is like Aurie's Doctor?" Howard asked.

"He has a personality and you can talk to him?"

"Oh yes," Py said. "He most definitely has a personality. But most of our conversations were *him* talking to *me*. And he doesn't exactly embrace his job the way the Doctor does."

A prophet is not without honor, quoted the Professor melodramatically. *Save in his own country and among his own kin ... and especially in his own host!*

Aurie hushed him. *Pipe down, I'm trying to listen.*

"Every time I've gone through a Change," Py went on, "I've felt sick and feverish, almost delirious. As I was going through this one, I must've found my way to the Birch Grove in the middle of the night. But it felt like a dream. I don't remember getting there or back, only waking up in bed the next morning."

"What happened at the Birch Grove?" asked Howard.

"The ants knew something was wrong with me, and they were worried. I told them I was Changing and they asked if I was still with them. I said, *I will always be with you. I will do anything for you, give you everything I have.* Then they swarmed all over me." Py paused. "I didn't know it then, but I had offered them my soul, my CRISPR machine, *everything.*"

"My goodness," said Abel mildly. "If I didn't know any better, I'd say you were *fond* of these ants."

"Well, the feeling wasn't mutual. The next day, I ran back to the colony to tell them about my Change, and instead of my trusting, cooperative ants, I found a hostile, sentient Colony. It had a new aura, it was aware of itself, and it wanted nothing to do with me."

"But you gave those ants your CRISPR machine," Jacqueline protested.

"Not to mention your immortal soul," Howard added dryly.

"That's why they didn't need me anymore," Py told her. "My mistake was to think of them as *friends.* They were simply organisms exploiting a golden opportunity to evolve, as all organisms do." A shadow of the old hurt darkened his face, and Aurie had to remind herself again that it wasn't real, just the god feeling the influence of Py's ghost.

"So the Colony got what it wanted and turned me away," Py went on. "But I had to find out what had happened to it—how it had gained this new aura and self-awareness. So I did a little exploring." He described his jumping talent and experimental dive into the Colony, where he had wound up in subatomic space.

"And yeah, I know how impossible that sounds," he said quickly, before Howard could jump in and say so. "But it's the truth."

Howard snorted. "I'd be the last person to say that anything you or Aurie did was *impossible. Crazy,* maybe ... "

"Well," Py said. "I was dying to see how deep I could go."

"Penetrating an atom is going pretty deep, I would say," said Howard. "And how did you manage to get out?"

"The Colony's aura came after me and dragged me out," Py told him. "It would've killed me right then, if it could have."

"But why?" Jacqueline sounded baffled. "You weren't doing anything to hurt the ants, were you?"

"I was trespassing on sacred ground," Py said quietly. "And the Colony could feel it. Would you want something like a sentient virus inside *you,* working its way to the very heart of your atoms? Anyway, the Professor helped me escape, but the Colony stationed an army on my body to kill me once I jumped back."

Abel grunted. "So that's why we found you all covered with ants."

"Creepiest thing I've ever seen," Howard muttered. "Aurie drove them away and we carried you home."

Py nodded. "But then the Colony sent some ants to take all of you hostage and force me to jump back to my body. At the same time, it was busy assimilating other nests, expanding into a powerful supercolony."

"Good God." Howard raked a hand through his unruly hair, then closed his eyes briefly. "To think I was *disappointed* at the idea of you just sitting in the woods, blissfully observing the wildlife and not accomplishing anything." He sighed. "So your sister captured the ants stationed on all of us, but you were flatlining and you never jumped back to your body. Aurie said that you jumped into the Colony instead and … somehow became one with it?"

Py didn't look away from his father's questioning eyes. He nodded.

"Why?" Howard asked.

"I saw its Vision, a sort of ant fantasy of evolution." Py was quiet for a moment. "I could try to describe it, but I don't think you would understand how compelling it was. How it *drew* me."

"That's what Aurie said about the Pattern," Jacqueline murmured. "She said I wouldn't understand it unless I saw it for myself. She was right."

"But there was another reason," Py said. "And it was even more important. I was *responsible* for those ants—for everything they might do." He glanced bleakly out the window. "I couldn't just go back to my body and let them run rampant. So I jumped into the light inside their aura, their Life Fire. It was a crazy thing to do … but it felt completely right."

He fell silent, and no one prodded him to speak.

"The next thing I knew, I *was* the Colony," Py said. "When the Professor found me, he said my soul was still human, but it would eventually become an ant soul and I would lose that sense of responsibility. I wouldn't be able to keep myself—the Colony— from running amok."

"So that's why he activated the Colony's god template," Howard muttered.

Py shook his head. "Oh no, he would never have done that. But Aurie had injected some of the ants with her Doctor. It was the Doctor who activated the god template."

They all turned to Aurie. She looked down at her empty plate, expecting a flood of recrimination which didn't come. Silence reigned again, more uncomfortable this time. Howard finally took a deep breath and looked his son in the eye.

"We've been talking to you all this time like you're Py," he said. "And God knows, we'd love to believe that. But you're really not, are you?"

"No," Py said quietly.

"No," Howard echoed. "You're a god who woke up inside an

ant colony possessed by my son. So what are you doing in *Py's* body? I mean, his human body?"

Py looked uncomfortable for the first time. "I wanted to know how I was awakened, and why. I revived this body—and made it my home—so its memories would be mine. And I wanted to understand ... what it is to be human."

Howard was still gazing at him fixedly. Aurie's stomach tightened as she waited for her dad to ask the obvious next question: *So where is Py? Is he still in the ants, or did he hitch a ride back to his old body with you?* But Howard was uncharacteristically silent.

Aurie glanced around and saw the same unspoken question burning in every face, the question no one dared to ask. They all hoped or believed that the real Py was hiding somewhere in his own head. If he wasn't, they didn't want to know. And if he was, the last thing they wanted to do was call the god's attention to him. Glancing at Jacqueline, Aurie could see that fear clearly in her mother's eyes. *She's remembering when my god was in control,* Aurie thought. *And I was powerless and hiding.*

"Well, now that you're awake," Howard said at last, "what are you planning to do? Are you going to fly off to seed life on another planet?"

The adults all looked hopeful, but Py shook his head.

"Then I guess you're here to stay," Howard muttered. "Well, maybe our human brains are too small to understand your Grand Vision, but could you give us a dumbed-down version? It must be something more than sitting around while your ants build a bunch of tiny temples dedicated to your worship."

Py rolled his eyes. "Whatever I do here, it won't be that."

Howard's brow furrowed. "You don't know what your ultimate goal is? Don't you have a master plan in mind?"

Py glanced out the windows at the silent woods. "My ultimate goal is to help this world grow ... but there's no blueprint for that."

"But aren't you infallible and omnipotent?" Howard said.

Py laughed shortly. "I'm not one of your mythical gods. *Real* gods have to contend with reality. We're limited by the materials and mechanisms of the world in which we awaken."

Everyone stared at him, Aurie included.

"Do you really think it was part of my master plan to kill off all the animals in the vicinity, including all of you?" Py demanded. When no one said anything, he sighed. "Think of Aurie's god. Before it flew off, it made sure her eggs were safe. But it needed a doctor to remove them and a cryotank to house them. Her god couldn't just whisk them out and preserve them by magic, could it?"

He's right, Aurie thought. While sharing her mind with that god, she had felt immensely capable … and yet she had needed help.

"But Aurie's god left this planet for a different one," Howard said. "And you want to stay here. Why?"

"Hers was a kind of pioneer god," Py said, looking speculatively at Aurie. "Driven to seed new worlds with new forms of life. I'm more of an engineer driven to *improve* life." He turned to Howard with a faint smile. "A tinkerer like you, only I have more tools at my disposal."

Howard's eyes widened a bit. Aurie thought her father looked almost envious.

"You built your CRISPR machine with the same ultimate goal," Py pointed out. "You wanted to improve your children in ways that normal evolution couldn't accomplish. But you didn't have a specific plan. You fashioned your machine with a general directive, then let it run free." He cocked his head at his father. "You were behaving more like a god than a human, you know."

Howard shook his head. "Nothing has ever made me feel *less* godlike than watching the results of my tinkering and realizing there was almost nothing I could do to help my kids. Surely gods have more control over their creations than humans do."

"We have much less," Py said, glancing briefly at Aurie. "Pioneer gods kindle the fires of life, but that fire is uncontrollable." He smiled briefly. "How else did you humans evolve to worship false gods and uncover real ones by accident?"

"But you're an *engineer* god," Howard said. "Don't you have some control over life?"

"I can only help to shape it," said Py. "I can quench one flame or nurture another, but I can't control the whole fire. And I can't afford to make a mistake."

"Why not?" Howard pressed. "Can't you just undo whatever you've done and try again?"

"No. I only have one chance to enact a world-altering change." Py's eyes darkened as he spoke, and Aurie caught a glimpse of the eternity behind them. It was a vista that made her ache with hopeless, thwarted longing.

"It's simple to start from scratch on a clean world," Py murmured. "Much harder to tinker with an existing world and make it better. To do that, you have to see deep and far."

Howard was staring at Py intently. "You're planning to do what I did, then ... only on a much bigger and more dangerous scale."

"Dangerous to whom?"

"To all of mankind," Howard said, glancing at Jacqueline and Abel as if for support of this obvious conclusion.

Py's smile was thin. Aurie thought the god's attachment to his humanity had also grown thin, at least for the moment. In his ascetic countenance, she no longer saw any trace of her brother, only something that burned like a harsh, pure flame in a cage of flesh.

"If I am a danger to mankind, it will not be by accident," said the god. "Thanks to *you,* I've realized the enormous danger humans pose to this world."

"Thanks to *me?*" Howard looked stunned.

The god nodded grimly. "The template that encodes my kind exists in every organism on this planet. It's made to awaken when a life form is ready. But you built a tool capable of activating it prematurely. If you managed that tinkering feat, others can and will, soon enough ... and the results of that may be disastrous."

"Because other gods will be awakened in this world, willy-nilly?" Howard asked.

"Yes," said the god. "When a god awakens in a host, it is

partly shaped by the nature of that host." He looked intently at Howard. "Can you imagine the consequences if a sociopath or a sadist awakened a god in himself?"

Howard stiffened. "But you're *gods!* Can't you overcome the influence of mere mortals?"

"Gods aren't inherently good or evil," said the god. "Our drive to create manifests according to the character of our hosts. We amplify that character, for better or worse ... but almost always for better. The seeds of our sleeping drive take different forms on different worlds, but they're made to awaken when a life form is a suitable host."

"And the ants weren't ready?" Abel said.

"It wasn't the ants who awakened me," the god responded coldly. "It was a tool engineered by a human and pressed into use by a human. And you humans are far from ready."

The atmosphere in the room had grown cooler with the talk of gods. Now it was chilly enough to make them shiver, and a dusky gloom hung over the empty plates with their scattered crumbs.

Howard frowned at the boy sitting across the table. "God knows humans have done a lot of harm ... to ourselves and the rest of the world. But we've done a lot of good, too."

"Some of you *try* to do good," the god allowed. "But your tinkering ability has grown rapidly while your wisdom has not. How could it? You live inside your skulls—the smallest of spaces!—and your lives are over in an eyeblink. None of you see clearly or far enough to engineer fruitful change."

"You think the world would be better off if we had never developed our cerebral cortex?" Howard snorted. "What would you have us do? Go back to hunting and gathering, and scratching pictures on cave walls?"

"Some would make the argument that everything we do is a natural product of our evolution," Abel said, glancing at Howard.

"Why do you treat evolution as a kind of god?" asked the god. "It's not manifest destiny; it's simply the way life propagates on this planet. On other worlds, life arises and grows by completely different means." He turned his attention to Jacqueline. "When you get down to brass tacks, what *is* natural selection?"

"A random mutation or event," she said. "That allows one organism to pass its genes down more effectively than others of its kind."

The god nodded. "So there's no pinnacle to the path of a species, only a moving line that joins and breaks with other lines. Dynamic threads on a growing, changing tapestry. But the human thread developed cognition without sight, learned to investigate and probe itself and the tapestry around it. Humans became blind gods fumbling in the dark. And now you've found a way to amplify your foolish natures, by prematurely waking the gods asleep in your own cells."

The fire in his eyes abruptly cooled to ashes. "So tell me ... why should I risk catastrophe for an entire world to preserve this rogue thread? What makes humans worth saving?"

The god's question, spoken with deceptive mildness, hung over the table like a thunderbolt. The tension in the room was an electric taste in the back of Aurie's throat, and she bristled instinctively. Almost against her will, she found herself brainstorming exemplary human qualities in defense of her species. Clearly the god didn't think intelligence was enough, but what about the things humans had built, the stories they had created? Cathedrals and art and music? Would anything be enough?

"What makes us worth saving?" Jacqueline's voice shook a little, but she spoke with surprising calm. "Our truth-seeking spirit."

"Human truths are no more than shadows seen through a veil," the god murmured. "Those who try to rend that veil are rare blossoms, and they are cut down like weeds. The majority of you will not stand for them."

"But they still blossom," she said, giving Howard and Abel a desperate look.

"What about our persistence, our drive?" Howard said. "Humans make plenty of mistakes, but they never stop trying to build and improve. And they'll do anything to achieve a noble end."

"What is a noble end?" The god's eyes flared. "Nothing ever ends! Life is a continuation, and if you create misery and suffering through your efforts, then what have you achieved?"

Jacqueline grunted in reluctant agreement.

"What about our courage?" Abel asked the god. "The courage to stand up against iniquity, to fight injustice, to speak the truth no matter what the consequences! You can't tell me that isn't worth saving."

The god regarded the former prosecuting attorney gravely. "How many of you embrace such qualities? The good of the few is subverted by the savagery of the rest. The most courageous among you are crushed; the most honest are silenced. The clearest lesson from human history is that humans don't learn from it. Your own nature won't allow it."

Silence descended, weighing heavily on the humans at the table.

"Maybe humankind as a whole doesn't look so good," Howard allowed, "but surely there are individuals who are worth saving. What about all the heroes and saints who have ever lived? Even the God of Abraham, Isaac, and Jacob agreed not to burn Sodom and Gomorrah to the ground if he could find ten righteous souls in those cities."

"Well, apparently he couldn't find even that many," the god said dryly. "But saving a few worthy souls is pointless while the defect in humanity remains."

"What about love?" said Jacqueline quietly. "Isn't love the best thing humans are capable of?"

The god turned adamantine eyes on her. "Romantic or possessive feelings, strong affinities, filial bonds ... these are what humans call love. But if a strong attachment is the best thing you're capable of, then it should lead you to behave in the best of ways. Does it?"

No one answered him immediately.

"Strong, twisted feelings can get mislabeled as love," Jacqueline ventured. "Those feelings might bring out the worst in people, but *real* love brings out the best in them."

The god snorted. "Between the two I would not dare to stick a pin. Look at how you love each other!"

In her mind's eye, unbidden, Aurie saw acts of great passion that were also terrible acts of cruelty, senseless atrocities that made her soul shrink inside of her. She saw acts of mercy and compassion that were also acts of cowardice, enabling great evil. She saw lives suffocated out of love, and souls abused in the most insidious of ways. She saw men and women trying to love and failing. Around the table, the faces of her parents and uncle looked grey and ill.

The god sighed as the scenes he had called forth disappeared. "Like all emotion-driven behavior, you act out of *love* in the best and worst of ways. And your love often turns to hate, or is accompanied by hate. Look at the wars you wage against yourselves! How can the best thing you're capable of be so easily perverted?" He shook his head. "What you call love is just another emotion that you've elevated to the highest status. You're not capable of real love."

Jacqueline looked stricken, but Howard's face flushed.

"I can't speak for the rest of mankind," he said sharply, "but I promise you my love for this family is very real!"

"So is mine," Jacqueline said, her green eyes flashing in the gloom.

"And mine," Abel added. The flatness of his tone took nothing away from its harsh certainty.

"Is it?" The god fixed his dark gaze on each of them in turn. When his eyes met hers, Aurie felt her soul examined for flaws like a rough gemstone. But that implacable gaze weighed longest on Howard.

"Then make the case for yourself," the god told Howard. "I'm listening."

Howard frowned. "What do you mean?"

The god spread his hands in a magnanimous gesture. "Tell me about real love! How have you loved in your life?"

Howard's frown deepened. "I guess you don't want me to rattle off a list of virtuous deeds, do you? Half of those were done for the wrong reasons, anyway. And you don't want to know who or what I've loved … you want to know *how* I've loved." He hesitated, looking down into his empty mug. "I'll have to start at the beginning."

But then he fell silent, as if unsure where the beginning was. When he finally looked up at the god and began to speak, Howard's voice had lost its usual edge. Aurie listened to her father in surprise. Without any trace of cynicism or irony, it was a simpler and younger voice than the one she knew.

"I was more than my parents bargained for," Howard said. "I know that much. I think they would've happily exchanged me for someone easier to raise, another kid like Abel. I was restless and bored with the things other kids liked. Impatient with everyone who didn't see things my way, or as quickly as I did. And more stubborn than God! If I didn't want to do something, nothing on earth could make me. And if there was something I wanted to do, nothing on earth could stop me.

"None of that changed as I got older. My dreams got bigger, but I was always driven to get what I wanted, no matter the cost. I wanted to see my own children evolve, and I stole Jacqueline's eggs to do it—because her needs weren't as important as mine. You say I behaved like a god, and maybe that's true. I had to bring my grand vision to life, come hell *and* high water."

They were all utterly still, watching him. Howard winced, as if venturing into some unpleasant, untraveled corner of his mind, but he never looked away from the god. "That's what I've always loved … my vision. I've been more faithful to that vision than to anyone. What *wouldn't* I have done for it?"

He paused, and his eyes took on a tortured gleam. "When Aurie fell from that balcony, everything changed. I didn't give a damn about CRISPR-evo anymore; it meant nothing compared to her. And I tell you now that nothing is as important to me as the people in this room. I would die for any one of you … and I would kill for you, too. But is that a sign of love? Or just my possessive nature saying, *No one will take what belongs to me—and I will wage war on anyone who tries.*"

There was a hint of acid mockery in Howard's voice. "Make the case for myself? I'm a selfish, stubborn man who has bulldozed his way through life. This family only exists because of the terrible things I've done, and I would do even worse if I had to. To save all of you. But am *I* worth saving?" Howard's eyes fell, as if the god had finally released his gaze. For a long moment, no one moved or spoke. Even the embryos hung dead-still in their tanks.

Py's eyes had lightened to their usual hazel and his face had lost its carven coldness. Still, his sigh was like a death sentence.

"You are all trapped by stone walls, and no one can love from inside a fortress," he said softly. "If there's a way to demolish those walls, I don't know what it is."

Howard's head jerked up and he looked bitterly at the god. "Then why didn't you let your damned ants finish the job?"

Py didn't reply, but as he got up and left the room, Aurie saw the flash of anguished frustration in his eyes. It was the frustration of a god, but it made him look, just for a moment, entirely human.

IX

In the days following that terrible breakfast, life in the Wake household somehow returned to its old patterns. On a certain level, Aurie understood this. There was comfort in routines; they kept the family from being paralyzed with fear. But the apparent normalcy was disturbing. It made reality seem thin and insubstantial, a delicate shell that might crack at any moment.

She had expected the god to abandon Py's mind and return to his ants, to make his plans for fixing or destroying the human race. But to her surprise, he stayed in his human form and spent all of his time at home. Over the next few weeks, he ate meals with the family, helped clean and cook—without dropping a single egg—and engaged them in every subject imaginable, with the notable exception of humanity's worth. Seeing what they believed to be the real Py emerging, the adults in the family did everything they could to encourage it. None of them ever addressed the god; they spoke only to Py. And the god interacted as Py, so comfortable was he in Py's skin and skull! Aurie should have hated him for that, but instead she found herself soothed by the easy familiarity.

The-god-who-was-Py also spent considerable time with his niece and nephew, who were growing daily and pushing tiny limb buds from their streamlined forms. The Fishes grew accustomed to his silent attention and no longer sought shelter in their mother's aura, but Aurie worried about their proximity to the god. At times she could feel the frustration emanating from him. She couldn't let herself forget that there was a merciless stranger behind those eyes, one who considered humanity a grave danger to his adopted world. He had already judged them and found them wanting, so what was he waiting for?

Fortunately, the Prof now had a clear window into Py's thoughts.

He used to do most of his thinking as his god-self, the captured Professor told Aurie. *But lately he's been using your brother's brain quite a bit, so I know exactly what he's thinking.*

Great! Aurie responded. *So what is he thinking?*

He is contemplating two choices: destroying humans or attempting to fix their essential flaw. If he destroys them, the danger of birthing a terrible god shaped by an evil human soul will be averted. On the other hand, there will be no chance to birth another creator shaped by a healthy human soul. He is well aware that he himself was shaped by your brother, as your pioneer god was shaped by you. He knows that the cost of human extinction might be high, and so his mind is bent on finding another way. At the same time, he distrusts his own motives because of his human attachments. If he didn't identify so completely with Py, would the answer be clear? Is he only delaying the inevitable because he can't bear to destroy his own family? In the Professor's sigh, Aurie heard the empathy and respect he had developed for the god. *Whenever he's alone, he does nothing but think, meditate, and agonize over possible solutions. He will not destroy a species that has gained self-awareness lightly; he knows such life forms are exceedingly rare. He thinks of them as jewels in the void.*

And so the days went by with no decision. As the rest of the family grew more relaxed around Py, Aurie began to chafe from the uncertainty. She felt like a condemned prisoner just waiting for the executioner's sword to fall.

One morning, Py came into the nursery lab while Aurie was replenishing stock solutions.

"I've got something to show you, if you're interested," he said. "But it's a bit of a hike. Can you leave that for later?"

"Sure," she said, surprised at the cryptic invitation. She capped a jar of potassium phosphate and stripped off her gloves. "What is it?"

"You'll see," he said, sounding more like her brother than ever.

As they stepped outside, Aurie asked Py how his ants were

doing.

"Oh, they're fine," he said. "A little bored at the moment, since they were all geared up to take over the world and I put a stop to that."

"How much time do you spend inside them?"

"Inside the ants? None at all."

She glanced at him in surprise. "Don't you miss them?"

He shook his head, smiling a little. "I don't have to be inside the Colony to know what it's doing and thinking and feeling. I *am* the Colony, so my connection to the ants exists no matter where I am. Just like my connection to *this*." He indicated all of himself with a self-deprecating flourish.

"So you never transfer your awareness to the Colony?"

"Are you kidding?" Py said. "Have you forgotten what happened the one time I did that? You know, the murderous rampage I hadn't planned on?"

"I thought that only happened because your human mind was dreaming," she said.

"That's right," he said grimly. "Which is why I stay in this treacherous head and I don't sleep."

She stopped under the shade of the oaks and stared at him. "You mean you haven't slept *at all* since that one time in the Birch Grove?"

"Nope. I can't risk it."

"But you can't keep that up forever!"

He shrugged. "I'll keep it up as long as I have to."

Aurie shook her head as she followed him out of the glade. *Must be nice to be a god ...*

As Py led the way into the woods, Aurie marveled at the extraordinary quiet. She hadn't taken any long treks since the god's awakening; she had wanted to stay close and keep an eye on him, for whatever that was worth. And so the aftermath of the ants' rampage struck her for the first time. As she and Py made their way east, no small life scurried away from their approach; no foxes poked their tawny heads up from the grass in the glades. Whatever life remained had picked the dead clean; they encountered not carcasses, but skeletons, stripped and gleaming like sculptures in ivory. Nature was resilient, but three weeks after the death of so many creatures, the Garden still had the feel of a graveyard. The near silence discouraged speech, as did the cathedral-like quality of the light. No matter what the time of day, twilight reigned within the sphere of the god's presence. The sun overhead could not penetrate the dome of the Garden and lay waste to that perfect light. Neither could the darkness of night dispel it.

"This light is driving Mom and Dad crazy," Aurie murmured, as they mounted the hillside above a small valley. "Three in the morning still feels like five in the afternoon to them."

Py grunted. "The human clock is so light-dependent."

"Well, they don't have a CRISPR calibrator to set them straight," Aurie said. "At least Uncle Abel seems to be fine."

"Sure," Py said. "He hardly sleeps anyway."

Reaching the top of the bluff, they looked down on emerald slopes adorned with amethyst pillars of lupine. Heading downhill, Aurie brushed the dewy blossoms gently with her threads. It seemed as if those perfect flowers would wither under her touch—or cut her like sharp-edged gems—but they were as soft and resilient as they had ever been. As the two of them continued east across the valley, Aurie became aware of an odd sensation, a tendency to stray in another direction. She found herself veering north or south, and had to constantly correct her path to stay with Py. The aversion to heading east grew stronger, becoming an unpleasant, metallic sensation. Minutes later, she came to a halt, trembling with revulsion. What felt like a strong electromagnetic field lay in front of her, sending its dissonant waves deep into her bones.

"Ugh," she said. "What is this? It's awful!"

"It's a boundary, of sorts," Py told her. "I'll explain the point in a minute. It's an effective barrier, but not impassable. It won't hurt you, and you can go through it if you want to."

Aurie steeled herself and took a step closer. Now her teeth were vibrating at a terrible frequency. Her whole body felt wrong, as if she'd stepped into a world completely unsuitable for flesh-

and-blood life forms. With a choked cry, she leapt through the Boundary and landed on the ground a few feet away. The intensity of the *wrongness* had gone down a notch; now there was only that maddening hum in her bones. She continued on, feeling relief and rightness flooding back with every step. Finally, she turned and saw Py still standing where she'd left him.

"Can't *you* go through?" she called in mocking challenge.

He grinned and walked toward her with no apparent discomfort at all.

"That didn't bother you?" she said incredulously.

"Well, it wasn't fun," he admitted. "And now you can see why anything that has a choice will never get close enough to this Boundary to know it's there."

"But anything that doesn't have a choice will get through? Like a fish swimming downstream, or a seed carried on the wind?"

Py nodded. "It's not a perfect barrier, but it's better than nothing. I'm glad the Fishes made it."

She gaped at him. "The *Fishes?*"

"Well, *I* didn't make it," Py said. "And how many other gods do we have kicking around? You do the math."

"But they're just embryos!"

"I'm not sure exactly what they are. Some strange hybrid of god and human? Whatever they are, we both know they aren't just embryos."

"But they've never done anything like this before. They've never done anything at all." Aurie shook her head in puzzlement. "Why would they make such a thing?"

"Because they're afraid of me," Py said simply. "I think they're trying to contain the consequences of my actions. They know I won't do anything intentional until I can overcome these human emotions and act on my will alone. But in the meantime, they're hoping this Boundary will mitigate any unintentional harm I might cause."

"Like another ant raid?" Aurie frowned. "If they had the power to put up a barrier like this, then why did they let your ants attack us in the first place?"

Py laughed. "First you say they're just embryos, and now you expect them to behave like full-grown gods! They're just beginning to learn what they can do ... but I think their abilities will grow faster than you think."

"They didn't even tell me about this!"

"They didn't ask your permission, you mean?"

Aurie snorted. "I don't expect *that,* but some notice would have been nice."

Py chuckled. "Does a baby give notice when it takes its first steps? I don't think they consider what they've done to be anything special. They just behaved instinctively. It didn't occur to them to ask permission or expect praise or reflect on what they've done. They just *acted*—and then moved on to something else."

"How do you know all this?"

"I got them to talk to me a little," he admitted, heading toward a stream that cut through the valley. "They were thinking of their home as McElligot's Pool, connected to the big ocean outside. They wanted something that would keep the fish in the pool from going out, and the fish in the ocean from coming in."

Aurie shook her head in wonder. "It's still hard to believe. They're so young and so small. They're so naïve."

"They are," Py said, "but don't underestimate them because of that. You've tried to educate them early, but it's their ignorance that allows them to be wise."

"Their *ignorance* allows them to be *wise?*"

"I know it sounds counter-intuitive, but if they act in their embryonic state, it will be in advance of their fallible human brains. They will be guided by eternity, by the deepest and surest wellspring of intent. It's a source of wisdom the human mind can never approach." He sighed. "I should've awakened in a life form that had grown close to that wellspring, but nothing on this planet was ready yet."

Aurie found herself bridling at that, just as she had before. "So what kind of advanced life forms are you used to waking up in? Enlightened gases? Wise and sophisticated crystals? Creatures of pure energy or consciousness?"

"Yes," Py said with utter seriousness. "Among many others."

Aurie gave him a deadpan look. "And you gods *never* take shape in anything that isn't ready for you? Anything evil?"

"It does happen," he admitted. "But very rarely. Pioneer gods—like yours—aren't concerned with good and evil at all. To them, the act of creation itself is the greatest good. So they spread the Life Fire to other worlds, plant seeds, awaken gods ... basically create a world of problems for the engineers to fix. And we do, but occasionally one of us works a great evil in concert with an evil host. I once incarnated on a world that was utterly ruined by such a god."

Aurie stared at him. "Did you manage to fix it?"

Py shook his head. "The Gift I gave changed it completely. I couldn't fix that world, so I sent it down a new path. But when I woke up on *this* world, I was faced with an even bigger challenge—to keep such a god from taking shape in the first place." He shot her a bitter glance. "And then I went and made my job even harder."

"By leaving the Colony, you mean?"

"By taking possession of this human mind with its clouding loyalties and emotions."

"Yeah, loyalties and emotions are a real drag," she said dryly. "But at least they keep a check on unbridled power."

"No!" he said vehemently, glaring at her from eyes that had darkened into coals. "They send power in the wrong directions, at the wrong times, for the wrong reasons! Don't you understand? The Colony went on a killing rampage because of the dreams and emotions of this human mind,"—he tapped his skull angrily—"not because I willed it! And just look at me now; I'm angry and frustrated like a human."

"So what makes you any better than one?" she demanded.

"I won't *act* on that anger and frustration. That's the difference!"

"So if you had stayed in the Colony, you would have destroyed us coldly and intentionally instead of doing it unwittingly in the throes of emotion?" She glared back at him. "Doesn't make much difference from where I'm standing."

Py took a deep breath and spoke with forced calm. "It makes all the difference in the world. And I don't know that I would have destroyed anything. I only know that my ability to see clearly and act rightly—for the good of creation—is compromised now."

Yes, she thought with ungodly satisfaction. *Now you're conflicted, forced to grapple with Py's brain. Forced to reckon with his ghost! To know what it means to be human.*

"I don't know why you defend human emotions," Py said. "They aren't reasonable, and they make you miserable when you don't need to be."

His direct gaze made it clear he was referring to her personally. Aurie stiffened at once. "What are you talking about?"

"You and Mom," he said frankly. "There's no reason for you to be upset with her."

Suddenly Aurie was furious, and the fact that her anger was overblown and thus evidence of unreasoning human emotion only made her madder.

"Stay out of my mind," she said through gritted teeth.

"I haven't been in your mind," he said, almost contemptuously. "How you feel when Mom's around is written all over your face ... and your aura."

"You don't understand," Aurie snapped. "She blames me for letting you—I mean *Py*—become the Colony! She's hardly said a word to me since then. She won't even look at me."

"But not because she's angry or disappointed with you. She's upset with herself." Py's eyes softened. "I heard her talking with Dad the other night, so I know what she said that upset you. She was crying, you know. She feels terrible about it. If you could just put aside your irrational feelings for a minute, you'd realize that she only spoke out of fear and desperation."

Aurie said nothing, only looked down at the stream without seeing it.

"For all their talk of love, humans don't know much about it," Py said. "But Mom loves us as well as she knows how ... and she'd do anything to keep us safe. You know that."

"I know," Aurie said in a small voice, still looking down at the water.

"You know, and you still harbor this pointless resentment?" Py shook his head. "Every human on this planet clings to pain like a leech. Nothing but foolishness!"

Well ... he was right. And although she would never admit it, he'd made her feel better about her mom. As Py moved downstream along the banks of the creek, Aurie followed slowly, thinking about irrational emotions and pride and attachment to pain. She had never felt more uncomfortably human than in company with this god who was also, in a strange way, the ghost of her brother. Then another disturbing thought occurred to her.

"Hey," she said, hastening to his side. "Why don't you just kill that troublesome human body you're in? Then you could go back to your emotionless ants and think clearly and rationally again ... for the good of creation."

He looked at her with undisguised shock. "You want me to do that?"

"Of course not! But it seems like an obvious solution to your problem. So why haven't you done it?"

He sighed. "It *is* an obvious solution, isn't it? Simply relinquish possession of this mind. I almost did it at the beginning, when I first realized I was hamstrung this way. But there are things I can only learn from inside a human mind ... and it feels right to be part of this family. To be patient and wait. I've learned quite a bit, but I still think I'm missing something."

In his face she saw the deep-seated frustration that came and went, but no sign of the bitter anger that had been there earlier. And there was a trace of something else—was it humility? Whatever it was, it gave her courage to speak more freely as they wandered alongside the creek. The tension between them eased, and they talked as equal, imperfect beings instead of god and human. At last, Py looked up at the sun, which had fallen from its zenith. Aurie realized that they'd been moving in a dome of Garden twilight, even outside the Boundary. And the world around them was still glorious.

He creates the Garden wherever he goes, she thought, glancing at Py in awe. *And he's not even aware of it.*

"Guess we'd better head back," Py said. "I promised Uncle Abel I'd make the stuffing for those rabbits."

'Those rabbits' were the last animals Aurie had caught before Py had turned these woods into a sanctuary—and then a cemetery. She could have hunted outside the Garden, beyond the limits of the god's light, but hunting no longer held any appeal for her.

"What are we going to do when we run out of meat?" she wondered.

"Well, we could go to the market in town, like normal people," Py suggested.

"Mom and Uncle Abel aren't going to like driving through *that.*" Aurie nodded towards the invisible Boundary.

"It won't be so bad in a car going thirty miles an hour. If only our human legs could run that fast."

"Speak for yourself," Aurie said, flexing her calves.

He grinned at her. "Race you through it?" Without waiting for an answer, he took off.

Aurie sprang after him at once. When they were younger, Py had always run circles around her, but Aurie's god had greatly enhanced her speed and strength. Now she pushed herself to her limits, exulting in the way her feet flew over the grass, in the feeling that she could launch herself into the sky on invisible wings. Racing towards the Boundary felt like running headlong into a stone wall, but she staunchly ignored her body's command to change direction. Bones thrumming, teeth singing, brain screaming, Aurie sprinted through the Boundary, not stopping or slowing until she reached the slope at the far end of the valley. Giddy with adrenaline, she collapsed on the ground, laughing.

"I just outran a god," she crowed to Py when he fell down beside her.

"No fair," he panted. "You're CRISPR-enhanced!"

"So what? You could turn yourself into a gazelle if you really wanted to outrun me. Why didn't you?"

"I can't work magic, remember?"

"Who said anything about magic? We both know a lot can be done just by tinkering with materials and mechanisms."

"And we both know there are limits to that." Py was still breathing hard.

"But if you decided to destroy the human species—?"

"I'd have to do it in a natural way," he said. "Not by waving a magic wand."

Aurie propped herself up on an elbow to look at him. "You said you only have one chance to enact a major change on this world. Why is that?"

Py lay with his eyes closed as the rhythms of his chest slowed. "Because a world-changing act requires more than my ability to tinker. It requires *all* of me."

"You mean ... it uses you up? It *kills* you?" Aurie was shocked and slightly horrified. Weren't gods immortal?

"Just this incarnation," he said easily. "My soul will move on to another."

Aurie rolled onto her back again and gazed at the sky above the dome of twilight, chastened by the thought of the god's death. Perhaps because—in spite of her best efforts—she still thought of him as Py. He was the closest thing to her brother, and if he died—

"Okay, no more breaks," Py said briskly. "Those rabbits aren't going to stuff themselves." He grunted as he sat up. "You're lucky I'm not one of those sore-loser Greek gods, or I'd turn you into a slug right now."

Aurie laughed. She put aside thoughts of death and sprang lightly to her feet. "Race you home? In the *extremely* unlikely event that I lose, I'll make the stuffing for you."

Py groaned in protest. But a moment later, he got up to continue their race up the hill.

Aurie held herself to a pace just slightly faster than what her brother could manage. When they arrived home, Py was flushed and winded. Abel, who was patting down three brined rabbits, looked at them in astonishment.

"If the two of you are running from something," he said, "then Armageddon must be here. Is there time for a last meal?"

"We didn't want to be late helping with dinner," Aurie said.

"Looks like we're just in time," wheezed Py, staggering to the sink and guzzling water from the faucet.

Shaking his head, Abel supplied them with ingredients. In short order, the rabbits were stuffed with chestnuts and potatoes, surrounded with shallots and garlic and fresh thyme, and set to bake in covered pots.

"Well, that's the last of the rabbits," Abel said as he set a timer. "There's still a few venison steaks and a brace of trout in the freezer, but I think it's time to stock up on meat. If hunting season is officially over?" He gave Aurie a questioning look, to which she nodded.

Abel sighed. "We've sure been spoiled! Farm-raised animals are going to be bland as porridge after all this game."

"There's a wholesale butcher in Bethel," Jacqueline said, coming in from the hall. "I'm about to head into town anyway; I'll pick up some meat while I'm there."

"I'll come with you," Aurie said, surprising herself as much as her mother.

"Great!" Jacqueline said. "I just need to check some stocks in the lab and the garage first. Leave in about twenty minutes?"

Aurie nodded and went to wash her hands at the kitchen sink.

"You okay doing all these dishes?" she asked Py, who was already scrubbing away. "I'd better warn Mom about the Boundary, so she's not caught off-guard."

"I'll try to manage," he said, smiling at her. "Have fun with Mom."

Aurie returned his smile, but as she followed Jacqueline to the lab, it occurred to her that she had never seen her brother look so tired ... even when he was nothing but a mere mortal.

X

It was fortunate, the god thought, that his soul retained such clear memories of its past lives. He could even feel the ghost imprint of each form he had taken; they whispered within him in voices sad or joyful. He knew he had helped many worlds, and also made many mistakes. Being incarnate was truly a double-edged sword—it allowed him to see some things more clearly, and others far less.

In each incarnation, he could only experience the full clarity of eternity three times. The first was upon awakening, when he used deepsight to understand his new world. The second was upon approaching the forge of creation to offer his Gift. Once he gained the necessary knowledge in his host form, a path to the forge would manifest before him, and he would use deepsight to see into the future of his world, what would befall it if he did nothing. Often, it was a future he had predicted, but there had been surprises that changed his intended course of action. The third time was upon bestowing his Gift, in the moment of his own death. Back in the embrace of eternity, the god used deepsight to see the altered future of his world. His Gift was like a new thread appearing in a complex tapestry of cause-and-effect that stretched far into the future of a world he had changed for better or worse.

He had told his human family, *I can't afford to make a mistake,* but learning from mistakes—one world at a time—was how a god perfected his craft. Lately, he had been brooding over those mistakes, errors of judgement in past lives. Many of them, it seemed, had been caused by a blindness to something seemingly small and unimportant. And he couldn't shake the nagging sense that something similar was happening here.

In the weeks following his Colony's rampage, the god had avoided sleep completely, afraid of what his dreams might unleash. During those sleepless nights, he had examined the dreams of his family and found a goulash of images and events with no cohesion. How humans rested themselves by staging a senseless play in the theater of their minds was a mystery to him, but he would have happily joined them ... if only his dreams weren't tied to the emotions that had once racked this boy's mind. The dreaming human brain was a lunatic at the mercy of raw emotions—and in the mind of one with the capacity to reshape the world, any dream was a dangerous one.

After finishing up the dishes, the god-who-was-Py made his way to the library. Although never the prolific reader that his sister was, Py had always liked the weight of a real book in his hands, and the woodsy smell of its pages. Thus, as an inheritance from the mind he occupied, the god found that he enjoyed the physical act of reading. This tactile pleasure was entirely human, but he saw no reason to resist it. Selecting the first volume that caught his eye—a heavy one full of Greek myths—he sat down in the armchair next to the open window. Heliotrope was starting to bloom in the garden, and its soporific scent drifted in on the afternoon breeze. Py opened the book to the story of Theseus in the Cretan Labyrinth. It was his favorite Greek myth, not because of the story, which featured the predictable slaying of a deadly monster by a prince, but because of its setting, a dark and unsolvable labyrinth. Straining to keep his eyes open, Py began to read.

Although aware of his physical exhaustion, the god paid it no mind. Being tired was simply the cost of staying awake, and staying awake was necessary. When he thought of his body at all, he thought of it as a shell sustained by his own essence, which never dimmed or faltered. Thus, it was a great surprise to him when, halfway through the story, without any warning at all, his body fell instantly and deeply asleep.

In the startling loss of his conscious awareness was a momentary thrill of freedom. With his human senses shut off, the god could almost believe himself adrift in the eternity of space. But the cage of his mind still hung in a dark net around him, and soon dream-fish would come swarming out of that net in all the violent colors of fear and desire.

The god tried to wake himself up, but his stubborn, stupid, feeble body refused to cooperate. Prod and tinker as he might, his neurons stayed locked in sleep—and these networks, precious repositories of self, could not simply be destroyed and remade. Having failed to awaken, the god wrestled with his pride—yet another human weakness!—and finally called on the Professor for help.

I've been trying, the distressed CRISPR machine protested. *But your cells are resistant to everything I do.*

This shouldn't be happening, the god thought. He had given this failing body a new lease on life; how hard could it be to simply stay awake?

The Professor sighed. *The organisms on this world require sleep. Even the smallest of worms needs its rest. You have already stayed awake longer than any human in history, and I've had all I can do just to keep you from hallucinating on your feet. Then you go for a hike and decide to race your sister home?* The Professor threw up his arms in frustration. *There are limits to what I can do to counter such abuse!*

Can you put me into deep sleep, with no dreaming?

The Professor shook his head. *No more than I can wake you up.*

Then do what you did before, the god said, *and give me a safe dream.*

A moment later, the god-who-was-Py found himself running and stumbling through the woods, following his sister's trail. Fear of the alien consciousness overtaking her pushed him to the limits of his endurance. He was hungry, thirsty, sore from a dozen cuts and bruises, and terribly afraid—but underneath everything, his love for Aurie burned brighter than the sun sinking behind the hills. It drove him on, though he despaired of ever catching her.

XI

Sitting in the passenger seat of her uncle's Chevy felt strange to Aurie, who hadn't used any mode of transportation other than her own legs for quite awhile. The ancient car had taken some time to start, but it seemed to be running fine now. As they turned from the old logging road onto the access road, Aurie glanced at her mother behind the wheel and felt an instant of strong *déjà vu*. It might have been the day they first met, when Jacqueline had agreed to help Aurie freeze her eggs and they had driven off before anyone could stop them. In this same rusty car, traveling the same overgrown road through these woods. Only the woods themselves—now graced by the god's twilight—were different.

Jacqueline caught Aurie's eye and smiled before turning her attention back to the road. The look in her mother's eyes made Aurie's chest tighten. It was so simple and undeniable, the love in those eyes. It had been there from the beginning, on the day they first met, and it was still there, unchanged, even though their relationship was different now. For the first time, it occurred to Aurie that she and her mother had only been close in those early days, when the need to save her eggs had consumed both of them. Once the high-pressure intensity of their lives had abated, the two of them had drifted apart.

Why? Aurie wondered. *Which one of us changed?*

From his integral place inside her, the Doctor laughed. Well, okay, maybe it was a stupid question—but Aurie had no idea why she herself might have changed. After all, nothing was happening ... not to her.

You lost your god, and you've never gotten over it, the Doctor said.

Well, that was true ... but it hadn't affected her relationship with her dad or her brother.

You have a longer history with them, the Doctor reminded her. *Your mother never had the chance to get to know you before you lost that vital part of yourself.*

Aurie looked surreptitiously at Jacqueline, taking in her beauty and age in one undivided instant. The hair swept into a loose knot was more silver than gold at the temples, and fine lines marked the corners of her eyes and mouth. Even the long-fingered hands on the wheel—hands that could still perform microinjections and dissections with keen precision—were no longer young. This woman should have had children who were normal adults by now, not nine-year-olds whose genetic engineering had precipitated one crisis after the next. In a moment of sudden empathy, Aurie reached out and took her mother's free hand.

Jacqueline looked at her in surprise, then squeezed Aurie's hand hard. "I'm so sorry, Aurie."

"For what?" Aurie asked.

"For what I said when Py jumped into those ants ... when he *became* those ants. I was just so upset! Afterwards, I realized what a terrible thing I'd done, what an unfair burden I had put on you."

Jacqueline didn't speak for a moment, but her eyes glistened. "I know how much you love him ... and if there was anything you could have done, you would have done it."

"I'm sorry I couldn't save him." Aurie's voice trembled and broke a little. "I really couldn't!"

"I know," Jacqueline said. "After I thought about it ... once I realized what he was facing, I knew you couldn't change his mind. No more than anyone could have changed yours when you were being pulled by the Pattern. I *saw* that Pattern. I should have understood."

Aurie swallowed hard and looked at her mother in relief. She had underestimated Jacqueline.

"You didn't know what those mushrooms would do," Jacqueline went on, still holding Aurie's hand firmly in her own. "But you were compelled to hunt them down. You couldn't have stopped yourself ... and I don't think he could've stopped himself from doing what he did."

"He had a choice," Aurie said. "It was a lot like the choice I had when I jumped off that balcony—to fall and stay human, or to fly and become something new. I chose to fall … and Py chose to fly." Her voice trembled, but the pressure of her mother's hand was warm and comforting.

"Do you ever regret it?" Jacqueline asked. Aurie opened her mouth to deliver her long-held answer, and then closed it again. Her mother deserved the truth, and having already told Py—or Py's god—somehow made it easier.

"On the balcony, I didn't have much time," Aurie said, "but I understood the choice. I knew that going with the god and becoming part of the Pattern meant giving up myself, but somehow that was okay." She tried to conjure up the feeling she could never recapture in her waking life, that sense of blissful freedom and joy in creation. "I would have been *more* than myself, not less. But do I regret giving that up?" She shook her head. "Regret means wishing you'd chosen differently. I don't wish that. I just wish it were easier to live with the choice I made."

Her mother gave her a sympathetic glance, then silently turned her attention back to the road.

"I dream about it all the time," Aurie murmured. "Almost every morning, I wake up thinking I've been flying through space."

Jacqueline sighed as they crossed a narrow deer path. "No wonder you've been so depressed. My poor girl!"

"I haven't been *depressed,*" Aurie protested. "Just a little down sometimes."

"Since we moved here, you've been like someone grieving over a death or a great loss."

Aurie was shocked. "Is that what everyone thinks?"

Jacqueline shook her head. "That's what *I* think. Your dad thinks taking care of the Fishes can be overwhelming and you just need some time to yourself. Which is true, but it's not the real reason you run off." She gave Aurie a keen glance. "I've seen the look in your eyes when you come back. It's the look of someone who's been torn out of a dream, someone who's just fallen back to earth."

"You saw that?"

"Of course I did," Jacqueline said with some asperity. "You're my daughter! I just wish I had a clue how to be a mother." In the god's perfect twilight, she looked sad and frustrated. "I should have talked with you about all this long before now ... but I didn't think you wanted to talk."

"I didn't," Aurie admitted. "It's too hard to explain—and I thought it would get easier to deal with, but it hasn't."

"No," Jacqueline said thoughtfully. She had slowed down until they were barely ambling along, and now she pulled off, letting the car idle along the side of the road. "That business about time healing all wounds is nonsense! Time can dull the pain of some wounds, but it causes others to fester. And it doesn't do a damn thing to solve problems."

"Why are we stopping?" Aurie asked, even though she had a pretty good idea why. She had warned her mother about the Boundary, and she could sense it now. It was an electric hum at the edge of her awareness, maybe half a mile away.

Jacqueline looked momentarily bewildered, then she chuckled a little. "It's that Boundary you were telling me about, isn't it? I'd almost forgotten."

"It's better if you go through fast," Aurie advised. "It'll feel like you're heading for a wall, but just ignore that."

"Drive fast and ignore the feeling that we're about to crash into a wall," her mother muttered.

"Trust your eyes," Aurie said. "There's no real obstacle, I promise!"

Shaking her head, Jacqueline pulled back onto the road and accelerated quickly, making the old car groan. As they sped forward, Aurie felt that same sense of impending collision. Her mother drove as if she were piloting an army tank straight into enemy lines, gripping the steering wheel tightly in both hands. Aurie wondered if this was a bad mistake, if her mother would lose her nerve at the last moment, yank the wheel, and crash them into the trees. But just as the feeling of *wrongness* grew too intense, they were through.

"God, that was awful!" Jacqueline shot a disbelieving glance at the empty road behind them. "And we have to do it again on the way back? Ugh!"

"It's even worse on foot," Aurie told her.

"I'll take your word for it. And Py says the Little Fishes made that thing? To keep him from unintentionally wreaking havoc in the world?"

"It sounds crazy, I know."

Jacqueline laughed. "After the things I've seen, what's crazy is that anything surprises me at all."

As they continued on, Aurie became aware of a distinct change in the air. The forest was no longer suffused in crystalline light, but bathed in the tired, flat radiance of mid-afternoon. The transition had been too gradual to notice, but now the woods around them were the old woods, dusty and faded under harsh shafts of sunlight. When they reached the main highway and saw a car up ahead, Aurie wondered what the folks in town would have thought if Py had come along on this excursion, bringing his enchanted twilight with him.

"It's a relief to see the real world again," Jacqueline murmured as they took the road to Bethel. "And sort of deflating at the same time. All this looks so rough and unfinished, doesn't it? Like God's first stab at creation."

In town, they passed a Vitablitz stand selling every artificial vitamin from A to K (plus Q and V, whatever those were) and two NutraShacks, where you could get artificial protein made to taste like anything from an abalone to a zebra steak. They drove past a strip mall containing a derelict salon, an Energee Station, and a drive-thru dispensary, then Jacqueline parked in an empty lot close to the butcher shop. Never eager to mingle with strangers, Aurie stayed in the car. After a few minutes of waiting, though, she decided to get some fresh air.

As soon as she opened the door, a wave of ants swelled around her feet, seeming to come from the undercarriage of the car. There was no mistaking them for anything ordinary—even in the flat daylight, they gleamed with their own internal fire. Aurie froze in her seat as the insects gathered. Wave after wave entered, running one atop the last until they had formed a bristling mass. There was no way to battle so many, but she sensed no hostility from them. For the span of a few heartbeats, the horde stood quivering before her. Then it dissolved with fluid speed as the ants all exited the car. They crossed the asphalt like a glittering, amorphous shadow.

You had a few hitchhikers along for the ride, said the Professor accusingly, as the ants disappeared into a tangle of brush behind the buildings. *And they're no longer in McElligot's Pool, if you know what I mean.*

With a sinking heart, Aurie realized exactly what he meant. *Why didn't you tell me earlier? Before we reached the Boundary!*

It's me he's upset with. The Doctor sounded both apologetic and resigned. *I've been keeping the Professor company in your stem cell ... and he told me that your brother has fallen asleep and can't be woken up. Quite reasonably, he gave Py what he considered a safe dream, the old memory of chasing you through the woods. That's why those ants stowed away under the car—they were following you. Chasing you through the woods, as it were. Acting on the emotions and motivations of Py's dream.*

That's exactly what he's been trying to prevent, Aurie snapped. *But how did those ants get to the car so fast? They couldn't have come from the Birch Grove!*

They didn't, the Professor told her. *They came from nests near the house—part of the supercolony that extends for miles in all directions. When I realized they were rushing to the car— which your mother was having trouble starting!—I made the great mistake of informing your good Doctor, who then proceeded to gag me like a hooligan. Now ask him why he thinks letting those ants escape was a good idea.*

The Doctor didn't explain right away, but Aurie could sense his feelings of guilt and uncertainty. *Call it instinct,* he said at last. *Or intuition. But I can feel the pressure in the Garden building.*

Aurie didn't ask what he meant by *pressure;* she knew. She had felt the tension of the god's unrelieved creative drive growing by the day. She gazed at the sparse woods across the street, where the giant contingent of ants had gone. *Why did they all stop and stare at me like that—and then run off?*

They were confused, the Professor said. *Actually finding you was beyond the scope of the dream.*

Well, this is just great, thought Aurie. The god was still at the mercy of Py's human emotions ... and now he had a hand in the outside world. Why would the Doctor have allowed such a thing?

The god can't contain himself forever, the Doctor said. *His need to shape the world is growing stronger, but he is suppressing it in an attempt to control his uncontrollable emotions. He is a powder keg about to burst. Correct me if I'm wrong, Professor.*

The Professor only heaved a disgruntled sigh.

So how does letting those ants out of the Garden help? Aurie demanded.

The ants that followed you are special, said the Doctor. *Unless I miss my guess, they were part of the group who went rampaging through the woods. Probably the ones who led that destructive rampage. Am I right, Professor?*

The Professor grudgingly conceded that he was.

I thought all of the ants went on that rampage, Aurie said.

No, said the Professor. *Not the queens and the males, not the very young ants and their nurses. Not even all the workers.*

So in every nest of the supercolony, said the Doctor, *some of the ants continued to behave like ants, protecting the nest itself. But all the others are vehicles for the god's creative energy. And the ants that followed you are probably the most receptive vehicles. Whatever he ends up doing ... I think it will be done through them.*

The Professor snorted. *And it's better to have this catastrophic event far from home?*

Yes, said the Doctor emphatically. *If those ants can be led somewhere safe, away from any towns. And so, my dreary friend, this is your chance to do what you do best.*

If you mean behave responsibly— began the Professor.

That's exactly what I mean, the Doctor said. *Dampen the danger. Curb the consequences. Infuse insanity with reason!*

Easier said than done, growled the Professor. *Considering those ants are still under the influence of Py's dream.*

Then give him another dream, said the Doctor. *Find one that leads those ants somewhere remote!*

The Professor grunted in agreement. He said nothing more, and Aurie imagined a billion copies of him bustling through all the cells of Py's sleeping brain, searching for the right dream.

She chuckled, turning her attention to the Doctor. *Another one of your elegant operations?*

It's only elegant if it works, he said. *Time will tell.*

You've turned into a bit of a rogue, haven't you? I never imagined you like this when I was little. How the Doctor could be a real personality was still a mystery to Aurie. He had originally been her imaginary playmate, and then an agent of the god asleep in her genome. Now that god was long gone, and yet the Doctor was himself ... as independent and unpredictable as any human.

And you still wouldn't imagine me like this now that you're a wise and worldly nine, said the Doctor. *But everything grows in unexpected ways. When your father first created us, the Professor and I were identical twins.*

While she waited for her mother, Aurie pondered the strangeness of Py's dreams influencing reality.

Don't real events normally create illusions in dreams? she said to the Doctor. *If you're asleep and you hear real thunder, you create a firecracker or a gunshot in your dream. But in Py's dreams, it's the opposite—the illusion is creating the reality.*

That's right, said the Doctor. *If he dreams of destruction as the stepping-stone to creation, God help anything in the path of his Colony. If he dreams that he is desperately chasing you and won't stop until he catches you, his ants will follow you to the ends of the earth.*

So no dream is really a safe one, Aurie thought.

Not when a god is involved, the Doctor agreed.

The escaped ants ran through scrub brush behind the strip mall, then crossed an alley and disappeared into a stand of birch and alder. From there, they found their way into deeper woods. The dream that had influenced them was over, but another dream was just beginning. They could feel the pull of it, drawing them into cooler, darker places.

The contingent roamed until it found a rocky hollow at the base of a hill. The cave was dry and empty, its stone floor seamed with cracks. The ants followed a series of shafts leading underground. Through narrow crevices they ran, stirring ancient dust. They passed through silent corridors where only the faded trails of worms and springtails whispered their old messages. Deeper and deeper they went, navigating the maze of Py's childhood dreams.

As the boy himself once had, they were searching ... not for a way out, but for a way in.

Part Four

The Labyrinth

The way leads neither east nor west,
but in.

- Rumi, "With You Here Between"

I

As soon as the Professor conjured his 'safe dream' in Py's unconscious mind, the god was instantly caught up in it. As before, he was borne along on the current of an old memory, chasing Aurie through the woods. But before long, the dream changed. The trees around him melded into stone walls, their canopies morphing into the ceiling of a vast tunnel.

The god checked himself and was startled to realize that he had actually stopped moving. He was no longer a passive participant in this new dream; he could move forward—or not—as he liked. This was not an ordinary human dream, then, but the dream of one of his own kind.

And there was something else … a faint sensation of heat that drew him, a song that called to him from far down the tunnel. He knew the fire that engendered that warmth and that music; it had marked the end of every incarnation on each of his adopted worlds. This was a path to the forge of creation! Which meant that it was time to choose his Gift. But as the god hastened down the tunnel, he soon realized that no straight path lay before him, only a convoluted labyrinth. The dark maze was familiar, and he recognized it from Py's memories. No human dream, indeed, but the dream of Py's sleeping god. It had drifted into the boy's subconscious mind while he was only an infant, becoming the most memorable and recurrent of all his dreams.

In that dream, Py had searched for the heart of the labyrinth without ever reaching it.

Glancing up, the god found a warning engraved on the ceiling arch above a dead-end gallery. *Only the free walk a straight path.* He looked down at himself and saw his own soul flaming with its true light—and another thing, a pale and pitiful thing that he recognized as the aura of his human host. The shell of Py's departed

261

soul. That empty shell, swarming with Py's memories and emotions, was connected to him by four thin cords.

The god understood, then. He had to be free of his tethers before he could approach the source of the Life Fire. But if this was a god's dream, then he could *act* in this dream ... and the laws that governed physical reality might not apply here. In the physical world, Py's emotional attachments were inextricably linked to the rest of his brain, uncuttable, but *here* they were simply four cords! Could he sever those cords in this god's dream? Sever them, and find his way to the forge of creation?

But I have no hands in this place, the god thought, looking down in frustration at his flaming self. Although he could conjure any tool imaginable, he lacked the ability to wield one.

And then an idea occurred to him.

II

Whenever he was alone in the lab, Howard talked to the Fishes. The fact that they didn't hold up their end of the conversation was no deterrent; in fact, he found it surprisingly helpful. Who could ever hear themselves in the buzz and hubbub of real conversations? With the Fishes, it was startling to actually *hear* his own thoughts. Their receptive silence echoed his words and feelings back to him, forcing him to reflect. When Py chose to become an ant colony instead of returning to his human body, Howard had turned to the Fishes the way another man might have turned to a psychiatrist or a priest. Too desperate to feel foolish, he had unburdened his soul to them. And now that a god was awake and inhabiting Py's mind, Howard found the company of his tiny grandchildren undeniably comforting. Although they never communicated with anyone but Aurie, he had the distinct impression that they were listening to him, too. And who could say that was implausible? They were godlings, after all.

So while Jacqueline and Aurie were out, Howard talked to his grandkids as he worked. He found himself thinking out loud about gods ... and wondering how the same template could give rise to different ones. Of course, a single genetic program gave rise to different humans, but that program lay encoded by fifty thousand genes on twenty-three pairs of chromosomes. By contrast, the god template was small indeed, just a scattering of strands in that giant web, with a small central hub. According to Aurie, it was this hub that could be activated, awakening one of the gods in the Pattern. Py's god had said that the nature of an awakened god was influenced by the soul of its host, which would explain why the gods that had awoken in Howard's children were so different from each other. But Aurie thought it was more complicated than that.

"According to the Doctor and the Professor, the reverse is

also true," she had told Howard. "They think a sleeping god influences its host by dreaming. Remember when I was always dreaming about flying into the sun? That was a dream of my sleeping god that drifted into my subconscious mind. I don't know if it was the only dream, or just the one I latched onto most strongly. And did I choose that dream, or did the dream shape who I am?" She had paused, looking at him curiously. "Have you ever wondered what sort of god is asleep inside of *you?* The Doctor said once that you were a powerful dreamer because you had dreamed up the blueprint for him. Maybe your own god gave you that vision of CRISPR evolution ... maybe it wanted all of this to happen."

The idea had been both fascinating and deeply troubling. Howard brooded on it now as he set up his culture flasks. He thought of Py's god saying that a terrible god might awaken one day in an evil man ... and felt a resurgence of his old guilt, flowing like acid through familiar channels. To think that he had enabled this!

When Py's god had asked him, *How have you loved?* Howard had looked into the mirror of his son's eyes and seen his own soul reflected back at him. Since then, he had never lost sight of that disturbing vista.

"What kind of a man am I?" he muttered to the Fishes. He had certainly never thought of himself as evil, but then, he had never thought much about the condition of his soul at all. Could a person be evil, not through malice, but through single-minded dedication to his own vision? Through being too blind or short-sighted to see the ultimate ends of his tinkering?

"But nothing ever ends," Howard murmured. "He said that too, and he was right." The god's words echoed in his head: *Life is a continuation, and if you create misery and suffering through your efforts, then what have you achieved?* Thus far, Howard Wake had created a considerable amount of misery and suffering for his own family; the jury was still out on whether all of mankind would be included in that tally.

Except there's no jury, Howard thought grimly. *Just one judge ... and executioner.*

And yet, as the days had gone on, he had grown increasingly hopeful. Which was undoubtedly foolish, but he couldn't help it. Seeing Py—the *real* Py—looking out of the boy's hazel eyes had sparked a hope that refused to die.

"That first morning, the god was in total control," Howard reminded the Fishes as he sparked a Bunsen burner. He dipped his inoculation loop in ethanol and sterilized it in the flame, then set it to cool. "Threatening to bring Judgement Day down on all of us! But Py was there, too. And now it's only Py all the time, with just a hint of the Grim Reaper now and then."

Yes, Py was sounding almost entirely like himself and doing a hundred little things the way only Py did them. It was a tremendous relief to all of them. And with any luck, Py would keep the god from doing something dire, help him find some gentler way of tinkering with the world. And with even more luck, the god would finally fly away, and Py would be only himself again. Changed by the experience, no doubt, but only himself, the way Aurie was only herself.

Howard glanced over at the tanks, wondering briefly how his grandkids would evolve, and what it would mean for them to be themselves.

"I suppose you'll have personalities," Howard allowed, as he inoculated his cultures. "And you'll be talking back to your elders. Probably demanding that I explain why mankind shouldn't be eradicated so we can start over and put all the fish in charge."

Setting his flasks in the shaking incubator, he went over to Casa del Utero to see if the Fishes were awake. They seemed to do an awful lot of sleeping lately, but according to Aurie, the embryos slept very little and were actually projecting their souls elsewhere.

"Hitching a ride into town with your mom?" Howard guessed. "Or hanging out with your apocalyptic uncle?"

At the mention of their uncle, both Fishes twitched in their tanks. Howard's breath fogged the glass as he peered closer, trying to get a good look at them. "Hanging out with Uncle Py, huh? What's he up to?"

Before the little embryos could answer—assuming they were

so inclined—the door to the lab opened, letting in a savory aroma from down the hall.

"Those rabbits got done a little early," Abel announced. "But Jacqueline and Aurie aren't back yet, and your son's asleep in the library. I'm just keeping everything warm in the meantime."

"Py's *asleep?*" Howard couldn't remember the last time either of his kids had taken a nap during the day.

Abel nodded. "He's been looking pretty tired lately, don't you think? God or no god? He and Aurie skipped lunch to run through the woods, then they got back and did all the prep work for dinner, and Py did all the washing up. If we needed any better proof that there's a human boy in there ... " With a wry smile, Abel jerked his head in the direction of the library before returning to the kitchen.

Howard turned back to his grandchildren. Were they following Py through his dreams, or had that synchronized twitch meant nothing at all? Suddenly—in the midst of the warm, brightly lit lab—he had the clear impression of running through cold, arid darkness on thousands of little feet. He blinked in surprise, and the bizarre sensation faded.

Howard waited, but nothing followed on the heels of that impression. With a last searching glance at the Fishes, Howard left the lab. He went to check on Py in the library, and found him asleep in the armchair by the window.

Howard took the open book from the boy's lap and glanced at the pages. *Theseus and the Minotaur?*

"It's getting darker out there," Abel called from the kitchen. "For the first time since ... " His voice trailed off and Howard turned to look through the open window. The constant twilight of the last few weeks had certainly deepened, leaching color from the shadowless world. As he watched, darkness began to fall—but not in the usual way. Instead of the light diminishing, blackness crept into the air like ink seeping through water.

Heart skittering, Howard put the book down and looked closely at his sleeping son. The angles of Py's face seemed harder than before, and the healthy tan of his skin had drained away. He might have been a carving in marble or alabaster, except for the eyes moving restlessly beneath their lids.

"Py," Howard said sharply, giving his son's shoulder a brisk shake. "Wake up, dammit! Come on, wake up!" But no amount of exhortation or shaking or even the mouthwatering odors coming from the kitchen had any effect on the sleeping boy.

A gust of chilly air made Howard turn. Abel had opened the French doors and was craning his neck outside, although he seemed afraid to step over the threshold. Howard joined him, and together they watched inky fibrils form and coalesce in thin air. Those dark fissures were filling the dome of twilight that Aurie called the Garden. In a weird juxtaposition, late afternoon sunlight still lit the skies above the dome.

Abel yelped, jolting Howard away from the specter overhead. His brother was hurriedly shutting the French doors.

"What happened?" Howard asked, peering through the open window.

"Those dark things are coming after us," Abel hissed. "Close all the windows, for God's sake!"

Together, they battened down all the hatches in the house, then rejoined each other in the kitchen. Abel turned on the overhead lamps and the one by the door. In the sudden illumination, black tendrils materialized outside, probing the window panes as if seeking entrance.

"Jacqueline and Aurie are out there," Howard said hoarsely. "And I can't wake him up! That damned god of his must be dreaming again."

Abel looked pained. "Hopefully the girls are still in town ... assuming it isn't like this everywhere."

"I think it's just our enchanted neck of the woods," Howard said, thinking of that faintly sunlit sky above the darkening dome of the Garden. "But we'd better warn them." He looked around. "Where's my damned Spider when I need it?"

"Mine's right here," Abel said. "I'll call them right now."

Abel tried to reach Jacqueline and then Aurie, but all they heard was silence.

"Goddamn calls aren't going through," Howard muttered.

"I'm guessing we've got no satellite, no Web, nothing. Can you connect to anything at all?"

"I'll try upstairs," Abel said, hurrying into the hall.

Howard turned toward the library, intending to smack Py awake from whatever god-cursed dream he was having, but his eyes were drawn again to the kitchen windows, where a darkness that bore no resemblance to night now pressed against the glass. Was he just imagining it, or were faint wisps of blackness coming inside ... seeping through the cracks between each window and its frame?

Feeling as if he'd been plunged into a terribly realistic nightmare, Howard crept toward the front door. In the glow of the halo lamp, he could clearly see thin creepers of darkness coming in through cracks in the doorframe. They looked like the many hyphae of a colossal fungus. When they touched one another, the hyphae grew together, thickening into serpentine tendrils. With horrified fascination, Howard watched them quest through the air like something alive. As if they were searching for something ... or someone.

As soon as the thought occurred to him, those dark feelers swerved toward him with snakelike speed. He stumbled backwards, but they were already wrapped around him. Like the eddies of a chill breeze, they pulled him toward the door.

Howard wasn't aware of opening the door, but somehow he was standing outside. The coldness filled his lungs and sank into his bones. Something in the dark whispered to him, compelling him to move forward. And part of him understood that there was no escaping it. Howard took a few blind steps onto the patio, then turned around. He could see nothing at all, no light in the skies above, no light from the house. If there even *was* a house. He might have stepped into another realm of existence.

Which way should he go?

All ways lead in, whispered the dark, pulling him with icy fingers.

Shivering and disoriented, Howard moved forward cautiously, but there were no rocks or roots to trip him. What had happened to the glade with its tall grasses? And where was the forest with its rough carpet of leaves and needles? The ground was hard and smooth beneath his feet, and the air oddly still. After a time, he heard the soft, dry rasp of many small feet scurrying ahead of him. With nothing else to guide him, Howard followed the scurrying sounds deeper into the dark.

III

When Jacqueline returned to the car, Aurie said nothing about the escaped ants. There was no point in worrying her mother when there was nothing either of them could do. Only the Professor could influence Py's dreams, and he was undoubtedly doing his best. Aurie tried to relax as they drove from the butcher shop to The Kitchen Sink on Main Street. At the all-hours vendoporium, Jacqueline bought dish soap, coffee beans, vacuum sealing film, stainless steel screws, fertilizer, and a dozen other things. Aurie loaded everything from the dispenser into the car while her mother paid with a card belonging to Alita Thurston (unofficial wife of one Robert P. Hartwell). Then, instead of heading straight home, Jacqueline turned the car down Grover Hill Road and pulled into the drive-through of the most decrepit Golden Oldies Aurie had ever seen.

"The folks in the butcher shop said this is the only one left on the Eastern seaboard," Jacqueline said, grinning at Aurie. "Might be our last chance to get the best chocolate shake in the universe. What size do you want?"

"Large," Aurie said promptly. "But how do you know these are the best shakes in the whole *universe?*"

"Well," said Jacqueline in her best lecture hall voice. "According to Roger Zelazny, the Vegan civilization considers the Coke formula to be Earth's great contribution to galactic culture. And given that proposition, I think we can safely extrapolate that humanity has cornered the cosmic market on junk food."

Aurie laughed. "Sounds like a big point in our favor." *We ought to get Py one of these milkshakes and save the human race!*

They slurped contentedly on the way back, and Aurie felt her tension easing with every sip. This really *was* the best shake ever. But a chocolate shake on a summer day was as short-lived as a steaming mug of cocoa in winter.

Maybe the pleasure of frozen desserts and hot drinks is partly their ephemeral nature, suggested the Doctor.

Aurie let the ice crystals melt on her tongue in silent agreement. She did love the way the chocolate flavor lingered, then faded to a memory.

And even these common pleasures are transient in the grand scheme of things, the Doctor mused. *In another fifty years, humans will likely refresh themselves with chemical bursts from artificial glands ... and milkshakes will be a thing of the distant past. People will read about them and wonder what they tasted like!*

Traffic thickened as their road drew alongside the Androscoggin River. As they waited at a stoplight, Aurie glanced into the auto-piloted cars around them. No one met her glance; most of the other drivers and passengers were looking at a virtual world projected by a Spider. Four kids shuffled across the street with their heads down, paying equally little attention to the world around them. Impossible to tell how old they were, since each was lost in a curtain of hair and the folds of some dark, baggy clothes. In startling contrast, two women with bright, open faces approached the intersection, conversing rapidly with each other. Their eyes shone with good cheer, but there was something false about the emotion, as if it were pasted on. Aurie looked closer and her sharp eyes caught a faint flickering about their features.

"What do those women have on their faces?" she wondered.

Jacqueline followed Aurie's gaze, but the women's faces were no longer in view. "Make-up?"

"I don't think they're wearing any make-up," Aurie said. "But there's some kind of alteration going on, like with Dad's glasses."

Her mother looked confused, so Aurie explained. "He wears them for distance scanners like the ones in tollbooths. Well, he *used* to wear them ... I guess he hasn't gone for a long drive in awhile. The glasses digitally alter his face so he looks like 'Robert P. Hartwell'."

"Ah," said Jacqueline. "I bet those ladies are wearing mood

masks! Abel was telling me about those."

"Mood masks?"

"They alter your expression to whatever mood you want on display. So even if you just lost your best friend, you can still look perfectly happy. And if you think that's weird, take a look at that girl coming up the street."

Aurie looked and saw a teenager whose face was nothing but a blur. Below this blatant digital masking, the girl was dressed in nothing but a few scraps of bright cloth. The fabric, which appeared to be real, was attached to her skin by some mysterious mechanism. The orange and violet swaths fluttered in the breeze, making her look like a garish, faceless butterfly.

"Do you think she's sending a mixed message?" Jacqueline murmured, as they moved forward on the road.

"Well, yeah," Aurie said. "Her clothes say, *Look at me,* and her face says, *Look away.*" Fascinated and appalled, she watched the butterfly in her face-canceling mask until the girl disappeared from view.

What's wrong with all of them? Having spent no real time with anyone outside the family, Aurie felt more bewilderment than empathy. And yet ... these people were as human as she was, and unhappy in some fundamental way. Sorrow for them lay beneath her general feeling of puzzlement. Jacqueline, too, looked slightly melancholy as they approached a park where an antiques fair was wrapping up for the day. A virtual concert was beginning on a stage by the river, drawing a small crowd to the real-as-life hologram crooning into the real-as-life mic. The distant strains of an old song drifted across the park.

"Do you miss them?" Aurie asked her mother.

"Who?"

"People," Aurie said.

Jacqueline gave her daughter an amused glance. "I *do* miss a few people, believe it or not. And I miss art shows and farmer's markets and real concerts."

On their left, the river shone in the last of the day's light. Aurie realized that she'd grown completely accustomed to the normal world again. *An hour outside the Garden,* she thought sadly, *and I can't even remember it anymore!*

"I miss other places, too," her mother said reflectively. "The kind most people think of as bleak and lonely. Rugged coast with capes and coves and headlands. Grey shores where you can hike for miles and never see another soul. My family visited British Columbia back when I was a kid, and I loved all the inlets and channels with their scattering of rocky islands. We live in a beautiful place here, but ... "

"But we're still hiding," Aurie said. She understood her mother's feelings, especially the sense of being trapped and unable to roam freely. "Because of *people.* Do you think Py's right, that humans are incapable of real love?" She expected Jacqueline to deny it emphatically, but her mother surprised her.

"I don't know," Jacqueline said. "After your dad made that terribly honest case for himself, I went out to the garden and asked myself the same question: *Who am I? And how have I loved?* And my answer wasn't any better than his. Do you know who your mother is?" She cast Aurie a brief, troubled look. "I spent most of my adult life being a hypocrite. I condemned rogue scientists even though I was a rogue myself, and I sustained a corrupt system by my own cowardice. I didn't even have the courage to use the kill switch I invented."

"You're not a coward!" Aurie was aghast at the harshness of her mother's self-appraisal. "You're brave ... look what you did for *my* eggs ... and you're smart and resourceful and—"

"Thank you," Jacqueline said, reaching over to squeeze her daughter's hand. "But my bravest moments could easily be classified as stupid. And I've always loved new ideas and my own vision more than anything, the same as your dad. It took this family to change that." She paused, considering. "I guess the question is, does the good in us outweigh the bad? It's kind of a strange question, since we didn't evolve to be good *or* bad. Like every other organism on this planet, we evolved to survive and we took a convoluted path to become what we are."

"But Py thinks we're no longer driven to survive," Aurie said, wondering what her mother would think of the god's view. "He thinks that humans are unconsciously bent on destroying themselves."

"Why? Because our technology has outpaced our wisdom in using it?"

Aurie thought about that, then shook her head. "He would say that we use a crude knife or a sophisticated genetic tool with the same lack of wisdom ... because we can't see ourselves as one with each other and with the rest of the world."

Jacqueline frowned. "But over the last century, people have been finding more and more connections with other species. Aren't we more aware of ourselves and our world than ever before?"

"Yes, but *knowing* we're connected hasn't brought the walls down. Py says we're like prisoners in solitary confinement, that we all live in our heads alone. It's not natural, though, and deep down we hate it, so we try to work together. We create artificial group identities to foster feelings of togetherness ... but what is a group identity? *Us* against *them*. Which is ultimately *me* against *you*. *Self* against *other*. He thinks there's no escape from the prison of our egos."

Other isolated humans, each imprisoned within a skull, passed by in their vehicles under the light of the dying sun. Aurie's gaze lingered on each of them.

"So he believes that evolution has driven us into a dead end," Jacqueline said. "But when he talked about this at breakfast that morning, it didn't sound like he wanted to *fix* people ... it sounded like he wanted to get rid of them." She glanced briefly at Aurie. "I mean the god, of course—not Py."

Aurie nodded. "He's an engineer god and he's driven to improve every world he takes shape in. He sees humans as the biggest danger to this world ... but he won't eliminate the human species if there's a way to save it."

Jacqueline gave her a curious glance. "When did you talk to him about all this?"

"On our hike today," Aurie said. "I didn't have the guts to

bring it up earlier."

Jacqueline snorted. "You had a lot more courage than the rest of us." Turning south from the river, they headed into thick woods again, driving in silence for awhile.

"It's terrifying to imagine what that god is capable of doing," Jacqueline said at last. "But I *know* Py is still in there, and I trust him. He hasn't lost his humanity or his love for us. Especially for you." She gave Aurie a meaningful glance. "Because of him, the god is struggling to control himself and not rush into anything. Whatever he ends up doing ... I think it will be a good thing."

She still thinks the real Py is hiding in his brain, Aurie thought with mixed affection and exasperation. Her dad and uncle did, too—it was the only reason they were all carrying on as normally as they were. And maybe Jacqueline was partly right. The god *was* struggling to control himself, although it wasn't for love of anyone. He wanted to act rightly for the good of creation. For love of the force that drove him to reform creation. But did that mean wiping out all of humanity?

Maybe he can't decide while he's tethered to Py's mind, she thought as the Boundary neared and her heart beat faster. And yet the god refused to leave Py's mind. What was it he'd said? *I've learned quite a bit ... but I still think I'm missing something.*

What was it the god still needed to learn? He had fallen asleep again, part of his Colony had escaped the Garden, and the Doctor was convinced that time was growing short.

"Well, here we go again," murmured Jacqueline, as the sense of wrongness from the Boundary intensified. Tightening her grip on the wheel, she stepped on the gas. The car shot forward on the empty road.

Aurie braced herself against the irrational feeling of impact. All the hairs on her neck stood up and her bones began to howl as they rushed toward the invisible barrier. Then they plunged through the Boundary—and into total blackness.

Jacqueline screamed and hit the brakes. Aurie cried out as she was jerked forward against her seat belt, then slammed back against the car seat. The stench of burned rubber permeated the suddenly icy air, and the only light came from the console and the Spider on Jacqueline's wrist. Then those, too, winked out.

"What in God's name!" breathed Jacqueline. "Are you okay?"

"Yeah ... I think so."

They sat in stunned silence, then Aurie heard the faint clicks of her mother pressing the ignition button with no result.

I don't know what your brother is doing, said the Doctor grimly. *But there's something terribly wrong with the air!*

Is it poisonous? Aurie looked apprehensively toward her open window. The blackness inside and out was impenetrable.

Well ... not exactly. The Doctor uttered a nervous, disbelieving chuckle. *I can't detect any toxic chemicals, but then, I can't detect any gases at all! Any air, if you can believe that. And yet you and your mother are still very much alive in this apparent vacuum. I don't know what to make of it.*

I can suggest one possibility, offered the Professor, sounding calmer than he had any right to be.

Let's have it, Aurie said.

We may have entered the world of Py's dream, the Prof said. *Where natural laws don't necessarily apply.*

"I must've damaged the driveshaft, braking that hard," Jacqueline muttered, tapping frantically on her Spider. "I could have killed us just now, if the road had happened to curve! This is all Py's doing, isn't it?"

"It has to be," Aurie said. "The Professor says he fell asleep, and we might've been pulled into his dream. The god's power must have made it real, somehow."

"The Professor? You mean *Py's* CRISPR machine? How are you able to talk with him too?"

"I, uh ... kidnapped a single copy of him from one of Py's ants. The Prof knows everything that's going on in the Colony and in Py's human body, which makes him a pretty useful informant."

Jacqueline grunted in agreement. "I thought that ant raid was bad, but this ... it's like we've been drawn into a nightmare!"

Aurie sighed. "And the Prof was trying to give Py a *safe* dream."

Her mother uttered a brittle laugh. "Tell him that being plunged into total blackness at thirty miles per hour leaves something to be desired in terms of safety." She expelled a harsh breath. "I guess electronics don't work in this safe dream. What the hell are we going to do? I can't even roll up the windows to keep us from freezing!"

"Stay here," Aurie said. "I'm going to see what's up the road."

"But you can't see a thing out there!"

"Don't worry, I'll be fine. Be back soon." Aurie found her mother's hand in the dark and gave it a squeeze. Before Jacqueline could argue or plead with her, Aurie got out and shut the door. Then she headed up the road in the icy darkness, using her threads to feel her way.

IV

In the corridors of the Labyrinth, the god felt none of the cold. As he drew his human family into the dream, he burned with the heat of anticipation. At the heart of this maze lay the fount of all life, waiting to be tapped ... and the path to it would be clear once he was freed of his emotional tethers. He had been wrong in thinking he could accomplish that in a conscious human mind, among other conscious human beings. It would take place here, in this dream-made-real. In the prophecy of a sleeping god made manifest by the power of an awakened one.

As he turned a sharp corner, it occurred to him that the specific form this maze had taken—a Cretan Labyrinth—was remarkably apt.

Complete with a Minotaur, thought the god. *Only this one is attached to me, and I can't slay it myself.* Fortunately, the ones who could were coming.

As he prepared for his first encounter, the god felt the pull of creation's forge, that smallest and brightest of all fires. Once he reached it, the raw materials of life would be his, to use in a single act of change upon this world.

One chance, he thought, burning with the desire to act and trembling with the need to act rightly. Soon he would be very close to eternity, unfettered at last ... and then he would see his course with perfect clarity.

Unconstrained by their physical forms, the Fishes had spent most of their young lives exploring and observing. Bold and innocent, they happily absorbed the vast world around them. With the coming of Py's god, they had known fear for the first time—fear of the pent-up energy brewing in this dangerous presence. Used to observing and not acting, the Fishes had clung to Aurie in fear during the ant raid. But afterwards, they were dissatisfied and a little ashamed of themselves.

We should have stopped that, Two Fish told her brother, who brooded in silent agreement. But how? Neither of them knew how to curb the machinations of a powerful god. And yet the feeling remained that they should have done something. Their mom had managed to keep the family safe ... but what if those ants had gotten out of the woods? The Fishes knew their mom was special, that other people in the world would have been helpless under such an attack.

We need a sign, One Fish murmured.

A sign? said Two Fish dubiously.

To keep things in or out, said her brother. He sent his sister an image of McElligot's Pool with a large sign planted next to it. On the ocean side it said, *Keep Out!* and on the pool side it said, *Stay In!*

Two Fish hummed with satisfaction, warming to the idea. *How do we make it?*

Like this, said One Fish, and he thought hard, focusing on the edges of the Garden. His sister caught on at once and the two of them bent their will on that place, the threshold of the god's light. They focused their will like sunlight through a magnifying glass— and the Boundary sprang into being, formed from the energies and elements of the Garden itself. The godlings had found their tinkering ability as easily as young fish learn to swim.

Wherever their souls happened to be, the Fishes knew whenever their Boundary was breached. They felt the disruption by small creatures that couldn't avoid it, by their mom and uncle jumping through it, and, most recently, by a car containing their mom and grandma—and a host of Py's ants—heading to town. Puzzled by the hitchhiking ants, the Fishes followed the car to the butcher shop. With alarm, they felt the growing power of Py's god surging through the escaped ants.

Something big is coming, said One Fish to his sister.

Through them, she said, watching anxiously as the ants massed at their mother's feet. Aurie was strong and capable—but she had never faced so many at once, all of them bristling with the energy of a god.

We can't let them hurt Mom! said Two Fish, growing warm with her own energy. Her brother emanated the same heat as they braced themselves to defend their mother.

But the ants abruptly dispersed, running off across the lot and into the woods. With uneasy curiosity, the Fishes followed them through the trees and into the subterranean darkness of a cave. Underground seemed like a good place for these dangerous escapees, but following cracks in a cave was slow going for such a massive contingent; they weren't moving nearly fast enough or far enough to suit the Fishes. In desperation, the godlings sent the force of their will like a laser into the rock—and the rock yielded.

Encouraged, the Fishes began to carve an underground way for the ants, burning through soil and stone with unwavering focus. They led the escaped ants on a straight course to the ocean, as far as possible from their family and any of the scattered towns in the vicinity.

With a path laid out before them, and filled with the energy of Py's god, the legion of ants streaked through the earth at a speed that would have put their Saharan silver cousins—formerly the fastest ants on the planet—to shame.

V

Swearing over his useless Spider, Abel returned to the kitchen to find the room empty and the front door gaping wide. He stared at the open door in disbelief. What could have possessed Howard to venture out into that abysmal night? Cursing, Abel went to fetch a flashlight from the utility closet and found himself somehow outside without it. He was moving blindly in the dark, his heart hammering in the cold. Grinding to a halt, he whirled around and saw nothing behind him, no sign of the house at all.

The god's magic, Abel thought grimly. He began to move more carefully, holding his hands out to keep from hitting a tree. But the ground underfoot wasn't earth at all; it was hard and smooth as stone. He bent down to touch it, and yes, he was walking over bare rock! The glade outside the house had been transformed into—what?

Feels like the floor of a cave, Abel thought, shivering. *And why should that be any stranger than the sun going out? Hell, if you're in a cave, it's no wonder you can't see the sun. Or the moon.* He realized he had no idea what time it was. And the temperature must have gone down forty degrees. It felt like he was wandering the bowels of the earth in the middle of winter.

Py's god must have wreaked some extreme changes in the woods ... or in the grey stuff between Abel's ears.

I'd like to cop an insanity plea, Your Honor, he thought somewhat hysterically as he shuffled along. *I'm either off my rocker, or I've fallen asleep.* But this bitter cold felt too real to be a dream. And then Abel heard something—the whisper of his own name in the dark. He turned toward the sound, straining in vain to see who had called him.

"Uncle Abel!" The voice was faint, but a spark was growing in the distance, like a single firefly brightening.

"Py?" Abel peered into the light, which began to illuminate his startling surroundings. Rather than the cave he had imagined, a stone tunnel loomed around him. As the light grew, Abel saw that the tunnel was as massive as an underground highway of ancient Europe. The wide corridor curved gradually, its inner wall resembling the coil of a gigantic snake, with numerous galleries and side-passages along its length. Abel hurried down the thoroughfare to find his nephew standing in the entrance to one of these passages. Py held the light source in his hands, a shining box. Abel's eyes widened in recognition. It was one of the small treasure chests he'd carved for the twins' upcoming birthday.

"Looks like you got hold of your present a little early," Abel said.

Py glanced down at the box in his hands, then back at Abel. "Is that what this looks like to you? A gift?"

"It's the wooden chest I made for you." Abel cast an appraising eye over it. The box was identical to the one he'd carved, down to its tracery of leaves and the giant ant adorning the lid.

"It's attached to me," Py said. "I need you to cut it free."

Abel looked closer and saw a slender cord growing from the wood of the box into the skin of Py's hand. And the box itself seemed to be alive. It pulsed like a heart, and it shone in many colors—from the softest rose to the deepest violet.

This is all a dream, Abel told himself, and yet the thought brought him no comfort.

"I can't cut that," he told Py. "It's a part of you! Why do you want to get rid of it?"

"Because it's *not* part of me," Py said as the strange growth shuddered in his hands. "This is a burden I accepted, but now it's time to relinquish it. Only I can't lay it down without your help."

That sounded like something Py's god might have said, and Abel looked up sharply.

"Who are you? Are you Py or his god?" He had never dared ask that question by the sane light of day, but here, in the darkness of this dream world, Abel felt possessed of more courage.

"You know the answer to that," Py replied, looking steadily

into Abel's eyes. "And you know my purpose here." He glanced down in frustration at the box that was fused to him. "I can't act until my hands are freed."

So this was the god, and not Py. And yet … during that breakfast interrogation, Py's god had been as cold and immovable as a Grand Inquisitor, but now he seemed almost human.

Disturbed, Abel returned his attention to the pulsing box and found himself thinking about the first days he'd spent getting to know his nephew. Whereas Aurie had been withdrawn and secretive on the brink of her god's awakening, Py had been completely open. He had told Abel the truth about his astonishing life, and he hadn't bothered to hide his feelings, his fear of an unknown mother and indignation at the way his father had treated her. If there was one word that summed Py up, Abel thought, it was *honest*. That had not changed through all of the Changes the boy had endured, none of which Abel fooled himself into thinking he understood.

God or human? he wondered again, feeling that the answer was somehow both. God *and* human, they were together in this soul … and the sum was still *Py*.

Abel looked at the cord connecting the glowing box to the soul he loved. "You can't give the right Gift to the world unless this cord is cut. Is that right?"

Py nodded.

I trust him, Abel thought in helpless wonder. *God help me, I do.* The soul in those eyes was warmer than a god's and wiser than any human's. This was Py … and something beyond Py, a source of will and authority that Abel's own soul responded to with unswerving devotion.

"I'll do what I can to help you," Abel said. "But I don't have anything to cut with." Then he saw the knife in his hand. It was the kitchen knife he'd used earlier, to make a dinner that hadn't been eaten.

Taking a deep breath, Abel cut the cord. The lid of the box cracked open and a flurry of gossamer leaves flew out. Abel was suddenly overwhelmed by memories of his nephew, from the day he had arrived at the old cabin until he had fallen asleep in the library that afternoon.

"What was all that?" Abel blinked as the luminous leaves drifted away into the gloom of the passage.

"I don't remember," Py answered. His voice had strengthened and his face had taken on a harder aspect. In his eyes, Abel saw great relief ... and a total lack of familiarity. Py might have been standing on his doorstep, gazing up at him for the first time. And yet, the soul Abel loved was still there, behind those eyes. And he was still—

"Honest," Py whispered. "Yes, that I am. Goodbye, Uncle Abel."

VI

Jacqueline waited in the car, her eyes sore from the strain of trying to see in the dark. For all she could tell, a giant beast might have swallowed the woods. It was hard to believe that she and Aurie had been sipping milkshakes in the summer sunshine only minutes ago. Or had it been hours? Jacqueline hugged herself for warmth, wishing she'd brought a heavy coat along. Because you never knew when your son's god might pull you into his dream of interstellar space or subterranean night. The bone-numbing cold had cleared away some of her shock, and Jacqueline couldn't believe she'd let Aurie run off alone.

Let her? How could you have stopped her?

Jacqueline sighed. *I should have gone with her!*

She was heading into the unknown, and she just wanted you to be safe. The thought drew a bitter chuckle. As if Aurie were the parent and Jacqueline the helpless child! Of course Aurie was more capable than any adult, but she didn't have a god in her head any longer; how could she protect herself against one? Sitting in darkness so thick it was almost tangible, Jacqueline's earlier assertions of Py's humanity returned to haunt her. *Whatever he ends up doing,* she had said, *I think it will be a good thing.* But this ancient night was something beyond human conceptions of good and evil. She felt lost and helpless in the midst of it.

And yet, sitting here and doing nothing was growing intolerable. She wanted to be outside and moving, exploring this dark dream world. Once the urge took her, the blackness inside the car *moved,* swirling like a breeze that had sprung up from nowhere. It pushed her firmly against the driver's door. Jacqueline found her hand resting on the door handle, and the next thing she knew, she was standing outside. Before she could stop herself, she had taken a half-dozen steps down the road.

What the hell are you doing? she demanded of herself. *You're not Aurie; you can't see in the dark!* She turned around and groped her way back, searching for the reassuring hardness of the car door ... but her hands encountered nothing.

"What an idiot you are," Jacqueline muttered out loud. Talking to herself seemed like a good way to stave off panic as she continued on with outstretched hands. "You'll bump into a tree soon enough ... and that'll keep you on the road, at least."

But she encountered no trees. And although she couldn't possibly have been walking a straight line, the road seemed to unroll, hard and smooth, beneath her feet. Bewildered, she bent down and felt, not the dirt of a little-used woods road, but solid stone.

Part of Py's dream? she thought uneasily, wondering where Aurie was and how she was faring. No sooner had she thought about Aurie than a faint voice called to her. Jacqueline froze, straining to hear.

"Mom!" came the call again, from somewhere up ahead. Not Aurie's voice, but Py's. Peering into the blackness, Jacqueline saw a pinpoint of illumination, no bigger than a pilot light, but growing steadily. She hurried toward it.

Py stood in the alcove of a great stone corridor—a corridor she had been blindly traversing—and he held a glowing book in his hands. It looked like the hardcover volume she was saving for his birthday: *A Northeastern Guide to Field Biology*. Even more surreal than her impossible surroundings, the book was fused to her son's hand by a tissue-like cord that made her think of a heartstring.

"This isn't real," Jacqueline whispered. "Just a dream."

"Reality and dreams aren't mutually exclusive," Py said. "You're in the midst of a god's dream, and it's very real."

Jacqueline stared at him. "Do you mean that I'm wide awake in this place?"

"Well, not exactly. You don't exist in this dream as you do in the physical world. But your soul is wide awake here."

Wanting to ground herself in something tangible, Jacqueline

looked down at the object attached to Py's hands. "What is that?"

"What does it look like to you?"

"A living book." Jacqueline bent down to get a closer look. The book shone with rich colors and throbbed like a vital organ. It was beautiful and full of life. By comparison, the boy holding it looked thin and frail.

"Is it hurting you?" she asked.

"It's crippling me." Py said. "I need you to cut it free."

Suddenly a small pair of scissors, sharp and gleaming, appeared in Jacqueline's hand. A piece of faded tape with her initials—*JW*—was fastened to one curved handle. Without any surprise at all, she realized they were her own dissecting scissors.

She looked up quickly, searching her son's eyes. Was this Py, or was it his god? In the past weeks, she had been surprised, relieved, and delighted to see much more of the boy she loved than of the god who had usurped his mind. She'd spent more time than ever with Py, testing and encouraging the presence of his human self. But looking at him now, Jacqueline saw god and boy together. One soul, one resolute will.

With her free hand, she reached out to touch the book. It was warm and trembled under her fingers, as if fearing the prospect of amputation.

"Cut the cord," Py said quietly.

Jacqueline withdrew her hand. Even in a dream, she balked at carrying out orders without any explanation. There was too much here that she didn't understand. "What is this, really? Tell me before I help you."

Py met her gaze steadily. "When you made that kill switch for your eggs—the Policeman—you did it to prevent the worst things from happening. And it worked perfectly. It was a vigilant protector of the cell, but Aurie had to get rid of it before she could Change. Because no real progress can be made under safeguard."

He glanced down at the shining object fused to his hands. "This is worse than the Policeman. Instead of overprotecting my cells, it's suffocating my soul—and I can't cut it out like a troublesome gene."

"But I can?"

"Yes." Py's eyes were bright with desperation. "You helped Aurie's god once, because it showed you the Pattern. I'm part of that Pattern, too, and I can't fulfill my purpose without your help."

Still, Jacqueline hesitated. Py had said this dream was real, and it certainly felt real. *More than real,* she thought nervously. *Momentous. The fate of the world hinges on this.* This was not a decision she could make lightly, trusting that it wouldn't matter once she—or Py—woke up.

"How can I decide this in a dream?" she muttered to herself. "Something so important deserves a conscious decision."

"You mean an *unconscious* decision," Py corrected. "A conscious decision is a choice of the mind, based on a narrow view of reality and subject to the winds of emotions. An unconscious decision is a choice of the soul, which sees much clearer than the mind ... and a dream is the best place to make it. Here in this dream, your conscious mind is asleep, and your soul is free to choose."

Jacqueline thought back to her first glimpse of the Pattern inside Aurie's cells. That had been a kind of waking dream, and she had known—*known,* without any consideration of cost or consequence—that she would do anything to help fulfill her daughter's destiny. If she had ever made a choice of the soul, that was it. But for whom or what had she chosen? Had she chosen to help Aurie, or Aurie's god, or the Pattern itself?

"This is your connection to us, isn't it?" she whispered, gesturing at the living book in his hands. "Everything that's human in you."

Py nodded, his eyes still burning into hers.

"What will you be without this? The death of our species?"

"A giver of the right Gift," he promised.

But not for humanity, she thought bleakly. *For the whole world.* And yet ... this was not the cold and impersonal arbiter who had cross-examined them at breakfast. This was Py-the-god and Py-her-son together, one being. The fusion filled her with awe and a strange sense of peace. At its core was the knowledge that she trusted her life—and the life of the world—in these hands.

Jacqueline looked down at the scissors in her own hand, then at the god who was also her son. For one brief, terrible moment, the mother in her—the mother who wanted her nine-year-old boy to live and grow and always be with her—cried out against this travesty. But it was no use; her soul had already chosen. Despair engulfed her and her stomach clenched, but her hands on the little pair of scissors were steady.

With a single snip, Jacqueline cut the cord binding the book. Its cover slipped open and a whirlwind of bright pages sailed out, fluttering away into the tunnel.

"What's written there?" she asked.

Py glanced at her, and Jacqueline saw that while he still recognized her, there was no love or familiarity in his eyes. Only gratitude. She might have been a stranger who had done him a great favor.

"I don't remember," he said, sounding relieved.

But Jacqueline suddenly knew. A thousand memories she shared with Py flashed through her mind, scenes from a book he would never read again. As her eyes blurred with tears, Jacqueline felt a light touch on her forehead that might have been a kiss. But when the last of Py's memories faded, she was alone in the dark with nothing but her own.

VII

Howard had been walking in the cold for so long that he could no longer feel his limbs. Chilled to the marrow, he trudged onward without stopping to rest. The small, scurrying sounds had long since faded away, leaving him guideless in the dark. He wondered for the umpteenth time where the hell he was. Not in the Maine woods, that was for sure.

You must've fallen asleep thinking of that Cretan Labyrinth, he told himself again, half-believing it. *And now you're having a nightmare. A pretty damn realistic one, but just a dream for all that.*

A glimmer in the distance caught his eye, and Howard heard the call of a familiar voice. He stopped and blinked, but the glimmer remained. It was a spark of lantern light that grew to illuminate the boy holding it, and the walls and ceiling of a vast tunnel. With a glad cry, Howard rushed down the corridor to meet his son.

Py was standing near the entrance to a chamber; the archway above him was inscribed with Greek writing. As Howard approached, he saw that Py was holding, not a lantern, but a bird's nest. It was the spherical kind made by ovenbirds; Py had found one when he was very young, and rushed home to show his father. But this nest seemed to be lit with an inner fire.

"What's going on?" Howard demanded, startled by the sound of his echoing voice. "And where the hell are we? I know you're asleep in the library—is this some part of your dream? The Cretan Labyrinth?"

Py nodded.

Then it isn't real, Howard thought with relief. A voice in his mind whispered that the ant raid had been real enough, but he dismissed it. Ants running amok were one thing, but this mythical labyrinth was surely the stuff of dreams. He looked up into the dim recesses of the ceiling far above. "Am I dreaming, too?"

"Not in the usual sense," Py said. "It would be more accurate to say that I've drawn you into a dream-made-real." He held out the dome-shaped nest. "I need you to cut this free."

Howard tried to take the nest and met resistance. He looked closer and saw a fleshy tendril connecting the nest to Py's hand. And then he realized that the nest itself was alive, its mud and grass shell pulsing with rich, warm colors. From within came a whispering murmur like the sound of nightingales.

"What is this?" Howard asked.

"It's the only thing keeping me from fulfilling my purpose," Py answered, and Howard felt something pressed into his hand. He looked down and saw his own straight razor, the one he had used to shave with that morning.

"Cut the cord," Py implored.

"What happens if I do?" Howard found himself very reluctant to sever what was clearly a bond of some kind—between Py and whatever was in this nest-like thing.

"CRISPR evolution is fulfilled," Py said. "Aurie's god took its place in the Pattern, but it needed help ... and so do I."

Howard looked hard at his son, trying to fathom who was behind those eyes. He had been so sure that Py was growing stronger and the god was weakening or preparing to leave ... but listening to him now, that certainty evaporated.

"Tell me," Howard said slowly, "exactly what I'd be cutting. What do I need to free you from?"

"The part of me that you know."

Howard looked at his son with a sinking heart. "And what will be left after that, just the god? You—the *real* you—will be gone for good?"

Py laughed a little. "What is the 'real' me? Your son was partly fashioned by the god asleep in his genome. The dreams of that god helped to shape him. And he, in turn, shaped the god that awoke in the Colony. We are, in a very real sense, each other's creations." He looked at Howard with naked intensity. "But everything you think of as the real Py will be gone when the last cord is cut."

Those were clearly the words of a god, but Howard was suddenly unsure of the line between boy and god ... and did such a distinction even matter? In his son's eyes, he saw a deeply conscientious power that was shaped by a human soul and by something beyond all souls. In that moment, Howard saw eternity itself, and the daunting force that moved within it. A moment later, the impression was gone and forgotten, but his soul had made its choice.

"I always knew you would change," Howard managed to say, his voice thick with emotion. "But I never thought I would lose you."

I was never yours to lose, said the eyes of the boy standing before him. Out loud, Py said, "I'm only shedding my skin, Dad. Don't grieve for me."

But Howard's hand trembled as he gripped the razor, and tears clouded his eyes. The gently throbbing nest in Py's hands blurred into shimmering swaths of amber, cobalt, copper, and chartreuse. As he took hold of it, Howard felt as if the cord of its attachment had sunk into his own flesh, and for one brief instant, he knew everything inside—they were the murmuring voices of his own memories, down to the smallest and most forgotten.

"I love you," he told his son, knowing that in another moment, Py would no longer care.

"I love you, too," Py said hoarsely.

As the tears ran down his face, Howard severed the cord with his razor. A flock of things that were not quite birds flew crying from the nest. Howard wiped his eyes hastily to see them better, but they were already gone, winging their way into the darkness of the tunnel and leaving nothing but their faint echoes behind.

"Thank you," Py breathed, and then he winked out like a flame, leaving Howard more alone and desolate than he had ever been.

VIII

After she left her mother in the car, Aurie moved cautiously up the road. Her sharp eyes were blind in this utter darkness, but her threads met no resistance. And the darkness itself felt strangely alive, an intangible presence that flowed with her, urging her forward.

You're not in the woods anymore, she reminded herself. *You're in Py's dream.* There was a sense of great space, yet the air felt close and still, like the air in a cavern. And the road itself was no longer dirt, but smooth stone. Even the sounds of the woods had vanished; not a single leaf could be heard stirring, and only her own footfalls rang out. If this was the world of Py's dream—brought to life by the god—it was certainly a barren one. She wondered how long it had been since she'd left the car. Time, if it even existed here, seemed insignificant and unreliable.

"Aurie!"

She stopped at once, alert in the silence.

Was that you? she asked the Doctor, but he didn't answer ... and it hadn't sounded like him. It had sounded like a voice coming from up ahead. She kept going, straining her acute senses until she saw a light flickering in the distance. The flame grew, dancing on the sides of a grotto carved into a stone wall. Barely noticing her surroundings, Aurie ran toward the light in dawning recognition of what it must be.

Trying to describe a person's aura had always frustrated Py, who reluctantly compared it to a cloak of shifting colors and textures, the shape of which was unique. Aurie had thought the image a beautiful one, but now she understood her brother's dissatisfaction. For the aura she was approaching defied the boundaries of known entities. Wind and water and fire were in its restless shape, and indescribable colors that made her think of dawns breaking on alien worlds. Aurie stared at the god's aura, mesmerized. He blazed before her in all his inhuman glory, yet when he spoke, his voice was one Aurie knew well. And god or human, she could only think of him as *Py*.

"I wanted to show you what you looked like once," Py said.

"I looked like *this?*" She could scarcely believe it.

"Well, not exactly. You were more … static. Like starlight caught in crystal. But then, your god was still in your head, and I'm almost free."

Aurie drew closer, scrutinizing the god's aura for any sign of Py. And there *was* something—a very small, pale shape inside that burning aura, like a ghost haunting a conflagration. At the same time, something hard materialized in her hand. Looking down, she saw the Doctor's CRISPR-evo multi-tool, with its scalpel blade extended. The metal gleamed coldly in the fulgent light.

"No," she said, backing away. She tried to drop the imaginary instrument, but it was glued to her hand. *"You're* the god—you figure out how to be a god on your own! Don't make me responsible for your mistakes."

"You know there won't be any mistakes once I am fully myself," Py said sternly. "And you know I can't get there on my own! You know exactly what's holding me back."

"Your emotional attachments? Your humanity?" She shook her head. "That's *your* problem. If you can't get rid of it yourself, find a way to live with it! I won't help you destroy it."

Py hissed with frustration. "I thought I'd have trouble with the rest of the family, not with you. You're the only one who understands!"

"Yeah, I understand," she snapped. "I understand that whatever you're doing can only be done once, for better or worse. If you lose your humanity … "

Py moved closer to her, and a surge of anger from his aura washed over her like a hot wind. "You know that my *humanity* is nothing but a ghost tied to my back! You know exactly what I am and where I came from. I'm brother to your winged god, but I'm not *your* brother—not the one you grew up with. That Py is gone!"

"I know that," she said, stricken. "But it's still … "

"Still what? Better than nothing?" Py's aura seethed and twisted in a fury of torment. "You would rather keep me hobbled this way because I *remind* you of Py?"

"No," Aurie cried. "That's not it at all!" She struggled to marshal her frustrated thoughts. This god was only awake because of her … and why had she said yes to that? Because Py had created a problem that only a god could solve. Because he had endangered the entire world. And now this god was posing an even graver danger, not to the world, but to the people in it. If she helped him, she would be directly responsible for whatever havoc he wreaked.

Unable to release the scalpel in her hand, Aurie shook it furiously at the god. "What am I supposed to do with this? Cut the ghost off your back?"

"Yes," Py said fiercely. "Do it now!"

"How is it even possible?" Yet even as she asked, her godbrother's aura reshaped itself, resolving into two distinct entities. Now the small, pale aura hovered beside the auroral one. The two auras were connected to each other by a single luminous tendril.

Aurie looked closely at the much fainter, humbler aura. The rest of the family might think *Py* was holding the god at bay, but she knew better. There was no Py, only this spectral thing he had left behind.

"What *is* that?" she asked. "Your human memories?"

"What's left of them," he affirmed. "Intertwined with your brother's talents and personality, his strengths and weaknesses, his sense of life, his sense of self."

"Sounds like his soul," she said, feeling very cold.

"More like the matrix that once held his soul."

"His humanity, then," she whispered. "And this cord is the only thing keeping you attached to that?" *The only thing protecting the human race!*

"The only thing keeping me from finding the right Gift." The god had regained his composure, but his voice was still harsh with desperation.

Trust him, she thought in the midst of her turmoil. That cool voice—her own, but not her own—stilled her thoughts briefly.

Trust who? she wondered. *I would have trusted Py with my life, but how can I trust this god?*

Aurie shifted her gaze from the remains of Py's humanity to the smoldering, vital aura that was bound to it. If each soul had shaped the other, then perhaps something human would remain in the god, cord or no cord. Some lasting impression of her brother's soul. And whether she cut this last cord or not, the god would make a decision. He would do *something* to change the world and the people in it. Whether he made that decision free or tethered was up to her. Would she keep him tethered out of fear?

Trust him, she thought again, in that voice that wasn't quite her own. It was a whispery, feathery voice that seemed to come from the deepest place inside her. Trembling, she looked into the wind and water and fire of the god's soul … and saw another light within, one that stirred the dust of an old memory.

"Cut the cord," begged the god.

"I trust you," she whispered. "I trust you to find a Gift that doesn't mean our death. Something other than destruction. I trust you to … "

What did she trust him to do? What was right? What was fair? What was merciful? None of those things was enough. That jewel of light blazed forth—light beyond the bounds of sight, music beyond all hearing—and she called upon it in an agony of faith; she entreated it with every fiber of her being.

I trust you to find the wisest Gift … the greatest one there is. Tightening cold fingers around the haft of her tool, Aurie severed the last of the god's bonds.

He cried out then in a unity of many voices. Aurie heard the eager rush of a wave above the sea, the boom of fire exploding into an opening, and the wild scream of a bird taking flight. At the same time, that feathery thing stirred inside her. It made an eager, rustling sound as it rose, higher and higher. She had the impression of bright fibrils trembling in an airless wind, and then the brightness grew, filling her mind with pure light and the unbridled desire to fly.

She rose up on remembered wings, truly herself again, as a fierce joy filled her. Above her, the god beat his flaming wings, sending the darkness flying in a madness of light. For a moment his golden eyes shone down on her, then he blew through the corridor like a terrible wind.

IX

Like a winged star, the god streaked down the corridor. His Minotaur had been vanquished and he was finally free! All twists and turns were behind him; this last stretch of the Labyrinth was as straight and true as a beam of light. The path widened in all directions until he was flying over a great plain of unbroken stone, which ended abruptly in a sheer drop.

He checked himself at the brink of the abyss, gazing out into eternity. Like the brightest of all stars, the heart of the void flamed before him. The source of all life. A single word sung into the dark. The god held still, overcome by his kinship with that fount of light. He, too, had been forged in its fires. Those fires burned hot within him, pulling him toward their source. At the same time, the cold inertia of empty space pressed in, trying to consume him, denying form and resisting movement. Between motion and stillness, between song and silence, the deepsight returned to him. And the world he had awoken to took shape in his consciousness with perfect fullness and clarity. He saw it as a great weaving on an invisible loom. Every thread touched many others in a wild pattern, but the human thread was tangled up in itself, snagging other threads in its path across the loom.

The god followed the human thread down its course and saw the shape of the future. He watched his greatest fear come to pass as the unwitting consequence of genetic tinkering—the awakening and shaping of a god by an evil human soul. From the vantage of his host, this god believed the greatest good could be achieved through a concentration of power, and thus he Gifted his human family with the knowledge of how to activate the god template. With an arrogant, controlling family as the new caretakers of Earth, three twisted gods rose up in succession. That alone would have been terrible enough in any time ... but it happened on the cusp of humanity becoming a spacefaring race that sought to leave its problems on Earth behind.

Two of the gods in their human forms took their constituents to the stars with dreams of starting over. The third god remained to shape the fortunes of those left on Earth, where a state of chronic war was the norm. At all levels of human society, from nations to individuals, life was ruled by a score of bitter and often senseless partisan struggles, of old enmities fueled by new conflicts. The Gift of this last god, intended to refashion the existing power structures, instead spurred the dissolution of civilization. Mobs and gangs took over what remained of cities and towns; cannibals and drug addicts roamed hills and countrysides. Many humans behaved worse than animals, delighting in the pain they caused, living for orgies of violence and destruction. Others sought to terrorize and control the helpless, who merely struggled to survive in a world that had become a living hell.

At the brink of the abyss, the god who saw with deepsight shuddered with horror. He followed the human thread from Earth to each new colony world, hoping for redemption. But the good and evil in human nature—qualities whose potency was amplified by the gods they awakened—ensured the rise and eventual ruin of every colony. Gods colluded or warred with each other, seeking to strengthen or weaken each other's Gifts, but the stubborn, persistent human species never quite destroyed itself. Like a cosmic virus, it managed to endure and spread, to adapt its destructive mentality to each new home it found.

Grief overwhelmed the god. His emotional attachments to humans had been severed, yet he was stricken with sorrow for them. The Gift he needed to bestow was clear; it would be a mercy to the universe to erase this species from existence. He pondered ways in which to do so ... fast ways and slow ways. Even if he took a gradual approach, the Earth's ecology would undergo massive changes, with many species dying and others flourishing. There would be sharp adaptations, the lessening of old pressures, and the creation of new ones. Life would rush to fill the gap, life free of the rogue thread that threatened Earth and so many other worlds.

The god closed his inner eye and took a moment to compose himself. But even in the dark, he wasn't entirely alone. He could sense his Colony and the embryonic gods waiting in underground darkness ... and his human family wandering in despair through the blackness of the Labyrinth. Those humans had slain his Minotaur, but why? Knowing what he was capable of, why had they helped him?

Love, he thought, knowing it was the simple truth. Howard, Jacqueline, and Abel had finally recognized Py's impression on the god's soul; because of it, the god was no longer an alien to be hated and feared. They had loved and trusted him. And in the moment of choice, each of them had sacrificed a future with Py to fulfill his deepest purpose. Their love was great enough to encompass his, even to their own grief.

And Aurie, who had known more than the others, had struggled more. With her brother truly gone, what would stop the god from destroying the human race if she freed him? What she wanted—an act that preserved humans and bettered their world, a miraculous Gift of both beneficence and integrity—seemed like the slimmest of chances, and yet her soul believed in it. In the end, she had served something beyond a human or a god, something beyond the evolutionary imperative that drove her world. She had served the eternal force that binds all of existence and drives it toward something *greater*. She had placed all of her faith in that force, trusting it to help him find the right Gift.

It was the purest expression of love the god had ever witnessed.

He opened his inner eye once more to the weaving on the invisible loom and looked closer, much closer, until the human thread was a skein composed of billions of fibers. And he saw with astonishment that there were other instances of such love. They were as rare as stars in the vastness of space, but they changed his perception the way constellations change a human's view of the night sky. These humans were all wandering blind, and yet there were moments when light pierced the darkness. The ego was a terrible prison, and yet it could be breached. As he beheld the weaving in its entirety, the god no longer saw the shape of the pattern-to-be-woven as final. He gazed long, and finally saw no pattern at all, only the glimmering path of a comet or an electron as it follows those wild, uncertain laws that have never been written.

Shaken, the god thought once more of Aurie's faith. Faith in his ability to tap that eternal force for *greater*. And suddenly a new plan came to him, a plan as reckless and imperfect and uncertain as the course of humanity. The human ego couldn't be removed ... but perhaps it could be outgrown.

The god considered carefully. If he embarked on this course, it would be the end of his immortality. As long as his Gift survived, there would be, for him, no death on Earth followed by life in another time and place. There would be no tinkering with other worlds, no shaping of other life.

My final incarnation. The knowledge brought no sadness, but a hopeful joy. The god felt strangely young, as excited as a child about to plunge into a pool that might lead anywhere through passages unknown. He opened his mind's eye to his ants, the ones who waited for him in the rocks beneath the sea.

One chance, he thought, marshaling the restless fires within him. As he took his final leap, the god understood that he was following in the footsteps of his human family.

And if his faith was justified, theirs would be, too.

Part Five

Ariadne's Thread

Gather the pieces,
so I can show you what is.

- Rumi, "Green Ears"

I

As the god flew off down the corridor, Aurie's Feather pulled her senses up and away. She followed like a fledgling behind the winged god, exulting in the sensation of flight, of being free at last. They left the tunnel behind and soared over a dark plain, emerging at the edge of an abyss. Like the sum of all stars embedded in that vast blackness, a familiar jewel blazed. It was a spark of fire, a pulse of music, and a single word that was the source of all life. But then the jewel winked out and she was no longer borne aloft. She stood alone in the stone chamber where the god had left her.

Aurie sank to the floor, too devastated to weep. That sense of ultimate freedom was slowly leaching away like a dying wind. She tried to beat her wings, but of course she had no wings of her own. Just a feather ... if there had ever been a feather.

I hate to interrupt, said the Doctor hesitantly. *But this isn't the best time and place for a breakdown.*

Go away, she cried, wishing that she could tear him out of her cells and be completely alone for once. *You can't help, so just leave me alone!*

He fell silent and Aurie huddled in the darkness, surrendering to the worst misery of her life. But even in her anguish, she wasn't alone; the Doctor was still with her. She could feel him waiting in every cell, his concern for her a life-sustaining warmth. And her desire for solitude was quickly replaced by gratitude for the Doctor's presence. How could she ever have wished him gone? He was her lifelong companion and advisor, her co-conspirator and best friend, literally her flesh and blood. He was closer to her than any sibling could ever be.

I'm sorry, she said. *I don't ever want you to leave. But I've lost Py and I've lost ...*

She didn't finish the thought, but she didn't need to. The

Doctor knew exactly what she had lost.

And I know I should get up and try to find my way out of here, she said, *but what's the point? All of mankind will probably be blown to hell any minute now.*

Now that sounds more like you, the Doctor said, with fond relief. *But maybe we could take a stab at getting out of this Cretan Labyrinth anyway. On the off-chance that our lives aren't over just yet.*

Aurie chuckled weakly. *Who can sulk for more than ten seconds with a slave driver like you in their cells?* With a sigh, she got up and cast her threads out to find the nearest wall. She had a feeling that what the Doctor called this place—a Cretan Labyrinth—was eerily correct, and there would be no straight path back to the woods and the car where she had left her mom. She tried to remember what she knew of the Greek myth ... something about Ariadne giving Theseus a ball of thread to help him find his way back. Of course she had nothing so useful in here, not even a trail of breadcrumbs.

But there are some interesting things nearby, the Doctor said encouragingly. *Can you see them?*

Peering around, Aurie *did* see something. A faint luminosity a short distance away. She went over to investigate and found what looked like a swatch of pale, transparent fabric lying on the stone floor.

What is it? she wondered.

I think it's your brother, the Doctor told her.

Aurie bent down and picked up the pale thing. It came apart in her hands, falling to the ground in a flurry of wisps. With a small cry, she crouched over them. Were these really the remains of Py's human aura? But surely they were useless without Py's soul ... and she couldn't put them back together again anyway. Or could she? The image of a ball of thread teased her, hovering in her mind. Deep inside her, something gave a feathery rustle.

I wonder if this is all of him, the Doctor muttered.

Aurie barely heard him. She was focused on that bright, whispery thing, really attuned to it for the first time. It was the part of herself that longed to be reunited with her god, the part she had always tried to ignore. The part of her that felt like a feather.

You're really there, aren't you? she thought. *I wish I could see you.* An instant later, it took shape, smooth as silk, in the palm of her hand. It was a wing feather, long and gently curved, shimmering with a deep and colorless fire.

Aurie's heart beat faster as she gazed at it. *Can you help me?*

In answer, a single barb near the base of the shaft stripped itself from the Feather and floated away. It drifted slowly towards the ground, settling atop the wisps of Py's aura. The shimmering barb was straight and sturdy, narrowing to a point at one end. It no longer looked like part of a feather; in fact, it resembled the spindle on an old spinning wheel. And those wisps of Py's aura looked like cotton fluff, waiting to be spun. But she didn't have any idea how to spin thread.

It may not matter, said the Doctor encouragingly. *That's hardly an ordinary spindle, after all.*

Aurie thought his voice seemed a tad fainter than usual. And oddly enough, she felt a little lighter, as if some burden she carried had just been eased a bit.

Why don't you just try wrapping those wisps around it? urged the Doctor.

Aurie laid the Feather down and picked up one of the wisps of Py's aura. It was lighter than the floss of a cocoon, but she carefully twisted it around the base of her barb-spindle. As she did so, the wisp and the base of the spindle melded, transforming into a thin, shining filament. Delighted, Aurie repeated the process until all the wisps and the remaining barb had been "spun" into filament. She coiled this filament into a small ball and picked up the Feather.

You think that was only part of his aura? she said to the Doctor. *Let's look for the rest!*

What are you going to do once you've spun all the bits and pieces together? the Doctor asked curiously.

Well, that was a good question. Aurie thought about it as she headed down the tunnel. *The god called this a matrix for Py's soul*

... so I guess all we need is Py's soul.

Is that all? the Doctor said with a smile in his voice. *And where do you suppose it ran off to?*

Eternity, she told him. *The god said Py's soul fled back to eternity. I think we're very close to that here. I saw the place the god flew to, where this maze opens up and falls off into space. I saw the light in the void—*

Yes, said the Doctor, sounding thoughtful now. *If there's a way to recover your brother's soul, and a place where such a thing is possible, it would be there.*

It was a long shot at best, and Aurie had no idea if she could even find the place. She had followed the god down a straight path, but there *was* no straight path here, only this curving tunnel with its many sharp-angled passages. She was probably wasting her time, but salvaging her brother's aura didn't feel useless or foolish, it felt right.

Using her threads to guide her along the walls, Aurie began to search the Labyrinth. On the Doctor's advice, she laid her own chemical trail like an ant to avoid covering the same ground twice, but it was impossible to tell how big the maze was. The giant passages twisted back on themselves, often leading to empty galleries. It was near one of these dead-end chambers that Aurie found another drift of familiar-looking wisps.

Look! she cried. The shreds of Py's aura trembled at her approach, like delicate leaves in a breeze. As her Feather released another barb, Aurie felt again that inexplicable lightening of heart and soul. Quickly, she crouched down and began spinning the wisps into filament.

Good, the Doctor said. *We're making progress.* But this time his voice was unmistakably softer, as if he were shrinking in size or getting farther away.

I can't hear you very well, Aurie said. *Are you okay?*

Of course I am, said the Doctor impatiently. *Hurry up and finish before those pieces disappear.*

The wisps on the stone floor were more ghostlike than ever. But once she spun them, the fading wisps grew brighter, suffused with the Feather's own light. And when she brought the new filament close to the one she'd coiled up, their two ends fused together quite naturally. Pleased, Aurie wrapped the new filament around the growing ball.

There are others close by, said the Doctor. *Hurry!*

Aurie rushed down the corridor until she found the next scattering of wisps, then focused fully on her task—spinning Py's aura and searching for more of it. In spite of her exhaustion, she felt lighter and freer every time the Feather released another barb. The incessant ache in her heart was lifting. And yet the Doctor's voice grew fainter with every barb that was lost. She wanted to stop and find out what was wrong with him, but there was no time. Each newfound scattering of wisps was dimmer than the last, only brightening once they were spun.

Aurie reminded herself that even if something happened to the Doctor, it wouldn't be permanent. He was a fixture in her genome—made to be degraded and born again.

That's right, agreed the Doctor, sounding like he was miles away. *I'll be with you as long as you draw breath, my dear. And that's likely to be a very long time, indeed. Goodness, it looks like you've found the mother lode!*

Aurie had stumbled upon the biggest drift of all, and her heart sank. There must be hundreds of wisps scattered along the tunnel! Surely it would take more barbs than she had left to join them all.

This had better be it, Aurie thought, spinning as fast as she could. She didn't stop until the last barb was used and only the shaft of the Feather remained, glowing on the stone floor like a moonbeam. It took the shape of a spindle and then waited there, unmoving.

This is the last of me, it seemed to whisper. *Are you sure?*

Last piece of Feather, she told the Doctor.

Use it, he said.

She spun and spun, and was beginning to think she could get all the wisps; the Feather's shaft was just long enough. But the wisps themselves were bare glimmers in the dark, and it was hard to be sure. As the last bit of spindle transformed into filament, Aurie felt the emptiness of a sudden silence inside her. That silence was like a wall; she could no longer hear the soft background hum of her own cells. But there was no time to investigate; she coiled the final length of filament around the ball, then scanned the dark chamber one more time.

As Aurie ran her threads blindly over the ground, hoping she hadn't missed anything, the stone floor trembled. Then the walls and ceiling rumbled, raining down dust. She flung her threads in a protective net around the ball of Py's aura as the dull thud of falling stones echoed through the tunnel. A massive tremor shook the ground, and she fell backwards with a cry. Then her head struck the wall and a black wave swept her away.

When she came to, the ball of filament was still in her grasp. It shone softly in the nest of her threads. The Labyrinth was still and quiet. Faint shafts of light fell through wide cracks in the ceiling, turning the darkness to gloom. She had hit her head—hard enough to knock her out!—but strangely, there was no pain at all. Cautiously, Aurie felt the back of her head, but the skin there was intact. No blood and no swelling?

Did you heal me already? she asked the Doctor, but he didn't respond. Then she tried to go inside herself ... and found that she couldn't. She tried again, to no avail. Bewildered, Aurie called to the Doctor, but there was no answer. Only the weight of that unfamiliar silence.

She had been able to enter her own cells as naturally as breathing ever since her god had awoken. What had happened to her now? And, more importantly, what had happened to the Doctor?

Where are you? she demanded fiercely as angry tears welled up in her eyes. *Don't disappear on me, I need you!*

In desperation, she called to the Professor and was met with the same silence. In frustration and anguish, Aurie broke down and cried.

Come now, murmured a voice in her head. It was her own voice, but it sounded just like the Doctor, chiding her for wasting time and indulging in useless self-pity. *If you're going to do something with that ball of filament, you'd better get moving!*

Aurie wiped her eyes and looked down at the shining ball nestled among her threads. *Not Py's soul,* she thought, remembering what the god had said. *But a matrix for his soul.* That matrix had been reassembled at random and lacked its proper shape, but it was whole again and it shone with life. All thanks to her Feather, which had come from the wing of her own god. Now unmade—or, perhaps, remade—its unearthly fire still burned in the coiled ball of Py's aura.

Was it the Feather that kept you alive? she asked the Doctor who wasn't there anymore. The dawning suspicion filled her with bitter sorrow. She had no idea when he'd become real and not just a figment of her imagination. Maybe when her god started stirring in its sleep. Or once it was fully awake and its powers were unleashed. But her god must have brought the Doctor to life! And its Feather must have kept him alive … and allowed her to keep some of the god's power, even after it flew away. She had been taking that power for granted all this time. And now it was gone, and so was her soul's companion. The price of expending her Feather.

Well, don't let it be for nothing, said her own voice, in gruff imitation of the Doctor. *You know where you have to go!*

To the brink of the abyss, the place that was closest to eternity. She could feel sorry for herself afterwards.

As she continued down the passageway, Aurie soon saw light up ahead … but not the brilliant fire of the god's aura or the pale glow of Py's wisps. Part of the ceiling had caved in, letting in a wash of ordinary moonlight. Her spirits lifted a little at the sight, and she scrambled atop the fallen stones in the corridor.

Maybe this isn't a god's dream, after all. Craning her neck to see the moonlit sky, Aurie could almost believe that this was just a nightmare of her own making. And if she climbed outside, maybe she would wake up. She might open her eyes to the relief of finding herself in her own bed, with all she had lost restored to her. She would tell the Doctor, *You wouldn't believe the dream I just had,* and he would laugh and say, *I'm in every one of your neurons, my dear—do you think you could dream up a jelly bean without me knowing its color?*

The slightest of breezes whispered through the gap, stirring the dead air of the tunnel. *This is a god's dream, not yours,* it seemed to say. *That earthquake put some holes in the walls, so you might be able to climb outside the dream. But if you do, what will happen to that thing you're carrying?*

Aurie glanced down at her brother's aura. In the moonlight it appeared insubstantial, a ball of ghost-filament. She could see right through it to her own threads clutching the underside of the ball. She couldn't leave the Labyrinth and risk losing Py's aura. And she couldn't waste any more time—who knew how much longer this dream would last?

Around her, the cracked walls rippled briefly, as if in warning. Yes, this dream was getting thin. Quickly, Aurie climbed down from the pile of rubble and hurried deeper into the Labyrinth.

She had no idea which way to go, but the ball she held seemed to know. As she picked her way around chunks of fallen rock, it pulsed warmly against her threads, and whenever she reached a junction, it pulled her, subtly but unmistakably, in a certain direction. She became increasingly sure that they were leaving the outer shell of the maze behind, working their way tortuously toward the center.

Gradually, the sharp turns became fewer, and the curve of the tunnel eased. Eventually, Aurie found herself moving down a straight passageway. This similarity to the god's path perked her spirits up considerably. But the shafts of moonlight that fell through gaps in the ceiling played tricks on her. At times, the half-fallen walls rearranged themselves, becoming thick woods on either side of her path. But when she looked hard at the ranks of trees, they were only stone walls again.

Maybe Mom did crash when we went through the Boundary. Aurie paused to run her hands over the rough edge of the broken wall. It felt as real as anything, but ... *Maybe I'm having this nightmare in a coma.* It wasn't exactly a comforting thought. Forcing it away, she continued on.

As the path widened, total darkness enveloped her once more. Aurie cradled Py's aura against her chest and used her threads to test the ground. But not a single pillar, tree, or stone crossed her way.

She walked on in icy blackness broken only by the light of the aura she carried. Her unease quickly deepened into fear. What had happened to Py's dream of the Labyrinth? Perhaps the god had done something devastating to the world, after all. She grew cold at the thought that all humankind was gone and only she was left, preserved by the last lingering traces of a god's power. Or maybe she had stumbled into some psychic void, the cellar of Py's dreaming mind. She would have given anything for a barked order from the Doctor—or even his reluctant admission that yes, they were completely lost in here, with no way back. Without the Doctor, she was truly alone for the first time in her life.

Calm down, she ordered herself, in Doctor-like fashion. *Remember where the god flew? To a place where the walls fall away! You haven't left the Labyrinth, you're only getting closer to its heart.*

But the darkness around her smothered even the thinnest ray of hope. And there was no sign at all of the god. She might have been moving over the surface of a sterile world, alone in the vacuum between the stars.

After the longest, loneliest, most miserable walk of her life, something very small or distant glimmered in the darkness up ahead. It was only a spark, but Aurie's heart leapt. She could hear the music that defied memory drifting through the void. The music of life itself, forming a single word that existed in no language at all.

Hope flared inside her, and she ran toward that jewel of light. By its growing luminosity, she saw the abrupt end of the stone plain far ahead ... and the boy lying motionless at the edge of the drop.

II

The boy ran through the woods.

The woods had no beginning and no end. His path led between colonnades of trees that sometimes looked like stone walls under the pale moon. His footfalls made no sound as they stirred dead leaves on the moonlit ground, or sometimes dust on a cracked stone floor. He didn't know who he was chasing or why, only that he couldn't stop running.

He was cold, hungry, thirsty, and tired; these seemed to be permanent conditions for which no relief was possible. If someone had asked his name, he would have answered quite honestly, *I am Cold, Hungry, Thirsty, and Tired.* If asked why he was running through these woods, he would have said, *To find what I'm looking for.* Beyond that, he had no thoughts at all, no purpose or reason for existing. He was running, he had always been running, and he would never stop running. He would run forever through this stony forest that had no end.

Then a voice broke the silence of the woods.

Pick up the thread.

Vaguely, he recognized it as a girl's voice. It came from far away, and from inside his own head at the same time.

Pick it up! The words were muted with distance, yet sharp and clear in his mind. *Come on, Py—you have to grab hold of it.*

Something materialized out of the darkness. Long and sinuous, the tail of a coiled ball of filament that drifted in the air. It seemed very real, more real than the woods. Even as he ran, unable to stop the movement of his feet, that glimmering thread hovered before him.

It's yours, said the voice of the girl. *Take it and don't let go!*

He had no idea what this strange thing was, but it was new, the first new thing he could remember. And the girl's voice was

314

very insistent. Curious, he reached for the end of the thread.

As soon as he touched it, a star appeared in the dark skies above. The star brightened and grew, and he realized it was falling through the darkness, hurtling towards him. He watched its descent in terror, but this star was no giant ball of flame. It was something much smaller that seemed to grow wings as it reached him. It alighted on the ball of filament, which began to uncoil, tumbling into his arms in a profusion of light.

Py cried out as his soul returned to him. As the filament unraveled, memories filled him like lifeblood, so that now he had two arms, two legs, and a beating heart—and then again, he had thousands of legs and antennae, and a mind that embraced many smaller minds. The story of his life murmured and shouted and whispered its way into him, in fragments that found their place inside him and wove themselves back together. He remembered everything, and he knew himself again.

Trees or stone walls were falling around him, stricken as if by lightning, but Py barely noticed. He was filled to the brim with *himself*—and with so much more. His soul had come home to roost, and yet it held the tang of unfamiliar winds and the warmth of sunlight on distant worlds. He had no memory of those places, but he sensed them. He felt his connection to every being that had left its trace on him, intangible wings brushing his. And Py knew that never again would he keep jealous watch over his soul.

Anything with such wings was meant to fly free.

III

After the shock of the earthquake, Jacqueline continued on through the broken corridor, not knowing what else to do. She finally came to a place where the upper half of the tunnel had caved in, letting in the fine warmth of sunlight. Dazed, she climbed out of the ruins and found herself on a familiar dirt road through the woods. The Labyrinth had disappeared like any dream, and there was Abel's car, right where she'd left it.

According to her Spider, it was almost seven in the morning. Apprehensively, Jacqueline checked the news. It was a relief to see that there *was* news, and no catastrophes of epic proportions in the daily headlines. Jacqueline got into the car, then hesitated, unsure what to do. Should she wait for Aurie here, or check in at home?

Better check in at home first. Jacqueline held her breath as she pressed the ignition, but for once, the old car started without a hitch. She headed slowly down the road, scanning the woods for any sign of her daughter. Passing a stand of second-growth pine and deadwood, it struck Jacqueline that the woods looked just as they had in Bethel.

"Normal sunlight," she murmured to herself. "What's happened to the enchanted twilight?"

When she got home, Howard and Abel were donning their coats by the door. They looked at her with surprise and relief.

"Thank God you're okay," Howard said softly, wrapping her in a fierce hug. "We were about to go looking for you. Where's Aurie?"

"I was hoping she'd be here," Jacqueline said. "But why are we whispering?"

"Py's asleep in there." Abel jerked his head in the direction of the library. "And he's having a *normal* sleep, thank God."

"What happened to Aurie?" Howard looked concerned. "Didn't she go into town with you?"

Jacqueline told them about driving back from Bethel and crossing the Boundary to find the woods pitch-black and freezing cold. Howard and Abel both nodded.

"We *saw* that weird darkness forming," Abel told her. "And it actually pulled us outside. Like a pair of idiots, we both went wandering off!"

"So did I, after awhile," Jacqueline said. "But Aurie went out to investigate right away. She said that Py was asleep, and the god had drawn us into his dream. And when I left the car, too—" She gave a short laugh. "What I remember is so bizarre that anyone would say *I* dreamed the whole thing."

Abel snorted. "Try us! Howard and I have already swapped stories, and I'm betting yours is pretty similar."

As Jacqueline described her time in the Labyrinth, Howard and Abel jumped in from time to time, recounting details of their own night.

"So he asked us all for the same thing," Howard said when Jacqueline had finished. "To cut the cords of his memories and emotional attachments. And we all did it. What the hell were we *thinking?*"

"We weren't thinking," Jacqueline said, remembering her conversation with Py. "I think that was the point of the Labyrinth. It was a place where our souls would make the choice, not our minds."

Abel looked uncomfortable. "Was it the god who was asking, or was it Py?"

Jacqueline shook her head. "I felt like I was talking to both of them ... that they were somehow joined together."

"I felt the same way," Howard said, looking troubled. "And I trusted him."

Abel murmured agreement. "But what did he do *after* all his cords were cut? And where did he go?"

"Maybe he finally flew away," Howard suggested hopefully. "Why else would Py be sleeping a normal sleep?"

"The woods are back to normal, too," Jacqueline said. "Did you see?"

Howard and Abel strode over to the windows.

"I'll be damned," Howard muttered. "That crazy twilight is gone! I walked out of that maze into the glade there, and I was so relieved to be back, I didn't even notice."

Abel grunted softly. "Did everything always look so dull and faded? The world looks like a painting left out in the sun too long."

"I wish Aurie would get home," Jacqueline said, feeling suddenly anxious.

"Give her some time," Howard said reasonably. "When we climbed out of Py's Labyrinth, we all re-entered the real world at the point where we ran off, didn't we? Abel and I came back to the glade here, and you came back to the road where you left the car. So Aurie will probably have to make her way home from the same place you did."

Jacqueline groaned. "I should've waited for her! That's an awfully long walk."

Howard snorted. "For one of us, maybe. Not for someone who runs thirty miles before dinner on a slow day! And there's no sense looking for her along the road now. Once she sees the car's gone, she'll cut straight through the woods for home."

Abel, who had been checking something on his Spider, whistled softly. "Look at this—there was an explosion in Casco Bay about an hour ago!"

"Where the hell is Casco Bay?" Howard asked. "It can't be anywhere close to this godforsaken Disorganized Territory."

"*Unorganized* Territory," Abel said. "The bay is in the Gulf, about eighty miles away. And didn't we all feel an earthquake in the Labyrinth?" He brought up the holo-feed and they gathered around to listen. A local reporter explained that the footage they were about to see was from a cruise ship heading to Bar Harbor and just off Orr's Island at the time of the explosion. The next thing they saw was a tower of white water rocketing up from the surface of the ocean to fall like a collapsing skyscraper back into the bay. While the source of the explosion was unknown, it was being attributed to the detonation of a sea mine, and radical political groups were already taking credit for the "warning to those who oppose us."

Howard rolled his eyes. "I'm sure all the fish in the Bay are shivering in their scales and canceling their nefarious plots as we speak. If that was an act of terror, it deserves a Darwin Award."

"There's no mention of an earthquake," Abel said. "Just an explosion in the Gulf. But I can't help thinking—"

"Whatever we felt in that Labyrinth has nothing to do with this," Howard interjected.

"You can't *know* that," said the former lawyer. "Maybe we experienced the explosion as an earthquake in Py's dream."

"Or maybe the physical world experienced the earthquake in Py's dream as an explosion," Jacqueline said. "Howard, you can't possibly think they're unrelated! Whatever happened to cause that explosion, I'm betting it was the god's doing."

"I'll admit my usual healthy skepticism is at a low ebb these days," Howard said, "but why would Py's god cause an explosion in a bay eighty miles away?"

Abel shrugged. "Who knows why gods do what they do? But if that was the destruction he was planning for all mankind, I'd say he missed his mark."

Howard snorted. "I guess we should be grateful that he only laid waste to some fish off the coast of Maine. Although that cruise ship was awfully damn close!"

As the men searched for other news, Jacqueline stepped into the library to see her son.

Py was sleeping in the armchair overlooking the garden. One look at him and Jacqueline knew the god was gone. It was hard to say exactly what was different ... but the lines of his face were softer, and a wholeness had come back into his flesh. Py looked entirely like himself again. Relief brought tears to Jacqueline's eyes. A moment later, Howard came up behind her.

"It's him," she whispered. "And *only* him."

"Yeah," Howard whispered back as he held her close. They watched the steady rise and fall of their son's breathing, then left him to sleep, closing the door softly behind them.

"I'm dying to find out what happened," Jacqueline admitted in the kitchen. "What his god did after we freed it."

"I know," Howard said. "But Py will wake up when he gets hungry, which can't be long."

"Speaking of which," Abel said, with his head buried in the fridge. "Are either of you as peckish as I am? There are three roasted rabbits in here that never got eaten last night."

"I'm so hungry I could eat one stone-cold," Howard said, heading down the hall to the nursery. "The Fishes were still asleep when I checked on them—asleep or off somewhere—but they ought to be ready for breakfast by now."

As they moved about the kitchen, heating up leftovers and brewing coffee, Jacqueline found herself listening for the sound of quick footsteps on the patio, and she caught Howard sneaking looks out the window. When their eyes met, Jacqueline saw her own worry reflected back at her.

"Thirty minutes," Howard muttered to Jacqueline as he handed her a cup of coffee. "If she isn't home by then, we'll turn the woods inside-out ... starting with that damned anthill."

IV

Aurie stood on a dirt road beside a stand of young aspens that looked very ordinary in the light of the morning sun.

She had no eyes for the trees, though, or for anything else in the physical world. The heart of the Labyrinth was still much too real. She looked around, half-expecting to see her brother sleeping at the edge of an abyss, reaching out in the midst of his dream for the filament she had spun. Before all of that vanished, she thought he had touched it … but had touching it been enough? It seemed ridiculous to hope that his aura had somehow found its way back inside him. And what about his soul? She couldn't call *that* back from eternity, and yet in the heart of the Labyrinth, it had seemed like anything was possible.

That place had been so terribly real! The arid darkness and cold, the feel of the pitted stone walls. Aurie glanced down at her clothes, which only bore a few grass stains from her hike of the previous day. Not a trace of the dust that had rained down during the earthquake in the Labyrinth. If even the dust hadn't lasted outside of the dream, then maybe—

Are you there? she asked the Doctor, hoping against hope that he would answer. But the only answer she got was the silence of an empty room. The silence of an empty *cell*. She had always felt his presence inside her—warm and keenly aware—and now she felt nothing. It was strange and awful to think of all her cells going about their usual business without their caretaker.

Your template is in my genome, she thought. *In every one of my cells. You* must *still be there!*

But maybe he had been reduced to something less. Not her Doctor anymore, only the insentient CRISPR machine her dad had engineered.

Aurie tried to go inside herself, but failed just as she had in the Labyrinth. The power of her god was really gone, then, lost with the sacrifice of the Feather. And how was she going to see what had become of the Doctor if she couldn't get inside her own cells?

There has to be a way, and I'll find it. I swear I will!

But first ... where was her mom and the car? Jacqueline might've gotten the car started and driven home, but Aurie couldn't feel the Boundary at all, which was odd. Maybe this wasn't the place where they'd stopped.

After a quick reconnaissance up and down the road, Aurie set off through the woods, taking the most direct route home. As she leapt over logs and deadfalls, she realized that her eyes were still as sharp as any predatory bird, even if the woods seemed especially drab—

It abruptly dawned on her that the drab woods were perfectly ordinary. The Garden was gone.

Then the god is gone, she thought with a flare of nervous excitement. *He must've given his Gift to the world, and used up his Earthly incarnation!* And what exactly did that mean? *She* was still alive, but maybe staying in the Labyrinth had protected her from whatever the god had done. What if she was returning to a home with no family? What if the entire world was devoid of human life, except for her?

Anxious now, Aurie ran as fast as she could, sprinting through narrow avenues in the forest. It was cold consolation to find her physical abilities still intact. Those didn't matter at all; nothing mattered if her family had been eradicated, along with every other human on Earth! Horrible what-ifs assailed her as she raced through the woods.

When she finally flung open the kitchen door, it was hard to believe the reassuring scene in front of her was real. Her parents were lacing up their hiking boots, and her uncle was clearing the dishes. Casa del Utero was in its usual place at the table, and the Fishes drifted quietly in their tanks. Suddenly drained of adrenaline, Aurie staggered inside.

"You're home," Jacqueline cried. The intense relief in her

voice echoed Aurie's own feelings.

"Told you she'd be back any minute," Howard said, but he, too, looked very relieved as he shucked his boots.

"Now don't start cross-examining her before she's eaten," Abel growled at them. He gave Aurie a wink, then began filling a plate.

"Who's cross-examining anyone?" Howard protested. "We're just glad she's okay!"

"Is *Py* okay?" Aurie asked, as fresh worry set in. "Where is he? Is he still asleep? Is he *alive?*"

They all hastened to assure her that Py was just fine.

"Go see for yourself," Jacqueline said gently. "He's in the library."

Aurie found her brother sleeping peacefully. Normal sunlight fell through the windows, brightening a very human face—a face that belonged to Py and no one else.

It worked, she thought in amazement. *I spun all those pieces of him, willy-nilly ... gave him that cobbled-together aura—and it was enough!*

She remembered searching blindly for the last wisps of Py's aura, and the shadow of a doubt crossed her mind. But then Py stirred in his chair; he drew a deep breath and opened his eyes. He looked up at Aurie and smiled.

"You saved me again," he said.

"Again?" Her voice was hoarse.

He nodded, eyes shining. "My first Change, remember? Your threads saved me after that condiment binge at Dixie's."

Aurie nodded, drinking in the sight and sound of her real brother. She could hear the rest of the family approaching, and hoped they would stay out for now and let her talk to Py alone. For a wonder, they did, gathering quietly near the library door.

"It's been so long since you were *you,*" she said, still gazing at him with relief. "Do you actually remember everything that happened?"

Py cocked his head, looking thoughtful. "My memories are more complicated now. I have my own memories—human and

Colony—and then the god awakened, and I have *his* memories. Like grilling everyone at breakfast, and lying awake at night thinking about possible Gifts and wondering how to fix human beings. I remember showing you the Boundary ... when was that?"

"Yesterday," Aurie said. "Just yesterday."

"Feels like a lifetime ago." Py took a deep breath and exhaled slowly. "Some of the god's experiences are imprinted in my Colony consciousness, and some are in my human brain. So now I remember those things, even though the memories aren't really *mine*."

Aurie tried to wrap her head around that. Py had human memories, ant memories, and god memories? How could he keep them all straight?

"And I remember my soul coming back," Py said wonderingly. "Thanks to that ball of thread you gave me!"

"That ball of thread wasn't your soul, was it? I spun it from bits of your aura ... which the god said were your memories and personality and abilities." Aurie paused, trying to remember. "A matrix for your soul. That's what he called it."

"He must be right," Py said. "Because as soon as I touched it, my soul came hurtling back like a falling star!"

"But where did it go in the first place?"

Py's eyes took on a far-away look. "Other places and times. Everywhere it went, my soul changed whatever it touched, and was changed by it."

Aurie looked at her brother doubtfully. Surely if his soul had changed, she would know the difference.

Py laughed as if he knew what she was thinking. "Don't worry, I'll always be myself. How could I be anything else? But my *self* isn't just defined by the parts that stay the same, it's defined by how I grow. Did you know that souls evolve? They do! In a way, I've come back as a very ancient man—who has also been many other things."

"And your soul left one of those incarnations to come back to this one?" Aurie gestured at him incredulously.

Py laughed. "Who said anything about leaving? Souls are like stories, you know—they can live in more than one place at a time.

I have it on good authority."

Only a day earlier, such a conversation would have driven Aurie mad with heartache and envy ... but that was before the loss of her Feather. It was the *Feather* that had been so miserable on Earth, lost without its wing and the god it belonged to. Now she was only fascinated. But there was something more pressing she had to understand.

"The Labyrinth your god drew us into ... was it taken from that old dream of yours? The one where you had to find your way through an underground maze?"

Py nodded. "I used to have that dream all the time. You were having the opposite dream, remember? About flying into the sun. And eventually you *did* have to fly—and I had to find my way to the center of the Labyrinth."

"What *was* that place, really?"

He paused, thinking. "I think the maze itself was a mental construct, but the heart of the Labyrinth is real. The forge of creation, the place where anything is possible."

"Your god flew there after I cut him free. Do you remember that?"

Py shook his head. "I remember finding each of you, and asking you to cut one of the cords that connected us. Those are the last of the god's memories in my mind. They ended when you cut the last cord."

"I almost didn't," she admitted.

"I know," he said, smiling. "You were the only one who really fought it. And in the end, it was *your* god who helped you choose. The last remnant of your god that you've been carrying all this time."

"It was a feather from one of its wings. It's what I used to spin the shreds of your aura together. They were fading pretty fast." She hesitated, then spoke quietly. "I hope I didn't miss any."

Py shifted his gaze to the bookshelf in front of him, and his eyes grew unfocused. A moment later, he looked at her and shrugged. "Well, I can't jump into things the way I used to—"

"Oh no," she said, stricken by his loss. If only she hadn't

wasted time sitting in the dark feeling sorry for herself! "Py, I'm so sorry!"

"Don't you dare be sorry," he said sharply. "You saved my *life*. Once the god was free, I was just a soulless brain locked in a dream that wouldn't end. It was a fusion of my strongest dream and my strongest memory—wandering that underground maze and chasing you through the woods."

"So that's why the stone walls looked like trees the closer I got to you," she said. "But when I finally found you, you were lying on the edge of—nothing. A black gulf, with one light flaming inside it. And that was the forge of creation? I know that light; my own god knew it too! *Your* god must've used it to engineer his Gift. But what did he do?"

The three adults, who had been hovering by the door, suddenly spilled over the threshold.

"We didn't want to interrupt," Howard said as they crowded around. "And you can explain all that philosophical stuff later, but this can't wait. What did your god *do?*"

"To the world?" Py shook his head. "I wish I knew! When Aurie cut the last cord, that was the end of my god's attachment to *this*." He pointed to his head. "So that's the last of his memories in my mind."

"He flew to the heart of the Labyrinth," Aurie added. "The forge of creation. But that's all *I* know. I have no idea what he did there."

There was a moment of stunned silence.

"Neither one of you knows *anything?*" Howard sounded incredulous. "You can't give us a single clue? Not even an idle speculation? I was half-expecting to be vaporized by now!"

Jacqueline gave Howard a wry look. "Are you complaining?"

"Of course not," Howard said. "But I'd sure like to know what cataclysmic Gift he gave to the world. Wouldn't you?"

"Of course," said Jacqueline. "But—"

"But if these two don't know, then no one does," Abel said with an air of finality. "Now, why don't we get a meal into the boy before he dies all over again?"

"He never actually—" Howard began.

"The Fishes!" Py exclaimed, interrupting his dad. He scrambled up from the armchair and rushed out of the room.

"They're in the kitchen," called Howard, as they all followed Py there. At their place by the table, the embryos still appeared to be sleeping in their tanks.

"They might not know anything," Py said, glancing at Aurie. "But they've been worried about what the god might do, and they've been keeping tabs on him. So let's ask them."

All eyes turned to Aurie, who felt her heart sink. She hadn't realized until now that her connection to the Fishes might be lost. That telepathic link had driven her crazy, but the idea of losing it was almost as bad as losing the Doctor.

Steeling herself for heartbreak, she reached out with her mind and felt for her children. They were far away from their tanks, but she could still sense them. With a sigh of relief, Aurie closed her eyes and focused on that link.

Where are you? she called to them. *Come home.*

She felt a dim stirring, but her children were deeply absorbed in something. And they were moving quickly, like fish scanning ocean currents for plankton.

Come back, we need to talk.

They weren't intentionally ignoring her; she was just too soft a voice to get their attention.

One Fish, Two Fish—this is your mother. Come home this instant!

The intensity of her command must have reached them, because she felt the startled shift in their attention. A moment later, they were home.

Mom, come! Help us look! In their excitement, the Fishes had apparently forgotten that she couldn't travel the way they did.

Look for what? Aurie wished she could join them; her children's enthusiasm was as infectious as always. She felt a tugging in her mind, like tiny hands pulling her, but then it stopped.

Mom … what happened to you?

They sounded as shocked as if she'd lost an arm, and Aurie

felt the pain of her losses afresh. She wondered what they were seeing—no Feather where a Feather should have been?

I lost something, she told them. *But it's okay, I'm not hurt. I'm fine.* They considered her in silence, then she felt that light touch again, probing, as if the Fishes needed to verify that she was still herself. Apparently reassured, they gave her a brisk mental pat.

I can't go with you, she said, *but tell me what you're looking for. What happened?*

The god changed the ants, they told her excitedly, then sent her a series of impressions. Aurie felt herself speeding through rocky darkness, then through sandy darkness, up through murky ocean depths, and finally exploding into the air in a watery catapult.

She laughed. *I guess he sent them flying sky-high. How did they survive the explosion?*

They didn't, Two Fish told her. *But he made something inside them.*

It blew away on the wind, One Fish added.

The god made something? Aurie grew tense and alert. *What did he make?*

The Fishes were quiet and Aurie felt them searching for the right images. The first one they sent her was nothing more than a haze ... grains of dirt or specks of dust in the air. Then the image shifted to bees scattering yellow pollen in the wind.

Pollen?

They hissed with frustration and the pollen morphed into seeds drifting on a breeze—billions of seeds.

But smaller, One Fish said. *Much smaller than the tiniest seeds.*

What are they for? Aurie asked.

We don't know, said One Fish impatiently. *They blew away and we've been trying to find them!*

You called us back too soon, Two Fish grumbled.

I'm sorry, she said. *I should have trusted you guys to come home when you were ready. Go back to your hunting.*

But the Fishes were already gone. Aurie opened her eyes to find the rest of the family watching her with barely contained impatience.

"Well?" Howard said. "What did they say?"

She relayed the conversation, which left everyone as mystified as she was.

"Microscopic seeds?" Jacqueline murmured. "Seeds of what?"

When the Fishes returned that evening, they were disconsolate. The winds over the coastal waters had picked up in capricious gusts, and the god's seeds were nowhere to be found. The godlings had searched all day in vain.

They could be anywhere, the Fishes complained to Aurie as she lay in bed. Everyone in the family had turned in early, emotionally and physically done in from their sleepless night in the Labyrinth. Everyone except the Fishes, whose energy never seemed to flag. *Sunk in the ocean, lost in the sand, trapped in rocks, blown across the mountains, anywhere!*

Okay, okay, said Aurie wearily. *I get it. But it's amazing you can see microscopic things at all. If it weren't for you two, we wouldn't even know about these seeds.*

We can see small things, One Fish said glumly. *We just can't find them!*

Speaking of small things, Aurie said, *I want to ask you guys about the Doctor. I know he's in every one of your cells, but can you find him? Can you talk with him?*

We never look inside ourselves, Two Fish said, as if the very idea were absurd. *But we'll find out.*

Aurie felt them leave her. Minutes later, they returned with no good news.

We searched inside ourselves, said Two Fish, *but we don't know what we're looking at.*

You never taught us about the insides of things, One Fish

reproached her.

I apologize for the oversight, Aurie said dryly. *We'll get started on cell and molecular biology first thing tomorrow. But did you hear the Doctor's voice? Did you try to get his attention?*

We called, Two Fish said. *But we didn't hear him answer.*

Well, why would they? Aurie thought gloomily. The Fishes might be godlings, but they had no connection to the Doctor in their cells. And even if they could communicate with him, what good would it do? She needed him in her own cells, his voice in her own head. As tears welled up in her eyes, she felt her children draw closer, trying to comfort her with the fin-like folds of their auras.

I love you both so much, she told them, as her tears fell to dampen the pillow.

We love you, too, they assured her. And for the first time, Aurie felt the stark power behind those words. Their love for her was a fiercely protective force, and woe to anyone who tried to hurt her. Then the dire feeling subsided, and the Fishes drew away with their customary restlessness.

We'll keep looking for the god's seeds, One Fish promised.

And for the god, added Two Fish.

I don't think you'll find him, Aurie told them. *I think he's gone for good.* His words came back to her clearly: *A world-changing act requires more than my ability to tinker. It requires all of me.* Whatever the god had accomplished by making his mysterious seeds, the act must have consumed him. But the Fishes seemed uncertain about this.

We can still feel him, said Two Fish.

Aurie's heart beat a little faster. *Really? Where do you think he is?*

Close, said One Fish.

And far away, his sister added.

Aurie caught their conflicting impression of the god's presence. He seemed to be far in the distance and also just over the next hill. He was like a light hovering at the edge of their vision, a ghost that disappeared when they tried to focus on it. Had the god actually survived somehow? Crazily, Aurie found herself hoping that he had, and that the Fishes would find him. Part of it was just her burning curiosity, but she also found herself missing the god.

I should've spent more time talking with him, she thought ruefully, *instead of worrying about what he might do!*

Part Six

The God's Seeds

Humanity is being led along an evolving course,
through this migration of intelligences,
and though we seem to be sleeping,
there is an inner wakefulness
that directs the dream,
and that will eventually startle us back
to the truth of who we are.

- Rumi, "The Dream that Must be Interpreted"

I

Although he hated what passed for journalism in the mainstream news, Abel read it religiously. And not just news reports, but blogs and op-eds. In addition to the old historical novels he enjoyed, Abel force-fed himself a strict diet of cutting-edge drivel and rant, agenda and misinformation. He listened to venomous podcasts and stared at incomprehensible images and one-liners on speed platforms. There was a whole lot of crazy flooding the air, but one could learn a good deal from studying why people behaved the way they did. And Abel took nothing at face value. He checked sources, facts, and context, considered the motivations of everyone involved, and determined their conflicts of interest. He also delved as deeply as he could into news regarding science and medicine. All of this was a huge pain in the ass, but he considered it his duty to keep on top of world events and shifts in the tide of human sentiment. For the safety of his family. But God, how he hated it! And never more than in the winter months, which were long and dreary enough already. The winter following the business with Py's ants and his god had been particularly harsh, and the news especially gloomy. By February, Abel was reduced to skimming headlines just to keep his peace of mind.

One morning at the end of the month, he noticed that the temperature gauge was registering an unlikely forty-two degrees outside. Poking his head out, he was delighted to find the air practically balmy. Just an unseasonable winter day—what his mother would have called a spring tease—but Abel was damned if he'd ruin it with the news. *Any* news. He decided to take a little break for once.

"Why don't you all go for a hike?" he suggested to his family after breakfast. "I'll keep an eye on the Fishes and get my bread going."

The others were all happy to get out of the house, and Abel was happy to have the kitchen to himself. In sunlit peace, he mixed the dough for his rosemary bread while his charges lay quietly in their double bassinet at the foot of the table. Having reached the end of fetal development ahead of schedule, the Fishes had been evicted from Casa del Utero a few weeks ago, much to their displeasure. They greatly preferred living in a warm, nutrient-rich liquid to living in thin air; Abel imagined most babies felt that way, if they could only say so. But while other babies were stuck in their infant bodies, the Fishes spent very little time in theirs. Keeping an eye on them was like watching two kennels while each dog came and went as it pleased.

"Isn't this nice?" he murmured to them as he set his dough to rise. "No one jabbering at us or hectoring us, no commotion at all! Peace and quiet, for a change. And nothing going on in the world, as far as I can see." Washing his hands, he gazed out the window. The skies were a fine cerulean blue above a tattered sweep of clouds, the glade gently gilded with sunlight. Stunning as the god's ever-twilight had been, Abel found himself thinking that the ordinary world—with its play of light and shadow and changing weather—suited him just fine. And how could he have truly appreciated this golden morning if the last few months hadn't been so dismal? With a light heart, he poured himself a fresh cup of coffee and settled down in his usual place at the kitchen table. He automatically reached for his Spider to check the news, then stopped himself in time.

"No, no!" he muttered. "No calamities, insanity, or sheer stupidity. Not today."

Small, restful sounds came from the bassinet, and Abel glanced down fondly. The Fishes looked like nothing more than two adorable human infants. Yet, while they appeared to be sleeping, they could have been doing just about anything, anywhere— from accompanying the others on their hike to exploring the farthest corners of the globe. Jacqueline had done her best to give them real names when they were "born," but nothing stuck. The babies wouldn't answer to anything except *One Fish* and *Two Fish*.

Abel sipped his coffee and looked around the empty kitchen. Maybe he'd sharpen up the knives while he waited for his bread to rise. And a little music would be nice. He turned to his Spider to search for something invigorating and spring-like—Beethoven's Pastoral Symphony might be just the ticket—and accidentally tapped on the science news. A headline flashed up at once, cutting through the tranquil morning as sharply as a town crier.

Abel pulled up the article and read quickly, all thoughts of music and springtime forgotten. Then he pulled up a slew of other articles. The alarm for his bread went off, but the ex-lawyer ignored it.

"Goddamn," he muttered as he read, then slapped his palm on the heavy table. "God*damn!*"

Two Fish opened her eyes and looked up at him inquiringly.

"Tell your uncle that his microscopic seeds have sprouted," Abel said. "Ye gods!" He shook his head and took a cold sip of coffee, then got up to shape his loaves.

At that moment, Py was perched on the lip of an icy ravine, watching his sister with admiration. Descending the treacherous slope, Aurie was an unlikely amalgam of simian, feline, and arachnid traits. As she climbed, loped, and scuttled toward the snowy bottom, Py found himself leaning over the drop, wishing he could penetrate the world with the full chemical sense he no longer possessed. His god had eliminated that sense in the interest of restoring his normal vision, and Py's talent for jumping into things had been lost in the Labyrinth. Most of the time now he was content to see the world through either visual or aura mode, and he no longer felt compelled to overuse the latter. But there were times when he felt the loss of his other abilities with an intensity that surprised him. Times when he longed to plunge through the snow and enter the burrows of hibernating creatures, or the great networks of roots and fungi that honeycombed the earth.

Aurie, too, could no longer venture into the world of her own cells. Py wondered if she felt the way he did—painfully handicapped now and then—but he kept those feelings to himself. Bringing them up would only make her feel guilty. Although Aurie had reassembled his scattered aura, she was convinced the pieces that held his jumping talent had been left behind. And Py knew she would never forgive herself for that.

As his sister reached the bottom of the gorge, Two Fish came swimming up from wherever she'd been—an alpine lake, Py thought. He sensed her coming a few moments before she reached him. It always surprised him how human his infant niece and nephew actually looked, when his mental impression of them was strongly piscine, complete with long fins, shining scales, and eyes like corona stars. When Two Fish entered his mind, he caught the zing of cold mineral waters, as bracing as if she'd splashed him with her tail.

Hey, he complained. *You're getting me all wet!*

As if to correct his definition of *all wet,* she unleashed a tidal wave of icy lake water on Py, then capped it off by flinging a piece of milfoil in his face. Py bore the mental drenching stoically, but had to stop himself from picking imaginary wet weeds off his cheek.

Two Fish giggled. *Do you want to dry off, Uncle Py?*

Before he could reprimand her, Py was scoured and sandblasted with hot desert winds. He growled at his impish niece, but abruptly her mood sobered.

Uncle Abel says that your microscopic seeds have sprouted, she informed him. Then she darted away, leaving Py bewildered.

His microscopic seeds? Uncle Abel could only be referring to the god's creation, whatever had been released following the explosion in the Gulf last summer. Suddenly anxious, Py called down to Aurie.

"Mom and Dad still working their way up that hill?" she hollered back with a grin, as if they couldn't hear Howard and Jacqueline huffing and puffing a quarter mile behind.

"We have to get back," he told her. "Something's happened."

"It's in the news!" Abel said, as they all rushed into the kitchen. Normally, everyone would have doffed their snowy, muddy boots at the back-door entrance, but today no one gave a thought to such niceties. Two loaves of fresh bread waited on the table, along with a crock of butter and a pitcher of iced tea, but the food and drink went unnoticed. The Wakes only had eyes for the holo-articles magnified on the far wall. As one, the family gathered around to read.

Together, the articles described a new virus that had spread through the general population. It had been discovered during standard scans of bodily fluids, and was thought to be transmitted in aerosolized droplets. Following its initial discovery in saliva, the virus had been found in the brains of people who had died and donated their bodies to research. Since the donors had all died of completely unrelated causes, this new virus was not thought to be complicit in their deaths. And yet it was causing quite a stir because this was not a natural virus, but an engineered variant—and it encoded a protein based loosely on first-generation CRISPR technology.

Named amarantha for its seedlike capsid shell and its tenacious ability to spread, the virus appeared to only infect humans, and—based on data from autopsies and biopsies—only the brains of humans. It did so in an unprecedented way, taking up residence in different neuronal subpopulations in different people. And what it was doing there, no one knew.

Wherever it had come from, amarantha had spread as quickly and quietly as the fast-evolving plant it was named for. Dr. Eric Melman, now Director of Operations for the Federal Institute for Biomedical Research, was quoted as saying that an estimated ninety-eight percent of the world was infected, based on global epidemiological surveys. Dr. Melman was leading the international team tasked with investigating the new virus—and specifically the CRISPR-based protein it encoded.

"Melman," Howard hissed. "Hell, he probably *engineered*

this damned virus—and released it himself."

Jacqueline gave him a skeptical look. "Why on earth would he do that?"

"Money, power, political reasons. Who knows?" Howard had begun to pace the length of the kitchen, casting suspicious glances back at the magnified articles. "With that asshole, anything is possible. Maybe he's in bed with those bioweapons manufacturers in China and Southeast Asia. An engineered human virus springs up everywhere, and this guy just happens to be front and center? Doesn't sound like a coincidence to me."

"But the virus isn't hurting anyone," Abel pointed out.

"It isn't *killing* anyone," Howard corrected.

"Never mind your obsession with Melman," Jacqueline snapped. "You're forgetting that Py's god made *microscopic seeds* in the ants and released them into the winds. That sounds like a virus to me. And those ants were full of Py's CRISPR machine, which means this 'CRISPR-based protein' in amarantha is probably your CRISPR-evo."

Howard recoiled visibly. Beneath his obvious agitation was a deep-seated fear that the others could clearly sense. For whatever reason, he seemed to be hoping that Melman—and not the god—was responsible for amarantha. "That's a pretty big leap, Jackie. This amarantha is just a virus engineered to cause trouble, which sounds a lot more like the work of some human than the work of a god."

"Oh, come on, Dad," Py protested. "You know it's CRISPR-evo! Look here—*'We still don't know the function of the CRISPR-based protein encoded by amarantha.'* They can't figure out what it does."

"Melman and his cronies are just pretending they don't know," Howard muttered. "Trying to cover their asses."

Abel shook his head. "It isn't just Melman's task force doing the work. All the leading research institutions around the world are studying this thing. So far, they're all stumped. Apparently this CRISPR machine doesn't look like anything a normal scientist could have dreamed up."

Jacqueline uttered a dry chuckle.

"That's gotta be the Prof!" Aurie elbowed her brother hard in her excitement. "Your god must've decided to keep him as part of his creation."

Py nodded agreement. "So what's the Prof doing in this virus?"

Before anyone could throw out a suggestion, a series of heart-wrenching whimpers came from the bassinet, and images of floating bottles entered every mind in the room.

"Oh, for the love of God," Aurie muttered.

"Both of them actually at home, awake, and hungry, for a wonder!" Jacqueline hurried to get two bottles of formula from the fridge. "If those two spend any more time away from their bodies, we'll have to feed them intravenously."

"Well, godlings can't be bothered with the petty needs of the flesh," Howard said, looking grateful for the interruption. He took one of the bottles and whisked Two Fish out of the bassinet. He and Jacqueline fed their grandkids at the table, while the others finally settled down to sate their own appetites ... although their eyes kept straying to the articles on the wall.

"Assuming this is the work of Py's god," Abel began, nodding toward the articles. Howard began to interject, but Abel cut him off. "Just humor me for a minute, will you? Forget about your old nemesis and consider the possibility that Py's god decided to tinker with your fancy CRISPR machine. What do you think he's programmed it to do in our grey matter? Brainwash us into behaving ourselves?"

Everyone laughed but Howard.

"What's wrong, Dad?" Py asked.

Howard shook his head. "*Everything* about this is wrong! You all want to believe this is the work of Py's god, and you want to speculate about his motivations. Fine, let's throw some ideas around. Starting with this—what if the god decided that the human species can't be fixed, after all? What if eradication is still the goal?" He shrugged at their incredulous expressions. "Wouldn't be hard, would it? A virus with the ability to sterilize the population is all it would take. That would explain why we haven't seen any obvious effects yet. And he could do it without harming his 'family,' without killing a single person on Earth." His expression turned bleak. "Just making sure the human race died a slow and painless death."

"But if that were the case, wouldn't this virus be sitting in our gonads instead of our brains?" Abel demanded.

"The brain controls the production of sex hormones," Jacqueline said. "It controls everything, really."

Howard sighed. "Whatever's going on, we need to get samples of this virus and analyze it ourselves. We certainly can't trust anyone else to do it."

Jacqueline snorted agreement. "But we might be part of the two percent of humans on the planet who are still uninfected. If we go out there … "

"You really think we're uninfected?" Howard shook his head. "That virus started in Casco Bay, just eighty miles from here! It probably hit the people on that cruise ship first, and everyone along the coast. You and Abel have been to town half a dozen times since then."

Jacqueline and Abel glanced at each other uneasily.

"So let's just spit in some tubes and find out," Howard said. "We can isolate DNA from the cells in our saliva, and if the CRISPR machine is there, we can amplify it before dinner. The kids are our positive controls."

"The virus will only be in our saliva if it's currently active," his wife pointed out. "A negative result won't tell us anything."

Abel looked puzzled, so Aurie explained. "If there's no CRISPR machine in your saliva, it *could* mean that you're not infected with the virus. Or it could mean that you *are* infected, but all the virus is living in your brain cells."

"Yes, yes," said Howard impatiently. "But a *positive* result will reveal a CRISPR machine. And then we can sequence the damned thing and see if it's really mine. If it's not, then someone—probably FIBR—is up to no good … and we can congratulate ourselves on staying the hell away from the world."

Very late that night, they had the negative result Jacqueline had predicted: no CRISPR transgene was detectable in anyone but Py and Aurie. Not knowing if they were infected with amarantha left the adults in the family dissatisfied. And not having the amarantha CRISPR DNA to sequence left Howard grimly resolved.

"We have to get our hands on some active virus," he said when they were all gathered in the library.

Jacqueline nodded. "Shouldn't be too hard, if amarantha is as infectious as everyone says it is. There's gotta be some active virus in *someone's* saliva. The simplest thing would be to run down to Bethel and steal a bag of restaurant trash ... but the roads won't be passable for at least a few more weeks."

"We can take the UTV now, if you don't want to wait until spring," Abel put in.

"Suppose we do that," Howard said. "And suppose it *is* my CRISPR-evo machine being made by this virus that has infected nearly all of mankind." He was quiet for a moment. "In that case, amarantha is clearly the god's work. But how do we figure out what it's doing?"

In the silence that followed, Py and Aurie glanced at each other, but neither of them said a word.

"FIBR and all the other institutions are studying this virus in isolation," Howard went on. "They're turning it inside-out and doing every experiment they can think of. But how can they really study something that only infects human brains? The most inaccessible tissue of all!"

"For ethical scientists," Jacqueline said uneasily.

"Yes," Howard said grimly. "And those are in short supply at FIBR."

Another moment of silence passed, this one longer and heavier than the last.

"Dammit," Howard said softly. "I would have sworn that nothing—I mean *nothing*—could have dragged me back into the world. Not after you spent that night in police custody, waiting for one of FIBR's detectives to torture you before breakfast."

"I won't ever forget that." Jacqueline gave her brother-in-law a grateful look before turning back to Howard. "But you're not thinking we should leave here, are you?"

"All of *you* are staying here," Howard said. "But I started this whole damned thing. I'm responsible—"

"Hang on a second," said Abel sharply. "If you're taking all the credit or blame for letting Py's god loose in the world, we're all responsible for that. You may have started the ball rolling, but the rest of us had a chance to stop it, and instead we greased the hill." He turned to his nephew. "We *all* cut one of those cords for your god. Weren't those the emotional attachments that were holding him back?"

Py nodded. Jacqueline glanced at her kids, noticing their unusual reticence, but Howard was still lost in self-reproach. He walked over to the French doors and appraised the darkness outside. Then he looked up into the clear night skies and shivered.

"It doesn't matter who cut what," he murmured. "*I* built CRISPR-evo and I am ultimately responsible for it. For every god that awakens. For whatever they do ... to this world or any other."

"You're forgetting that CRISPR-evo would never have worked without the tinkering of another irresponsible scientist," Jacqueline reminded him. "Who saved ... how many other dangerous gods *in ovo*? Eight hundred and fifty-nine thousand?"

"And seven hundred and twenty-two," Aurie added, sharing a conspiratorial glance with her mother. "Including the Little Fishes. And *I'm* responsible for waking Py's god, we all know that."

"And I made that necessary in the first place," Py said, "by turning my ants into a super-aggressive, self-aware Colony."

"And all of you reprobates would be safe behind bars," said Abel, "if it weren't for the meddling of an ex-lawyer turned outlaw."

Howard uttered a reluctant laugh. "So what you're all saying is, there's plenty of blame to go around?"

"It's pointless to talk about blame," Jacqueline said. She looked at her children with a love that overrode the emotions racking her troubled mind. "We're a CRISPR-evo family, for better or worse. For better *and* worse. Whatever we have to deal with, we'll deal with it together."

Howard looked around at his family and a muscle near his jaw quivered. Then his expression tightened and he turned back to the window. "That doesn't mean all seven of us are trekking down to Bethesda and into the lion's den."

"Bethesda?" Jacqueline expelled a frustrated breath. "What in the world are you planning to do? Break into FIBR and have a look at their secret files? Search for unwilling research subjects and set them free? You were a hell of a rogue scientist, but you're not a spy or a government operative."

"I'll have a talk with Alé," Howard muttered, "and we'll figure something out."

"*We* will figure something out." Jacqueline strode over to grasp his hand. "All of us. Not just you!"

Howard nodded and kissed the top of her head, but his gaze had drifted back to the dark skies outside. Low in the southeast, a world that humans had named for the ancient god of dissolution, renewal, and liberation shone steadily down on them, brighter than any star.

II

Early the next morning, Aurie went looking for Py and finally found him in the Birch Grove. He was sitting on a thermopad against his favorite tree. His ants, apparently roused from their winter diapause by yesterday's spring tease, swarmed over and around him. It was a sight that never failed to mesmerize her. She lingered just outside the grove, remembering an old conversation that had taken place here, a day or two after the Labyrinth.

"Looks like you have your old friends back," Aurie said as the motley crew ran over her brother in waves. The Birch Grovers were joined by many more, black and russet and honey-colored ants from other nests in Py's supercolony. These were the ones who had stayed behind when their hitchhiking sisters followed her to town under the influence of Py's dream.

"I know you can't go inside them now," she said. "But can you still communicate? Can you work with them the way you used to?"

Py chuckled. "You're thinking of these ants as something separate, but we're really extensions of each other."

Once he said it, Aurie saw what he meant. The ants on and around Py were not behaving like individual creatures at all. They moved like the tendrils of an enormous jellyfish, or the drifting leaves of a seagrass.

"We share a soul," Py told her. "And we're not fighting that anymore."

"I thought the god displaced your soul from the Colony," she said, puzzled. "Didn't your soul fly back to eternity and incarnate in other places and times? And then come back to your human body when I returned your aura?"

"Yeah, but my soul came back to the Colony, too," Py said.

"That thread you spun from my aura held all my memories, human and ant. And when my soul returned, I was myself again—my human self and my Colony self. I know it's hard to believe, but I am the Colony, Aurie. We share the Prof, and we share a soul."

"Forever?" She found the idea hard to accept.

"My human body won't live forever." He glanced at the fluid sheath of his second skin, and Aurie caught a glimpse of the ant-soul in his eyes. "But my Colony might. Even an ordinary super-colony can live for thousands of years and span hundreds of generations ... and this Colony is CRISPR-evo."

The idea of her brother outliving her by thousands of years was a daunting one. Aurie wasn't sure how she felt about it.

"And what is Colony Py going to do now?" she asked him. "When you gave the ants your soul, they wanted to dominate all other species. Then you became the Colony and wanted to evolve with other species. Then your god awoke and engineered his one mysterious change for the good of all life on Earth."

Py grinned at her. "The idea of evolution keeps evolving, doesn't it?" But his smile faded quickly, leaving him looking strangely time-worn. For a moment, Aurie saw her brother as a very old man, his eyes sunken and weary. In the next instant, he was his nine-year-old self again, but a trace of that deep fatigue remained.

"I think Colony Py is worn out," he said quietly. "When it comes to evolution, I'm ready for a rest."

Musing on that conversation, Aurie entered the grove and laid claim to a corner of Py's pad, careful not to crush any ants.

"Finally coming over to say hi? Thought you were going to stand there all morning like a turkey hunter." Py sounded amused. "What are you doing up so early?"

"Couldn't sleep," she said, but her attention was fixed on the insects running over him in burnished waves of topaz and garnet and onyx. These restless little organisms were a part of him, and he could no longer see inside them!

"Why doesn't your Prof give you back your last Change?" she murmured. "Let you see everything in chemical form again? You could at least *see* inside your ants ... even if you can't *jump* inside them anymore."

"You're not still beating yourself up over that, are you?"

"No," she lied. "Just curious."

He looked down at the ants enveloping his arm. "It would be fun if the world were my playground again ... but I don't *need* to peer into things, or see the forge of creation, or jump into the heart of another atom. And I don't need to meddle with these pieces of myself. I'll Change again when it's time."

His calm acceptance of his own fate confounded her. "How can you be so relaxed about that? After everything you've done, everything you've *been?*"

"That's why," he said simply.

Aurie laughed a little bitterly. "I guess we can't complain, can we? I mean, we've already had our share. More than our share."

Her brother gave her a keen glance. "You still miss the Doctor, don't you?"

"Don't you ever miss the Prof?" she countered. "He's still in your cells, too. You just can't talk to him anymore."

"I actually *would* like to talk to him, now that things have calmed down." Py reached toward the ground to receive a new group of ants, which quickly melded with the rest. "He tried so hard to teach me things, but I wasn't all that receptive, you know? I was busy trying to escape the Colony, or become the Colony, or keep it from overrunning the world ... and he always said things that scared or upset me. Never what I wanted to hear."

"The Doctor never said what I wanted to hear, either," Aurie admitted. "But I miss him so much."

"Maybe if I'd had more time with the Prof, we would have become friends, like you and the Doctor."

'Friends' wasn't an adequate word, Aurie knew, but neither was any other. The Doctor had been more than her friend and teacher and co-conspirator; he had been an essential part of her. It was terrible to think of his transgene still being expressed in her cells, no longer producing new copies of the Doctor, only of the original insentient tool her dad had engineered. Without the god-fire of the Feather, it was impossible to believe that her CRISPR-evo machine would ever be anything more than a lifeless protein. She felt as if a piece of her own soul had died and been entombed inside her.

Trying to dispel her melancholy, Aurie looked around at the familiar grove, painted with ordinary twilight. She tried to remember the Garden in its glory, but all she could conjure up was a gilded picture, static as a painting rendered with colors too vivid to be believable. The reality of the Garden couldn't be captured and preserved on the canvas of her mind. But knowing this produced only a trace of the old discontent; since the loss of her god's Feather, Aurie no longer felt the intense, aching hunger for other-worldly things. Just then, she understood Py's contentment to be what he was—not a god, but a human boy who had once surrendered himself to a god, and cast an unknown Gift into the world.

"You were pretty quiet last night," she said, finally broaching the subject she had come there to talk about. "Didn't really say a word during that whole discussion."

"Neither did you," Py reminded her, giving her a sidelong look.

Aurie nodded. "I figured it was better to let them hash it out on their own. It's kind of funny, if you think about it."

"What?"

"Mom and Dad and Uncle Abel," she said. "They're all upset over the idea that the god made a virus. Especially Dad. But when they were in the Labyrinth, caught up in the god's dream, they trusted him. Enough to cut his ties to humanity ... knowing he had the power to obliterate the human species. They put the fate of mankind in the hands of a god!"

"Well, they certainly didn't trust the god on his own. And I'm not sure they would've trusted *me* on my own. They trusted us together." Py frowned. "The god's memories are clear on that."

"They actually thought you were sharing your head with the god," Aurie marveled. "And able to influence him!"

"That's what their minds believed," Py said. "But in the Labyrinth, they saw our souls as one. A fusion of human and god. I think they saw the shape of my soul in the god's own. And maybe he changed a bit during his time in my head, his time as *Py*. Anyway, they trusted that soul to do what was best."

Aurie snorted. "That's a pretty big gamble."

"You took a pretty big gamble yourself," Py said. "You saw through to the source of their faith, the source of the god's power ... and you believed in it. Completely. You staked the fate of the world on it."

Aurie was quiet for a moment, a little awed by the memory.

"But what's happened to *their* faith?" she said at last. "It was there in the god's dream ... but as soon as they stepped out of the Labyrinth, their minds took over again. And now they're back to doubting and worrying and trying to control things."

Py nodded. "Trying to put the god in a test tube."

"The god? You mean the Professor, don't you?"

Py's eyes took on a sudden gleam. "I don't think the Prof is working on his own."

Aurie stared at him, wondering if they suspected the same thing.

"I don't think the god died when he created that virus," Py went on. "I think he's *in* it."

"But he said that a world-changing act would kill him," Aurie reminded her brother.

"I know," Py admitted. "All those memories of his are ingrained in my head, so I know he believed that. It must have been a death he experienced many times before. But I think this time was different. I think he's *part* of amarantha."

"So instead of destroying the human race," Aurie mused, "your god demoted himself? He made a virus from the DNA of those escaped ants and sealed himself inside ... with his own devil's advocate?" It was a crazy theory, and it sounded even crazier spoken out loud, but Py only nodded.

"And if he *is* inside people's heads, what's he doing in there?" Aurie wondered. "Does he still have the tinkering ability of a god, or is he more limited now? Is he just directing the Prof to carry out his plans?"

"I doubt it." Py chuckled. "Whatever's going on, I have a feeling that the Prof isn't just the god's tool. I think they're a dichotomous deity ... and polar opposites when it comes to risk versus reward."

"So the amarantha virus might contain your CRISPR machine *and* your god." Aurie was quiet for a moment, thinking. "Why didn't you say any of this last night?"

"It wouldn't have made any difference," Py said, with a trace of his father's cynicism. "All of them would still be in a tizzy ... and Dad would still be making plans to run off and try to save the world."

"Yeah, but you ought to tell them what you're thinking."

Py shrugged. "I don't have any proof ... and I don't really *know* if the god is inside this virus. It's just a feeling."

"The Fishes can still feel him, too," Aurie said. "Very faintly. Even though they don't pay much attention to human events, and they didn't know a thing about amarantha."

"Where *are* the Fishes? They ought to be rounding us up for breakfast by now."

Aurie glanced up at the brightening sky above the treetops. "Yeah ... guess we ought to head back."

Py leaned forward and all the ants trailed away, gliding through the leaf litter back to their many nests. The two of them headed home, lost in their own thoughts. When their house came into view between the leafless branches of the oak grove, Py paused to gaze at it.

"Uncle Abel's CRISPR-evo Farm," he murmured. "I made that up as a joke, remember? But now ... I guess the entire world might be a CRISPR-evo farm."

III

Twilight was a good word, Aurie thought—one of those rare words that means more by being imprecise. Either the first light of day or the last. Heralding the beginning or the end … and who really knew one from the other?

While the others engaged in a general discussion of viruses over dinner, Aurie looked out the window, losing herself in the silence of the dusky glade. She had been lonely for the Doctor all day, and distracted by speculations about amarantha. Despite her mother's insistence that they'd discuss it as a family, Howard and Jacqueline had been making furtive calls and having private discussions and arguments all day long. Aurie knew that even if they collected some active virus from a nearby town, there was only so much they could do with it in a garage lab. And her dad wanted to study amarantha with every tool he could get his hands on. More, he yearned to infiltrate the world's most exclusive and self-contained science city. Howard had always been madly curious about what went on inside FIBR's high walls, and now he had a pressing reason to find out. So it was just a matter of time before he ventured back into the world on his own … to study and try to control the god's creation. And to thwart those who would hurt others in their efforts to do the same.

I'm the one who should be studying this thing, she thought as her uncle pulled a dried fig tart out of the oven. *And not in a lab … inside my own cells.* If only she could go inside herself and make changes the way she used to! With that ability restored, she would have less to fear from an unknown virus than anyone on Earth. She could run to town this very minute and get her own sample of amarantha. The Grand Harvest Market in Gorham ought to be crawling with live virus.

When sleep finally came that night, Aurie was troubled by

strange dreams. In one, she lay marooned on an endless plain, pressed flat by the weight of the sky. In another, she wandered through a tunnel marked with countless closed doors. Through the chinks between each door and its frame spilled the fire of a distant sun. Aurie glimpsed the light of green dawns and saffron dusks; she caught the scent of winds passing over fertile plains and mineral seas. But every door she tried to open was locked.

At last she came to a much smaller door. It opened easily and Aurie found herself in the familiar wilderness of her cartoon cell. It was the way she'd imagined it when she was very young. The molecular inhabitants of the nucleus were rendered with childish abandon, as fanciful as the creatures in *McElligot's Pool*. Festooned seahorses drifted by, and jellyfish that trailed impossibly long tentacles. Giant, X-shaped rafts whizzed past in wild streaks of blue and purple. Two fish were approaching at a more sedate speed, and she smiled as she recognized them.

Hello, fishlings, she said. *What mischief are you up to in here?*

No mischief, said One Fish innocently, but his eyes gleamed with excitement.

His sister hovered beside him, twitching her long golden fins. *We have a message from the Doctor!*

Aurie felt her heartbeat quicken. *The Doctor in your cells? He finally spoke to you?*

He said he's been trying to get our attention for a long time, said One Fish, sounding abashed. *But we were so busy going places and doing things ... we didn't hear him until now.*

Well, what did he say? Aurie demanded.

He wants to try an experiment, said One Fish, looking excited again. *Take one of our scales.*

Aurie looked closer at her children, whose piscine bodies were sheathed in fine scales of opaline colors. *You mean, I should pull one out?*

It won't hurt us, One Fish assured her. *Go ahead! Take one of mine.*

So Aurie reached out and touched her son's side, just above

his gills. She felt for the crisp edge of a single scale and gave it a little tug. The scale came free. In her hands, it glowed like a drop of fire and she felt the stirring of an old memory.

What should I do with it? she asked, but the Fishes were already swimming away.

Wait! Aurie called out, chasing them through the hubbub of the cell. In her haste, she collided with a giant scaffold. Toppling end-over-end, she knocked into a bundle of actin filaments, which scattered like twigs.

You haven't lost it, have you? asked a sourly familiar voice.

Dizzy, Aurie looked up to see a scholarly head peering around the scaffold. Then she looked down at her hands, which still held the shimmering scale.

Ah, good, said the Professor. He was apparently still tied to the scaffold, with Aurie's emergency alarm system unperturbed.

You haven't managed to get free of that? she said, a bit horrified.

It's a dastardly piece of engineering, sighed the Professor. *Thanks to your quality work, I've been incarcerated in this wretched stem cell for nearly a year now! What I wouldn't have given for the dignity of a timely death.*

I wouldn't have left you like that, Aurie said. *But I can't go inside myself anymore ... and the Doctor is gone. I mean, he's still here somewhere, but he isn't himself. And this is all just a dream, anyway.*

Dreams can be powerful things, the Professor reminded her. *Or I wouldn't be able to help you at all. As for your Doctor, I assure you he is still very much himself. We've had many fascinating discussions in this otherwise uninspiring room with no windows.*

He's really alive—and still himself? Aurie scarcely dared to believe it. *But I can't communicate with him anymore!*

When you used up that Feather, your connection was lost, the Professor told her. *But you have everything you need to restore it in the palms of your hands.*

Aurie looked down at the god-fire she held. It had lost its

scale shape and now looked like a scrap of dancing sunlight or a flame. *This is like my Feather, isn't it? The fire that made him real!*

The Professor shook his head and his expression softened. *That Feather only sustained your connection to him. You and your god together made the Doctor real. You dreamed him up, and your god gave him life and a voice. And you both gave him the wisdom of your past lives.*

Aurie was shocked into silence. *Then who made you real?* she asked at last. *Py never imagined you like this, did he?*

Py isn't as visual as you are, admitted the Professor. *But his imagination is larger, deeper, and more terrifying by far. What he might have done to the world!*

But you are so much the opposite, Aurie pointed out. *How could Py and his god have created ... you?*

The Professor smiled. *The lament of many a parent. Humans are always shocked when their creations don't turn out to be carbon copies of themselves. But that's life, my girl—it never manifests or grows according to plan.* In the dancing light of the flame, his face blurred as the dream began to fade.

Don't go, not yet! Aurie looked down at the god-fire in her hand as she fought to stay in the dream. *How do I use this to connect with the Doctor again?*

You need to see him as clearly as you see me, the Professor said, but he was dissolving along with the cell around him. *Go back to the beginning. Recreate him in your mind.*

Aurie woke abruptly, blinking in the dark. The dream was gone, but the sense of its importance hadn't faded. And if there was even the slightest chance ...

Closing her eyes again, she took a deep breath.

The beginning.

When had she spun those threads that her god had cast onto the loom of creation? When had she first imagined her CRISPR machine as a real person?

Aurie thought back to the first time she'd envisioned the Doctor, building the cartoon cell—his office—around him. She pictured the white coat and stethoscope, the cotton-ball puffs of hair above his ears. She imagined his scalpel and bright blue eyes. She allowed that visage to evolve as the real Doctor had, losing his cartoonish qualities and becoming as human as she was. She filled her mind with his gruff voice, his no-nonsense briskness, his occasional lapses into tenderness. He had looked after her in the hardest possible way, always driving her toward her best self. He had been stern and wise and unafraid, never hesitating to plunge into the deepest part of life's pool. When she had the real Doctor firmly in mind, she called forth the flame the Fishes had given her. A Scale and not a Feather ... yet it burned with the same fire. Her vision of the Doctor was bathed in its radiance, and Aurie found herself wondering what their relationship really *was*. Not simply creator and creation; they felt more like symbionts or two halves of a whole. Were they evolving as one, or forging separate, intertwining paths as they spurred each other's growth? Aurie didn't know, but she knew instantly when her connection was restored. The god-fire reshaped itself, contracting its wild, expansive light, finally settling into a single spark of consciousness that shone from the depths of the blue eyes regarding her.

The Doctor smiled at her. *I see my experiment was a success!*

It's you—it's really you! Joy filled Aurie to overflowing, and she found herself unable to say anything more.

Of course it's me, the Doctor said, but he gazed at her with obvious relief. *I can't tell you how good it is to see you again, my dear. That Professor is a worthy fellow, but I've missed your company greatly. It was truly terrible to know everything you were thinking and feeling, and be unable to communicate! I'm only sorry it took me so long to come up with the solution. Using the power of dreams and gods ... well, such things are not exactly in my wheelhouse.*

I thought you were gone for good! Aurie gazed at the Doctor intensely, half-afraid he would regress into an insentient protein if she looked away. *I thought you might be yourself in the Fishes, because they have the god-fire to sustain you. I was so envious of them!*

The Doctor snorted. *Yes, plenty of god-fire, but no connection to me whatsoever. And those children of yours are the worst hosts imaginable—they are almost never home. But listen to me complaining when you've been disabled all this time! That's behind us too, thank the gods.*

Aurie wondered what the Doctor was talking about. Surely he couldn't mean her ability to—

Certainly that's what I mean, he said. *Did you think that god-fire was only good for restoring our lost connection? It restored all of your lost abilities, naturally! Oh … your captured Professor entreats you to give him his well-earned rest. Do I have your permission to do so? As much as he's enjoyed our discussions, I think he's very uncomfortable living in an organism that's not his host.*

Yes, of course. Aurie remembered the Prof's chagrin in her dream. *Tell him thank you, too … for everything he's done.*

The Doctor nodded. *I think you'd better get some rest yourself, now. Your dreams have not been peaceful ones.*

I don't want to sleep, Aurie said hotly. *I want to stay up and talk! Do you realize it's been almost a year since we talked?*

Yes, indeed, the Doctor said. *A very long year!*

I need to tell you about amarantha, Aurie said.

No need, my dear. I've been here all this time, remember? Listening to everything. The Doctor's voice was both gentle and unyielding. *We can skip the introduction and begin the discussion … tomorrow.*

And before Aurie could go inside herself and do anything about it, she was immersed in deep and dreamless sleep, the most restful sleep she'd ever had.

IV

Aurie awoke to bright winter sunlight filling her room. She raised her head in surprise, inhaling the aromas of coffee and a savory casserole, and listening to the murmur of voices from the kitchen. She had never overslept like this! It was even harder to believe that everyone had let her do it, even the Fishes.

With a sigh, Aurie sank back onto her pillow and closed her eyes. The clear memory of a dream drifted through her mind, one that was far too good to be true. She had taken a scale from one of the Fishes—blazing with god-fire—and restored her connection with the Doctor! But she had dreamed of reviving him before, and always woken up to bitter disappointment. No miracle had ever lasted beyond the veil of sleep.

Well, this one has, came the Doctor's crisp voice from inside her. *Do you really think you could've overslept on your own?*

Aurie's eyes flew open. That certainly sounded like the Doctor ... but it was still too good to be true. If her overactive imagination was playing tricks on her—

For the love of all the gods, the Doctor groaned. *Our connection is fully restored, and so are you, my dear. Now come in here and say a proper hello!*

With a glad cry, Aurie sent her consciousness sailing inward. How good it was to travel her inner world again! She glided through her cells like the softest of winds, thrilling to the textures and murmurs of each healthy tissue. She gave herself a fever and chills, started a fire of inflammation in her big toe, then set her pulse racing, just for the fun of it. After setting everything back to rights, she finally entered the realm of her cartoon cell.

The Doctor was waiting for her in his protein armchair, looking as if he he'd never left it. He raised an eyebrow at her.

Enjoying yourself?

Just knocking the rust off, she said, delighted to see him. *But look at you—portlier than ever! What were you doing all this time, stuffing yourself silly?*

I was keeping your captive Professor entertained. And thinking up plans to restore our lost connection, not to mention trying my hardest to get the attention of your children.

Who are never home, I know.

You do not know! The Doctor shook his head in exasperation. *If you had any inkling of the wild flights they've taken ...*

I thought you couldn't follow their souls out of their bodies, she reminded him.

I can't, he acknowledged. *And when their souls leave their bodies, those journeys aren't recorded in the brains they leave behind. However, after returning home, their souls' out-of-body memories and all subsequent thoughts are recorded. Now that your children's brains have developed, I know everything they experience after the fact. It's a wonder I have any hair left at all.*

Aurie laughed. *Lucky Fishes! Why would they spend time in their own cells with all of the world to explore?*

Speaking of which, said the Doctor sternly. *We need to talk before you set foot in the Grand Harvest Market in Gorham.*

At first Aurie had no idea what he was talking about, but then she remembered her plans to get hold of some live amarantha virus. She chuckled. *I'm not used to having my mind read anymore. Or my thoughts spelled out before I can get them in order.*

Well, let's get them in order before you head to town, shall we? This amarantha ... we don't know what it is.

That's the point; we need to find out! What do you think it is? Do you think the god and the Prof coexist, or are they a single entity?

Impossible to say, the Doctor said.

Amarantha could be the Professor with Py's god giving orders, Aurie mused. *Or it could be the god in the form of a CRISPR machine. Hey, what does the Prof know about amarantha? Oh, crap ... I guess we should've asked him before you gave him his well-earned rest. We don't have our spy anymore.*

No, the Doctor agreed. *But he and I had many months in which to speculate about amarantha. I'm afraid speculation was all it was; he doesn't know anything more than we do. Which means that whatever form he's taken in the virus is different enough that our Professor can't communicate with those altered copies of himself.*

Aurie thought back to her conversation with Py the previous day. *Maybe amarantha is something we can't even imagine.*

Exactly, said the Doctor. *So we can't assume that I can protect you from it, or that you can protect yourself. It's unlikely either one of us could supersede this entity, whatever it is.*

You make the god sound like our enemy. Don't you trust him?

I trust him to do what he believes is in the best interests of this world, the Doctor said. *That may not always coincide with your best interests—and we'd be fools to forget it.*

Aurie grunted in agreement. *That's why I have no intention of getting infected … at least not right away. I'm going to kidnap amarantha the same way I kidnapped the Prof.*

You're going to bring a single virion into one of your cells? The Doctor sounded dubious.

And keep it under lock and key, she assured him.

Viruses replicate quickly!

But they can't do anything without the host's machinery.

This is hardly a normal virus.

Biologically, it's normal enough, Aurie countered. *FIBR and the rest of the world have been studying it for months. Except for the CRISPR machine it encodes, amarantha is a virus like any other.*

If worse comes to worst, and you do get infected—

Then I'll be in the same boat as the rest of humanity, Aurie admitted. *Except that our boat has some pretty sophisticated surveillance, repair systems, and communications capabilities.*

Even the best-equipped boat in the world can still be dashed to pieces and sunk, the Doctor warned her.

He was beginning to sound like the Prof, and Aurie glared at him. *And what would you call the best-equipped boat in the world if it sat in a sheltered harbor and never ventured out on the open seas?*

The Doctor chuckled. *I'd call it a waste of engineering. But if this boat is planning to sneak out of the harbor, I would suggest waiting until tonight, when all the other boats are asleep.*

That sounded like a good idea until Aurie remembered how worried and upset her parents had been every time she ran off at a critical juncture. They would be beside themselves if she left in the middle of the night without a word. Leaving a message with the Fishes seemed just as cowardly, and Py ... Py would never forgive her.

I won't sneak off, she said. *I'll talk to them all right now.*

The Doctor looked surprised, and then he smiled—the smile of a parent who realizes his child is growing up. *What are you going to tell them?*

That I can communicate with you and make changes to my cells again—which means I'm in the best and safest position to get the answers we want. That I'm leaving after breakfast and I'll be home by dinner. And it'll be fastest if I go alone. It was unlikely the conversation would go that smoothly, but one could always hope.

Fair enough, said the Doctor. *But let's steer clear of becoming a test subject, shall we? Because heaven only knows what amarantha is doing in the human brain.*

Gods aren't magicians, she murmured. *They're more like expert tinkerers.*

That still leaves a Pandora's Box of possibilities, the Doctor said. *And we don't know what the god's purpose is.*

Aurie had been mulling that over, remembering the horrific scenes the god had shown them ... and the history she'd learned while teaching her children. Humans inflicted the worst suffering on each other, then vowed never to repeat the mistakes of the past. People might shut their eyes to the brute inside them, but the brute remained. That unsleeping monster—with ever more sophisticated weapons in its grasp—promised that every horror would be repeated again and again.

He said we didn't know how to love each other, Aurie reminded the Doctor. *Maybe he wants to teach us how.*

Or maybe he's planning to sterilize the human race, as your dad suggested, said the Doctor grimly.

It was a sobering thought, but Aurie didn't think it was true. *Remember what the god said? His greatest fear was that another god would awaken and be shaped by an evil human soul. Maybe he's keeping watch in all of us to make sure that doesn't happen.*

Let's hope it really is that simple, sighed the Doctor.

Returning her awareness to the outer world, Aurie got dressed quickly. Catching the flash of her eyes in the window pane, she saw her own excitement and nervousness mirrored there. She imagined drawing the amarantha virus into one of her cells like a tiny spaceship ... and going to meet its god-captain. Aurie tried to envision the god's intrepid soul shining from the cautious Professor's eyes. But for once her imagination failed her, and the figure lurking in the darkness of its alien craft remained faceless.

It may be *faceless, for all we know,* murmured the Doctor inside her. *Faceless, voiceless, unapproachable. How will you handle that, my dear?*

Aurie smiled as she headed down the hall to breakfast and the heated discussion that was surely coming. Her family would be afraid for her, and she couldn't blame them for that. The world outside these sheltered woods was a labyrinth full of unknown dangers, after all. But she wouldn't be navigating it alone.

Let's talk about it on the way to town, she told the Doctor. *And whatever we find there, we'll handle it together.*

Which means you'll do whatever you want and I'll be hard pressed to keep you alive, he groused, but she could hear the protective warmth in his voice. It was the warmth of the fire that joined them, a fire that would never go out again.

Glossary of Terms with Examples

*contains spoilers

***aura**:* the energy matrix of a soul. Depending on the organism, an aura can include memories, personality, character traits, and emotions.

***awareness/consciousness**:* the way a mind perceives reality. A soul also has its own awareness, as with the embryonic Fishes, whose minds are still undeveloped.

***Change**:* a powerful ability bestowed on Py or Aurie by a CRISPR-evo machine.

    ***Aurie**:* Aurie has only undergone one Change: the awakening of the god in her genome. That god gave her the power to project her soul into the microcosm of her own cells and modify them. Aurie kept this ability even after her god flew away to seed life on a distant planet.

    ****Py**:* Py has undergone three Changes: 1) the ability to see auras, including certain biological chemicals; 2) the ability to see auras through any object, and 3) the ability to see all chemicals through any object. When the god in the Colony awakened and took possession of Py's human mind, it undid this third Change in the interest of restoring normal human vision. In addition to his CRISPR-evo-conferred abilities, Py has a natural talent for projecting his soul outside of his body, a talent that was lost as a result of events in the Labyrinth.

****CRISPR-evo machine**:* the powerful protein engineered by Howard to drive evolution in his children. Aurie's Doctor and Py's Professor have evolved self-awareness and distinct personalities of their own. Each is endowed with the conscious and unconscious knowledge of his host, along with some of the wisdom of the sleeping god encoded in his host's genome. Thus, these protein entities know a good deal more than their hosts do.

Feather: a fragment of the soul of Aurie's god, which she pulled from its wing on the brink of its flight. *Prior to events in the Labyrinth, the Feather gave Aurie the continued power to project her soul internally and make biological changes to her cells; it also sustained her connection with the Doctor, allowing them to communicate.

god: a powerful, sentient being that is driven to create, nurture, and shape life in all its forms. *Gods fall into two general categories: *pioneer* (e.g., Aurie's god) and *engineer* (e.g., Py's god). Although vastly capable, gods are not omnipotent. They are limited by the materials and mechanisms of the world in which they awaken.

god template: a space-faring seed that gives rise to gods. On Earth, this seed manifests as a dormant template scattered throughout the genome of every terrestrial organism. Unlike ordinary DNA, the god template is protected from loss and mutation. Although the same template exists in every organism, it gives rise to very different gods when activated. While asleep in the genome of an organism, a god dreams, and some of those dreams influence its host. The soul of the host then influences the nature of the god, if and when it awakens.

Little Fishes: Aurie's children, created from her own eggs in which she awakened the god template. The Fishes have souls that are part god and part human. Because Aurie's eggs contain the transgene for her CRISPR-evo machine, the Doctor lives in her children just as he lives in her. Unlike her, however, the Fishes have no special connection to the Doctor, or any interest in their own physical forms.

soul: essential spiritual self. The souls of both creatures and gods reincarnate in various forms, times, and places.

absence: A body cannot survive long in the absence of a soul. One exception to this is the host body of a god, which can survive for extended periods if the god's soul is elsewhere.

***assimilation/eviction**: A soul can be assimilated by a stronger one, as when Py's soul absorbed the weaker soul of the Birch Grove ant colony, transforming it into a self-aware Colony. A soul can also be evicted by a stronger one, as when the god in the Colony awoke and displaced Py's soul, which fled back to eternity.

***possession**: the infusion of a soul into a living creature. When the god in the Colony awoke, it took possession of the Colony. After the god subsequently repaired Py's dying human body, it took possession of Py's human mind, as well.

***projection**: The ability to project one's soul is universal among gods and rare among humans. As god-human hybrids, the Fishes have the ability to leave their bodies for extended periods of time. Py also has an innate talent for projecting his soul, but the time he can spend away from his body is limited. The first time he projected his soul was by accident, when he touched the aura of the Birch Grove ant colony; this forged a spiritual connection that allowed for mutual communication with his ants. Following his third Change, Py projected his soul into the newly sentient Colony; this allowed him to meet and communicate with the Professor. Aurie can also project her soul, but only within herself; this is the central ability conferred by her god.

***split soul**: a soul that exists in more than one place. When the Birch Grove ant colony acquired Py's soul, that soul was split between Py and the Colony. A highly unusual and uncomfortable state, the split soul longs to be reunited, but is repulsed by its twin self. A split soul does not share awareness with its twin self. Gods are exceptions to this; when a god possesses multiple creatures, it can send its awareness into any of them, and it doesn't suffer the agonies of a split soul.

Acknowledgements

I am deeply grateful to those who gave so much time and energy to this book. Editing this difficult story was a challenge, and I am indebted to my trio of exceptional editors: Marla Himeda (who also crafted interior images and did the meticulous work of formatting), Dawn Hollison, and Peter Jones. Thanks also to Jeff Brown for his incredible cover art and to fans of *CRISPR Evolution* who hounded me to finish the sequel.

About the Author

Charis Jones (aka Charis Himeda, PhD) is a research professor and co-founder of Renogenyx, a company dedicated to developing treatments for facioscapulohumeral muscular dystrophy. She won the FSHD Society's inaugural Young Investigator award, and has been interviewed by *The Washington Post, The Huffington Post,* and *The Boston Business Journal* for engineering FSHD therapeutics using CRISPR gene modifying technology.

At night, Dr. Himeda doffs her lab gloves to pen speculative fiction about renegade scientists who do things she would never dream of doing. Her short fiction has appeared in a number of literary magazines and in *The Best American Mystery and Suspense 2021*. *CRISPR Evolution* was a first-place winner in the PNWA literary contest, a semifinalist for the BookLife Prize, and a finalist for the Eric Hoffer First Horizon Award and Grand Prize, the American Book Fest Best Book Awards, the Foreword INDIES Awards, the Indies Today Awards, the National Indie Excellence Awards, the Readers' Favorite Awards, and the Page Turner Awards.

Visit the author at charisjonesbooks.com.